THE
PUSHCART PRIZE, XI:
BEST OF THE
SMALL PRESSES

THE PUSHCART PRIZE XI:

#6

BEST OF THE SMALL PRESSES

BEST OF THE SMALL PRESSES

. . . WITH AN INDEX TO THE FIRST ELEVEN VOLUMES

An annual small press reader

EDITED BY BILL HENDERSON

with The Pushcart Prize editors

Introduction by Cynthia Ozick

Poetry Editors: Philip Levine, David Wojahn

published by THE PUSHCART PRESS
1986-87 Edition

THE PUSHCART PRIZE, XI:

Note: nominations for this series are invited from any small, independent, literary book press or magazine in the world. Up to six nominations—tear sheets or copies selected from work published in the calendar year—are accepted by our October 15 deadline each year. Write to Pushcart Press, P.O. Box 380, Wainscott, N.Y. 11975 if you need more information.

Pushcart Press sends special thanks to The Helen Foundation of Salt Lake City for its generous awards to the authors of our lead short story, poem, and essay.

Library of Congress Card number: 76-58675
ISBN: 0-916366-39-1
ISSN: 0149-7863

First printing, July 1986
Manufactured in The United States of America
by Ray Freiman and Co., Stamford, Connecticut

Acknowledgments

The following works are reprinted by Permission of the author and publisher.

"Lawns" © 1985 Paris Review
"Not-Knowing" © 1985 The Georgia Review
"Off Port Townsend, One Month Before The Arrival of The U.S.S. Ohio" © 1985 Sea Pen Press and Paper Mill
"The Throne of the Third Heaven of the Nations Millennium General Assembly" © 1985 The Paris Review
"Other Lives" © 1985 Antaeus
"Lyrics for Puerto Rican Salsa and Three Soneos By Request" © 1985 New England Review and Bread Loaf Quarterly
"Communist" © 1985 Antaeus
"Property, Patriotism and National Defense" © 1985 Guardian Press, North Point Press
"Sunday At St. Christine's In Budapest and A Fruitstand Nearby" © 1985 Red Dust Press
"Mid-Plains Tornado" © 1985 Ahsahta Press
"Eating Together" © 1985 The Iowa Review
"Jury Selections" © 1985 Ironwood
"Tide of Voices" © 1985 Tendril
"The Flowers of Bermuda" © 1985 Sewanee Review
"Rose" © 1985 Ploughshares
"Friends and Fortunes" © 1985 Seal Press
"My Legacy" © 1985 Kenyon Review
"In A Polish Home for the Aged" © 1985 Grand Street
"Morro Rock" © 1985 Field
"Delfina Flores and Her Niece Modesta" © 1985 Shenandoah
"Don't Go To The Barn" © 1985 Antaeus
"The Island of Ven" © 1985 Ploughshares
"Leviathan" © 1985 Triquarterly
"Today Will Be A Quiet Day" © 1985 Missouri Review
"Quarter to Six" © 1985 Five Fingers Review
"I Send Mama Home" © 1985 The Southern Review
"Plain Song" © 1985 The Greenfield Review
"Writing In The Cold" © 1985 Granta
"Elegy on Independence Day" © 1985 University of Pittsburgh Press
"The Biblical Garden" © 1985 Missouri Review
"Amaryllis" © 1985 The Bennington Review
"The Paperboys" © 1985 American Poetry Review
"Somewhere Geese Are Flying" © 1985 The Georgia Review
"The Merry Chase" © 1985 The Antioch Review
"In The Country of Last Things" © 1985 The Paris Review
"The Victims" © 1985 Mississippi Review
"X" © 1985 The Georgia Review
"At the Death of Kenneth Rexroth" © 1985 New Directions
"Turtle, Swan" © 1985 Crazyhorse
"The Foundry Garden" © 1985 The Ohio Review
"It" © 1985 The Antioch Review
"Cooking" © 1985 Bloomsbury Review
"The Poet At Seventeen" © 1985 Quarterly West
"Molly's Dog" © 1985 Ontario Review and Alfred Knopf Inc.
"Something Good for Ginnie" © 1985 The Georgia Review
"The Noise The Hairless Make" © 1985 Sonora Review
"What The Days Are" © 1985 Poetry Northwest
"The Theme of the Three Caskets" © 1985 Iowa Review
"Maria Mitchell in The Great Beyond With Marilyn Monroe" © 1985 Alice James Books and Prairie Schooner

This book is for
John Baker
and Myrna M. Sheely

THE
PEOPLE WHO HELPED

FOUNDING EDITORS—*Anaïs Nin (1903-1977), Buckminster Fuller (1895-1983), Charles Newman, Daniel Halpern, Gordon Lish, Harry Smith, Hugh Fox, Ishmael Reed, Joyce Carol Oates, Len Fulton, Leonard Randolph, Leslie Fiedler, Nona Balakian, Paul Bowles, Paul Engle, Ralph Ellison, Reynolds Price, Rhoda Schwartz, Richard Morris, Ted Wilentz, Tom Montag, William Phillips. Poetry editor: H. L. Van Brunt.*

EDITORS—*Walter Abish, Ai, Elliott Anderson, John Ashbery, Russell Banks, Robert Bly, Robert Boyers, Harold Brodkey, Joseph Brodsky, Wesley Brown, Hayden Carruth, Raymond Carver, Frank Conroy, Malcolm Cowley, Paula Deitz, Steve Dixon, Andre Dubus, M. D. Elevitch, Loris Essary, Ellen Ferber, Carolyn Forché, Stuart Friebert, Jon Galassi, Tess Gallagher, Louis Gallo, George Garrett, Jack Gilbert, Reginald Gibbons, Louise Glück, David Godine, Jorie Graham, Linda Gregg, Barbara Grossman, Donald Hall, Michael Harper, DeWitt Henry, J. R. Humphreys, David Ignatow, John Irving, June Jordan, Edmund Keeley, Karen Kennerly, Galway Kinnell, Carolyn Kizer, Jerzy Kosinski, Richard Kostelanetz, Seymour Krim, Maxine Kumin, Stanley Kunitz, James Laughlin, Seymour Lawrence, Naomi Lazard, Herb Leibowitz, Denise Levertov, Philip Levine, Stanley Lindberg, Thomas Lux, Mary MacArthur, Daniel Menaker, Frederick Morgan, Howard Moss, Cynthia Ozick, Jayne Anne Phillips, Robert Phillips, George Plimpton, Stanley Plumly, Eugene Redmond, Ed Sanders, Teo Savory, Grace Schulman, Harvey Shapiro, Leslie Silko, Charles Simic, Dave Smith, William Stafford, Gerald Stern, David St. John, Bill and Pat Strachan, Ron Sukenick, Barry Targan, Anne Tyler, John Updike, Samuel Vaughan, David Wagoner, Derek Walcott, Ellen Wilbur, David Wilk, Yvonne, Bill Zavatsky.*

CONTRIBUTING EDITORS FOR THIS EDITION—*Diane Ackerman, John Allman, Philip Appleman, Bo Ball, Jim Barnes, Barbara Bedway,*

Antonio Benitez-Rojo, Suzanne Berger, Gina Berriault, D. C. Berry, Clark Blaise, Michael Blumenthal, Philip Booth, Michael Dennis Browne, T. Coraghessan Boyle, Christopher Buckley, Richard Burgin, Frederick Busch, Jared Carter, Kelly Cherry, Amy Clampitt, Naomi Clark, Stephen Corey, Gerald Costanzo, Martha Collins, Peter Cooley, Douglas Crase, Robert Creeley, Philip Dacey, John Daniel, Susan Strayer Deal, Terrence Des Pres, Sharon Doubiago, Rita Dove, Stuart Dybek, Richard Eberhart, Michael Finley, Jane Flanders, H. E. Francis, Kenneth Gangemi, Celia Gilbert, Patricia Goedicke, Barry Goldensohn, Matthew Graham, Patrick W. Gray, John Haines, James Baker Hall, Yuki Hartman, Lyn Hejinian, Don Hendrie Jr., Brenda Hillman, Andrew Hudgins, Elizabeth Inness-Brown, Josephine Jacobsen, Laura Jensen, William Kittredge, August Kleinzahler, Maxine Kumin, Doris Lessing, Gerry Locklin, David Madden, Dan Masterson, Cleopatra Mathis, Robert McBrearty, Michael McFee, Thomas McGrath, Heather McHugh, Joe-Anne McLaughlin, Wesley McNair, Sandra McPherson, Lorenzo W. Milam, Barbara Milton, Mark Crispin Miller, Susan Mitchell, Judy Moffett, Mary Morris, Lisel Mueller, Joan Murray, Leonard Nathan, Sheila B. Nickerson, Naomi Shihab Nye, Mary Oliver, Jonathan Penner, Mary Peterson, Joe Ashby Porter, Tony Quagliano, Bin Ramke, Donald Revell, Pattiann Rogers, Vern Rutsala, Michael Ryan, Sherod Santos, Philip Schultz, Lynne Sharon Schwartz, Bob Shacochis, Jim Simmerman, Nat Sobel, Elizabeth Spires, Ann Stanford, Maura Stanton, Felix Stefanile, Pamela Stewart, Mary Tallmountain, Elizabeth Tallent, Eleanor Ross Taylor, Elizabeth Thomas, Barbara Thompson, Sarah Vogan, Michael Waters, Gordon Weaver, Bruce Weigl, Susan Welch, Harold Witt, Christina Zawadiwsky, Patricia Zelver.

DESIGN AND PRODUCTION—*Ray Freiman*

EUROPEAN EDITORS—*Kirby and Liz Williams*

MANAGING EDITOR—*Helen Handley*

ROVING EDITORS—*Genie Chipps, Lily Francis*

ESSAYS EDITOR—*Anthony Brandt*

POETRY EDITORS—*Philip Levine, David Wojahn*

EDITOR AND PUBLISHER—*Bill Henderson*

PRESSES FEATURED IN THE PUSHCART PRIZE EDITIONS

Agni Review
Ahsahta Press
Ailanthus Press
Alcheringa/Ethnopoetics
Alice James Books
Amelia
American Literature
American PEN
American Poetry Review
Amnesty International
Anaesthesia Review
Antaeus
Antioch Review
Apalachee Quarterly
Aphra
The Ark
Ascent
Aspen Leaves
Aspen Poetry Anthology
Assembling
Barlenmir House
Barnwood Press
The Bellingham Review
Beloit Poetry Journal
Bennington Review
Bilingual Review
Black American Literature Forum

Black Rooster
Black Scholar
Black Sparrow
Black Warrior Review
Blackwells Press
Bloomsbury Review
Blue Cloud Quarterly
Blue Wind Press
Bluefish
BOA Editions
Bookslinger Editions
Boxspring
Brown Journal of the Arts
Burning Deck Press
Caliban
California Quarterly
Calliopea Press
Canto
Capra Press
Cedar Rock
Center
Chariton Review
Charnel House
Chelsea
Chicago Review
Chouteau Review
Chowder Review

Cimarron Review
Cincinnati Poetry Review
City Lights Books
Clown War
CoEvolution Quarterly
Cold Mountain Press
Columbia: A Magazine of Poetry
    and Prose
Confluence Press
Confrontation
Conjunctions
Copper Canyon Press
Cosmic Information Agency
Crawl Out Your Window
Crazy Horse
Crescent Review
Cross Cultural Communications
Cross Currents
Cumberland Poetry Review
Curbstone Press
Cutbank
Dacotah Territory
Daedalus
Decatur House
December
Dragon Gate Inc.
Domestic Crude
Dreamworks
Dryad Press
Duck Down Press
Durak
East River Anthology
Empty Bowl
Epoch
Fiction
Fiction Collective
Fiction International
Field
Firelands Art Review
Five Fingers Review
Five Trees Press
Frontiers: A Journal of Women
    Studies

Gallimaufry
Genre
The Georgia Review
Ghost Dance
Goddard Journal
David Godine, Publisher
Graham House Press
Grand Street
Granta
Graywolf Press
Greenfield Review
Greensboro Review
Guardian Press
Hard Pressed
Hills
Holmgangers Press
Holy Cow!
Home Planet News
Hudson Review
Icarus
Iguana Press
Indiana Writes
Intermedia
Intro
Invisible City
Inwood Press
Iowa Review
Ironwood
The Kanchenjuga Press
Kansas Quarterly
Kayak
Kenyon Review
Latitudes Press
L'Epervier Press
Liberation
Linquis
The Little Magazine
Living Hand Press
Living Poets Press
Logbridge-Rhodes
Lowlands Review
Lucille
Lynx House Press

Manroot
Magic Circle Press
Malahat Review
Massachusetts Review
Michigan Quarterly
Milk Quarterly
Missouri Review
Montana Gothic
Montana Review
Mho & Mho Works
Micah Publications
Mississippi Review
Missouri Review
Montemora
Mr. Cogito Press
MSS
Mulch Press
Nada Press
New America
New England Review and Bread
    Loaf Quarterly
New Directions
New Letters
North American Review
North Atlantic Books
North Point Press
Northwest Review
O. ARS
Obsidian
Oconee Review
October
Ohio Review
Ontario Review
Open Places
Orca Press
Oyez Press
Painted Bride Quarterly
Paris Review
Parnassus: Poetry In Review
Partisan Review
Penca Books
Pentagram
Penumbra Press

Pequod
Persea: An International Review
Pipedream Press
Pitcairn Press
Ploughshares
Poet and Critic
Poetry
Poetry Northwest
Poetry Now
Prairie Schooner
Prescott Street Press
Promise of Learnings
Quarry West
Quarterly West
Rainbow Press
Raritan: A Quarterly Review
Red Cedar Review
Red Clay Books
Red Dust Press
Red Earth Press
Release Press
Revista Chicano-Riquena
River Styx
Rowan Tree Press
Russian *Samizdat*
Salmagundi
San Marcos Press
Sea Pen Press and Paper Mill
Seal Press
Seamark Press
Seattle Review
Second Coming Press
The Seventies Press
Shankpainter
Shantih
Shenandoah
A Shout In The Street
Sibyl-Child Press
Small Moon
The Smith
Some
The Sonora Review
Southern Poetry Review

Southern Review
Southwestern Review
Spectrum
The Spirit That Moves Us
St. Andrews Press
Story Quarterly
Stuart Wright, Publisher
Sun & Moon Press
Sun Press
Sunstone
Tar River Poetry
Telephone Books
Telescope
Tendril
Texas Slough
13th Moon
THIS
Threepenny Review
Thorp Springs Press
Three Rivers Press
Thunder City Press
Thunder's Mouth Press
Toothpaste Press
Transatlantic Review
TriQuarterly

Truck Press
Tuumba Press
Undine
Unicorn Press
University of Pittsburgh Press
Unmuzzled Ox
Unspeakable Visions of the
    Individual
Vagabond
Virginia Quarterly
Wampeter Press
Washington Writers Workshop
Water Table
Western Humanities Review
Westigan Review
Wickwire Press
Wilmore City
Word Beat Press
Word-Smith
Wormwood Review
Writers Forum
Xanadu
Yale Review
Yardbird Reader
Y'Bird

CONTENTS

INTRODUCTION

by CYNTHIA OZICK

Best of the Small Presses. What, nowadays, is a small press? Partly it's really a *press:* one thinks of the burgeoning, all over America, of those artists who are active artisans, who care for beautiful paper (and sometimes even fabricate their own) and beautiful type (and sometimes set it themselves, the old-fashioned way), and with their own hands turn out pleasing sewn folios that, while they are certainly *books*, are at the same time art objects of high dedication. In the crush of a lightning technology that slams out computerized volumes stuck together with a baleful glue, it is good now and then to be reminded of a book as something worthy of body-love. The nostrils also read.

A small press means something else as well: a publisher who is a woman or a man (or a living handful of men and women), not a "corporate entity." Big companies are compelled to attend to "markets"; the bigger the house, the deeper the compulsion. Small-press publishers, unless they operate out of the pocket of some maverick philanthropist indifferent to the pinch of economics, are not averse to making a bit of money either; but they also concentrate on making *room:* for eccentricity, for risk, for the *idée fixe*, for poetry, for the odd essay and the odder fiction; for the future. They are on the watch for originality—even though originality, like any watched pot, often ends by blowing off steam identical to all other steam. It is a vigilance, a readiness, for which nothing can be predicted: one day (the saying goes) a tedium, the next a Te Deum. Still, when the big publishers look for a miracle, they are usually thinking of dollars. For the small presses a miracle is more often a literary dream: Willa Cather rising out of an unlikely Red Cloud; the obscure Malamud, teacher and father in Oregon, patiently constructing his magic barrel of stories—of a kind never put into the world before; Barthelme, editor of a forgotten organ called *locations,* closeted in a dusky cubicle at the top of a staircase in New York, imagining new locutions for a new art. Unexpectedness is what the small presses are open to. They are like the little shoemakers who come unseen at night to stitch the leather no one else can master. No wonder they have Rumpelstiltskin goldspinner names—*Unmuzzled Ox,* and *Mho and Mho Works,* and *Unspeakable Visions of the Individual,* and *Shankpainter,* and *Mr. Cogito Press,* and *Antaeus* and *Persea* and *Shantih* and *Pequod* and *Sun and Moon*—names that announce their intent to turn the invisible visible. Some of these little-shoemaker presses are in fact conventionally ambitious publishing houses working on a shoestring. But many are little magazines.

Little magazines! These may not be the real right words any more; they have a faintly anachronistic resonance, and have been sensibly replaced by the more capacious term small press, which in its democratic egalitarianism omits nothing on the American scene, whatever its aim, mood, tone, "school," literary or political coloration. But with the words little magazine we are in another place; we are in the history of our literary culture. It isn't simply that without *Poetry,* without the fabled *Dial,* those antique particularist precursors of our current abundance, we would not have had a vehicle for the first glimmers of modernism in American poetry and criticism. The little magazines began as an elitist movement favoring high art, in contradistinction to the big popular magazines; in this sense they were programmatic, didactic. They were intended as sanctuaries away from what was once thought of, dismissively and uncomplicatedly, as "midcult" (an out-of-date notion in a time when even kitsch is a resource, when graduate students in philosophy solemnly deconstruct the language of MacDonald's hamburger advertisements and serious literary critics look to reruns of *The Honeymooners* for cultural signifiers). It wasn't so much what they were, or what they were meant to be— they were meant to be an aristocracy of letters, and sometimes they were. But their best case lay in what they weren't. They weren't *Life* or *Look* or the *Saturday Evening Post* or *Esquire,* or even *Harper's* or *Atlantic.* They were, by and large (I'm reflecting now on the little magazines of the forties and fifties), coterie journals: all, however, with the same ideal—the loftiest peaks of what was said and thought. In a 1946 essay (it reads with fresh relevance this very minute) called "The Function of the Little Magazine," Lionel Trilling undertook to defend the little magazines against "populist critics" who "denounce the coterie and the writer who does not write for 'the many' ":

> The matter is not so simple as these earnest minds would have it. From the democratic point of view, we must say that in a true democracy nothing should be done *for* the people. The writer who defines his audience by its limitations is indulging in the unforgivable arrogance. The writer must define his audience by its abilities, by its perfections . . . He does well, if he cannot see his right audience within immediate reach of his voice, to direct his words to his spiritual ancestors, or to posterity, or even, if need be, to a coterie. The writer serves his daemon and his subject. And the democracy that does not know that the daemon and the subject must be served is not, in any ideal sense of the word, a democracy at all.

"The word coterie should not frighten us too much," Trilling warned. "Neither should it charm us too much; writing for a small group does not insure integrity any more than writing for the many; the coterie can corrupt as surely, and sometimes as quickly, as the big advertising appropriation."

If anything has changed in the life of the little magazines in the last four decades, it is their proliferation; and also the meaning of their proliferation. The little magazine as a form no longer stands for a single idea: the retreat to art and high culture. If Trilling's justification for the coterie journal—that "the daemon and the subject must be served"—is still even minimally viable, if little magazines are still founded to promote and pursue an "agenda" (and surely they are), then what has happened is—a marvelous thing—the multiplying of coteries, hence of purposes and agendas. And of daemons. *I hear America singing, the varied carols I hear,* one might cry, and—because not every daemon will be congenial—without sentimentality.

It may be that the little magazines no longer define themselves as uniformly as they once did because they cannot. Once they were the heralds and couriers of modernism—in advance of modernism's inclusion in the literary curricula of the universities. Their agenda, prevalent and single-minded, *was* modernism, and with it the now-archaic passions of the New Criticism, inspiring ranks and ranks of tertiary imitators—every poet a sub-Pound, every writer of fiction a neo-Kafka, every critic a pseudo-Eliot. Not that, forty or fifty years later, we have left the parrots behind, but the question is: parrot whom, parrot what? With the famous exhaustion of modernism, who knows where we are now? Aspiring to the cadences of James Joyce is one thing; aspiring to the sound of Ann Beattie is another, and may represent us more honestly. We live on a nameless planet. To give it a name—postmodernism—is only to confirm these thickets in the wilderness of no man's land, which turns out to be everyone's turf.

And so the little magazines increase their numbers. Where there were twenty little magazines with a single modernist idea, there are now a hundred, with a hundred different daemons. If you believe in the power of the Zeitgeist, then they may be more alike than they realize, these different daemons; but they *assume* singularity. This puts me in mind of my five zealously individualistic uncles. Each uncle demanded to be regarded as absolutely unlike the others; but they *all* demanded this, and in just the same style. And so they march by, our Rumpelstiltskins, some devoted to intellectual puzzlements of a recognizably professorial kind, others to startling Pan into kicking up his goat-feet: *Salmagundi, Raritan, Grand Street, Granta, Parnassus; Holy Cow!, Home Planet News, Crawl Out Your Window, Toothpaste Press*. The range in Reviews is from *Anaesthesia* to *Yale*, with *Lowlands, Mulch, Nada*, and *Ploughshares* in between. And just here it may be salubrious to look at still another passage in Trilling's small-press report:

> To the general lowering of the status of literature and of the interest in it [and Trilling is writing before television!], the innumerable "little magazines" have been a natural and heroic response. Since the beginning of the century, meeting difficulties of which only their editors can truly conceive, they have tried to keep the roads open. From the elegant and brilliant *Dial* to the latest little scrub from the provinces, they have done their

work, they have kept our culture from being cautious and settled, or merely sociological, or merely pious. They are snickered at and snubbled, sometimes deservedly, and no one would venture to say in a precise way just what effect they have—except that they keep the new talents warm until the commercial publisher with his customary air of noble resolution is ready to take his chance, except that they make the official representatives of literature a little uneasy, except that they keep a countercurrent moving which perhaps no one will be fully aware of until it ceases to move.

These are words that might have been cut from the hide of our own moment. But there is one ingredient in our moment that no one could have foreseen—not even Trilling, who invented the term adversary culture, and showed us how the established institutions of our society have digested their opposition. For us in America, bohemia and all its works are vanished; or, more exactly, bohemia has migrated to the middle class, and is alive and well in condo and suburb. So the little magazines have not only lost their elitism—beginning, one supposes, with the turning from Eliot and the long-range impact of Allen Ginsberg's *Howl*. But they have also lost (though some of them may resist admitting to it) their bohemianism, the glamor of outsiderness and marginality. Citizens of a free country with a free press, we don't have a *samizdat*; anybody can publish anything, including righteous rage of a political sort, which rather limits the spectrum of anti-establishment emotion. All this Trilling *did* more or less predict, and taught us to figure out for ourselves.

The new ingredient, however, is ours alone, and no one could have predicted it. In fact, when its first drop fell it was difficult even to understand that it *was* a new ingredient. I am talking about this book, this very book, the one in your hands, the *Pushcart Prize* anthology, subtitled *Best of the Small Presses*. The reason I am not one of the Founding Editors listed on page XI is that eleven years ago, when approached, I didn't recognize what precisely was being founded; probably (to my lasting humiliation) I shrugged. It's possible that Bill Henderson himself didn't entirely fathom his own revolution. George Plimpton in his Introduction to the Tenth Anniversary *Pushcart Prize* quotes Henderson: "I didn't know there was going to be such feeling for it."

What was it, then, that Bill Henderson, and I, and all of us, didn't know there was going to be such feeling for? The truth is, though *Pushcart Prize* is an anthology, it is something else besides. And to call it an institution (after a dozen years it might be called that) is not to see it with full clarity. *Pushcart Prize* is a handle on a whole society; and not simply a handle to get hold of something, but to make an idea go. *Pushcart Prize* is a new literary ingredient; and a revolution; and a great Ear; and a Voice braiding many voices. But this is broad and noisy Whitmanesque language, and I am not comfortable with it: it has a way of descending to an easy populism, like the hootenannies of my college days.

Henderson's *Pushcart Prize* hears America singing—its varied carols—but not in the open yawping Whitman fashion. I think, rather, of the private, the secret, nuanced and tendril-like, rife with hints and whispers; flashes of *What Maisie Knew*, or of the river scene in *The Ambassadors*. Aloneness. Contemplation and calculation. Literary America, for all its variegated strands and noble pluralism, is never really a public caroling; we mainly don't have, especially now, a public sort of literature; and almost not at all in fiction and poetry. Writers epitomize private lives. Here, in the eleventh collection of *Pushcart Prize*, are so many solitary night breathings: everything in this volume flew out from the underbrush of a bosky mind in its aloneness. Well, you'll say, that's true of every other book; every story, every essay, every poem is charged with singleness.

But *Pushcart Prize* is a living current that unites all these. Moreover, each story, essay, or poem has been flung out from an earlier anthology, since every little magazine is itself a collection. *No one would venture to say just what effect they have.* The effect is not of a chorus, those varied carols, but somehow of a . . . the word I want is *literature*, in the sense of the work of our period. This is the sound of how we write now. It is the sound of our time, our decade, our moment. It is, after all, a large sound. Each story herein—the stories are all very good—holds a life in its completeness, dyed in the peculiar resources of our language (to a greater or a lesser degree), and pressed out of the ferocity of imagination. The poems are, as poems ought to be—and the poems are all very good—fires of seeings, fusing sight with insight. The essays are real essays—they know that Hazlitt lived; they are not that shabby, team-driven, ugly, truncated, undeveloped, speedy, breezy, cheap thing: the "article." I ought to speak of each story, poem, and essay one by one; no writer wants to be talked about in this "generic" way, as part of a culture-pattern, as an instance of a time, or even of a literature. There are robust writers here who have earned high distinction, and others with acclaim to come. Still, my theme is not the particular content of this volume, idiosyncratically distinguished, but the harvest of these unusual collections; of their meaning.

What does it mean, this *Pushcart Prize* invention, this new idea, this new cultural ingredient that no one knew there was going to be such feeling for? It means that a way has been found to seize an ocean in a cup. A way has been found to hear, one year at a time, the sound—it *is* a sound above all—of America writing. You may protest that the other fine annual anthologies—notably, William Abrahams' *O. Henry Prize Stories* and Shannon Ravanel's *Best American Short Stories*—have been doing this right along. And they have, in part, by concentrating on the short story. But *Pushcart Prize* sweeps out its long arms (the arms of nearly 200 contributing editors) and rakes in the poets and the essayists along with the ficiton-writers: the whole American writing-sound. If I were disposed to quarrel at all with Trilling, it would be with his belief (essentially a comment on career) that the little magazines "keep the new talents warm until the commercial publisher . . . is ready to take his chance." Whatever the career chances, the good or bad luck, of any single writer, the American writing sound is an intrinsic multiple chord; it belongs to the nation; rather (considering the jumbled sort of nation we are, without a genuine nationality along the lines, say, of Swedish or Italian homogeneity), it *makes* the nation. The American writing sound gives us our nationality. And this, while it hasn't very much to do with keeping talents warm for the big trade publishers (though it certainly doesn't stand as an obstacle), is precisely the nature of Bill Henderson's revolution. Two hundred years after the other Revolution, we still haven't arrived at something that can count indivisibly as an, or the, American nationality. Nationality is a version of temperament and character. We are still creating ours; it is ours to uncover. And whatever, or however, it turns out to be, one thing is plain: it will be a sound, and it will come from the writers; from all the writers there are.

That, it seems to me, is the cumulative significance—the nearest thunder—of Bill Henderson's invention, and what he didn't know there was going to be such feeling for.

One last word: about the American essay. Though its history is brilliant enough—Emerson to Edmund Wilson—the essay has been dormant for a long time. For a long time it hardly recognized itself for what it was; it was often confused with the magazine article (see vilification above). The essay is waking up now; it appears in its most muscular form in this volume in the hands of a fiction writer writing about the writing of fiction. Donald Barthelme's "Not-Knowing" is sinewed throughout with dazzling knowings—even principles—in surprising sentences. I offer three admirable fragments from it as evidence not only of the American sound, but of the American character: the building (or call it *Bildung*, meaning education) of nationality.

> First, there is art's own project, since Mallarmé, of restoring freshness to a much-handled language, essentially an effort toward finding a language in which making art is possible at all. This remains a ground theme, as potent, problematically, today as it was a century ago.
>
> • • •
>
> Art is not difficult because it wishes to be difficult, but because it wishes to be art. However much the writer might long to be, in his work, simple, honest, and straightforward, these virtues are no longer available to him. [Here I break in parenthetically to call your attention, for instance, to Gordon Lish's "The Merry Chase." *C.O.*] He discovers that in being simple, honest, and straightforward, nothing much happens: he speaks the speakable, whereas what we are looking for is the as-yet unspeakable, the as-yet unspoken.
>
> • • •
>
> Style enables us to speak, to imagine again. . . . It's our good fortune to be able to imagine alternative realities, other possibilities. We can quarrel with the world, constructively (no one alive has quarreled with the world more extensively or splendidly than Beckett). "Belief in progress," says Baudelaire, "is a doctrine of idlers and Belgians." Perhaps. But if I have anything unorthodox to offer here, it's that I think art's project is fundamentally meliorative. The aim of meditating about the world is finally to change the world. It is this meliorative aspect of literature that provides its ethical dimension.

THE
PUSHCART PRIZE XI:
BEST OF THE
SMALL PRESSES
(1986-87 edition)

LAWNS

fiction by MONA SIMPSON

from THE IOWA REVIEW

I STEAL. I've stolen books and money and even letters. Letters are great. I can't tell you the feeling, walking down the street with twenty dollars in my purse, stolen earrings in my pocket. I don't get caught. That's the amazing thing. You're out on the sidewalk, other people all around, shopping, walking, and you've got it. You're out of the store, you've done this thing you're not supposed to do, but no one stops you. At first it's a rush. Like you're even for everything you didn't get before. But then you're left alone, no one even notices you. Nothing changes.

I work in the mailroom of my dormitory, Saturday mornings. I sort mail, put the letters in these long narrow cubbyholes. The insides of mailboxes. It's cool there when I stick in my arm.

I've stolen cash—these crisp, crackling, brand new twenty-dollar bills the fathers and grandmothers send, sealed up in sheets of wax paper. Once I got a fifty. I've stolen presents, too. I got a sweater and a football. I didn't want the football, but after the package was messed up on the mail table, I had no choice, I had to take the whole thing in my daypack and throw it out on the other side of campus. I found a covered garbage can. It was miles away. Brand new football.

Mostly, what I take are cookies. No evidence. They're edible. I can spot the coffee cans of chocolate chip. You can smell it right through the wrapping. A cool smell, like the inside of a pantry. Sometimes I eat straight through a can during just my shift.

Tampering with the United States mail is a Federal Crime, I know. Listen, let me tell you, I know. I got a summons in my

3

mailbox to go to the Employment Office next Wednesday. Sure I'm scared.

The University cops want to talk to me. Great. They think, suspect is the word they use, that one of us is throwing out mail instead of sorting it. Wonder who? Us is the others. I'm not the only sorter. I just work Saturdays, mail comes, you know, six days a week in this country. They'll never guess it's me.

They say this in the letter, they think it's out of LAZINESS. Wanting to hurry up and get done, not spend the time. But I don't hurry. I'm really patient on Saturday mornings. I leave my dorm early, while Lauren's still asleep, I open the mailroom—it's this heavy door and I have my own key. When I get there, two bags are already on the table, sagging, waiting for me. Two old ladies. One's packages, one's mail. There's a small key opens the bank of doors, the little boxes from the inside. Through the glass part of every mail slot, I can see. The astroturf field across the street over the parking lot, it's this light green. I watch the sky go from black to grey to blue while I'm there. Some days just stay foggy. Those are the best. I bring a cup of coffee in with me from the vending machine—don't want to wake Lauren up—and I get there at like seven-thirty or eight o'clock. I don't mind it then, my whole dorm's asleep. When I walk out it's as quiet as a football game day. It's eleven or twelve when you know everyone's up and walking that it gets bad being down there. That's why I start early. But I don't rush.

Once you open a letter, you can't just put it in a mailbox. The person's gonna say something. So I stash them in my pack and throw them out. Just people I know. Susan Brown, I open, Annie Larsen, Larry Helprin. All the popular kids from my high school. These are kids who drove places together, took vacations, they all ski, they went to the prom in one big group. At morning nutrition—nutrition, it's your break at ten o'clock for donuts and stuff. California State law, you have to have it.

They used to meet outside on the far end of the math patio, all in one group. Some of them smoked. I've seen them look at each other, concerned at ten in the morning. One touched the inside of another's wrist, like grown-ups in trouble.

And now I know. Everything I thought those three years, worst years of my life, turns out to be true. The ones here get letters. Keri's at Santa Cruz, Lilly's in San Diego, Kevin's at Harvard and

4

Beth's at Stanford. And like from families, their letters talk about problems. They're each other's main lives. You always knew, looking at them in high school, they weren't just kids who had fun. They cared. They cared about things.

They're all worried about Lilly now. Larry and Annie are flying down to talk her into staying at school.

I saw Glenn the day I came to Berkeley. I was all unpacked and I was standing there leaning into the window of my father's car, saying "Smile, Dad, jeez, at least try, would you?" He was crying because he was leaving. I'm thinking oh, my god, some of these other kids, carrying in their trunks and backpacks are gonna see him, and then finally, he drives away and I was sad. That was the moment I was waiting for, him gone and me alone and there it was and I was sad. I took a walk through campus and I'd been walking for almost an hour and then I see Glenn, coming down on a little hill by the infirmary, riding on one of those lawn mowers you sit on, with grass flying out of the side and he's smiling. Not at me but just smiling. Clouds and sky behind his hair, half of Tamalpais gone in fog. He was wearing this bright orange vest and I thought, fall's coming.

I saw him that night again in our dorm cafeteria. This's the first time I've been in love. I worry. I'm a bad person, but Glenn's the perfect guy, I mean for me at least, and he thinks he loves me and I've got to keep him from finding out about me. I'll die before I'll tell him. Glenn, OK, Glenn. He looks like Mick Jagger, but sweet, ten times sweeter. He looks like he's about ten years old. His father's a doctor over at UC Med. Gynecological surgeon.

First time we got together, a whole bunch of us were in Glenn's room drinking beer, Glenn and his roommate collect beer cans, they have them stacked up, we're watching TV and finally everybody else leaves. There's nothing on but those grey lines and Glenn turns over on his bed and asks me if I'd rub his back.

I couldn't believe this was happening to me. In high school, I was always ending up with the wrong guys, never the one I wanted. But I wanted it to be Glenn and I knew it was going to happen, I knew I didn't have to do anything. I just had to stay there. It would happen. I was sitting on his rear end, rubbing his back, going under his shirt with my hands. His back felt so good, it was smooth and warm, like cement around a pool.

All of a sudden, I was worried about my breath and what I

smelled like. When I turned fourteen or fifteen, my father told me once that I didn't smell good. I slugged him when he said that and didn't talk to him for days, not that I cared about what I smelled like with my father. He was happy, though, kind of, that he could hurt me. That was the last time, though, I'll tell you.

Glenn's face was down in the pillow. I tried to sniff myself but I couldn't tell anything. And it went all right anyway.

I don't open Glenn's letters but I touch them. I hold them and smell them—none of his mail has any smell.

He doesn't get many letters. His parents live across the Bay in Marin County, they don't write. He gets letters from his grandmother in Michigan, plain, even handwriting on regular envelopes, a sticker with her return address printed on it, Rural Route #3, Guns Street. See, I got it memorized.

And he gets letters from Diane, Di, they call her. High school girlfriend. Has a pushy mother, wants her to be a scientist, but she already got a C in Chem 1A. I got an A +, not to brag. He never slept with her, though, she wouldn't, she's still a virgin down in San Diego. With Lilly. Maybe they even know each other.

Glenn and Di were popular kids in their high school. Redwood High. Now I'm one because of Glenn, popular. Because I'm his girlfriend, I know that's why. Not 'cause of me. I just know, OK, I'm not going to start fooling myself now. Please.

Her letters I hold up to the light, they've got florescent lights in there. She's supposed to be blonde, you know, and pretty. Quiet. The soft type. And the envelopes. She writes on these sheer cream-colored envelopes and they get transparent and I can see her writing underneath, but not enough to read what it says, it's like those hockey lines painted under layers of ice.

I run my tongue along the place where his grandmother sealed the letter. A sharp, sweet gummy taste. Once I cut my tongue. That's what keeps me going to the bottom of the bag, I'm always wondering if there'll be a letter for Glenn. He doesn't get one every week. It's like a treasure. Cracker Jack prize. But I'd never open Glenn's mail. I kiss all four corners where his fingers will touch, opening it, before I put it in his box. Sometimes I hold them up and blow on it.

I brought home cookies for Lauren and me. Just a present. We'll eat 'em or Glenn'll eat 'em. I'll throw them out for all I care.

6

They're chocolate chip with pecans. This was one good mother. A lucky can. I brought us coffee, too. I *bought* it.

Yeah, OK, so I'm in trouble. Wednesday, at ten-thirty, I got this notice I was supposed to appear. I had a class, Chem 1C, pre-med staple. Your critical thing. I never missed it before. I told Glenn I had a doctor's appointment.

OK, so I skip it anyway and I walk into this room and there's these two other guys, all work in the mailroom doing what I do, sorting. And we all sit there on chairs on this green carpet. I was staring at everybody's shoes. And there's a cop. University cop, I don't know what's the difference. He had this sagging, pear-shaped body. Like what my dad would have if he were fat, but he's not, he's thin. He walks slowly on the carpeting, his fingers hooked in his belt loops. I was watching his hips.

Anyway, he's accusing us all and he's trying to get one of us to admit we did it. No way.

"I hope one of you will come to me and tell the truth. Not a one of you knows anything about this? Come on, now."

I shake my head no and stare down at the three pairs of shoes. He says they're not going to do anything to the person who did it, right, wanna make a bet, they say they just want to know, but they'll take it back as soon as you tell them.

I don't care why I don't believe him. I know one thing for sure and that's they're not going to do anything to me as long as I say, NO, I didn't do it. That's what I said, no, I didn't do it, I don't know a thing about it. I just can't imagine where those missing packages could have gone, how letters got into garbage cans. Awful. I just don't know.

The cop had a map with Xs on it every place they found mail. The garbage cans. He said there was a group of students trying to get an investigation. People's girlfriends sent cookies that never got here. Letters were missing. Money. These students put up xeroxed posters on bulletin boards showing a garbage can stuffed with letters.

Why should I tell them, so they can throw me in jail? And kick me out of school? Four-point-oh average and I'm going to let them kick me out of school? They're sitting there telling us it's a felony. A Federal Crime. No way, I'm gonna go to medical school.

This tall, skinny guy with a blonde mustache, Wallabees, looks kind of like a rabbit, he defended us. He's another sorter, works Monday/Wednesdays.

"We all do our jobs," he says. "None of us would do that." The rabbity guy looks at me and the other girl, for support. So we're going to stick together. The other girl, a dark blonde, chewing her lip, nodded. I loved that rabbity guy that second. I nodded too.

The cop looked down. Wide hips in the coffee-with-milk-colored pants. He sighed. I looked up at the rabbity guy. They let us all go.

I'm just going to keep saying no, not me, didn't do it and I just won't do it again. That's all. Won't do it anymore. So, this is Glenn's last chance for homemade cookies. I'm sure as hell not going to bake any.

I signed the form, said I didn't do it, I'm OK now. I'm safe. It turned out OK after all, it always does. I always think something terrible's going to happen and it doesn't. I'm lucky.

I'm afraid of cops. I was walking, just a little while ago, today, down Telegraph with Glenn, and these two policemen, not the one I'd met, other policemen, were coming in our direction. I started sweating a lot. I was sure until they passed us, I was sure it was all over, they were there for me. I always think that. But at the same time, I know it's just my imagination. I mean, I'm a four-point-oh student, I'm a nice girl just walking down the street with my boyfriend.

We were on our way to get Happy Burgers. When we turned the corner, about a block past the cops, I looked at Glenn and I was flooded with like this feeling. It was raining a little and we were by People's Park. The trees were blowing and I was looking at all those little gardens coming up, held together with stakes and white string.

I wanted to say something to Glenn, give him something. I wanted to tell him something about me.

"I'm bad in bed," that's what I said, I just blurted it out like that. He just kind of looked at me, he was nervous, he just giggled. He didn't know what to say, I guess, but he sort of slung his arm around me and I was so grateful and then we went in. He paid for my Happy Burger, I usually don't let him pay for me, but I did and it was the best goddamn hamburger I've ever eaten.

I want to tell him things.

I lie all the time, always have, but I keep track of each lie I've ever told Glenn and I'm always thinking of the things I can't tell him.

Glenn was a screwed up kid, kind of. He used to go in his

backyard, his parents were inside the house I guess, and he'd find this big stick and start twirling around with it. He'd dance, he called it dancing, until if you came up and clapped in front of him, he wouldn't see you. He'd spin around with that stick until he fell down dead on the grass, unconscious, he said he did it to see the sky break up in pieces and spin. He did it sometimes with a tire swing, too. He told me when he was spinning like that, it felt like he was just hearing the earth spinning, that it really went that fast all the time but we just don't feel it. When he was twelve years old or something, his parents took him in the city to a clinic t'see a psychologist. And then he stopped. See, maybe I should go to a psychologist. I'd get better, too. He told me about that in bed one night. The ground feels so good when you fall, he said to me. I loved him for that.

"Does anything feel that good now?" I said.

"Sex sometimes. Maybe dancing."

Know what else he told me that night? He said, right before we went to sleep, he wasn't looking at me, he said he'd been thinking what would happen if I died, he said he thought how he'd be at my funeral, all my family and my friends from high school and my little brother would all be around at the front and he'd be at the edge in the cemetery, nobody'd even know who he was.

I was in that crack, breathing the air between the bed and the wall. Cold and dusty. Yeah, we're having sex. I don't know. It's good. Sweet. He says he loves me. I have to remind myself. I talk to myself in my head while we're doing it. I have to say, it's OK, this is just Glenn, this is who I want it to be and it's just like rubbing next to someone. It's just like pushing two hands together, so there's no air in between.

I cry sometimes with Glenn, I'm so grateful.

My mother called and woke me up this morning. Ms. I'm-going-to-be-perfect. Ms. anything-wrong-is-your-own-fault. Ms. if-anything-bad-happens-you're-a-fool.

She says if she has time, she MIGHT come up and see my dorm room in the next few weeks. Help me organize my wardrobe, she says. She didn't bring me up here, my dad did. I wanted Danny to come along, I love Danny.

But my mother has NO pity. She thinks she's got the answers. She's the one who's a lawyer, she's the one who went back to law

9

school and stayed up late nights studying while she still made our lunch boxes. With gourmet cheese. She's proud of it, she tells you. She loves my dad, I guess. She thinks we're like this great family and she sits there at the dinner table bragging about us, to us. She xeroxed my grade card first quarter with my Chemistry A+ so she's got it in her office and she's got the copy up on the refrigerator at home. She's sitting there telling all her friends that and I'm thinking, you don't know it, but I'm not one of you.

These people across the street from us. Little girl, Sarah, eight years old. Maybe seven. Her dad, he worked for the army, some kind of researcher, he decides he wants to get a sex-change operation. And he goes and does it, over at Stanford. My mom goes out, takes the dog for a walk, right. The mother CONFIDES in her. Says the thing she regrets most is she wants to have more children. The little girl, Sarah, eight years old, looks up at my mom and says, "Daddy's going to be an aunt."

Now that's sad, I think that's really sad. My mom thinks it's a good dinner table story, proving how much better we are than them. Yeah, I remember exactly what she said that night. "That's all Sarah's mother's got to worry about now, is that she wants another child. Meanwhile, Daddy's becoming an aunt."

She should know about me.

So my dad comes to visit for the weekend. Glenn's dad came to speak at UC one night, he took Glenn out to dinner to a nice place, Glenn was glad to see him. Yeah, well. My dad. Comes to the dorm. Skulks around. This guy's a BUSINESSMAN, in a three-piece suit, and he acts inferior to the eighteen-year-old freshmen coming in the lobby. My dad. Makes me sick right now thinking of him standing there in the lobby and everybody seeing him. He was probably looking at the kids and looking jealous. Just standing there. Why? Don't ask me why, he's the one that's forty-two years old.

So he's standing there, nervous, probably sucking his hand, that's what he does when he's nervous, I'm always telling him not to. Finally, somebody takes him to my room. I'm not there, Lauren's gone, and he waits for I don't know how long.

When I come in he's standing with his back to the door looking out the window. I see him and right away I know it's him and I have this urge to tip-toe away and he'll never see me.

My pink sweater, a nice sweater, a sweater I wore a lot in high

10

school was over my chair, hanging on the back of it and my father's got one hand on the sweater shoulder and he's like rubbing the other hand down an empty arm. He looks up at me, already scared and grateful when I walk into the room. I feel like smashing him with a baseball bat. Why can't he just stand up straight?

I drop my books on the bed and stand there while he hugs me.

"Hi, Daddy, what are you doing here?"

"I wanted to see you." He sits in my chair now, his legs crossed and big, too big for this room, and he's still fingering the arm of my pink sweater. "I missed you so I got away for the weekend," he says. "I have a room up here at the Claremont Hotel."

So he's here for the weekend. He's just sitting in my dorm room and I have to figure out what to do with him. He's not going to do anything. He'd just sit here. And Lauren's coming back soon so I've got to get him out. It's Friday afternoon and the weekend's shot. OK, so I'll go with him. I'll go with him and get it over with.

But I'm not going to miss my date with Glenn Saturday night. No way. I'd die before I'd cancel that. It's bad enough missing dinner in the cafeteria tonight. Friday's eggplant, my favorite, and Friday nights are usually easy, music on the stereos all down the hall. We usually work, but work slow and talk and then we all meet in Glenn's room around ten.

"Come, sit on my lap, honey." My dad like pulls me down and starts bouncing me. BOUNCING ME. I stand up. "OK, we can go somewhere tonight and tomorrow morning, but I have to be back for tomorrow night. I've got plans with people. And I've got to study, too."

"You can bring your books back to the hotel," he says. "I'm supposed to be at a convention in San Francisco, but I wanted to see you. I have work, too, we can call room service and both just work."

"I still have to be back by four tomorrow."

"All right."

"OK, just a minute." And he sat there in my chair while I called Glenn and told him I wouldn't be here for dinner. I pulled the phone out into the hall, it only stretches so far, and whispered. "Yeah, my father's here," I said, "he's got a conference in San Francisco. He just came by."

Glenn lowered his voice, sweet, and said, "Sounds fun."

My dad sat there, hunched over in my chair, while I changed my

11

shirt and put on deodorant. I put a nightgown in my shoulder pack and my toothbrush and I took my chem book and we left. I knew I wouldn't be back for a whole day. I was trying to calm myself thinking, well, it's only one day, that's nothing in my life. The halls were empty, it was five o'clock, five-ten, everyone was down at dinner.

We walk outside and the cafeteria lights are on and I see everyone moving around with their trays. Then my dad picks up my hand.

I yank it out. "Dad," I say, really mean.

"Honey, I'm your father." His voice trails off. "Other girls hold their fathers' hands." It was dark enough for the lights to be on in the cafeteria, but it wasn't really dark out yet. The sky was blue. On the tennis courts on top of the garage, two Chinese guys were playing. I heard that thonk-pong and it sounded so carefree and I just wanted to be them. I'd have even given up Glenn, Glenn-that-I-love-more-than-anything, at that second, I would have given everything up just to be someone else, someone new. I got into the car and slammed the door shut and turned up the heat.

"Should we just go to the hotel and do our work? We can get a nice dinner in the room."

"I'd rather go out," I said, looking down at my hands. He went where I told him. I said the name of the restaurant and gave directions. Chez Panisse and we ordered the most expensive stuff. Appetizers and two desserts just for me. A hundred and twenty bucks for the two of us.

OK, this hotel room.

So, my dad's got the Bridal Suite. He claimed that was all they had. Fat chance. Two-hundred-eighty room hotel and all they've got left is this deal with the canopy bed, no way. It's in the tower, you can almost see it from the dorm. Makes me sick. From the bathroom, there's this window, shaped like an arch, and it looks over all of Berkeley. You can see the bridge lights. As soon as we got there, I locked myself in the bathroom, I was so mad about that canopy bed. I took a long bath and washed my hair. They had little soaps wrapped up there, shampoo, may as well use them, he's paying for it. It's this deep old bathtub and wind was coming in from outside and I felt like that window was just open, no glass, just a hole cut out in the stone.

12

I was thinking of when I was little and what they taught us in catechism. I thought a soul was inside your chest, this long horizontal triangle with rounded edges, made out of some kind of white fog, some kind of gas or vapor. I could be pregnant. I soaped myself all up and rinsed off with cold water. I'm lucky I never got pregnant, really lucky.

Other kids my age, Lauren, everybody, I know things they don't know. I know more for my age. Too much. Like I'm not a virgin. Lots of people are, you'd be surprised. I know about a lot things being wrong and unfair, all kinds of stuff. It's like seeing a UFO, if I ever saw something like that, I'd never tell, I'd wish I'd never seen it.

My dad knocks on the door.

"What do you want?"

"Let me just come in and talk to you while you're in there."

"I'm done, I'll be right out. Just a minute." I took a long time towelling. No hurry, believe me. So I got into bed, with my nightgown on and wet already from my hair. I turned away. Breathed against the wall. "Night."

My father hooks my hair over my ear and touches my shoulder. "Tired?"

I shrug.

"You really have to go back tomorrow? We could go to Marin or to the beach. Anything."

I hugged my knees up under my nightgown. "You should go to your conference, Dad."

I wake up in the middle of the night, I feel something's going on, and sure enough, my dad's down there, he's got my nightgown worked up to like a frill around my neck and my legs hooked over his shoulders.

"Dad, stop it."

"I just wanted to make you feel good," he says and looks up at me. "What's wrong? Don't you love me anymore?"

I never really told anybody. It's not exactly the kind of thing you can bring up over lunch. "So, I'm sleeping with my father. Oh, and let's split a dessert." Right.

I don't know, other people think my dad's handsome. They say he is. My mother thinks so, you should see her traipsing around the balcony when she gets in her romantic moods, which, on her

13

professional lawyer schedule, are about once a year, thank god. It's pathetic. He thinks she's repulsive, though. I don't know that, that's what I think. But he loves me, that's for sure.

So next day, Saturday—that rabbity guy, Paul's his name, he did my shift for me—we go downtown and I got him to buy me this suit. Three hundred dollars from Saks. Oh, and I got shoes. So I stayed later with him because of the clothes, and I was a little happy because I thought at least now I'd have something good to wear with Glenn. My dad and I got brownie sundaes at Sweet Dreams and I got home by five. He was crying when he dropped me off.

"Don't cry, Dad. Please," I said. Jesus, how can you not hate someone who's always begging from you.

Lauren had Poly Styrene on the stereo and a candle lit in our room. I was never so glad to be home.

"Hey," Lauren said. She was on her bed, with her legs propped up on the wall. She'd just shaved. She was rubbing in cream.

I flopped down on my bed. "Ohhhh," I said, grabbing the sides of the mattress.

"Hey, can you keep a secret about what I did today?" Lauren said. "I went to that therapist, up at Cowell."

"You have the greatest legs," I said, quiet. "Why don't you ever wear skirts?"

She stopped what she was doing and stood up. "You think they're good? I don't like the way they look, except in jeans." She looked down at them. "They're crooked, see?" She shook her head. "I don't want to think about it."

Then she went to her dresser and started rolling a joint. "Want some?"

"A little."

She lit up, lay back on her bed and held her arm out for me to come take the joint.

"So, she was this really great woman. Warm, kind of chubby. She knew instantly what kind of man Brent was." Lauren snapped her fingers. "Like that." Brent was the pool man Lauren had an affair with, home in LA.

I'm back in the room maybe an hour, putting on mascara, my jeans are on the bed pressed, and the phone rings and it's my dad and I say, "Listen, just leave me alone."

"You don't care about me anymore."

"I just saw you. I have nothing to say. We just saw each other."

"What are you doing tonight?"

"Going out."

"Who are you seeing?"

"Glenn."

He sighs. "So you really like him, huh?"

"Yeah, I do and you should be glad. You should be glad I have a boyfriend." I pull the cord out into the hall and sit down on the floor there. There's this long pause.

"We're not going to end up together, are we?"

I felt like all the air's knocked out of me. I looked out the window and everything looked dead and still. The parked cars. The trees with pink toilet paper strung between the branches. The church all closed up across the street.

"No, we won't, Daddy."

He was crying. "I know, I know."

I hung up the phone and went back and sat in the hall. I'm scared, too. I don't know what'll happen.

I don't know. It's been going on I guess as long as I can remember. I mean, not the sex, but my father. When I was a little kid, tiny little kid, my dad came in before bed and said his prayers with me. He kneeled down by my bed and I was on my back. PRAYERS. He'd lift up my pajama top and put his hands on my breast. Little fried eggs, he said. One time with his tongue. Then one night, he pulled down the elastic of my pajama pants. He did it for an hour and then I came. Don't believe anything they ever tell you about kids not coming. That first time was the biggest I ever had and I didn't even know what it was then. It just kept going and going as if he was breaking me through layers and layers of glass and I felt like I'd slipped and let go and I didn't have myself anymore, he had me, and once I'd slipped like that I'd never be the same again.

We had this sprinkler in our back lawn, Danny and me used to run through it in summer and my dad'd be outside, working on the grass or the hedge or something and he'd squirt us with the hose. I used to wear a bathing suit bottom, no top—we were this modern family, our parents walked around the house naked after showers and then Danny and I ended up both being these modest kids, can't stand anyone to see us even in our underwear, I always dress

15

facing the closet, Lauren teases me. We'd run through the sprinkler and my dad would come up and pat my bottom and the way he put his hand on my thigh, I felt like Danny could tell it was different than the way he touched him, I was like something he owned.

First time when I was nine, I remember, Dad and me were in the shower together. My mom might have even been in the house, they did that kind of stuff, it was supposed to be OK. Anyway, we're in the shower and I remember this look my dad had. Like he was daring me, knowing he knew more than I did. We're both under the shower. The water pasted his hair down on his head and he looked younger and weird. "Touch it. Don't be afraid of it," he says. And he grabs my thighs on the outside and pulls me close to him, pulling on my fat.

He waited till I was twelve to really do it. I don't know if you can call it rape, I was a good sport. The creepy thing is I know how it felt for him, I could see it on his face when he did it. He thought he was getting away with something. We were supposed to go hiking but right away that morning when we got into the car, he knew he was going to do it. He couldn't wait to get going. I said I didn't feel good, I had a cold, I wanted to stay home, but he made me go anyway and we hiked two miles and he set up the tent. He told me to take my clothes off and I undressed just like that, standing there in the woods. He's the one who was nervous and got us into the tent. I looked old for twelve, small but old. And right there on the ground, he spread my legs open and pulled my feet up and fucked me. I bled. I couldn't even breathe the tent was so small. He could have done anything. He could have killed me, he had me alone on this mountain.

I think about that sometimes when I'm alone with Glenn in my bed. It's so easy to hurt people. They just lie there and let you have them. I could reach out and choke Glenn to death, he'd be so shocked, he wouldn't stop me. You can just take what you want.

My dad thought he was getting away with something but he didn't. He was the one that fell in love, not me. And after that day, when we were back in the car, I was the one giving orders. From then on, I got what I wanted. He spent about twice as much money on me as on Danny and everyone knew it, Danny and my mom, too. How do you think I got good clothes and a good bike and a good stereo? My dad's not rich, you know. And I'm the one who got to go away to college even though it killed him. Says it's the saddest thing that ever happened in his life, me going away and leaving him. But when I was a little kid that day, he wasn't in love with me, not like he is now.

Only thing I'm sad about isn't either of my parents, it's Danny. Leaving Danny alone there with them. He used to send Danny out of the house. My mom'd be at work on a Saturday afternoon or something or even in the morning and my dad would kick my little brother out of his own house. Go out and play, Danny. Why doncha catch some rays. And Danny just went and got his glove and baseball from the closet and he'd go and throw it against the house, against the outside wall, in the driveway. I'd be in my room, I'd be like dead, I'd be wood, telling myself this doesn't count, no one has to know, I'll say I'm still a virgin, it's not really happening to me, I'm dead, I'm blank, I'm just letting time stop and pass, and then I'd hear the sock of the ball in the mitt and the slam of the screen door and I knew it was true, it was really happening.

Glenn's the one I want to tell. I can't ever tell Glenn.

I called my mom. Pay phone, collect, hour long call. I don't know, I got real mad last night and I just told her. I thought when I came here, it'd just go away. But it's not going away. It makes me weird with Glenn. In the morning, with Glenn, when it's time to get up, I can't get up. I cry.

I knew it'd be bad. Poor Danny. Well, my mom says she might leave our dad. She cried for an hour, no jokes, on the phone.

How could he DO this to me, she kept yelping. To her. Everything's always to her.

But then she called an hour later, she'd talked to a psychiatrist already, she's kicked Dad out, and she arrives, just arrives here at Berkeley. But she was good. She says she's on my side, she'll help me, I don't know, I felt OK. She stayed in a hotel and she wanted to know if I wanted to stay there with her but I said no, I'd see her more in a week or something, I just wanted to go back to my dorm. She found this group. She says, just in San Jose, there's hundreds of families like ours, yeah, great, that's what I said. But there's groups. She's going to a group of other thick-o mothers like her,

17

these wives who didn't catch on. She wanted me to go to a group of girls, yeah, molested girls, that's what they call them, but I said no, I have friends here already, she can do what she wants.

I talked to my dad, too, that's the sad thing, he feels like he's lost me and he wants to die and I don't know, he doesn't know what he's doing. He called in the middle of the night.

"Just tell me one thing, honey. Please tell me the truth. When did you stop?"

"Dad."

"Because I remember once you said I was the only person who ever understood you."

"I was ten years old."

"OK, OK. I'm sorry."

He didn't want to get off the phone. "You know, I love you, honey. I always will."

"Yeah, well."

My mom's got him lined up for a psychiatrist, too, she says he's lucky she's not sending him to jail. I *am* a lawyer, she keeps saying, as if we could forget. She'd pay for me to go to a shrink now, too, but I said no, forget it.

It's over. Glenn and I are, over. I feel like my dad's lost me everything. I sort of want to die now. I'm telling you I feel terrible. I told Glenn and that's it, it's over. I can't believe it either. Lauren says she's going to hit him.

I told him and we're not seeing each other anymore. Nope. He said he wanted to just think about everything for a few days. He said it had nothing to do with my father but he'd been feeling a little too settled lately. He said we don't have fun anymore, it's always so serious. That was Monday. So every meal after that, I sat with Lauren in the cafeteria and he's there on the other side, messing around with the guys. He sure didn't look like he was in any kind of agony. Wednesday, I saw Glenn over by the window in this food fight, slipping off his chair and I couldn't stand it, I got up and left and went to our room.

But I went and said I wanted to talk to Glenn that night, I didn't even have any dinner, and he said he wanted to be friends. He looked at me funny and I haven't heard from him. It's, I don't know, seven days, eight.

I know there are other guys. I live in a dorm full of them, or half-full of them. Half girls. But I keep thinking of Glenn 'cause of happiness, that's what makes me want to hang onto him.

There was this one morning when we woke up in his room, it was light out already, white light all over the room. We were sticky and warm, the sheet was all tangled. His roommate, this little blonde boy, was still sleeping. I watched his eyes open and he smiled and then he went down the hall to take a shower. Glenn was hugging me and it was nothing unusual, nothing special. We didn't screw. We were just there. We kissed, but slow, the way it is when your mouth is still bad from sleep.

I was happy that morning. I didn't have to do anything. We got dressed, went to breakfast, I don't know. Took a walk. He had to go to work at a certain time and I had that sleepy feeling from waking up with the sun on my head and he said he didn't want to say good-bye to me. There was that pang. One of those looks like as if at that second, we both felt the same way.

I shrugged. I could afford to be casual then. We didn't say good-bye. I walked with him to the shed by the Eucalyptus Grove. That's where they keep all the gardening tools, the rakes, the hoes, the mowers, big bags of grass seed slumped against the wall. It smelled like hay in there. Glenn changed into his uniform and we went to the North Side, up in front of the Chancellor's manor, that thick perfect grass. And Glenn gave me a ride on the lawn mower, on the handlebars. It was bouncing over these little bumps in the lawn and I was hanging onto the handlebars, laughing. I couldn't see Glenn but I knew he was there behind me. I looked around at the buildings and the lawns, there's a fountain there, and one dog was drinking from it.

See, I can't help but remember things like that. Even now, I'd rather find some way, even though he's not asking for it, to forgive Glenn. I'd rather have it work out with him, because I want more days like that. I wish I could have a whole life like that. But I guess nobody does, not just me.

I saw him in the mailroom yesterday, we're both just standing there, each opening our little boxes, getting our mail—neither of us had any—I was hurt but I wanted to reach out and touch his face. He has this hard chin, it's pointy and all bone. Lauren says she wants to hit him.

I mean, I think of him spinning around in his backyard and that's why I love him and he should understand. I go over it all and think

19

I should have just looked at him and said I can't believe you're doing this to me. Right there in the mailroom. Now when I think that, I think maybe if I'd said that, in those words, maybe it would be different.

But then I think of my father—he feels like there was a time when we had fun, when we were happy together. I mean, I can remember being in my little bed with Dad and maybe cracking jokes, maybe laughing, but he probably never heard Danny's baseball in his mitt the way I did or I don't know. I remember late in the afternoon, wearing my dad's navy blue sweatshirt with a hood and riding bikes with him and Danny down to the diamond.

But that's over. I don't know if I'm sorry it happened. I mean I am, but it happened, that's all. It's just one of the things that happened to me in my life. But I would never go back, never. And what hurts so much is that maybe that's what Glenn is thinking about me.

I told Lauren last night. I had to. She kept asking me what happened with Glenn. She was so good, you couldn't believe it, she was great. We were talking late and this morning we drove down to go to House of Pancakes for breakfast, get something good instead of watery eggs for a change. And on the way, Lauren's driving, she just skids to a stop on this street, in front of this elementary school. "Come on," she says. It's early, but there's already people inside the windows.

We hooked our fingers in the metal fence. You know, one of those aluminum fences around a playground. There were pigeons standing on the painted game circles. Then a bell rang and all these kids came out, yelling, spilling into groups. This was a poor school, mostly black kids, Mexican kids, all in bright colors. There's a Nabisco factory nearby and the whole air smelled like blueberry muffins.

The girls were jumproping and the boys were shoving and running and hanging onto the monkey bars. Lauren pinched her fingers on the back of my neck and pushed my head against the fence.

"Eight years old. Look at them. They're eight years old. One of their fathers is sleeping with one of those girls. Look at her. Do you blame her? Can you blame her? Because if you can forgive her you can forgive yourself."

"I'll kill him," I said.

"And I'll kill Glenn," Lauren says.

So we went and got pancakes. And drank coffee until it was time for class.

I saw Glenn yesterday. It was so weird after all this time. I just had lunch with Lauren. We picked up tickets for Talking Heads and I wanted to get back to the lab before class and I'm walking along and Glenn was working, you know, on the lawn in front of the Mobi Building. He was still gorgeous. I was just going to walk, but he yelled over at me.

"Hey, Jenny."

"Hi, Glenn."

He congratulated me, he heard about the NSF thing. We stood there. He has another girlfriend now. I don't know, when I looked at him and stood there by the lawnmower, it's chugging away, I felt the same as I always used to, that I loved him and all that, but he might just be one of those things you can't have. Like I should have been for my father and look at him now. Oh, I think he's better, they're all better, but I'm gone, he'll never have me again.

I'm glad they're there and I'm here, but it's strange, I feel more alone now. Glenn looked down at the little pile of grass by the lawnmower and said, "Well, Kid, take care of yourself," and I said, "You too, bye," and started walking.

So, you know what's bad, though, I started taking stuff again. Little stuff from the mailroom. No packages and not people I know anymore.

But I take one letter a Saturday, I make it just one and someone I don't know. And I keep 'em and burn 'em with a match in the bathroom sink and wash the ashes down the drain. I wait until the end of the shift. I always expect it to be something exciting. The two so far were just everyday letters, just mundane, so that's all that's new, I-had-a-porkchop-for-dinner letters.

But something happened today. I was in the middle, three-quarters way down the bag, still looking, I hadn't picked my letter for the day, I'm being really stern, I really mean just one, no more, and there's this little white envelope addressed to me. I sit there, trembling with it in my hand. It's the first one I've gotten all year. It was my name and address, typed out, and I just stared at it. There's no address. I got so nervous, I thought maybe it was from

21

Glenn, of course. I wanted it to be from Glenn so bad, but then I knew it couldn't be, he's got that new girlfriend now, so I threw it in the garbage can right there, one of those with the swinging metal door and then I finished my shift. My hands were sweating, I smudged the writing on one of the envelopes.

So all the letters are in boxes, I clean off the table, fold the bags up neat and close the door, ready to go. And then I thought, I don't have to keep looking at the garbage can, I'm allowed to take it back, that's my letter. And I fished it out, the thing practically lopped my arm off. And I had it and I held it a few minutes, wondering who it was from. Then I put it in my mailbox so I can go like everybody else and get mail.

nominated by The Iowa Review, *Raymond Carver,*
DeWitt Henry and Mary Morris

NOT-KNOWING

by DONALD BARTHELME

from THE GEORGIA REVIEW

L ET US suppose that someone is writing a story. From the world of conventional signs he takes an azalea bush, plants it in a pleasant park. He takes a gold pocket watch from the world of conventional signs and places it under the azalea bush. He takes from the same rich source a handsome thief and a chastity belt, places the thief in the chastity belt and lays him tenderly under the azalea, not neglecting to wind the gold pocket watch so that its ticking will, at length, awaken the now-sleeping thief. From the Sarah Lawrence campus he borrows a pair of seniors, Jacqueline and Jemima, and sets them to walking in the vicinity of the azalea bush and the handsome, chaste thief. Jacqueline and Jemima have just failed the Graduate Record Examination and are cursing God in colorful Sarah Lawrence language. What happens next?

Of course, I don't know.

It's appropriate to pause and say that the writer is one who, embarking upon a task, does not know what to do. I cannot tell you, at this moment, whether, Jacqueline and Jemima will succeed or fail in their effort to jimmy the chastity belt's lock, or whether the thief, whose name is Zeno and who has stolen the answer sheets for the next set of Graduate Record Examinations, will pocket the pocket watch or turn it over to the nearest park employee. The fate of the azalea bush, whether it will bloom or strangle in a killing frost, is unknown to me.

A very conscientious writer might purchase an azalea at the Downtown Nursery and a gold watch at Tiffany's, hire a handsome thief fresh from Riker's Island, obtain the loan of a chastity belt from the Metropolitan, inveigle Jacqueline and Jemima in from Bronxville, and arrange them all under glass for study, writing up the results in honest, even fastidious prose. But in so doing he places himself in the realm of journalism or sociology. The not-knowing is crucial to art, is what permits art to be made. Without the scanning process engendered by not-knowing, without the possibility of having the mind move in unanticipated directions, there would be no invention.

This is not to say that I don't know anything about Jacqueline or Jemima, but what I do know comes into being at the instant it's inscribed. Jacqueline, for example, loathes her mother, whereas Jemima dotes on hers—I discover this by writing the sentence that announces it. Zeno was fathered by a—what? Polar bear? Roller skate? Shower of gold? I opt for the shower of gold, for Zeno is a hero (although he's just become one by virtue of his golden parent). Inside the pocket watch there is engraved a legend. Can I make it out? I think so: *Drink me*, it says. No no, can't use it, that's Lewis Carroll's. But could Zeno be a watch-swallower rather than a thief? No again, Zeno'd choke on it, and so would the reader. There are rules.

Writing is a process of dealing with not-knowing, a forcing of what and how. We have all heard novelists testify to the fact that, beginning a new book, they are utterly baffled as to how to proceed, what should be written and how it might be written, even though they've done a dozen. At best there's a slender intuition, not much greater than an itch. The anxiety attached to this situation is not inconsiderable. "Nothing to paint and nothing to paint with," as Beckett says of Bram van Velde. The not-knowing is not simple, because it's hedged about with prohibitions, roads that may not be taken. The more serious the artist, the more problems he takes into account and the more considerations limit his possible initiatives—a point to which I shall return.

What kind of a fellow is Zeno? How do I know until he's opened his mouth?

"Gently, ladies, gently," says Zeno, as Jacqueline and Jemima bash away at the belt with a spade borrowed from a friendly park employee. And to the park employee: "Somebody seems to have lost this-here watch."

Let us change the scene.

Alphonse, the park employee from the preceding episode, he

who lent the spade, is alone in his dismal room on West Street (I could position him as well in a four-story townhouse on East Seventy-second, but you'd object, and rightly so, verisimilitude forbids it, nothing's calculated quicker than a salary). Alphonse, like so many toilers in the great city, is not as simple as he seems. Like those waiters who are really actors and those cab drivers who are really composers of electronic music, Alphonse is sunlighting as a Parks Department employee although he is, in reality, a literary critic. We find him writing a letter to his friend Gaston, also a literary critic although masquerading pro tem as a guard at the Whitney Museum. Alphonse poises paws over his Smith-Corona and writes:

Dear Gaston,

Yes, you are absolutely right—Postmodernism is dead. A stunning blow, but not entirely surprising. I am spreading the news as rapidly as possible, so that all of our friends who are in the Postmodernist "bag" can get out of it before their cars are repossessed and the insurance companies tear up their policies. Sad to see Postmodernism go (and so quickly!). I was fond of it. As fond, almost, as I was of its grave and noble predecessor, Modernism. But we cannot dwell in the done-for. The death of a movement is a natural part of life, as was understood so well by the partisans of Naturalism, which is dead.

I remember exactly where I was when I realized that Postmodernism had bought it. I was in my study with a cup of tequila and William Y's new book, *One-Half*. Y's work is, we agree, good—*very* good. But who can make the leap to greatness while dragging after him the burnt-out boxcars of a dead aesthetic? Perhaps we can find new employment for him. On the roads, for example. When the insight overtook me, I started to my feet, knocking over the tequila, and said aloud (although there was no one to hear), "What? Postmodernism, too?" So many, so many. I put Y's book away on a high shelf and turned to the contemplation of the death of Plainsong, A.D. 958.

By the way: Structuralism's tottering. I heard it from Gerald, who is at Johns Hopkins and thus in the thick of things. You don't have to tell everybody. Frequently, idle talk is enough to give a movement that last little "push" that topples it into its grave. I'm convinced that's what happened to the New Criticism. I'm persuaded that it was Gerald, whispering in the corridors.

On the bright side, one thing that is dead that I don't feel too bad about is Existentialism, which I never thought was anything more than Phenomenology's bathwater anyway. It had a good run, but how peeving it was to hear all those artists going around talking about "the existential moment" and similar claptrap. Luckily, they have stopped doing that now. Similarly, the Nouveau Roman's passing did not disturb me overmuch. "Made dreariness into a religion," you said, quite correctly. I know this was one of your pared-to-the-bone movements and all that, but I didn't even like what they left out. A neat omission usually raises the hairs on the back of my neck. Not here. Robbe-Grillet's only true success, for my money, was with *Jealousy*, which I'm told he wrote in a fit of.

Well, where are we? Surrealism gone, got a little sweet toward the end, you could watch the wine of life turning into Gatorade. Sticky. Altar Poems—those constructed in the shape of an altar for the greater honor and glory of God—have not been seen much lately: missing and presumed dead. The Anti-Novel is dead; I read it in the *Times*. The Anti-Hero and the Anti-Heroine had a thing going which resulted in three Anti-Children, all of them now at M.I.T. The Novel of the Soil is dead, as are Expressionism, Impressionism, Futurism, Imagism, Vorticism, Regionalism, Realism, the Kitchen Sink School of Drama, the Theatre of the Absurd, the Theatre of Cruelty, Black Humor, and Gongorism. You know all this; I'm just totting up. To be a Pre-Raphaelite in the present era is to be somewhat out of touch. And, of course, Concrete Poetry—sank like a stone.

So we have a difficulty. What shall we call the New Thing, which I haven't encountered yet but which is bound to be out there somewhere? Post-Postmodernism sounds, to me, a little lumpy. I've been toying with the Revolution of the Word, II, or the New Revolution of the Word, but I'm afraid the Jolas estate may hold a copyright. It should have the word *new* in it somewhere. The New Newness? Or maybe the Post-New? It's a problem. I await your comments and suggestions. If we're going to slap a saddle on this rough beast, we've got to get moving.

Yours,
Alphonse

If I am slightly more sanguine than Alphonse about Postmodernism, however dubious about the term itself and not altogether clear as to who is supposed to be on the bus and who is not, it's because I locate it in relation to a series of problems, and feel that the problems are durable ones. Problems are a comfort. Wittgenstein said, of philosophers, that some of them suffer from "loss of problems," a development in which everything seems quite simple to them and what they write becomes "immeasurably shallow and trivial." The same can be said of writers. Before I mention some of the specific difficulties I have in mind, I'd like to at least glance at some of the criticisms that have been leveled at the alleged Postmodernists—let's say John Barth, William Gass, John Hawkes, Robert Coover, William Gaddis, Thomas Pynchon, and myself in this country, Calvino in Italy, Peter Handke and Thomas Bernhard in Germany, although other names could be invoked. The criticisms run roughly as follows: that this kind of writing has turned its back on the world, is in some sense not about the world but about its own processes, that it is masturbatory, certainly chilly, that it excludes readers by design, speaks only to the already tenured, or that it does not speak at all, but instead, like Frost's Secret, sits in the center of a ring and Knows.

I would ardently contest each of these propositions, but it's rather easy to see what gives rise to them. The problems that seem to me to define the writer's task at this moment (to the extent that he has chosen them as his problems) are not of a kind that make for ease of communication, for work that rushes toward the reader with outflung arms—rather, they're the reverse. Let me cite three such difficulties that I take to be important, all having to do with language. First, there is art's own project, since Mallarmé, of restoring freshness to a much-handled language, essentially an effort toward finding a language in which making art is possible at all. This remains a ground theme, as potent, problematically, today as it was a century ago. Secondly, there is the political and social contamination of language by its use in manipulation of various kinds over time and the effort to find what might be called a "clean" language, problems associated with the Roland Barthes of *Writing Degree Zero* but also discussed by Lukács and others. Finally, there is the pressure on language from contemporary culture in the broadest sense—I mean our devouring commercial culture— which results in a double impoverishment: theft of complexity from the reader, theft of the reader from the writer.

These are by no means the only thorny matters with which the writer has to deal, nor (allowing for the very great differences among the practitioners under discussion) does every writer called Postmodern respond to them in the same way and to the same degree, nor is it the case that other writers of quite different tendencies are innocent of these concerns. If I call these matters "thorny," it's because any adequate attempt to deal with them automatically creates barriers to the ready assimilation of the work. Art is not difficult because it wishes to be difficult, but because it wishes to be art. However much the writer might long to be, in his work, simple, honest, and straightforward, these virtues are no longer available to him. He discovers that in being simple, honest, and straightforward, nothing much happens: he speaks the speakable, whereas what we are looking for is the as-yet unspeakable, the as-yet unspoken.

With Mallarmé the effort toward mimesis, the representation of the external world, becomes a much more complex thing than it had been previously. Mallarmé shakes words loose from their attachments and bestows new meanings upon them, meanings which point not toward the external world but toward the Absolute, acts of poetic intuition. This is a fateful step; not for nothing does Barthes call him the Hamlet of literature. It produces, for one thing, a poetry of unprecedented difficulty. You will find no Mallarmé in Bartlett's *Familiar Quotations*. Even so ardent an admirer as Charles Mauron speaks of the sense of alienation enforced by his work. Mauron writes: "All who remember the day when first they looked into the *Poems* or the *Divagations* will testify to that curious feeling of *exclusion* which put them, in the face of a text written with *their* words (and moreover, as they could somehow feel, magnificently written), suddenly outside their own language, deprived of their rights in a common speech, and, as it were, rejected by their oldest friends." Mallarmé's work is also, and perhaps most importantly, a step toward establishing a new ontological status for the poem, as an object in the world rather than a representation of the world. But the ground seized is dangerous ground. After Mallarmé the struggle to renew language becomes a given for the writer, his exemplary quest an imperative. Mallarmé's work, "this whisper that is so close to silence," as Marcel Raymond calls it, is at once a liberation and a loss to silence of a great deal of territory.

The silencing of an existing rhetoric (in Harold Rosenberg's phrase) is also what is at issue in Barthes's deliberations in *Writing Degree Zero* and after—in this case a variety of rhetorics seen as actively pernicious rather than passively inhibiting. The question is, what is the complicity of language in the massive crimes of Fascism, Stalinism, or (by implication) our own policies in Vietnam? In the control of societies by the powerful and their busy functionaries? If these abominations are all in some sense facilitated by, made possible by, language, to what degree is that language ruinously contaminated (considerations also raised by George Steiner in his well-known essay "The Hollow Miracle" and, much earlier, by George Orwell)? I am sketching here, inadequately, a fairly complex argument; I am not particularly taken with Barthes's tentative solutions but the problems command the greatest respect. Again, we have language deeply suspicious of its own behavior; although this suspicion is not different in kind from Hemingway's noticing, early in the century, that words like *honor*, *glory*, and *country* were perjured, bought, the skepticism is far deeper now, and informed as well by the investigations of linguistic philosophers, structuralists, semioticians. Even conjunctions must be inspected carefully. "I read each word with the feeling appropriate to it," says Wittgenstein. "The word 'but' for example with the but-feeling. . . ." He is not wrong. Isn't the but-feeling, as he calls it, already sending us headlong down a greased slide before we've had the time to contemplate the proposition it's abutting? Quickly now, quickly—when you hear the phrase "our vital interests" do you stop to wonder whether you were invited to the den, Zen Klan, or coven meeting at which these were defined? Did you speak?

In turning to the action of contemporary culture on language, and thus on the writer, the first thing to be noticed is a loss of reference. If I want a world of reference to which all possible readers in this country can respond, there is only one universe of discourse available, that in which the Love Boat sails on seas of passion like a Flying Dutchman of passion and the dedicated men in white of *General Hospital* pursue, with evenhanded diligence, triple bypasses and the nursing staff. This limits things somewhat. The earlier newspaper culture, which once dealt in a certain amount of nuance and zestful, highly literate hurly-burly, has deteriorated shockingly. The newspaper I worked for as a raw youth, thirty years ago, is today a pallid imitation of its former self. Where once we could put spurious quotes in the paper and attribute them to Ambrose Bierce and be fairly sure that enough readers would get the joke to make the joke worthwhile, from the point of view of both reader and writer, no such common ground now exists. The situation is not peculiar to this country. Steiner remarks of the best current journalism in Germany that, read against an average number of the *Frankfurter Zeitung* of pre-Hitler days, it's difficult at times to believe that both are written in German. At the other end of the scale much of the most exquisite description of the world, discourse about the world, is now being carried on in mathematical languages obscure to most people—certainly to me—and the contributions the sciences once made to our common language in the form of coinages, new words and concepts, are now available only to specialists. When one adds the ferocious appropriation of high culture by commercial culture—it takes, by my estimate, about forty-five minutes for any given novelty in art to travel from the Mary Boone Gallery on West Broadway to the display windows of Henri Bendel on Fifty-seventh Street—one begins to appreciate the seductions of silence.

Problems in part define the kind of work the writer chooses to do, and are not to be avoided but embraced. A writer, says Karl Kraus, is a man who can make a riddle out of an answer.

Let me begin again.

Jacqueline and Jemima are instructing Zeno, who has returned the purloined GRE documents and is thus restored to dull respectability, in Postmodernism. Postmodernism, they tell him, has turned its back on the world, is not about the world but about its own processes, is masturbatory, certainly chilly, excludes readers by design, speaks only to the already tenured, or does not speak at all, but instead—

Zeno, to demonstrate that he too knows a thing or two, quotes the critic Perry Meisel on semiotics. "Semiotics," he says, "is in a position to claim that no phenomenon has any ontological status outside its place in the particular information system from which it draws its meaning"—he takes a large gulp of his Gibson— "and therefore, all language is finally groundless." I am eavesdropping and I am much reassured. This insight is one I can use. Gaston, the critic who is a guard at the Whitney Museum, is in love with an IRS agent named Madelaine, the very IRS agent, in fact, who is auditing my return for the year 1982. "Madelaine," I say kindly to her over lunch, "semiotics is in a position to claim that no phenomenon has any ontological status outside its place in the particular information system from which it draws its meaning, and therefore, all language is finally groundless, including that of those funny little notices you've been sending me." "Yes," says Madelaine kindly, pulling from her pocket a large gold pocket watch that Alphonse has sold Gaston for twenty dollars, her lovely violet eyes atwitter, "but some information systems are more enforceable than others." Alas, she's right.

If the writer is taken to be the work's way of getting itself written, a sort of lightning rod for an accumulation of atmospheric disturbances, a St. Sebastian absorbing in his tattered breast the arrows of the Zeitgeist, this changes not very much the traditional view of the artist. But it does license a very great deal of critical imperialism.

This is fun for everyone. A couple of years ago I received a letter from a critic requesting permission to reprint a story of mine as an addendum to the piece he had written about it. He attached the copy of my story he proposed to reproduce, and I was amazed to find that my poor story had sprouted a set of tiny numbers—one to eighty-eight, as I recall—an army of tiny numbers marching over the surface of my poor distracted text. Resisting the temptation to tell him that all the tiny numbers were in the wrong places, I gave him permission to do what he wished, but I did notice that by a species of literary judo the status of my text had been reduced to that of footnote.

There is, in this kind of criticism, an element of aggression that

31

gives one pause. Deconstruction is an enterprise that announces its intentions with startling candor. Any work of art depends upon a complex series of interdependences. If I wrench the rubber tire from the belly of Rauschenberg's famous goat to determine, in the interest of a finer understanding of same, whether the tire is a B. F. Goodrich or a Uniroyal, the work collapses, more or less behind my back. I say this not because I find this kind of study valueless but because the mystery worthy of study, for me, is not the signification of parts but how they come together, the tire wrestled over the goat's hind legs. Calvin Tomkins tells us in *The Bride and the Bachelors* that Rauschenberg himself says that the tire seemed "something as unavoidable as the goat." To see both goat and tire as "unavoidable" choices, in the context of art-making, is to illuminate just how strange the combinatorial process can be. Nor was the choice a hasty one; Tomkins tells us that the goat had been in the studio for three years and had appeared in two previous versions (the final version is titled "Monogram") before it met the tire.

Modern-day critics speak of "recuperating" a text, suggesting an accelerated and possibly strenuous nursing back to health of a basically sickly text, very likely one that did not even know itself to be ill. I would argue that in the competing methodologies of contemporary criticism, many of them quite rich in implications, a sort of tyranny of great expectations obtains, a rage for final explanations, a refusal to allow a work that mystery which is essential to it. I hope I am not myself engaging in mystification if I say, not that the attempt should not be made, but that the mystery exists. I see no immediate way out of the paradox—tear a mystery to tatters and you have tatters, not mystery—I merely note it and pass on.

We can, however, wonder for a moment why the goat girdled with its tire is somehow a magical object, rather than, say, only a dumb idea. Harold Rosenberg speaks of the contemporary artwork as "anxious," as wondering: Am I a masterpiece or simply a pile of junk? (If I take many of my examples here from the art world rather than the world of literature it is because the issues are more quickly seen in terms of the first: "goat" and "tire" are standing in for pages of prose, pounds of poetry.) What precisely is it in the coming together of goat and tire that is magical? It's not the surprise of seeing the goat attired, although that's part of it. One might say, for example, that the tire *contests* the goat, *contradicts* the goat, as a mode of being, even that the tire *reproaches* the goat, in some sense. On the simplest punning level, the goat is *tired*. Or that the unfortunate tire has *been caught by* the goat, which has been fishing in the Hudson—goats eat anything, as everyone knows—or that the goat is being *consumed by* the tire; it's outside, after all, mechanization takes command. Or that the goateed goat is protesting the fatigue of its friend, the tire, by wearing it as a sort of STRIKE button. Or that two contrasting models of infinity are being presented, tires and goats both being infinitely reproducible, the first depending on the good fortunes of the B. F. Goodrich Company and the second upon the copulatory enthusiasm of goats—parallel production lines suddenly met. And so on. What is magical about the object is that it at once invites and resists interpretation. Its artistic worth is measurable by the degree to which it remains, after interpretation, vital—no interpretation or cardiopulmonary push-pull can exhaust or empty it.

In what sense is the work "about" the world, the world that Jacqueline and Jemima have earnestly assured Zeno the work has turned its scarlet rump to? It is to this vexing question that we shall turn next.

Let us discuss the condition of my desk. It is messy, mildly messy. The messiness is both physical (coffee cups, cigarette ash) and spiritual (unpaid bills, unwritten novels). The emotional life of the man who sits at the desk is also messy—I am in love with a set of twins, Hilda and Heidi, and in a fit of enthusiasm I have joined the Bolivian army. The apartment in which the desk is located seems to have been sublet from Moonbeam McSwine. In the streets outside the apartment melting snow has revealed a choice assortment of decaying et cetera. Furthermore, the social organization of the country is untidy, the world situation in disarray. How do I render all this messiness, and if I succeed, what have I done?

In a common-sense way we agree that I attempt to find verbal equivalents for whatever it is I wish to render. The unpaid bills are easy enough. I need merely quote one: FINAL DISCONNECT NOTICE. Hilda and Heidi are somewhat more difficult. I can say that they are beautiful—why not?—and you will more or less agree, although the bald statement has hardly stirred your senses. I can describe them—Hilda has the map of Bolivia tattooed on her

33

right cheek and Heidi habitually wears, on her left hand, a set of brass knuckles wrought of solid silver—and they move a step closer. Best of all, perhaps, I can permit them to speak, for they speak much as we do.

"On Valentine's Day," says Hilda, "he sent me oysters, a dozen and a half."

"He sent me oysters too," says Heidi, "two dozen."

"Mine were long-stemmed oysters," says Hilda, "on a bed of the most wonderful spinach."

"Oh yes, spinach," says Heidi, "he sent me spinach too, miles and miles of spinach, wrote every bit of it himself."

To render "messy" adequately, to the point that you are enabled to feel it—it should, ideally, frighten your shoes—I would have to be more graphic than the decorum of the occasion allows. What should be emphasized is that one proceeds by way of particulars. If I know how a set of brass knuckles feels on Heidi's left hand it's because I bought one once, in a pawnshop, not to smash up someone's face but to exhibit on a pedestal in a museum show devoted to cultural artifacts of ambivalent status. The world enters the work as it enters our ordinary lives, not as world-view or system but in sharp particularity: a tax notice from Madelaine, a snowball containing a résumé from Gaston.

The words with which I attempt to render "messy," like any other words, are not inert, rather they are furiously busy. We do not mistake the words *the taste of chocolate* for the taste of chocolate itself, but neither do we miss the tease in *taste*, the shock in *chocolate*. Words have halos, patinas, overhangs, echoes. The word *halo*, for instance, may invoke St. Hilarius, of whom we've seen too little lately. The word *patina* brings back the fine pewtery shine on the saint's halo. The word *overhang* reminds us that we have, hanging over us, a dinner date with St. Hilarius, that crashing bore. The word *echo* restores to us Echo herself, poised like the White Rock girl on the overhang of a patina of a halo— infirm ground, we don't want the poor spirit to pitch into the pond where Narcissus blooms eternally, they'll bump foreheads, or maybe other parts closer to the feet, a scandal. There's chocolate smeared all over Hilarius' halo—messy, messy. . . .

34

The combinatorial agility of words, the exponential generation of meaning once they're allowed to go to bed together, allows the writer to surprise himself, makes art possible, reveals how much of Being we haven't yet encountered. It could be argued that computers can do this sort of thing for us, with critic-computers monitoring their output. When computers learn how to make jokes, artists will be in serious trouble. But artists will respond in such a way as to make art impossible for the computer. They will redefine art to take into account (that is, to exclude) technology—photography's impact upon painting and painting's brilliant response being a clear and comparatively recent example.

The prior history of words is one of the aspects of language the world uses to smuggle itself into the work. If words can be contaminated by the world, they can also carry with them into the work trace elements of world which can be used in a positive sense. We must allow ourselves the advantages of our disadvantages.

A late bulletin: Hilda and Heidi have had a baby, with which they're thoroughly displeased, it's got no credit cards and can't speak French, they'll send it back. . . . Messy.

Style is not much a matter of choice. One does not sit down to write and think: Is this poem going to be a Queene Anne poem, a Biedermeier poem, a Vienna Secession poem, or a Chinese Chippendale poem? Rather it is both a response to constraint and a seizing of opportunity. Very often a constraint is an opportunity. It would seem impossible to write *Don Quixote* once again, yet Borges has done so with great style, improving on the original (as he is not slow to tell us) while remaining faithful to it, faithful as a tick on a dog's belly. I don't mean that whim does not intrude. Why do I avoid, as much as possible, using the semicolon? Let me be plain: the semicolon is ugly, ugly as a tick on a dog's belly. I pinch them out of my prose. The great German writer Arno Schmidt, punctuation-drunk, averages eleven to a page.

Style is of course *how*. And the degree to which *how* has become *what*—since, say, Flaubert—is a question that men of conscience wax wroth about, and should. If I say of my friend that on this issue his marbles are a little flat on one side, this does not mean that I do not love my friend. He, on the other hand, considers that I am ridden by strange imperatives, and that the little piece I gave to

35

the world last week, while nice enough in its own way, would have been vastly better had not my deplorable aesthetics caused me to score it for banjulele, cross between a banjo and a uke. Bless Babel.

Let us suppose that I am the toughest banjulele player in town and that I have contracted to play "Melancholy Baby" for six hours before an audience that will include the four next-toughest banjulele players in town. We imagine the smoky basement club, the hustling waiters (themselves students of the jazz banjulele), Jacqueline, Jemima, Zeno, Alphonse, Gaston, Madelaine, Hilda, and Heidi forming a congenial group at the bar. There is one thing of which you may be sure: I am not going to play "Melancholy Baby" as written. Rather I will play something that is parallel, in some sense, to "Melancholy Baby," based upon the chords of "Melancholy Baby"—commentary, exegesis, elaboration, contradiction. The interest of my construction, if any, is to be located in the space between the new entity I have constructed and the "real" "Melancholy Baby," which remains in the mind as the horizon which bounds my efforts.

This is, I think, the relation of art to world. I suggest that art is always a meditation upon external reality rather than a representation of external reality or a jackleg attempt to "be" external reality. If I perform even reasonably well, no one will accuse me of not providing a true, verifiable, note-for-note reproduction of "Melancholy Baby"—it will be recognized that this was not what I was after. Twenty years ago I was much more convinced of the autonomy of the literary object than I am now, and even wrote a rather persuasive defense of the proposition that I have just rejected: that the object is itself world. Beguiled by the rhetoric of the time—the sculptor Phillip Pavia was publishing a quite good magazine called *It Is*, and this was typical—I felt that the high ground had been claimed and wanted to place my scuffed cowboy boots right there. The proposition's still attractive. What's the right answer? Bless Babel.

A couple of years ago I visited Willem de Kooning's studio in East Hampton, and when the big doors are opened one can't help seeing—it's a shock—the relation between the rushing green world outside and the paintings. Precisely how de Kooning manages to distill nature into art is a mystery, but the explosive relation is there, I've seen it. Once when I was in Elaine de

Kooning's studio on Broadway, at a time when the metal sculptor Herbert Ferber occupied the studio immediately above, there came through the floor a most horrible crashing and banging. "What in the world is that?" I asked, and Elaine said, "Oh, that's Herbert thinking."

Art is a true account of the activity of mind. Because consciousness, in Husserl's formulation, is always consciousness *of* something, art thinks ever of the world, cannot not think of the world, could not turn its back on the world even if it wished to. This does not mean that it's going to be honest as a mailman; it's more likely to appear as a drag queen. The problems I mentioned earlier, as well as others not taken up, enforce complexity. "We do not spend much time in front of a canvas whose intentions are plain," writes Cioran, "music of a specific character, unquestionable contours, exhausts our patience, the over-explicit poem seems . . . incomprehensible." Flannery O'Connor, an artist of the first rank, famously disliked anything that looked funny on the page, and her distaste has widely been taken as a tough-minded put-down of puerile experimentalism. But did she also dislike anything that looked funny on the wall? If so, a severe deprivation. Art cannot remain in one place. A certain amount of movement up, down, across, even a gallop toward the past, is a necessary precondition.

Style enables us to speak, to imagine again. Beckett speaks of "the long sonata of the dead"—where on earth did the word *sonata* come from, imposing as it does an orderly, even exalted design upon the most disorderly, distressing phenomenon known to us? The fact is not challenged, but understood, momentarily, in a new way. It's our good fortune to be able to imagine alternative realities, other possibilities. We can quarrel with the world, constructively (no one alive has quarreled with the world more extensively or splendidly than Beckett). "Belief in progress," says Baudelaire, "is a doctrine of idlers and Belgians." Perhaps. But if I have anything unorthodox to offer here, it's that I think art's project is fundamentally meliorative. The aim of meditating about the world is finally to change the world. It is this meliorative aspect of literature that provides its ethical dimension. We are all Upton Sinclairs, even that Hamlet, Stéphane Mallarmé.

nominated by Philip Booth

OFF PORT TOWNSEND, ONE MONTH BEFORE THE ARRIVAL OF THE U.S.S. OHIO

by HENRY CARLILE

from SEA PEN PRESS AND PAPER MILL

Down Haro Strait and the Strait of Juan De Fuca
the killer whales would breach and roll,
lifting tall dorsals free of the water, breath
popping like steam valves on old boilers.
Black and white they were, like a giant string quartet.

Not vicious as we'd thought,
but tameable and, captive, aiming only to please.
Once, lonely sailors rocked from sleep
by their music through a ship's hull
mistook them for mermaids.

Now, if you put your ear to the water
you might listen to the hiss of electrons,
the turbine's deep nuclear hum,
and pulse of propellers at each revolution
whispering no to the hope of cities.

The morning I saw my first Poseidon
I forgot the salmon I had come to fish for
and rammed the throttle open, closing
at twenty knots, quartering on its bow,
my ragged ban-the-Trident flag unfurled.

From their high place surrounded by periscopes
the curious officers looked down.
I was no Bogart, my boat no African Queen.
I only wished to keep this Poseidon safe
in some post-nuclear museum,

a tame nose we might pat
disarming as the whale's, but for now
it holds course through reaches darkened
by its pace, staining the scenery
it slips through like grease.

Tacking from that wake, I bore toward a reef
of gulls and auklets, candlefish and rising salmon,
white sand cliffs where madronas start and whisper,
blue sky, a red bell hanging on slack tide,
the only black, exposed rock, the whale's dorsal.

Once there was a city state that promised everything,
white as the sand cliffs, with olive trees, promenades
framed in marble, and statues of the old, cruel gods.
Poseidon was one, his weapon the trident—names
we thought we could use because they meant nothing.

nominated by Sandra McPherson and Vern Rutsala

THE THRONE OF THE THIRD HEAVEN OF THE NATIONS MILLENNIUM GENERAL ASSEMBLY

by DENIS JOHNSON

from THE PARIS REVIEW

James Hampton, 1909, Elloree, S.C.—1964, Washington, D.C.
Custodian, General Services Administration
Maker of The Throne

I

I dreamed I had been dreaming,
And sadness did descend.
And when from the first dreaming
I woke, I walked behind

The window crossed with smoke and rain
In Washington, D.C.,
The neighbors strangling newspapers
Or watching the TV

Down on the rug in undershirts
Like bankrupt criminals.
The street where Revelation
Made James Hampton miserable

Lay wet beyond the glass,
And on it moved streetcorner men
In a steam of crossed-out clues
And pompadours and voodoo and

Sweet Jesus made of ivory;
But when I woke, the headlights
Shone out on Elloree.

Two endless roads, four endless fields,
And where I woke, the veils
Of rain fell down around a sign:
FRI & SAT JAM W/ THE MEAN

MONSTER MAN & II.
Nobody in the Elloree,
South Carolina, Stop-n-Go,
Nobody in the Sunoco,

Or in all of Elloree, his birthplace, knows
His name. But right outside
Runs Hampton Street, called probably
For the owners of his family.

God, are you there, for I have been
Long on these highways and I've seen
Miami, Treasure Coast, Space Coast,
I have seen where the astronauts burned,

I have looked where the Fathers placed the pale
Orange churches in the sun,
Have passed through Georgia in its green
Eternity of leaves unturned,

But nothing like Elloree.

41

II

Sam and I drove up from Key West, Florida,
Visited James Hampton's birthplace in South Carolina,
And saw The Throne
At The National Museum of American Art in Washington.
It was in a big room. I couldn't take it all in,
And I was a little frightened.
I left and came back home to Massachusetts.
I'm glad The Throne exists:
My days are better for it, and I feel
Something that makes me know my life is real
To think he died unknown and without a friend,
But this feeling isn't sorrow. I was his friend
As I looked at and was looked at by the rushing-together
    parts
Of this vision of someone who was probably insane
Growing brighter and brighter like a forest after a rain,
And if you look at the leaves of a forest,
At its dirt and its heights, the stuttering mystic
Replication, the blithering symmetry,
You'll go crazy, too. If you look at the city
And its spilled wine
And broken glass, its spilled and broken people and hearts,
You'll go crazy. If you stand
In the world you'll go out of your mind.
But it's all right,
What happened to him. I can, now
That he doesn't have to,
Accept it.
I don't believe that Christ, when he claimed
The last will be first, the lost life saved—
When he implied that the deeply abysmal is deeply
    blessed—
I just can't believe that Christ, when faced
With poor, poor people hoping to become at best
The wives and husbands of a lonely fear,
would have spoken redundantly.
Surely he couldn't have referred to some other time

Or place, when in fact such a place and time
Are unnecessary. We have a time and a place here,
Now, abundantly.

III

He waits forever in front of diagrams
On a blackboard in one of his photographs,
Labels that make no sense attached
To the radiant, alien things he sketched,
Which aren't objects, but plans.
Of his last dated
Vision he stated:
"This design is proof of the Virgin Mary descending
Into Heaven . . ."
The streetcorner men, the shaken earthlings—
It's easy to imagine his hands
When looking at their hands
Of leather, loving on the necks
Of jugs, sweetly touching the dice and bad checks,
And to see in everything a making
Just like his, an unhinged
Deity in an empty garage
Dying alone in some small consolation.
Photograph me photograph me photo
Graph me in my suit of loneliness,
My tie which I have been
Saving for this occasion,
My shoes of dust, my skin of pollen,
Addressing the empty chair; behind me
The Throne of the Third Heaven
Of the Nations Millennium General Assembly.
i AM ALPHA AND OMEGA THE BEGiNNiNG
AND THE END,
The trash of government buildings,
Faded red cloth,
Jelly glasses and lightbulbs,
Metal (cut from coffee cans),
Upholstery tacks, small nails

And simple sewing pins,
Lightbulbs, cardboard,
Kraft paper, desk blotters,
Gold and aluminum foils,
Neighborhood bums the foil
On their wine bottles,
The Revelation.
And I command you not to fear.

nominated by Jim Simmerman and Maura Stanton

OTHER LIVES

fiction by FRANCINE PROSE

from ANTAEUS

CLIMBING UP with a handful of star decals to paste on the bathroom ceiling, Claire sees a suspect-looking shampoo bottle on the cluttered top shelf. When she opens it, the whole room smells like a subway corridor where bums have been pissing for generations. She thinks back a few days to when Miranda and Poppy were playing in here with the door shut. She puts down the stars and yells for the girls with such urgency they come running before she's finished emptying it into the sink.

From the doorway, Poppy and her best friend Miranda look at Claire, then at each other. "Mom," says Poppy. "You threw it *out?*"

Claire wants to ask why they're saving their urine in bottles. But sitting on the edge of the tub has lowered her eye level and she's struck speechless by the beauty of their kneecaps, their long suntanned legs. How strong and shaky and elegant they are! Like newborn giraffes! By now she can't bring herself to ask, so she tells them not to do it again and is left with the rest of the morning to wonder what they had in mind.

She thinks it has something to do with alchemy and with faith, with those moments when children are playing with such pure concentration that anything is possible and the rest of the world drops away and becomes no more real than one of their 3-D Viewmaster slides. She remembers when she was Poppy's age, playing with her own best friend Evelyn. Evelyn's father had been dead several years, but his medical office in a separate wing of their house was untouched, as if office hours might begin any minute. In his chilly consulting room, smelling of carpet dust and furniture

45

polish and more faintly of gauze and sterilizing pans, Claire and Evelyn played their peculiar version of doctor. Claire would come in and from behind the desk Evelyn would give her some imaginary pills. Then Claire would fall down dead and Evelyn would kneel and listen to her heart and say, "I'm sorry, it's too late."

But what Claire remembers best is the framed engraving on Evelyn's father's desk. It was one of those trompe l'oeil pieces you see sometimes in cheap art stores. From one angle, it looked like two Gibson girls at a table sipping ice cream sodas through straws. From another, it looked like a skull. Years later, when Clare learned that Evelyn's father had actually died in jail where he'd been sent for performing illegal abortions, she'd thought what an odd picture to have on an abortionist's desk. But at the time, it had just seemed marvelous. She used to unfocus her eyes and tilt her head so that it flipped back and forth. Skull, ladies. Skull, ladies. Skull.

Dottie's new hairdo, a wide corolla of pale blond curls, makes her look even more like a sunflower—spindly, graceful, rather precariously balanced. At one, when Dottie comes to pick up Miranda, Claire decides not to tell her about the shampoo bottle.

Lately, Dottie's had her mind on higher things. For the past few months, she's been driving down to the New Consciousness Academy in Bennington where she takes courses with titles like "Listening to the Inner Silence" and "Weeds for Your Needs." Claire blames this on one of Dottie's friends, an electrician named Jeanette. Once at a party, Claire overheard Jeanette telling someone how she and her boyfriend practice birth control based on lunar astrology and massive doses of wintergreen tea.

"Coffee?" says Claire tentatively. It's hard to keep track of what substances Dottie's given up. Sometimes, most often in winter when Joey and Raymond are working and the girls are at school, Dottie and Claire get together for lunch. Walking into Dottie's house and smelling woodsmoke and wine and fresh-baked bread, seeing the table set with blue bowls and hothouse anemones and a soup thick with sausage, potatoes, tomatoes put up from the fall, Claire used to feel that she must be living her whole life right. All summer, she's been praying that Dottie won't give up meat.

Now Dottie says, "Have you got any herbal tea?" and Claire

says, "Are you kidding?" "All right, coffee," says Dottie. "Just this once."

As Claire pours the coffee, Dottie fishes around in her enormous parachute-silk purse. Recently, Dottie's been bringing Claire reading material. She'd started off with Krishnamurti, Rajneesh, the songs of Milarepa; Claire tried but she just couldn't, she'd returned them unread. A few weeks back, she'd brought something by Dashiell Hammett about a man named Flitcraft who's walking to lunch one day and a beam falls down from a construction site and just misses him, and he just keeps walking and never goes to his job or back to his wife and family again.

When Claire read that, she wanted to call Dottie up and make her promise not to do something similar. But she didn't. The last time she and Dottie discussed the Academy, Dottie described a technique she'd learned for closing her eyes and pressing on her eyelids just hard enough to see thousands of pinpricks of light. Each one of those dots represents a past life, and if you know how to look, you can see it. In this way, Dottie learned that she'd spent a former life as a footsoldier in Napoleon's army on the killing march to Moscow. That's why she so hates the cold. Somehow Claire hadn't known that Dottie hated the winter, but really, it follows: a half-starved, half-frozen soldier cooking inspired sausage soup three lives later.

"I meant to bring you a book," says Dottie. Then she says, "A crazy thing happened this morning. I was working in front of the house, digging up those irises by the side of the road so I could divide them. I didn't hear anything but I must have had a sense because I turned around and there was this old lady—coiffed, polyestered, dressed for church, it looked like. She told me she'd come over from Montpelier with some friends for a picnic and got separated. Now she was lost and *so* upset.

"I said, Well, okay, I'll drive you back to Montpelier. We got as far as Barre when suddenly her whole story started coming apart and I realized: She hadn't been in Montpelier for twenty years. She was from the Good Shepherd House, that old folks' home up the road from us. I drove her back to the Good Shepherd, what else could I do? The manager thanked me, he was very embarrassed she'd escaped. Then just as I was pulling out, the old lady pointed up at the sky and gave me the most hateful triumphant smile, and I looked up through the windshield and there was this flock of geese heading south." Dottie catches her breath, then says, "You know what? It's August. I'd forgotten."

What Claire can't quite forget is that years ago, the first time she and Joey met Dottie and Raymond, afterwards Joey said, "They don't call her dotty for nothing." It took them both a while to see that what looked at first like dottiness was really an overflow of the same generosity which makes Dottie cook elegant warming meals and drive senile old ladies fifty miles out of her way to Montpelier. On Tuesdays and Thursdays, when Dottie goes down to the Academy, she's a volunteer chauffeur service, picking up class-mates—including Jeanette the electrician—from all over central Vermont. Even Joey's come around to liking her, though Claire's noticed that he's usually someplace else when Dottie's around.

Now he's in the garden, tying up some tomatoes which fell last night in the wind. Finding them this morning—perfect red toma-toes smashed on top of each other—had sent her straight to the bathroom with her handful of star decals. That's the difference between me and Joey, Claire thinks. Thank God there's someone to save what's left of the vines.

Joey doesn't see Claire watching him but Dottie does and starts to flutter, as if she's overstayed. She calls up to Miranda, and just when it begins to seem as if they might not have heard, the girls drag themselves downstairs.

"Why does Miranda have to go?" says Poppy.

"Because it's fifteen miles and Miranda's mom isn't driving fifteen miles back and forth all day," says Claire.

"But I don't want to go," says Miranda.

They stand there, deadlocked, until Poppy says, "I've got an idea. I'll go home with Miranda and tonight her mom and dad can come to dinner and bring us both back and then Miranda can sleep over."

"That's fine with me," says Claire.

"Are you sure?" says Dottie.

Claire's sure. As Dottie leans down to kiss her good-bye, Claire thinks once more of sunflowers, specifically of the ones she and Joey and Poppy plant every summer on a steep slope so you can stand underneath and look up and the sunflowers look forty feet tall.

Washing his hands at the sink, Joey says, "One day she's going to show up in saffron robes with a begging bowl and her hair shaved down to one skanky topknot and then what?"

Claire thinks: Well, then we'll cook up some gluey brown rice and put a big glob in Dottie's bowl. But this sounds like something they'd say at the New Consciousness Academy, some dreadful homily about adaptation and making do. All she can think of is, "I cried because I had no shoes until I met a man who had no feet," and that's not it.

One night, not long after Dottie started attending the Academy, they were all sitting outside and Dottie looked up and said, "Sometimes I feel as if my whole life is that last minute of the planetarium show when they start showing off—that is, showing off what their projector can do—and the moon and planets and stars and even those distant galaxies begin spinning like crazy while they tell you the coming attractions and what time the next show begins. I just want to find someplace where it's not rushing past me so fast. Or where, if it is, I don't care."

"I hope you find it," Joey said. "I really do." Later that night, he told Claire that he knew what Dottie meant. "Still," he said, "it was creepy. The whole conversation was like talking to someone who still thinks *El Topo* is the greatest movie ever made."

Joey had gone through his own spiritual phase: acid, Castenada, long Sunday afternoons in front of the tonkas in the Staten Island Tibetan museum. All this was before he met Claire. He feels that his having grown out of it fifteen years ago gives him the right to criticize. Though actually, he's not mocking Dottie so much as protecting her husband Raymond, his best friend. Remote as the possibility seems, no one wants Dottie to follow in Flitcraft's footsteps.

Now Claire says, "I don't think she'd get her hair permed if she was planning to shave it." Then she steels herself, and in the tone of someone expecting bad news asks if any tomatoes are left. Joey says, "We'll be up to our *ears* in tomatoes," and Claire thinks: He'd say that no matter what.

One thing she loves about Joey is his optimism. If he's ever discontent, she doesn't know it. Once he'd wanted to be on stage, then he'd worked for a while as a landscaper, now he's a junior-high science teacher—a job which he says requires the combined talents of an actor and a gardener. His real passion is for the names of things: trees, animals, stars. But he's not one of those people who use such knowledge to make you feel small. It's why he's a popular teacher and why Poppy so loves to take walks with him, naming the wildflowers in the fields. Claire knows how rare it is for children to want to learn anything from their parents.

When Claire met Joey, she'd just moved up to Vermont with a semi-alcoholic independently wealthy photographer named Dell. Dell hired Joey to clear a half-acre around their cabin so they could have a garden and lawn. Upstairs there's a photo Dell took of them at the time and later sent as a wedding present to prove there were no hard feelings. It shows Claire and Joey leaning against Joey's rented backhoe; an up-rooted acacia tree is spilling out of the bucket. Joey and Claire look cocky and hard in the face, like teen-age killers, Charlie Starkweather and his girl. Claire can hardly remember Dell's face. He always had something in front of it—a can of beer, a camera. If he had only put it down and looked, he'd have seen what was going on. Anyone would have. In the photo, it's early spring, the woods are full of musical names: trillium, marsh marigold, jack in the pulpit.

On the day they learned Claire was pregnant and went straight from the doctor's to the marriage license bureau in Burlington, Joey pulled off the road on the way home and took Claire's face in his hands and told her which animals mated for life. Whooping cranes, snow geese, macaws, she's forgotten the rest. Now they no longer talk this way, or maybe it goes without saying. Claire's stopped imagining other lives; if she could, she'd live this one forever. Though she knows it's supposed to be dangerous to get too comfortable, she feels it would take a catastrophe to tear the weave of their daily routine. They've weathered arguments, and those treacherous, tense, dull periods when they sneak past each other as if they're in constant danger of sneezing in each other's faces. Claire knows to hold on and wait for the day when what interests her most is what Joey will have to say about it.

Some things get better. Claire used to hate thinking about the lovers they'd had before; now all that seems as indistinct as Dell's face. Though they've had eight years to get used to the fact of Poppy's existence, they're still susceptible to attacks of amazement that they've created a new human being. And often when they're doing something together—cooking, gardening, making love—

Claire comes as close as she ever has to those moments of pure alchemy, that communion Poppy and Miranda must share if they're storing their pee in bottles.

Soon they'll get up and mix some marinade for the chickens they'll grill outside later for Dottie and Raymond. But now Joey pours himself some coffee and they sit at the table, not talking. It is precisely the silence they used to dream of when Poppy was little and just having her around was like always having the bath water running or something about to boil over on the stove.

First the back doors fly open and the girls jump out of the car and run up to Poppy's room. Then Dottie gets out, then Raymond. From the beginning, Raymond's reminded Claire of the tin woodsman in *The Wizard of Oz*, and often he'll stop in the middle of things as if waiting for someone to come along with the oil can. He goes around to the trunk and takes out a tripod and something wrapped in a blanket which looks at first like a rifle and turns out to be a telescope.

"Guess what!" When Raymond shouts like that, you can see how snaggletoothed he is. "There's a meteor shower tonight. The largest concentration of shooting stars all year."

The telescope is one of the toys Raymond's bought since his paintings started selling. Raymond's success surprises them all, including Raymond. His last two shows were large paintings of ordinary garden vegetables with skinny legs and big feet in rather stereotypical dance situations. It still surprises Claire that the New York art world would open its heart—would have a heart to open—to work bordering on the cartoonish and sentimental. But there's something undeniably mysterious and moving about those black daikon radishes doing the tango, those little cauliflowers in pink tutus on points before an audience of sleek and rather parental-looking green peppers. And there's no arguing with Raymond's draftmanship or the luminosity of his color; it's as if Memling lived through the sixties and took too many drugs. What's less surprising is that there are so many rich people who for one reason or another want to eat breakfast beneath a painting of the dancing vegetables.

Claire has a crush on Raymond; at least that's what she thinks it is. It's not especially intense or very troublesome; it's been going on a long time and she doesn't expect it to change. If anything did change, it would probably disappear. She doesn't want to live with

Raymond and now, as always when he hugs her hello, their bones grate; it's not particularly sexual.

She just likes him, that's all. When it's Raymond coming to dinner, she cooks and dresses with a little more care than she otherwise might, and spends the day remembering things to tell him which she promptly forgets. Of course, she's excited when Dottie or anyone is coming over. The difference is: With Dottie, Claire enjoys her food. With Raymond, she often forgets to eat.

Barbecued chicken, tomatoes with basil and mozzarella, pasta with chanterelles Joey's found in the woods—it all goes right by her. Luckily, everyone else is eating, the girls trekking back and forth from the table to the TV. The television noise makes it hard to talk. It's like family dinner, they can just eat. Anyway, conversation's been strained since Dottie started at the Academy. Claire fears that Joey might make some semi-sarcastic remark which will hurt Raymond more than Dottie. Raymond's protective of her; they seem mated for life. It's occurred to them all that Dottie is the original dancing vegetable.

What does get said is that the meteor shower isn't supposed to pick up till around midnight. But they'll set up the telescope earlier so the girls can have a look before they're too tired to see.

Joey and Raymond and the girls go outside while Dottie and Claire put the dishes in the sink. Claire asks if Poppy was any trouble that afternoon and Dottie says, "Oh, no. They played in the bathroom so quiet, I had to keep yelling up to make sure they were breathing. Later they told me they'd been making vanishing cream from that liquidy soap at the bottom of the soap dish. I said, You're eight years old, what do you need with vanishing cream? They said, to vanish. I told them they'd better not use it till they had something to bring them back from wherever they vanished to, and they said, yeah, they'd already thought of that."

"Where did they *hear* about vanishing cream?" says Claire. She feels she ought to tell Dottie—feels disloyal for not telling her—to watch for suspicious-looking shampoo bottles on the upper shelves. But she doesn't. It's almost as if she's saving it for something.

"Speaking of vanishing," says Dottie. She hands Claire the book she'd forgotten that afternoon. It's Calvino's *The Baron in the Trees*. Claire's read it before, and it seems like the right moment to ask, so she says, "Does this mean that you're going to get up from

52

the table one night and climb up in the trees and never come down again?"

Dottie just looks at her. "Me in the trees?" she says. "With *my* allergies?"

They're amazed by how dark it is when they go outside. "I told you," says Dottie. "It's August."

The grass is damp and cool against their ankles as they walk across the lawn to where Miranda and Poppy are taking turns at the telescope. "Daddy," Claire hears Poppy say. "What's that?"

Joey crouches down and looks over her shoulder. Claire wonders what they see. Scorpio? Andromeda? Orion? Joey's told her a thousand times but she can never remember what's in the sky when.

Before Joey can answer, Raymond pulls Poppy away from the telescope and kneels and puts one arm around her and the other around Miranda. "That one?" he says, pointing. "That one's the Bad Baby. And it's lying in the Big Bassinet."

"Where?" cry the girls, and then they say, "Yes, I see!"

"And that one there's the Celestial Dog Dish. And that"—he traces his finger in a wavy circle—"is the Silver Dollar Pancake."

"What's that one?" says Miranda.

"Remember *Superman II*?" Raymond's the one who takes the girls to movies no one else wants to see. "That's what's left of the villains after they get turned to glass and smashed to smithereens."

"Oh, no," say the girls, and hide their faces against Raymond's long legs.

Claire's tensed, as if Raymond's infringed on Joey's right to name things, or worse, is making fun of him. But Joey's laughing, he likes Raymond's names as much as the real ones. Claire steps up to the telescope and aims it at the thin crescent moon, at that landscape of chalk mountains and craters like just-burst bubbles. But all she sees is the same flat white she can see with her naked eye. Something's wrong with the telescope, or with her. The feeling she gets reminds her of waking up knowing the day's already gone wrong but not yet why, of mornings when Poppy's been sick in the night, or last summer when Joey's father was dying.

By now the others have all lain down on the hillside to look for shooting stars. There aren't any, not yet. Claire wonders if Dottie is listening to the inner silence or thinking of past lives, if Raymond is inventing more constellations. She can't imagine what Joey's thinking. She herself can't get her mind off Jeanette the electrician and her boyfriend, drinking penny-royal tea and checking that sliver of moon to see if this is a safe night for love.

On the way in, Joey says, "Lying out there, I remembered this magazine article I haven't thought of in years, about Jean Genet at the '68 Democratic convention in Chicago. The whole time, he kept staring at the dashboard of the car they were driving him around in. And afterwards, when they asked him what he thought of it—the riots, the beatings and so forth—he just shrugged and said, 'What can you expect from a country that would make a car named Galaxy?' "

Over coffee, the conversation degenerates into stories they've told before, tales of how the children tyrannize and abuse them, have kept them prisoner in their own homes for years at a time. The reason they can talk like this is that they all know: The children are the light of their lives. A good part of why they stay here is that Vermont seems like an easy place to raise kids. Even their children have visionary names: Poppy, Miranda. O brave new world!

When Claire first moved here with Dell, she commuted to New York, where she was working as a free-lance costume designer. She likes to tell people that the high point of her career was making a holster and fringed vest and chaps for a chicken to wear on "Hee Haw." Later she got to see it on TV, the chicken panicky and humiliated in its cowboy suit, flapping in circles while Grandpa Jones fired blanks at its feet and yelled, "Dance!" Soon it will be Halloween and Claire will sew Poppy a costume. So far she's been a jar of peanut butter, an anteater with pockets full of velveteen ants, Rapunzel. Last fall Claire made her a caterpillar suit with a back which unzipped and reversed out into butterfly wings. Poppy's already told her that this year she wants to be a New Wave, so all Claire will have to do is rip up a T-shirt and buy tights and wraparound shades and blue spray-on washable hair dye.

Dottie is telling about the girls making vanishing cream when Joey pretends to hear something in the garden and excuses himself and goes out. Dottie says she wants to stay up for the meteor shower but is feeling tired so she'll lie down awhile on the living-room couch.

Claire and Raymond are left alone at the table. It takes them so long to start talking, Claire's glad her crush on Raymond will never be anything more; if they had to spend a day in each other's company, they'd run out of things to say. Still it's exciting. Raymond seems nervous, too.

Finally he asks how her day was, and Claire's surprised to hear herself say, "Pretty awful." She hadn't meant to complain, nor had she thought her day was so awful. Now she thinks maybe it was. "Nothing really," she says. "One little thing after another. Have you ever had days when you pick up a pen and the phone rings and when you get off, you can't find the pen?"

"Me?" says Raymond. "I've had decades like that."

Claire says, "I woke up thinking I'd be nice and cook Poppy some French toast. So I open the egg carton and poke my finger through one of those stuck-on leaky eggs. When I got through cleaning the egg off the refrigerator, the milk turned out to be sour. I figured, Well, I'll make her scrambled eggs with coriander, she likes that. I went out to the garden for coriander and all the tomatoes were lying on the ground. The awful part was that most of them looked fine from on top, you had to turn them over to see they were smashed. You know: first you think it's all right and then it isn't all right."

"I almost never think it's all right," says Raymond. "That's how I take care of that."

"Know how *I* took care of it?" says Claire. "I went crying to Joey. Then I went upstairs and got out these star decals I'd been saving, I thought it would make me feel better. I'd been planning to paste them on the ceiling over the tub so I could take a shower with all the lights out and the stars glowing up above and even in winter it would be like taking a shower outside." Suddenly Claire is embarrassed by this vision of herself naked in the warm steamy blackness under the faint stars. She wonders if Dottie is listening from the other room and is almost glad the next part is about finding the shampoo bottle.

"That's life," says Raymond. "Reach for the stars and wind up with a bottle of piss."

"That's what I thought," says Claire. "But listen." She tells him about calling the girls in and when she says, "Like newborn giraffes," she really does feel awful, as if she's serving her daughter up so Raymond will see her as a complicated person with a daily life rich in similes and astonishing spiritual reverses. Now she understands why she hadn't mentioned the incident to Dottie or Joey. She was saving it for Raymond so it wouldn't be just a story she'd told before. But Raymond's already saying, "I know. Sometimes one second can turn the whole thing around.

"One winter," he says, "Miranda was around two, we were living in Roxbury, freezing to death. We decided it was all or nothing. We sold everything, got rid of the apartment, bought tickets to some dinky Caribbean island where somebody told us you could live on fish and mangoes and coconuts off the trees. I thought, I'll paint shells, sell them to the tourists. But when we got there, it wasn't mango season, the fish weren't running, and the capital city was one giant cinderblock motel. There was a housing shortage, food shortage, an everything shortage.

"So we took a bus across the island, thinking we'd get off at the first tropical paradise, but no place seemed very friendly and by then Miranda was running another fever. We wound up in the second-biggest city, which looked pretty much like a bad neighborhood in L.A. We were supposed to be glad that our hotel room had a balcony facing main street. Dottie put Miranda to bed, then crawled in and pulled the covers over her head and said she wasn't coming out except to fly back to Boston.

"At that moment, we heard a brass band, some drums. By the time I wrestled the balcony shutters open, a parade was coming by. It was the tail end of carnival, I think. The whole island was there, painted and feathered and glittered to the teeth, marching formations of guys in ruffly Carmen Miranda shirts with marimbas, little girls done up like bumblebees with antennae bobbing on their heads. Fever or no fever, we lifted Miranda up to see. And maybe it was what she'd needed all along. Because by the time the last marcher went by, her fever was gone.

"Miranda fell asleep, then Dottie. I went for a walk. On the corner, a guy was selling telescopes. Japanese-made, not like that one out there, but good. They must have been stolen off some boat, they were selling for practically nothing. So I bought one and went down to the beach. The beach was deserted. I stayed there I don't know how long. It was the first time I ever looked through a telescope. It was something."

For the second time that day, Claire's struck speechless. Only this time, what's astonishing is, she's in pain. She feels she's led her whole life wrong. What did she think she was doing? If only she could have been on that beach with Raymond looking through a telescope for the first time, or even at the hotel when he came back. Suddenly her own memories seem two-dimensional, like photographs, like worn-out duplicate baseball cards she'd trade all at once for that one of Raymond's. She tells herself that if she'd married Raymond, she might be like Dottie now, confused and restless and wanting only to believe that somewhere there is a weed for her need. She remembers the end of the Hammett story: After Flitcraft's brush with death, he goes to Seattle and marries a woman exactly like the wife he left on the other side of that beam. There's no guarantee that another life will be better or even different from your own, and Claire knows that. But it doesn't help at all.

There's a silence. Claire can't look at Raymond. At last he says, "If I could paint what I saw through that telescope that night, do you think I'd ever paint another dancing vegetable in my whole fucking life?"

For all Raymond's intensity, it's kind of a funny question, and Claire laughs, mostly from relief that the moment is over. Then she notices that Dottie has come in. Dottie looks a little travel-worn, as if she might actually have crossed the steppes from Moscow to Paris. She seems happy to be back. As it turns out, she's been closer than that. Because what she says is, "Suppose I'd believed that old lady and dropped her off in the middle of Montpelier? What would have happened then?"

Claire wants to say something fast before Raymond starts inventing adventures for a crazy old lady alone in Montpelier. Just then, Joey reappears. Apparently, he's come back in and gone upstairs without their hearing; he's got the girls ready for bed, scrubbed and shiny, dressed in long white cotton nightgowns like slender Edwardian angels. Claire looks at the children and the two sets of parents and thinks a stranger walking in would have trouble telling: Which one paints dancing vegetables? Which one's lived before as a Napoleonic soldier? Which ones have mated for life? She thinks they are like constellations, or like that engraving on Evelyn's father's desk, or like sunflowers seen from below. Depending on how you look, they could be anything.

Then Raymond says, "It's almost midnight," and they all troop outside. On the way out, Raymond hangs back and when Claire catches up with him, he leans down so his lips are grazing her ear

57

and says, "I hope this doesn't turn out to be another Comet Kohoutek."

Outside, Claire loses sight of them, except for the girls, whose white nightgowns glow in the dark like phosphorescent stars. She lays down on the grass. She's thinking about Kohoutek and about that first winter she and Joey lived together. How excited he was at the prospect of seeing a comet, and later, how disappointed! She remembers that the Museum of Natural History set up a dial-in Comet News Hot-line which was supposed to announce new sightings and wound up just giving data about Kohoutek's history and origins. Still Joey kept calling long distance and letting the message run through several times. Mostly he did it when Claire was out of the house, but not always. Now, as Claire tries not to blink, to stretch her field of vision wide enough for even the most peripheral shooting star, she keeps seeing how Joey looked in those days when she'd come home and stamp the snow off her boots and see him—his back to her, his ear to the phone, listening. And now, as always, it's just when she's thinking of something else that she spots it—that ribbon of light streaking by her so fast she can never be sure if she's really seen it or not.

nominated by Antaeus

LYRICS FOR PUERTO RICAN SALSA AND THREE SONEOS BY REQUEST

fiction by ANA LYDIA VEGA

translated by Mark McCaffrey

from NEW ENGLAND REVIEW AND BREAD LOAF QUARTERLY

THERE'S A HOLY FEAST DAY FEVER of fine asses on De Diego Street. Round in their super-look panties, arresting in tube-skirt profile, insurgent under their fascist girdles, abysmal, Olympian, nuclear, they furrow the sidewalks of Rio Piedras like invincible national airships.

More intense than a Colombia buzz, more persevering than Somoza, He tracks Her through the snaking river of derrieres. He is as faithful as a Holy Week procession with his hey little fox litany, his you're fine, you're lookin' good, those pants dress you up nice, that's a lush woman, man, packed to load limit, all that meat and me livin' on slim pickins.

And in fact She is a good looker. Brassiere showing through, Bermuda triangle traced with every jiggle of her spike heels. On the other hand, he would settle for a broomstick in a baseball jersey.

59

Sssssay, fine asssss woman. He comes undone in sensual hissing as he leans his mug perilously close to the technicolor curls of his prey. She then kicks in the secondaries and, with her rear end in overdrive, momentarily removes her virtue to safety.

But the salsa chef wants his Christmas ham and turns on his relentless street song: what a chassis, baby, a walkin' pound cake, raw material, a sure enough hunk of woman, what legs, if I were rain I'd fall on you.

The siege goes on for two biblical days. Two days of dogged pursuit and unnerving ad lib. Two long days of hey, delicious, hey honeycakes, I could light you up, she's an animal that woman, I'm all yours, for you I'd even work, who are you staying in deep-freeze for, man-killer?

On the third day, directly in front of the Pitusa Five and Ten, and with the spicy noontime sizzle of sofrito in the air, the victim takes a deep breath, pivots spectacularly on her precarious heels and slam dunks one.

"Whenever you're ready."

Thrown from his mount, the rider does an emotional head-over-heels. Ready nevertheless to risk it all for his national virility, he alights on his feet and blurts out in telling formality, "as you wish."

At this point she solemnly takes over. A metallic, red '69 Ford Torino sits in the parking lot at the Plaza del Mercado. They get in. They take off. The radio howls a senile bolero. She drives with one hand on the steering wheel and the other on the window, with a couldn't-care-less air about her. He begins violently to wish for a seaside bachelor's pad, a kind of discotheque/slaughterhouse where he could process the grade-A prime that life sometimes drops in one's lap like free food stamps. But unemployment fuels no dreams and he is kicking himself, thinking if I had known about this ahead of time I'd have hit up Papo Quisqueya for his room, Papo is blood, he's Santo Domingo soul, a high-steppin' no-jive street sultan and we're thick with our chicks. Damn, he says to himself, giving up. Then, sporting his best soap opera smile, he attempts to sound natural giving directions.

"Head for Piñones."

But she one-ups him again, taking instead the Caguas Highway as if it were a golden thigh of Kentucky Fried Chicken.

The motel entrance lies hidden in the shrubbery. Guerrilla warfare surroundings. The Torino slides vaseline-like up the narrow entranceway. The clerk nods from a coy distance, gazing coolly ahead like a horse with blinders. The car squeezes into the garage. She gets out. He tries to open the door without unlocking it, a herculean task. At last he steps out in the name of Homo Sapiens.

The key is shoved all the way into the lock and they penetrate the entrance to the room. She turns on the light. It is a merciless neon, a revealer of pimples and blackheads. He jumps at the sight of the open black hand sticking out through the pay window. He remembers the interplanetary void in his wallet. An agonizing and secular moment at the end of which She deposits five pesos in the black hand, which closes up like a hurt oyster and disappears, only to reappear again instantly. Godfather-like gravel voice:

"It's seven. Two more."

She sighs, rummages through her purse, takes out lipstick, compact, mascara, Kleenex, base, shadow, pen, perfume, black lace bikini panties, Tampax, deodorant, toothbrush, torrid romance and two pesos which she chucks at the insatiable hand like so many bones. He feels the socio-historical compulsion to remark:

"It's tough on the street, eh?"

From the bathroom comes the rushing sound of an open faucet. The room feels like a closet. Mirrors, though, everywhere. Half-sized single bed. Sheets clean but punished with wear. Zero pillows. Red light overhead. He like freaks at the thought of all the people that must have blushed under the loud red lights, all the horny Puerto Rican thrills spilled out in that room, the orgies the mirror must have witnessed, the bouncing the bed has taken. He parks his thoughts at the Plaza Convalescencia, aptly named for the hosts of sickies who get their daily cure there, oh, Convalescencia, where the cool stroll of the street lizards is a tribal rite. It is his turn now, and it won't be campaign rhetoric he's spouting. He stands before the group, walking back and forth, rising and falling on his epic mount: She was harder than a mafioso's heart, bro'. I just looked at her and she turned into jelly right there. I took her to a motel, man. They hit you for seven pesos now just to blast a cap.

She comes out of the bathroom. Her goddess complex not undeserved. Not a stitch on her. An awesome Indian queen. Brother, there was more ass on her than you could put up on a movie screen.

"Don't you intend to take your clothes off," thunders Guabancex from the pre-Columbian heights of El Yunque.

He turns to the task at hand. Off comes the undershirt. Off

comes the belt. Down come the pants. She lies back, the better to grasp you. At last his underwear drops with the metallic weight of a chastity belt. Remote-controlled from the bed, a projectile closes the strip-tease act. He catches it and—oh, must we not blush—it is a condescending condom and an indisposable one at that.

In the Pine-Sol-saturated bathroom the stud ram engages nature. He wants to go into this in full warrior splendor. Retroactive cerebral functions are no help. Cracks spied through barely open doorways: zip. Social science teacher in black panties: zip. Gringo female sunning her Family Size tits on a terrace: zip. A couple feeling each other up inside and out in the back row at the Paradise Theater: zip. Stampeding women rubbed against and desired on the streets and freely deflowered in his mind; recall of memorized pages of Mexican porno rags; incomparable Playboy centerfolds, rewind, replay; the old hot and heavy war lingo: nail me, negrito; devastate me, daddy, melt me down, big man. But . . . zip. There's not a witch doctor alive who can raise this dead body up.

She is calling him. In vain Clark Kent seeks the Emergency Exit. His Superman suit is at the cleaner's.

From within a Marlboro smoke cloud she is saying her final prayers. It's all up to luck now, you might say, and she is on the threshold of life's own phenomenal cleansing ritual. Since Hector's wedding with that shit-eating white baby doll from Condado, having a hymen is a crime that drags her down. Seven years in a playboy dentist's hip pocket. Seven years filling cavities and scraping tartar. Seven years staring down gaping throats, breathing septic tank breath for a wink or a limp pass or a Tinkerbell tease or a hollow hope. But today the convent lets go. Today the vows of chastity take the tomato pickers' flight out. She changes the channel and tunes in to the cheap deal destiny has dealt her for this date: a plump little cork of a man, stiff-comb Afro, bandana-red T-shirt and battle-weary jeans. Truly light years away from her glittering, dental assistant dreams. But truly, too, the historic moment has come, is banging down the door like a drunken husband, and it's getting later all the time and she already missed the big ride once; there was Viet Nam and there was emigration and that left rationing in between, and statehood is for the poor, and you jog or you get fat though after all it's not the gun that counts but the shot it fires. So there it is, the whole thing, scientifically programmed right down to the radio that will drown out her vestal cries. And then back to society sans tasseled debutante gown, and let the impenetrable veil of anonymity forever swallow up her portable emergency mate.

Suddenly, there is a wrenching scream. She rushes to the bathroom. He is straddled and half-bent over the bidet, pale as a gringo in February. When He sees her he falls to the floor, epileptically writhing and moaning as if possessed. Dawning realization that She may have gotten herself involved with a junkie, an actual, hard-core dope addict. When the moaning reaches all but a death rattle, She asks if perhaps it wouldn't be wise to call the motel clerk. As if by magic, his wailing ceases. He straightens up, maternally cooing and soothing his hurt tummy.

"I've got a stomach ache," he says, giving her his mangy-dog-looking-at-kennelmaster look.

Soneo I

First aid. Mouth-to-mouth resuscitation. Caressing the crisis-stricken belly, She breaks into a full-blown rap on historical materialism and classless society. Vigorous dictatorship-of-proletariat rubdown. Party Program hallelujah chorus. First on a small, then a medium, then a large scale, He experiences a gradual strengthening of his long-napping consciousness. They unite. Intoning the Fifth International in emotional unison, they bring their infrastructures to shuddering excitation. Nature answers the call of the mobilized masses and the act is dialectically consummated.

Soneo II

Heavyduty confrontation: Her on Him. She sits him down on the bed, sitting cross-legged next to him. Inspiringly fluent, dazzlingly lucid, She tears a millenium of oppression to shreds; all those centuries of ironing, comrade, and all that forced kitchen work. She gets carried away in her own eloquence, using her brassiere as an ashtray while emphatically demanding genital equality. Caught in the implacable spotlight of reason, He confesses, repents, firmly resolves to mend his ways and fervently implores communion with her. Their emotions stirred, they join hands and unite in a long, egalitarian kiss, inserting exactly the same amount of tongue into their respective bucal cavities. Nature answers the unisex call and the act is equitably consummated.

Soneo III

She gets dressed. He is still holding out in the bathroom. She throws his clothes to him. They split from the motel without a word to each other. When the metallic red '69 Ford stops at De Diego Street to unload its cargo, the holiday of rideable rear ends is still in full cinematic swing. Intense as a Colombian buzz, as persevering as Somoza and as shameless as the Shah, He falls basely back into it. And He's a rogue combing the streets again, a part of the endless daybreak litany that says bless my soul, brown Sally, my but you do move, baby, say, what do you eat to stay so healthy, those are some lamb chops, man, God bless rice and beans, a prime cut I'd say, Momma, watch out if I catch you . . .

nominated by New England Review and Bread Loaf Quarterly
and Antonio Benítez-Rojo

COMMUNIST

fiction by RICHARD FORD

from ANTAEUS

MY MOTHER ONCE had a boyfriend named Glen Baxter. This was in 1961. We—my mother and I—were living in the little house my father had left her up the Sun River, near Victory, Montana, west of Great Falls. My mother was thirty-one at the time. I was sixteen. Glen Baxter was somewhere in the middle, between us, though I cannot be exact about it.

We were living then off the proceeds of my father's life insurance policies, with my mother doing some part-time waitressing work up in Great Falls and going to the bars in the evenings, which I know is where she met Glen Baxter. Sometimes he would come back with her and stay in her room at night, or she would call up from town and explain that she was staying with him in his little place on Lewis Street by the GN yards. She gave me his number every time, but I never called it. I think she probably thought that what she was doing was terrible, but simply couldn't help herself. I thought it was all right, though. Regular life it seemed and still does. She was young, and I knew that even then.

Glen Baxter was a Communist and liked hunting, which he talked about a lot. Pheasants. Ducks. Deer. He killed all of them, he said. He had been to Vietnam as far back as then, and when he was in our house he often talked about shooting the animals over there—monkeys and beautiful parrots—using military guns just for sport. We did not know what Vietnam was then, and Glen, when he talked about that, referred to it only as "the far east." I think now he must've been in the CIA and been disillusioned by something he saw or found out about and had been thrown out, but that kind of thing did not matter to us. He was a tall, dark-eyed man with thick black hair, and was usually in a good humor. He had gone halfway through college in Peoria, Illinois, he said, where he grew up. But when he was around our life he worked wheat farms as a ditcher, and stayed out of work winters and in the bars drinking with women like my mother, who had work and some money. It is not an uncommon life to lead in Montana.

What I want to explain happened in November. We had not been seeing Glen Baxter for some time. Two months had gone by. My mother knew other men, but she came home most days from work and stayed inside watching television in her bedroom and drinking beers. I asked about Glen once, and she said only that she didn't know where he was, and I assumed they had had a fight and that he was gone off on a flyer back to Illinois or Massachusetts, where he said he had relatives. I'll admit that I liked him. He had something on his mind always. He was a labor man as well as a Communist, and liked to say that the country was poisoned by the rich, and strong men would need to bring it to life again, and I liked that because my father had been a labor man, which was why we had a house to live in and money coming through. It was also true that I'd had a few boxing bouts by then—just with town boys and one with an Indian from Choteau—and there were some girlfriends I knew from that. I did not like my mother being around the house so much at night, and I wished Glen Baxter would come back, or that another man would come along and entertain her somewhere else.

At two o'clock on a Saturday, Glen drove up into our yard in a car. He had had a big brown Harley-Davidson that he rode most of the year, in his black-and-red irrigators and a baseball cap turned backwards. But this time he had a car, blue Nash Ambassador. My mother and I went out on the porch when he stopped inside the olive trees my father had planted as a shelter belt, and my mother had a look on her face of not much pleasure. It was starting to be cold in earnest by then. Snow was down already onto the Fairfield Bench, though on this day a chinook was blowing, and it could as easily have been spring, though the sky above the Divide was turning over in silver and blue clouds of winter.

"We haven't seen you in a long time, I guess," my mother said coldly.

"My little retarded sister died," Glen said, standing at the door of his old car. He was wearing his orange VFW jacket and canvas shoes we called wino shoes, something I had never seen him wear before. He seemed to be in a good humor. "We buried her in Florida near the home."

"That's a good place," my mother said in a voice that meant she was a wronged party in something.

"I want to take this boy hunting today, Aileen," Glen said. "There're snow geese down now. But we have to go right away or they'll be gone to Idaho by tomorrow."

"He doesn't care to go," my mother said.

"Yes I do," I said and looked at her.

My mother frowned at me. "Why do you?"

"Why does he need a reason?" Glen Baxter said and grinned.

"I want him to have one, that's why." She looked at me oddly. "I think Glen's drunk, Les."

"No, I'm not drinking," Glen said, which was hardly ever true. He looked at both of us, and my mother bit down on the side of her lower lip and stared at me in a way to make you think she thought something was being put over on her and she didn't like you for it. She was very pretty, though when she was mad her features were sharpened and less pretty by a long way. "All right then, I don't care," she said to no one in particular. "Hunt, kill, maim. Your father did that too." She turned to go back inside.

"Why don't you come with us, Aileen?" Glen was smiling still, pleased.

"To do what?" my mother said. She stopped and pulled a package of cigarettes out of her dress pocket and put one in her mouth.

"It's worth seeing."

"See dead animals?" my mother said.

"These geese are from Siberia, Aileen," Glen said. "They're not like a lot of geese. Maybe I'll buy us dinner later. What do you say?"

"Buy what with?" my mother said. To tell the truth, I didn't know why she was so mad at him. I would've thought she'd be glad to see him. But she just suddenly seemed to hate everything about him.

"I've got some money," Glen said. "Let me spend it on a pretty girl tonight."

"Find one of those and you're lucky," my mother said, turning away toward the front door.

"I already found one," Glen Baxter said. But the door slammed behind her, and he looked at me then with a look I think now was helplessness, though I could not see a way to change anything.

My mother sat in the back seat of Glen's Nash and looked out the window while we drove. My double gun was in the seat between us beside Glen's Belgian pump, which he kept loaded with five shells in case, he said, he saw something beside the road he wanted to shoot. I had hunted rabbits before, and had ground-sluiced pheasants and other birds, but I had never been on an actual hunt before, one where you drove out to some special place and did it formally. And I was excited. I had a feeling that something important was about to happen to me and that this would be a day I would always remember.

My mother did not say anything for a long time, and neither did I. We drove up through Great Falls and out the other side toward Fort Benton, which was on the benchland where wheat was grown.

"Geese mate for life," my mother said, just out of the blue, as we were driving. "I hope you know that. They're special birds."

"I know that," Glen said in the front seat. "I have every respect for them."

"So where were you for three months?" she said. "I'm only curious."

"I was in the Big Hole for a while," Glen said, "and after that I went over to Douglas, Wyoming."

"What were you planning to do there?" my mother asked.

"I wanted to find a job, but it didn't work out."

"I'm going to college," she said suddenly, and this was something I had never heard about before. I turned to look at her, but she was staring out her window and wouldn't see me.

"I knew French once," Glen said. "Rose's pink. Rouge's red." He glanced at me and smiled. "I think that's a wise idea, Aileen. When are you going to start?"

"I don't want Les to think he was raised by crazy people all his life," my mother said.

"Les ought to go himself," Glen said.

"After I go, he will."

"What do you say about that, Les?" Glen said, grinning.

"He says it's just fine," my mother said.

"It's just fine," I said.

Where Glen Baxter took us was out onto the high flat prairie that was disked for wheat and had high, high mountains out to the east, with lower heartbreak hills in between. It was, I remember, a day for blues in the sky, and down in the distance we could see the small town of Floweree and the state highway running past it toward Fort Benton and the high line. We drove out on top of the prairie on a muddy dirt road fenced on both sides, until we had gone about three miles, which is where Glen stopped.

"All right," he said, looking up in the rearview mirror at my mother. "You wouldn't think there was anything here, would you?"

"*We're* here," my mother said. "You brought us here."

"You'll be glad though," Glen said, and seemed confident to me. I had looked around myself but could not see anything. No water or trees, nothing that seemed like a good place to hunt anything. Just wasted land. "There's a big lake out there, Les," Glen said. "You can't see it now from here because it's low. But the geese are there. You'll see."

"It's like the moon out here, I recognize that," my mother said, "only it's worse." She was staring out at the flat, disked wheatland as if she could actually see something in particular and wanted to know more about it. "How'd you find this place?"

"I came once on the wheat push," Glen said.

"And I'm sure the owner told you just to come back and hunt any time you like and bring anybody you wanted. Come one, come all. Is that it?"

"People shouldn't own land anyway," Glen said. "Anybody should be able to use it."

"Les, Glen's going to poach here," my mother said. "I just want you to know that, because that's a crime and the law will get you for it. If you're a man now, you're going to have to face the consequences."

"That's not true," Glen Baxter said, and looked gloomily out over the steering wheel down the muddy road toward the mountains. Though for myself I believed it was true, and didn't care. I didn't care about anything at that moment except seeing geese fly over me and shooting them down.

"Well, I'm certainly not going out there," my mother said. "I like towns better, and I already have enough trouble."

"That's okay," Glen said. "When the geese lift up you'll get to see them. That's all I wanted. Les and me'll go shoot them, won't we, Les?"

"Yes," I said, and I put my hand on my shotgun, which had been my father's and was heavy as rocks.

"Then we should go on," Glen said, "or we'll waste our light."

We got out of the car with our guns. Glen took off his canvas shoes and put on his pair of black irrigators out of the trunk. Then we crossed the barbed-wire fence and walked out into the high, tilled field toward nothing. I looked back at my mother when we were still not so far away, but I could only see the small, dark top of her head, low in the back seat of the Nash, staring out and thinking what I could not then begin to say.

On the walk toward the lake, Glen began talking to me. I had never been alone with him and knew little about him except what my mother said—that he drank too much, or other times that he was the nicest man she had ever known in the world and that some day a woman would marry him, though she didn't think it would be her. Glen told me as we walked that he wished he had finished college, but that it was too late now, that his mind was too old. He said he had liked "the far east" very much, and that people there knew how to treat each other, and that he would go back some day but couldn't go now. He said also that he would like to live in Russia for a while and mentioned the names of people who had gone there, names I didn't know. He said it would be hard at first, because it was so different, but that pretty soon anyone would learn to like it and wouldn't want to live anywhere else, and that Russians treated Americans who came to live there like kings. There were Communists everywhere now, he said. You didn't know them, but they were there. Montana had a large number and he was in touch with all of them. He said that Communists were always in danger and that he had to protect himself all the time. And when he said that he pulled back his VFW jacket and showed me the butt of a pistol he had stuck under his shirt against his bare skin. "There are people who want to kill me right now," he said, "and I would kill a man myself if I thought I had to." And we kept walking. Though in a while he said, "I don't think I know much about you, Les. But I'd like to. What do you like to do?"

70

"I like to box," I said. "My father did it. It's a good thing to know."

"I suppose you have to protect yourself too," Glen said.

"I know how to," I said.

"Do you like to watch TV?" Glen said, and smiled.

"Not much."

"I love to," Glen said. "I could watch it instead of eating if I had one."

I looked out straight ahead over the green tops of sage that grew at the edge of the disked field, hoping to see the lake Glen said was there. There was an airishness and a sweet smell that I thought might be the place we were going, but I couldn't see it. "How will we hunt these geese?" I said.

"It won't be hard," Glen said. "Most hunting isn't even hunting. It's only shooting. And that's what this will be. In Illinois you would dig holes in the ground to hide in and set out your decoys. Then the geese come to you, over and over again. But we don't have time for that here." He glanced at me. "You have to be sure the first time here."

"How do you know they're here now?" I asked. And I looked toward the Highwood Mountains twenty miles away, half in snow and half dark blue at the bottom. I could see the little town of Floweree then, looking shabby and dimly lighted in the distance. A red bar sign shone. A car moved slowly away from the scattered buildings.

"They always come November first," Glen said.

"Are we going to poach them?"

"Does it make any difference to you?" Glen asked.

"No, it doesn't."

"Well then we aren't," he said.

We walked then for a while without talking. I looked back once to see the Nash far and small in the flat distance. I couldn't see my mother, and I thought that she must've turned on the radio and gone to sleep, which she always did, letting it play all night in her bedroom. Behind the car the sun was nearing the rounded mountains southwest of us, and I knew that when the sun was gone it would be cold. I wished my mother had decided to come along with us, and I thought for a moment of how little I really knew her at all.

Glen walked with me another quarter mile, crossed another barbed-wire fence where sage was growing, then went a hundred yards through wheatgrass and spurge until the ground went up and formed a kind of long hillock bunker built by a farmer against the wind. And I realized the lake was just beyond us. I could hear the sound of a car horn blowing and a dog barking all the way down in the town, then the wind seemed to move and all I could hear then and after then were geese. So many geese, from the sound of them, though I still could not see even one. I stood and listened to the high-pitched shouting sound, a sound I had never heard so close, a sound with size to it—though it was not loud. A sound that meant great numbers and that made your chest rise and your shoulders tighten with expectancy. It was a sound to make you feel separate from it and everything else, as if you were of no importance in the grand scheme of things.

"Do you hear them singing?" Glen asked. He held his hand up to make me stand still. And we both listened. "How many do you think, Les, just hearing?"

"A hundred," I said. "More than a hundred."

"Five thousand," Glen said. "More than you can believe when you see them. Go see."

I put down my gun and on my hands and knees crawled up the earthwork through the wheatgrass and thistle until I could see down to the lake and see the geese. And they were there, like a white bandage laid on the water, wide and long and continuous, a white expanse of snow geese, seventy yards from me, on the bank, but stretching onto the lake, which was large itself—a half mile across, with thick tules on the far side and wild plums farther and the blue mountain behind them.

"Do you see the big raft?" Glen said from below me, in a whisper.

"I see it," I said, still looking. It was such a thing to see, a view I had never seen and have not since.

"Are any on the land?" he said.

"Some are in the wheatgrass," I said, "but most are swimming."

"Good," Glen said. "They'll have to fly. But we can't wait for that now."

And I crawled backwards down the heel of land to where Glen was, and my gun. We were losing our light, and the air was purplish and cooling. I looked toward the car but couldn't see it, and I was no longer sure where it was below the lighted sky.

"Where do they fly to?" I said in a whisper, since I did not want anything to be ruined because of what I did or said. It was important to Glen to shoot the geese, and it was important to me.

"To the wheat," he said. "Or else they leave for good. I wish your mother had come, Les. Now she'll be sorry."

I could hear the geese quarreling and shouting on the lake surface. And I wondered if they knew we were here now. "She might be," I said with my heart pounding, but I didn't think she would be much.

It was a simple plan he had. I would stay behind the bunker, and he would crawl on his belly with his gun through the wheatgrass as near to the geese as he could. Then he would simply stand up and shoot all the ones he could close up, both in the air and on the ground. And when all the others flew up, with luck some would turn toward me as they came into the wind, and then I could shoot them and turn them back to him, and he would shoot them again. He could kill ten, he said, if he was lucky, and I might kill four. It didn't seem hard.

"Don't show them your face," Glen said. "Wait till you think you can touch them, then stand up and shoot. To hesitate is lost in this."

"All right," I said. "I'll try it."

"Shoot one in the head, and then shoot another one," Glen said. "It won't be hard." He patted me on the arm and smiled. Then he took off his VFW jacket and put it on the ground, climbed up the side of the bunker, cradling his shotgun in his arms, and slid on his belly into the dry stalks of yellow grass out of my sight.

Then for the first time in that entire day I was alone. And I didn't mind it. I sat squat down in the grass, loaded my double gun, and took my other two shells out of my pocket to hold. I pushed the safety off and on to see that it was right. The wind rose a little then, scuffed the grass and made me shiver. It was not the warm chinook now, but a wind out of the north, the one geese flew away from if they could.

Then I thought about my mother in the car alone, and how much longer I would stay with her, and what it might mean to her for me to leave. And I wondered when Glen Baxter would die and if someone would kill him, or whether my mother would marry him and how I would feel about it. And though I didn't know why, it occurred to me then that Glen Baxter and I would not be friends when all was said and done, since I didn't care if he ever married my mother or didn't.

Then I thought about boxing and what my father had taught me

73

about it. To tighten your fists hard. To strike out straight from the shoulder and never punch backing up. How to cut a punch by snapping your fist inwards, how to carry your chin low, and to step toward a man when he is falling so you can hit him again. And most important, to keep your eyes open when you are hitting in the face and causing damage, because you need to see what you're doing to encourage yourself, and because it is when you close your eyes that you stop hitting and get hurt badly. "Fly all over your man, Les," my father said. "When you see your chance, fly on him and hit him till he falls." That, I thought, would always be my attitude in things.

And then I heard the geese again, their voices in unison, louder and shouting, as if the wind had changed and put all new sounds in the cold air. And then a *boom*. And I knew Glen was in among them and had stood up to shoot. The noise of geese rose and grew worse, and my fingers burned where I held my gun too tight to the metal, and I put it down and opened my fist to make the burning stop so I could feel the trigger when the moment came. *Boom*, Glen shot again, and I heard him shuck a shell, and all the sounds out beyond the bunker seemed to be rising—the geese, the shots, the air itself going up. *Boom*, Glen shot another time, and I knew he was taking his careful time to make his shots good. And I held my gun and started to crawl up the bunker so as not to be surprised when the geese came over me and I could shoot.

From the top I saw Glen Baxter alone in the wheat field, shooting at a white goose with black tips of wings that was on the ground not far from him, but trying to run and pull into the air. He shot it once more, and it fell over dead with its wings flapping.

Glen looked back at me and his face was distorted and strange. The air around him was full of white rising geese and he seemed to want them all. "Behind you, Les," he yelled at me and pointed. "They're all behind you now." I looked behind me, and there were geese in the air as far as I could see, more than I knew how many, moving so slowly, their wings wide out and working calmly and filling the air with noise, though their voices were not as loud or as shrill as I had thought they would be. And they were so close! Forty feet, some of them. The air around me vibrated and I could feel the wind from their wings and it seemed to me I could kill as many as the times I could shoot—a hundred or a thousand—and I raised my gun, put the muzzle on the head of a white goose and

74

fired. It shuddered in the air, its wide feet sank below its belly, its wings cradled out to hold back air, and it fell straight down and landed with an awful sound, a noise a human would make, a thick, soft, *hump* noise. I looked up again and shot another goose, could hear the pellets hit its chest, but it didn't fall or even break its pattern for flying. *Boom*, Glen shot again. And then again. "Hey," I heard him shout. "Hey, hey." And there were geese flying over me, flying in line after line. I broke my gun and reloaded, and thought to myself as I did: I need confidence here, I need to be sure with this. I pointed at another goose and shot it in the head, and it fell the way the first one had, wings out, its belly down, and with the same thick noise of hitting. Then I sat down in the grass on the bunker and let geese fly over me.

By now the whole raft was in the air, all of it moving in a slow swirl above me and the lake and everywhere, finding the wind and heading out south in long wavering lines that caught the last sun and turned to silver as they gained a distance. It was a thing to see, I will tell you now. Five thousand white geese all in the air around you, making a noise like you have never heard before. And I thought to myself then: This is something I will never see again. I will never forget this. And I was right.

Glen Baxter shot twice more. One shot missed, but with the other he hit a goose flying away from him and knocked it half-falling and flying into the empty lake not far from shore, where it began to swim as though it was fine and make its noise.

Glen stood in the stubbly grass, looking out at the goose, his gun lowered. "I didn't need to shoot that, did I, Les?"

"I don't know," I said, sitting on the little knoll of land, looking at the goose swimming in the water.

"I don't know why I shoot 'em. They're so beautiful." He looked at me.

"I don't know either," I said.

"Maybe there's nothing else to do with them." Glen stared at the goose again and shook his head. "Maybe this is exactly what they're put on earth for."

I did not know what to say because I did not know what he could mean by that, though what I felt was embarrassment at the great number of geese there were, and a dulled feeling like a hunger because the shooting had stopped and it was over for me now.

Glen began to pick up his geese, and I walked down to my two that had fallen close together and were dead. One had hit with such an impact that its stomach had split and some of its inward parts were knocked out. Though the other looked unhurt, its soft white belly turned up like a pillow, its head and jagged bill-teeth and its tiny black eyes looking as if it were alive.

"What's happened to the hunters out here?" I heard a voice speak. It was my mother, standing in her pink dress on the knoll above us, hugging her arms. She was smiling though she was cold. And I realized that I had lost all thought of her in the shooting. "Who did all this shooting? Is this your work, Les?"

"No," I said.

"Les is a hunter, though, Aileen," Glen said. "He takes his time." He was holding two white geese by their necks, one in each hand, and he was smiling. He and my mother seemed pleased.

"I see you didn't miss too many," my mother said and smiled. I could tell she admired Glen for his geese, and that she had done some thinking in the car alone. "It *was* wonderful, Glen," she said. "I've never seen anything like that. They were like snow."

"It's worth seeing once, isn't it?" Glen said. "I should've killed more, but I got excited."

My mother looked at me then. "Where's yours, Les?"

"Here," I said and pointed to my two geese on the ground beside me.

My mother nodded in a nice way, and I think she liked everything then and wanted the day to turn out right and for all of us to be happy. "Six, then. You've got six in all."

"One's still out there," I said and motioned where the one goose was swimming in circles on the water.

"Okay," my mother said and put her hand over her eyes to look. "Where is it?"

Glen Baxter looked at me then with a strange smile, a smile that said he wished I had never mentioned anything about the other goose. And I wished I hadn't either. I looked up in the sky and could see the lines of geese by the thousands shining silver in the light, and I wished we could just leave and go home.

"That one's my mistake there," Glen Baxter said and grinned. "I shouldn't have shot that one, Aileen. I got too excited."

My mother looked out on the lake for a minute, then looked at Glen and back again. "Poor goose." She shook her head. "How will you get it, Glen?"

"I can't get that one now," Glen said.

My mother looked at him. "What do you mean?" she said.

"I'm going to leave that one," Glen said.

"Well, no. You can't leave one," my mother said. "You shot it. You have to get it. Isn't that a rule?"

"No," Glen said.

And my mother looked from Glen to me. "Wade out and get it, Glen," she said, in a sweet way, and my mother looked young then for some reason, like a young girl, in her flimsy short-sleeved waitress dress, and her skinny, bare legs in the wheatgrass.

"No." Glen Baxter looked down at his gun and shook his head. And I didn't know why he wouldn't go, because it would've been easy. The lake was shallow. And you could tell that anyone could've walked out a long way before it got deep, and Glen had on his boots.

My mother looked at the white goose, which was not more than thirty yards from the shore, its head up, moving in slow circles, its wings settled and relaxed so you could see the black tips. "Wade out and get it, Glenny, won't you please?" she said. "They're special things."

"You don't understand the world, Aileen," Glen said. "This can happen. It doesn't matter."

"But that's so cruel, Glen," she said, and a sweet smile came on her lips.

"Raise up your own arms, Leeny," Glen said. "I can't see any angel's wings, can you Les?" He looked at me, but I looked away.

"Then you go on and get it, Les," my mother said. "You weren't raised by crazy people." I started to go, but Glen Baxter suddenly grabbed me by my shoulder and pulled me back hard, so hard his fingers made bruises in my skin that I saw later.

"Nobody's going," he said. "This is over with now."

And my mother gave Glen a cold look then. "You don't have a heart, Glen," she said. "There's nothing to love in you. You're just a son of a bitch, that's all."

And Glen Baxter nodded at my mother as if he understood something that he had not understood before, but something that he was willing to know. "Fine," he said, "that's fine." And he took his big pistol out from against his belly, the big blue revolver I had only seen part of before and that he said protected him, and he pointed it out at the goose on the water, his arm straight away from him, and shot and missed. And then he shot and missed again. The goose made its noise once. And then he hit it dead, because there was no splash. And then he shot it three times more until the gun was empty and the goose's head was down and it was floating toward the middle of the lake where it was empty and dark blue. "Now who has a heart?" Glen said. But my mother was not there when he turned around. She had already started back to the car and was almost lost from sight in the darkness. And Glen smiled at me then and his face had a wild look on it. "Okay, Les?" he said.

"Okay," I said.

"There're limits to everything, right?"

"I guess so," I said.

"Your mother's a beautiful woman, but she's not the only beautiful woman in Montana." I did not say anything. And Glen Baxter suddenly said, "Here," and he held the pistol out at me. "Don't you want this? Don't you want to shoot me? Nobody thinks they'll die. But I'm ready for it right now." And I did not know what to do then. Though it is true that what I wanted to do was to hit him, hit him as hard in the face as I could, and see him on the ground bleeding and crying and pleading for me to stop. Only at that moment he looked scared to me, and I had never seen a grown man scared before—though I have seen one since—and I felt sorry for him, as though he was already a dead man. And I did not end up hitting him at all.

A light can go out in the heart. All of this went on years ago, but I still can feel now how sad and remote the world was to me. Glen Baxter, I think now, was not a bad man, only a man scared of something he'd never seen before—something soft in himself—his life going a way he didn't like. A woman with a son. Who could blame him there? I don't know what makes people do what they do or call themselves what they call themselves, only that you have to live someone's life to be the expert.

My mother had tried to see the good side of things, tried to be hopeful in the situation she was handed, tried to look out for us both and it hadn't worked. It was a strange time in her life then and after that, a time when she had to adjust to being an adult just when she was on the thin edge of things. Too much awareness too early in life was her problem, I think.

And what I felt was only that I had somehow been pushed out into the world, into the real life then, the one I hadn't lived yet. In a year I was gone to hardrock mining and no-paycheck jobs and not to college. And I have thought more than once about my mother saying that I had not been raised by crazy people, and I don't know what that could mean or what difference it could make, unless it means that love is a reliable commodity, and even that is not always true, as I have found out.

Late on the night that all this took place I was in bed when I heard my mother say, "Come outside, Les. Come and hear this." And I went out onto the front porch barefoot and in my underwear, where it was warm like spring, and there was a spring mist in the air. I could see the lights of the Fairfield Coach in the distance on its way up to Great Falls.

And I could hear geese, white birds in the sky, flying. They made their high-pitched sound like angry yells, and though I couldn't see them high up, it seemed to me they were everywhere. And my mother looked up and said, "Hear them?" I could smell her hair wet from the shower. "They leave with the moon," she said. "It's still half wild out here."

And I said, "I hear them," and I felt a chill come over my bare chest, and the hair stood up on my arms the way it does before a storm. And for a while we listened.

"When I first married your father, you know, we lived on a street called Bluebird Canyon, in California. And I thought that was the prettiest street and the prettiest name. I suppose no one brings you up like your first love. You don't mind if I say that, do you?" She looked at me hopefully.

"No," I said.

"We have to keep civilization alive somehow." And she pulled her little housecoat together because there was a cold vein in the air, a part of the cold that would be on us the next day. "I don't feel part of things tonight, I guess."

"It's all right," I said.

"Do you know where I'd like to go?" she said.

"No," I said. And I suppose I knew she was angry then, angry with life but did not want to show me that.

"To the Straits of Juan de Fuca. Wouldn't that be something? Would you like that?"

"I'd like it," I said. And my mother looked off for a minute, as if she could see the Straits of Juan de Fuca out against the line of mountains, see the lights of things alive and a whole new world.

"I know you liked him," she said after a moment. "You and I both suffer fools too well."

"I didn't like him too much," I said. "I didn't really care."

"He'll fall on his face. I'm sure of that," she said. And I didn't say anything because I didn't care about Glen Baxter anymore, and was happy not to talk about him. "Would you tell me something if I asked you? Would you tell me the truth?"

"Yes," I said.

And my mother did not look at me. "Just tell the truth," she said.

"All right," I said.

"Do you think I'm still very feminine? I'm thirty-two years old now. You don't know what that means. But do you think I am?"

And I stood at the edge of the porch, with the olive trees before me, looking straight up into the mist where I could not see geese but could still hear them flying, could almost feel the air move below their white wings. And I felt the way you feel when you are on a trestle all alone and the train is coming, and you know you have to decide. And I said, "Yes, I do." Because that was the truth. And I tried to think of something else then and did not hear what my mother said after that.

And how old was I then? Sixteen. Sixteen is young, but it can also be a grown man. I am forty-one years old now, and I think about that time without regret, though my mother and I never talked in that way again, and I have not heard her voice now in a long, long time.

nominated by Antaeus, *T. Coraghessan Boyle, Edmund Keeley, Mary Morris, and Joyce Carol Oates*

PROPERTY, PATRIOTISM AND NATIONAL DEFENSE

by WENDELL BERRY

from GUARDIAN PRESS and NORTH POINT PRESS

Man cannot so far know the connexion of causes and events, as that he may venture to do wrong in order to do right.

Samuel Johnson, Rasselas, Chapter XXXIV

If it were a question of defending rivers, hills, mountains, skies, winds, rains, I would say, 'Willingly, that is our job. Let us fight. All our happiness in life is there.' No, we have defended the sham name of all that.

Jean Giono, *Blue Boy* (North Point Press)

THE PRESENT SITUATION with regard to "national defense," as I believe that we citizens are now bidden to understand it, is that we, our country, and our governing principles of religion and politics are so threatened by a foreign enemy that we must prepare for a sacrifice that makes child's play of the "supreme sacrifices" of previous conflicts. We are asked, that is, not simply to "die in defense of our country," but to accept and condone the deaths of virtually the whole population of our country, of our political and religious principles, and of our land itself, as a reasonable cost of national defense.

That a nation should purchase at an exorbitant price, and rely upon, a form of defense inescapably fatal to itself is, of course, absurd. That good citizenship should then be defined as willing acceptance of such a form of defense can only be ruinous of the political health of that nation. To ask intelligent citizens to believe an argument that in its essentials is not arguable, and to approve results that are not imaginably good, and in the strict sense are not imaginable at all, is to drive wedges of disbelief and dislike

81

between those citizens and their government. And so the effect of such a form of defense is ruinous, whether or not it is ever used.

The absurdity of the argument lies in a little-noted law of the nature of technology: that, past a certain power and scale, we do not dictate our terms to the tools we use; rather, the tools dictate their terms to us. Past a certain power and scale, we may choose the means, but not the ends. We may choose nuclear weaponry as a form of defense, but that is the last of our "free choices" with regard to nuclear weaponry. By that choice we largely abandon ourselves to terms and results dictated by the nature of nuclear weapons. To take up weapons has, of course, always been a limiting choice, but never before has the choice been made by so few with such fatal implications for so many and so much. Once we have chosen to rely on such weapons, the only free choice we have left is to change our minds; to choose *not* to rely on them. "Good" or "humane" choices short of that choice involve a logic that is merely pitiful.

In order to attack our enemies with nuclear weapons, we must hate those enemies enough to kill them, and this hatred must be prepared in advance of any occasion or provocation. To exist, that is, this hatred must be aroused in response to a cause that does not yet exist, for, in order to work, the hatred must be formalized ahead of time in devices, systems and procedures.

And this hatred must be complete: there can be nothing selective about it. In this way the technology dictates terms to its users. Our nuclear weapons articulate a perfect hatred, such as none of us has ever felt, or can feel, or can imagine feeling. In order to make a nuclear attack against the Russians we must hate them *all* enough to kill them *all:* the innocent as well as the guilty, the children as well as the grownups. Thus, though it may be humanly impossible for us to propose it, we allow our technology to propose for us the defense of Christian love and justice (as we invariably put it) by an act of perfect hatred and perfect injustice. Or, as a prominent "conservative" columnist once put it, in order to save civilization we must become uncivilized.

But the absurdity does not stop with the death of all our enemies and all of our principles. It does not stop anywhere. Our nuclear weapons articulate for us a hatred of the Russian country itself: the land, water, air, light, plants and animals of Russia. Those weapons will enact for us a perfect political hatred of birds and fish and trees. And they will enact for us too a perfect hatred of ourselves, for a part of the inescapable meaning of those weapons is that we must hate our enemies so perfectly that in order to destroy them we are willing to destroy ourselves.

The intention to use nuclear weapons appears to nullify every reason to use them. There is no ostensible or imaginable reason to use them that could hope to survive their use. They would destroy all that they are meant to protect. There is no peace in them, or hope, or freedom, or health, or neighborliness, or justice, or love.

Except in the extremity of its immediate threat, nuclear weaponry is analogous to the inflated rhetoric of factional and political quarrels. It is too general and too extreme to be meant by any individual person. Belief in the propriety of its use requires personal abandonment to a public passion not validated by personal experience. Nuclear behavior is thus like the behavior of the prejudices of race or class or party: it issues a general condemnation for a cause that, in the nature of things, cannot prove sufficient.

As against political and factional rhetoric, the only defense against nuclear weaponry is dissent: the attempt once again, to bring the particularizing intelligence to the real ground of the problem.

Since I am outlining here the ground of my own dissent, I should say that I am not by principle a passive man, or by nature a pacific one. I understand hatred and enmity very well from my own experience. Defense, moreover, is congenial to me, and I am willing and sometimes joyfully, a defender of some things—among them, the principles and practices of democracy and Christianity that nuclear weapons are said to defend. I do not want to live under a government like that of Soviet Russia and I would go to considerable trouble to avoid doing so.

I am not dissenting from the standing policy on national defense because I want the nation—that is, the country, its lives and its principles—to be undefended. I am dissenting because I no longer believe that the standing policy on national defense can defend the nation. And I am dissenting because the means employed, the threatened results, and the economic and moral costs have all become so extreme as to be unimaginable.

It is, to begin with, impossible for me to imagine that our "nuclear preparedness" is well understood or sincerely meant by its advocates in the government, much less by the nation at large. What we are proposing to ourselves and to the world is that we are prepared to die, to the last child, to the last green leaf, in defense of our dearest principles of liberty, charity and justice. It would normally be expected, I think, that people led to the brink of total annihilation by so high and sober a purpose would be living lives of great austerity, sacrifice and selfless discipline. That *we* are not doing so is a fact notorious even among ourselves. Our leaders are not doing so, nor are they calling upon us or preparing us to do so. As a people, we are selfish, greedy, dependent, negligent of our duties to our land and to each other. We are evidently willing to sacrifice our own lives, and the lives of millions of others, born and unborn—but not one minute of pleasure. We will have more arms, but not more taxes; we will aggrandize the military-industrial establishment, but not at the cost of self-aggrandizement. We will have defense and self-indulgence, which is to say, defense and debt. Which is to say, that, willy nilly, we propose to defend ourselves by destroying ourselves. Surely not many nations before us have espoused suicide as a form of self-defense.

This policy of national defense by national debt, so ruinous to the country as a whole, is exploited for profit and power by a subversive alliance of politicians, military officers, industrialists and financiers—who, secure in their assumption that they will be the last to suffer or die as a result of their purposes, shift the real burden of industrial militarism onto the livelihoods of working people and onto the lives of young recruits.

And so our alleged willingness to die for high principles is all whitewash. What we are prepared to die for, if for anything, is resignation to the sham piety and the real greed of those in power.

What would make this willingness, this "state of nuclear preparedness" believable? It is easy enough to make a list of possible measures, both reasonable and necessary:

1. Forbid all taking of profit from military industries. Put an end to the possibility that anyone could get rich from any military enterprise. If all are asked to sacrifice their lives, why should not a few be asked to sacrifice their profits? If high principle is thought a sufficient motive for many, why should the profit motive be considered indispensable for a few?

2. Recognize that the outbreak of war in any form is a *failure* of government and of statesmenship. Let those who make or allow any war to be first into battle.

3. Require *all* the able-bodied to serve. Old and young alike have fought before in wars of national defense, such as the American Revolution, and should be expected to do so again. "Able bodied" should mean "able to walk and to work." So far as possible, exemptions should be granted to the young, who have the greatest number of useful years still to live, and who have had least time to understand the principles we wish to defend.

But let us assume, for the moment, that the argument of our present defense policy is valid. Let us assume that our country, our lives and our principles are indeed under threat of absolute destruction, and that our only possible defense against this threat is to hold the same absolute threat over our enemies—that is, that we have no choice but to accede to, and to pay for, the industry, the bureaucracy, and the politics of nuclear war. Let us assume that nuclear war is survivable and can be won. And, let us assume, further, that the credibility of our will to wage such war might be established beyond suspicion. *Then* would those of us who care about the defense of the country, its lives and its principles have anything to worry about?

We would still have a great deal to worry about, for we would not yet have shown that the present version of national defense could really defend what we must necessarily mean when we speak of the country, its lives and its principles. We must ask if the present version of national defense is, if fact, national defense.

To make sense of that question, and to hope to answer it, we must ask first what kind of country is defensible, militarily or in any other way. And we may answer that a defensible country has a large measure of practical and material independence: that it can live, if it has to, independent of foreign supplies and of long distance transport within its own boundaries; that it rests upon the broadest possible base of economic prosperity, not just in the sense of a money economy, but in the sense of properties, materials and practical skills; and, most important of all, that it is generally loved and competently cared for by its people, who, individually, identify their own interest with the interest of their neighbors and of the country (the land) itself.

To a considerable extent, that is the kind of country we had from the Revolution through World War II, and to a more considerable extent, that is the kind of country a great many people *hoped* to have during that time—which largely explains why the country was then so well defended. The remains and relics of that country

85

are still scattered about us. The ideal or the fact of local independence is still alive in some individuals, some communities and some small localities. There remains, here and there, a declining number of small farms, shops, stores and other small enterprises that suggest the possibility of a broad, democratic distribution of usable property. And, if one hunts for them, one can still find small parcels and plots of our land that have been cared for and safeguarded in use, not by the abstract political passion that now disgraces the name of patriotism, for such passion does not do such work, but by personal knowledge, affection, responsibility and skill.

And, even today, against overpowering odds and prohibitive costs, one does not have to go far in any part of the country to hear voiced the old hopes that moved millions of immigrants, freed slaves, westward movers, young couples starting out: a little farm, a little shop, a little store—some kind of place and enterprise of one's own, within and by which one's family could achieve a proper measure of independence, not only of its own economy, but of satisfaction, thought and character.

That our public institutions have not looked with favor upon these hopes is sufficiently evident from the results. In the twenty-five years after World War II, our farm people were driven off their farms by economic pressure at the rate of about 1,000,000 a year. They are still going out of business at a rate of 1,400 farm families per week, or 72,800 families per year. That the rate of decline is now less than it was does not mean that the situation is improving; it means that the removal of farmers from farming is nearly complete. Less than 3% of the population of our country is left on the farms; that tiny percentage is presently declining, and, if present conditions continue, will certainly decline further. And of that tiny percentage, a percentage still tinier now owns most of the land and produces most of the food. *Farming*, the magazine of the Production Credit Association, told farmers in its issue for March/April 1984: "Projections are that within the next 10-15 years, there'll be 200,000 to 300,000 of you farming big enough to account for 90% of the nation's gross farm receipts."

But this is not happening just on the farm. A similar decline is taking place in the cities. According to Jack Havemann, in the *Los Angeles Times*, December 10, 1983, "The percentage of households that own their own homes fell from 65.6 percent in 1980 to

86

64.5 at the end of 1982." Those percentages are too low in a country devoted to the defense of private ownership, and the decline is ominous. The reasons were the familiar ones of inflation and usury: "During the 1970's the value of a median-priced home nearly tripled, while family income only doubled and mortgage interest rates rocketed to a peak of more than 16 percent in late 1981." And in *The Atlantic Monthly* of September 1984, Philip Langdon wrote: "Most families are priced out of the new-home market and have been for years. In April the median price of a new single-family house rose above $80,000—an increase of 24 percent since 1979 . . ."

Those of us who can remember as far back as World War II do not need statistics to tell us that in the last 40 years the once plentiful small, privately owned neighborhood groceries, pharmacies, restaurants and other small shops and businesses have become endangered species, in many places extinct. It is this as much as anything that has rotted the hearts of our cities and surrounded them with shopping centers built by the corporate competitors of the small owners. The reasons again, are inflation and usury, as well as the legally sanctioned advantages of corporations in their competition with individuals. Since World War II, the money interest has triumphed over the property interest, to the inevitable decline of the good care and the good use of property.

As a person living in a rural, agricultural community, I need no statistics to inform me of the decline of availability of essential goods and services in such places. Welders, carpenters, masons, mechanics, electricians, plumbers, are all in short supply, and their decline in the last ten years has been precipitous. Because of high interest rates and inflation, properties, tools and supplies have become so expensive as to put a beginning out of reach of many who would otherwise be willing. And high interest works directly to keep local capital from being put to work locally. Why take a chance by investing in a small local store or shop when certificates of deposit are bringing ten percent.

When inflation and interest rates are high, young people starting out in small businesses or on small farms must pay a good living every year for the privilege of earning a poor one. People who are working are paying an exorbitant tribute to people who are, as they say, "letting their money work for them." The abstract value of money is preying upon and destroying the particular values that inhere in the lives of the land and of its human communities. For many years now, our officials have been bragging about the immensity of our gross national product and of the growth of our national economy, apparently without recognizing the possibility that the national economy as a whole can grow (up to a point) by depleting or destroying the small local economies within it.

The displacements of millions of people over the last forty or fifty years have, of course, been costly. The costs are not much talked about by apologists for our economy, and they have not been deducted from national or corporate incomes, but the costs exist nevertheless and they are not to be dismissed as intangible; to a considerable extent they have to do with the destruction and degradation of property. The decay of the "inner" parts of our cities is one of the costs; another is soil erosion, and other forms of land loss and land destruction; another is pollution.

There seems to be no escape from the requirement that intensive human use of property, if it is not to destroy the property, must be accompanied by intensive, which is to say intimate, human care. It is often assumed that ownership guarantees good care. But that is not necessarily true. It has long been understood that absentee ownership is a curse upon property. Corporate ownership is plagued by the incompetence, irresponsibility, or antipathy of employees. And among us, at least, public ownership, as of waterways and roads, amounts virtually to an invitation to abuse. Good use of property seems to require *both* ownership and personal occupation and use by the owner. That is to say that the good use of property requires the widest possible distribution of ownership.

When urban property is gathered into too few hands, and the division between owners and users becomes therefore too great, a sort of vengeance is exacted upon urban property: people litter their streets and destroy their dwellings. When rural property is gathered into too few hands, even when, as in farming, the owners may still be the users, there is an inevitable shift of emphasis from maintenance to production, and the land deteriorates. People displaced from farming have been replaced by machines and chemicals and other technological "labor savers" which, of themselves, contribute to production, but do not, of themselves, contribute to maintenance and often, of themselves, contribute to the degradation both of the land and of human care for it. Our extremely serious problems of soil erosion and of pollution by agricultural chemicals are, thus, both attributable to the displacement of people from agriculture. The technologies of "agri-business" are enabling less than 3% of our people to keep the land in production (for the time being), but they do not and cannot enable them to take care of it.

Increasing the number of property owners is not in itself, of course, a guarantee of better use. People who do not know how to care for property cannot care for it, no matter how willing they may be to do so. But good care is potential in the presence of people, no matter how ignorant; there is no hope of it at all in their absence. The question bearing ever more heavily upon us is how this potential for good care in people may be developed and put to use. The honest answer, at present, seems to be that we do not know how. Perhaps we will have to begin by answering the question negatively. For example, people who move from place to place every few years will never learn to care well for any place, nor will people who are long alienated from all responsibility for usable property. Such people, moreover, cannot be taught good care by books or classroom instruction, nor can it be forced upon them by law. A people as a whole, can learn good care only by long experience of living and working, learning and remembering, in the same places generation after generation, experiencing and correcting the results of bad care.

It may be, also, that people who do not care well *for* their land will not care enough *about* it to defend it well. It seems certain that any people who hope to be capable of national defense in the true sense—not by invading foreign lands, but by driving off invaders of its own land—must love their country with a particularizing passion with which deeply settled people have always loved, not their nation, but their *homes*, their daily lives and daily bread.

An abstract nationalist patriotism may be esay to arouse, if the times offer a leader sufficiently gifted in the manipulation of crowds, but it is hard to sustain, and it has the seed of a foolishness in it that will become its disease. Our great danger at present is that we have no defensive alternatives to this sort of hollow patriotic passion and its inevitable expression in nuclear warheads; this is both because our people are too "mobile" to have developed strong local loyalties and strong local economies, and because the nation is thus made everywhere locally vulnerable—indefensible except as a whole. Our life no longer rests broadly upon our land, but has become an inverted pyramid resting upon the pinpoint of a tiny, dwindling, agricultural minority critically dependent upon manufactured supplies and upon credit. Moreover, the population as a whole is now dependent upon goods and services that are not and often cannot be produced locally, but must be transported, often across the entire width of the continent, or from the other side of the world. Our national livelihood is everywhere pinched into wires, pipelines and roads. A fact that cannot have eluded our military experts is that this "strongest nation in the world" is almost pitifully vulnerable on its own ground. A relatively few well-directed rifle shots, a relatively few well-placed sticks of dynamite could bring us to darkness, confusion and hunger. And this civil weakness serves and aggravates the military obsession with megatonnage. It is only logical that a nation weak at home should threaten abroad with whatever destructions its technology can contrive. It is logical, but it is mad.

Nor can it have eluded our military experts that our own Revolution was won, in spite of the gravest military disadvantages, by a farmer-soldiery, direct share-holders in their country, who were therefore, as Jefferson wrote, "wedded to its liberty and its interests, by the most lasting bonds." The persian Wars, according to Aubrey de Selincourt, "proved to the Greeks what a handful of free men, fighting for what they loved, could achieve against a horde of invaders advancing to battle 'under the lash . . .'," And though the circumstances are inevitably different, we should probably draw similar conclusions from our experience in Vietnam, and from the Soviet Union's in Afghanistan. People tend to fight well in defense of their homes—the prerequisite being, of course that they must have homes to defend. That is, they must not look on their dwelling places as dispensible or disposable camp sites on the way to supposedly better dwelling places. A highly mobile population is predisposed to retreat; its values purpose no sufficient reason for anyone to stay anywhere. The hope of a defensive *stand* had better rest on settled communities, whose ways imply their desire to be permanent.

I have been arguing from what seems to me a reasonable military assumption: that a sound policy of national defense would have its essential foundation and its indispensable motives in widespread, settled, thriving local communities each having a proper degree of independence, living so far as possible from local sources, and using its local sources with a stewardly care that would sustain its life indefinitely, even through times of adversity. But now I would like to go further, and say that such communities are not merely the prerequisites or supports of a sound national defense; they *are* a sound national defense. They defend the country daily and hourly in all their acts by taking care of it, by causing it to thrive, by giving it the health and the satisfaction that make it worth defending, and by teaching these things to the young. This, to my mind, is *real* national defense, and military national defense would be forthcoming from it, as if by nature, when occasion demanded, as the history of our Revolution suggests. To neglect such national defense, to destroy the possibility of it, in favor of a highly specialized, expensive, unwieldly, inflexible, desperate and suicidal reliance on nuclear weapons, is already to be defeated.

And it is not as though the two kinds of national defense are compatible; it is not as though settled, stewardly communities can thrive and at the same time support a nuclear arsenal. In fact, the present version of national defense is destroying its own supports in the land and in human communities. It is doing this in the apathy, cynicism and despair that it fosters, especially in the young, but it is directly destructive of land and people by the inflation and usury that it encourages. The present version of national defense, like the present version of agriculture, rests upon debt—a debt that is driving up the cost of interest and driving down the worth of money, putting the national government actively in competition against good young people who are striving to own their own small farms and small businesses.

People who are concerned with the work of what I have called real national defense will necessarily have observed that it must be carried out often against our national government, and unremittingly against our present national economy. And our political and military leaders should have noticed, if they have not, that whereas the citizenry now submit apathetically or cynically to the demands and costs of so-called national defense, works and acts of real national defense are being carried out locally in all parts of the country every day with firm resolve and with increasing skill. People, local citizens, are getting together, without asking for, or needing government sanction, to defend their rivers, hills, mountains, skies, winds and rains. They are doing this ably, peaceably, and many times successfully, though still far from the success that they desire.

The costs of this state of affairs to our instituted government are many and dangerous, and they may perhaps be best suggested by questions. To what point, for instance, do we defend from foreign enemies a country that we are destroying ourselves? In spite of all our propagandists can do, the foreign threat inevitably seems diminished when our drinking water is unsafe to drink, when our rivers carry tonnages of topsoil that make light of the frieght they carry in boats, when our forests are dying from air pollution and acid rain, when we are sick from poisons in the air. Who *are* the enemies of this country? That is a question dangerous to instituted government when people begin to ask it for themselves. Many who have seen forests clear-cut on steep slopes, who have observed the work of the strip-miners, who have watched as corporations advance their claim on private property "in the public interest," are asking that question already. Many more are going to ask.

Millions of people, moreover, who have lost small stores, shops and farms to corporations, money merchants and usurers, will continue to be asked to defend capitalism against communism. Sooner or later they are going to demand to know why. If one must spend one's life as an employee, what difference does it make whether one's employer is a government or a corporation?

People, as history shows, will fight willingly and well to defend what they perceive as their own. But how willingly and how well will they fight to defend what has already been taken from them?

But we must ask, at last, if international fighting as we have known it has not become obsolete in the presence of such omnivorous weapons as we now possess. There will undoubtedly always be a need to resist aggression, but now, surely, we must think of changing the means of such resistance.

In the face of all-annihilating weapons, the natural next step may be the use of no weapons. It may be that the only possibly effective defense against the ultimate weapon is no weapon at all. It may be that the presence of nuclear weapons in the world serves notice that the command to love one another is an absolute practical necessity, such as we never dreamed it to be before, and that our choice is not to win or lose, but to love our enemies or die.

nominated by James Baker Hall

SUNDAY AT ST. CHRISTINE'S IN BUDAPEST AND A FRUITSTAND NEARBY

by ANTONIO CISNEROS

translated by Maureen Ahern, William Rowe and David Tipton

from AT NIGHT THE CATS (Red Dust Press)

It's raining among the peaches and the pears,
their skins shining in their hampers
like Roman helmets beneath the river.
It's raining between the roaring undertow
and the iron cranes. The priest
wears Advent green and a microphone.
I don't know what language he speaks or
in what century this church was founded.
But I know that the Lord is on his lips:
the lutes, the fattest calf,
the richest tunic, the sandals
are all for me,
because once I was more lost
than a grain of sand at Punta Negra

93

or this rain on the waters
of the tossing Danube.
Because I was dead and then reborn.

It's raining among the peaches and the pears,
fruits in season whose names I don't know, but I do know
their flavors and aromas, the colors
that change with the seasons,
I don't know the customs or the fruitvendor's face
—his name is a placard—
but I do know that these feasts and the fatted calf
await him at the end of the labyrinth
as they do for all birds
tired of beating against the wind.
Because I was dead and then reborn,
praised be the name of the Lord,
praised be any name under this good rain.

nominated by Red Dust Press

MID-PLAINS TORNADO

by LINDA BIERDS

from FLIGHTS OF THE HARVEST-MARE (Ahsahta Press)

I've seen it drive straw straight through a fence post—
sure as a needle in your arm—the straws all erect
and rooted in the wood like quills.
Think of teeth being drilled, that enamel and blood
burning circles inside your cheek. That's like the fury.
Only now it's quail and axles, the northeast bank
of the Cedar River, every third cottonwood.

It's with you all morning. Something wet in the air.
Sounds coming in at a slant, like stones
clapped under water. And pigs, slow to the trough.
One may rub against your leg, you turn with a kick
and there it is, lurching down from a storm cloud:
the shaft pulses toward you across the fields
like a magician's finger.
You say goodbye to it all then, in a flash over
your shoulder, with the weathervane so still
it seems painted on the sky.

The last time, I walked a fresh path toward the river.
Near the edge of a field I found our mare, pierced
through the side by the head of her six-week-foal.
Her ribs, her great folds of shining skin
closed over the skull. I watched them forever it seemed:
eight legs, two necks, one astonished head curved
back in a little rut of hail. And across the river
slim as a road, a handful of thrushes set down
in an oak tree, like a flurry of leaves
drawn back again.

nominated by Ahsahta Press and Pamela Stewart

EATING TOGETHER

by LI-YOUNG LEE

from THE IOWA REVIEW

In the steamer is the trout
seasoned with slivers of ginger,
two sprigs of green onion, and sesame oil.
We shall eat it with rice for lunch,
brothers, sister, my mother who will
taste the sweetest meat of the head,
holding it between her fingers
skillfully, the way my father did
weeks ago. Then he lay down
to sleep like a snow-covered road
winding through pines older than him,
without any travelers, and lonely for no one.

nominated by The Iowa Review

JURY SELECTION

by LUCIA PERILLO

from IRONWOOD

If they only could have put that in the papers, how the winter
    light hangs thickly in those southern Massachusetts towns,
sucking orange at four p.m. from the last spasm of daylight, then
    glowing morbid and humming
with a sound barely audible—not human, more like some rasping
    harmonic twanged
from the animated hulk of machinery that somewhere keeps it
    all running: this town
where the fish have been abandoned for over a century, the old
    men left

with just the memory of fish swimming in their bones, telling
    stories about the Azores
from their perch on rusted forty-gallon drums that have come to
    rest on the riprap
that's been brought in to seal the village from the sea. And what
    it would feel like to be a man
walking around smothering inside the fester of all that—you can
    almost understand why they did it,
raped that woman on the pool table at Big Dan's, in the broad
    daylight of Bobby Darrin singing Volare for a quarter
then Mack the Knife on the replay,
        . . . *cause old mackie's back in town* . . .
                            and the mown green felt
    smelling of wet wool and—yes, sweet jesus—even fish, their
    blood stirring with the sea.
You can almost understand why a woman might have needed it.

But before it gets too complicated, remember: we're supposed to
    work with only the available labels
to construct questions that will discern shades of meaning,
    measure culpability. Whether this woman
has a houseful of gray babies in dirty sleepers, which one's
    father has been named,
where it has happened before, who had drunk which kind of
    liquor
and how much. She says she only went into the tavern for a
    minute
to tug on the silver nozzles of the cigarette machine, but the thin
    curtains that line her bedroom windows
are clearly visible from the street. The whole town knows. Even
    some of these young men carry the blue nickels of her
    thumbprints on the back of their thighs, from this time,
but also the times before. Who whimpered, which ones came in
    her
and how often, which ones merely watched without speaking
    from the threshold.
The men were of a darker race, refusing to speak our language
    and moving their dark arms
in the ancestral motions of urging we only dimly remember,
    which still arouse us even in our embarrassment, through the
    electric current
of testimony. Whether a crime has been committed (because the
    woman has her Chesterfields, her change coins clenched &
    sweaty in her palm)
or not, their long-boned faces make this offense more
    palpable—the slick skin
and elegant hard moustaches recalling to us the brown eyes of our
    own lives, when in darkness
the vestiges of something we do not claim to know rise out from
    our bodies
and we seize it and do violence.

We all do violence.

Because the woman was as dark as any of the others,
with no green card and a name you won't find in the phone book.
What is on trial here is a thousand years of women plodding on
    thick legs, arms draped with string baskets,

towards some market in another continent, where boats pull into
  the waiting lips of shore
to meet these women and laud the correctness of their sexless
  march with fruit and cod and men come home
with the musk of Ecuadorian whores still riding on their loins.
In the end, the real trial takes place in words exchanged
in pissed-up alleyways between tight stone buildings, in words
that are to us gutteral and pronounced with too much tongue.
In the end the jury forgives everything but the pool table.
And on the streets of town, in the late afternoon light,
mothers tear their dresses away from their stout provincial
  breasts, and carry placards, and weep,
and spit at no one in particular,
for the love of their sons,
not the love of their daughters.

nominated by Ironwood *and Michael Waters*

TIDE OF VOICES

by LYNDA HULL

from TENDRIL

At the hour the streetlights come on, buildings
turn abstract. The Hudson, for a moment, formal.
We drink bourbon on the terrace and you speak
in the evening voice, weighted deep in the throat.

They plan to harvest oysters, you tell me,
from the harbor by Jersey City, how the waters
will be clean again in twenty years. I imagine nets
burdened with rough shells, the meat dun and sexual.

Below, the river and the high rock
where boys each year jump from bravado
or desperation. The day flares, turns into itself.
And innocently, sideways, the way we always fall

into grace or knowledge, we watched the police
drag the river for a suicide, the third this year.
The terrible hook, the boy's frail whiteness.
His face was blank and new as your face

in the morning before the day has worked
its pattern of lines and tensions. A hook
like an iron question and this coming
out of the waters, a flawed pearl—

a memory that wasn't ours to claim.
Perhaps, in a bedroom by lamplight,
a woman waits for this boy. She may riffle drawers
gathering photographs, string, keys to abandoned rooms.

Even now she may be leaving,
closing the door for some silence. I need
to move next to you. Water sluiced
from the boy's hair. I need to watch you

light your cigarette, the flickering
of your face in matchlight, as if underwater,
drifting away. I take your cigarette
and drag from it, touch your hand.

Remember that winter of your long fever,
the winter we understood how fragile
any being together was. The wall sweated
behind the headboard and you said you felt

the rim where dreams crouch
and every room of the past. It must begin in luxury—
do you think—a break and fall into the glamour
attending each kind of surrender. Water must flood

the mind, as in certain diseases, the walls
between the cells of memory dissolve, blur
into a single stream of voices and faces.
I don't know any more about this river or if

it can be cleaned of its tender and broken histories—
a tide of voices. And this is how the dead
rise to us, transformed: wet and singing,
the tide of voices pearling in our hands.

nominated by Maura Stanton and Elizabeth Spires

THE FLOWERS
OF BERMUDA

fiction by D. R. MACDONALD

from SEWANEE REVIEW

In memory of M. D. M.

Bilkie Sutherland took the postcard from behind his rubber bib and slowly read the message one more time: "I'm going here soon. I hope your lobsters are plentiful. My best to Bella. God bless you. Yours, Gordon MacLean." Bilkie flipped it over: a washed out photograph in black and white. *The Holy Isle. Iona. Inner Hebrides.* On the land stood stone ruins, no man or woman anywhere, and grim fences of cloud shadowed a dark sea. So this was Iona.

"You want that engine looked at?" Angus Carmichael, in his deepwater boots, was standing on the wharf above Bilkie's boat.

"Not now. I heard from the minister."

"MacLean?"

"He's almost to Iona now."

Angus laughed, working a toothpick around in his teeth. "Man dear, *I've* been to Iona, was there last Sunday." Angus meant where his wife was from, a Cape Breton village with a Highland museum open in the summer.

"It's a very religious place," Bilkie said, ignoring him. "Very ancient, in that way."

"Like you, Bilkie."

"I'm the same as the rest of you."

"No, Bilkie. Sometimes you're not. And neither is your Reverend MacLean."

Angus's discarded toothpick fluttered down to the deck. Bilkie picked it up and dropped it over the side. Angus never cared whether his own deck was flecked with gurry and flies. Nor was he keen on Gordon MacLean. Said the man was after putting in a good word for the Catholics. But that wasn't the minister's point at all. "We're all one faith, if we go back to Iona," is what he'd said. And nothing much more than that.

As Bilkie laid out his gear for the next day's work, he heard singing. No one sang around here anymore. Radios took care of that. He stood up to listen. Ah! It was Johnny, Angus's only boy, home from Dalhousie for the summer. He had a good strong voice, that boy, one they could use over at the church. But you didn't see him there, not since college. No singer himself, Bilkie could appreciate a good tune. His grandfather had worked the schooners in the West Indies trade, and Johnny's song had the flavor of that, of those rolling vessels . . . " 'He could smell the flowers of Bermuda in the gale, when he died on the North Rock Shoal. . . . ' " Bilkie stared into the wet darkness underneath the wharf where pilings were studded with snails. Algae hung like slicked hair on the rocks. He had saved Gordon MacLean under that wharf, when the man was just a tyke. While hunting for eels, Gordon had slipped and fallen, and Bilkie heard his cries and came down along the rocks on the other side to pull him out, a desperate boy clutching for his hand.

Bilkie's car, a big salt-eaten Ford, was parked at the end of the wharf, and whenever he saw it he wished again for horses who could shuck salt like rain. At home the well pump had quit this morning and made him grumpy. He'd had to use the woods, squat out there under a fir, the birds barely stirring overhead, him staring at shoots of Indian Pipe wondering what in hell they lived on, leafless, white as wax, hardly a flower at all. Up by the roadside blue lupines were a little past their prime. What flowers, he wondered, grew on Iona?

The car swayed through rain ruts, past clumps of St. Johnswort (*allas Colmcille* his grandfather had called them) that gave a wild yellow border to the driveway. His house appeared slowly behind a corridor of tall maples. In their long shade red cows rested. Sometimes everything seemed fixed, for good. His animals, his life. But God had taken away his only boy, and Bilkie could not fathom that even yet. For a time he had kept sheep, but quit because killing the lambs bothered him.

104

Bella was waiting at the front door, not the back, her palm pressed to her face. He stopped shy of the porch, hoping it wasn't a new well-pump they needed.

"What's wrong?"

"Rev. MacLean's been stabbed in Oban," his wife said, her voice thin.

Bilkie repeated the words to himself. There was a swallow's nest above the door. The birds swooped and clamored. "Not there?" he said. "Not in Scotland?" A mist of respect, almost of reverence, hovered over the old country. You didn't get stabbed there.

"Jessie told me on the phone, not a minute ago. Oh, he'll live all right. He's living."

Over supper Bella related what she knew. Gordon MacLean had been walking in Oban, in the evening it was, a woman friend with him. Two young thugs up from Glasgow went for her handbag, right rough about it too. Gordon collared one but the other shoved a knife in his back.

"He's not a big man either," Bilkie said, returning a forkful of boiled potato to his plate. He had known Gordon as a child around the wharf, a little boy who asked hard questions. He had pulled him from the water. He'd seen him go off to seminary, thinking he would never come back to Cape Breton, not to this corner of it, but after awhile he did. To think of him lying in blood, on a sidewalk in Oban. "Did they catch the devils?"

"They did. He'll have to testify."

"What, go back there?"

"When he's able. Be a long time until the trial."

Bilkie felt betrayed. A big stone had slipped somehow out of place. Certain things did not go wrong there, not in the Islands where his people came from. Here, crime was up, too few caring about a day's work, kids scorning church. Greedier now, more for themselves, people were. But knives, what the hell. There in the Hebrides they'd worked things out, hadn't they, over a long span of time? It had seemed to him a place of hard wisdom, hard won. Not a definite place, for he had never been there, but something like stone about it: sea-washed, nicely worn, and high cliffs where waves whitened against the rocks. He knew about the Clearances, yes, about the bad laws that drove his grandfather out of Lewis where he'd lived in a turf house. But even then they weren't knifing people. Gordon MacLean, a minister of God, couldn't return there and come to no harm? To Mull first he'd been headed,

105

to MacLean country. And then to Iona, across a strait not much wider than this one. But a knife stopped him in Oban, a nice sort of town by the sea.

From his parlor window Bilkie could see a bit of the church in the east, the dull white shingles of its steeple above the dark spruce. *We all have Iona inside us,* the man had said. *Our faith was lighted there.* Why then did this happen?

Bilkie had asked such a question before and found no answer. They'd had a son, he and Bella, so he knew about shock, and about grief. Even now, thinking of his son and the schoolhouse could suck the wind right out of him. The boy was born late in their lives anyway, and maybe Bilkie's hopes had come too much to rest in him. Was that the sin? Tormod they called him, an old name out of the Hebrides, after Bella's dad. But one October afternoon when the boy was nine, he left the schoolhouse and forgot his coat, a pea coat, new, with a big collar turned up like a sailor's. So he went back to get it, back to the old white schoolhouse where he was learning about the world. It was just a summer house now, owned by strangers. But that day it was locked tight, and the teacher gone home. A young woman. No blame to her. His boy jimmied open the window with his knife. They were big, double-hung windows, and you could see them open yet on a warm weekend, hear people drunk behind the screens. But Tormod had tried to hoist himself over the sill, and the upper half of the window unjammed then and came down on his neck. Late in the day it was they found him, searching last the grounds of the school. A time of day about now. The sash lay along his small shoulders like a yoke, that cruel piece of wood, blood in his nose like someone had punched him. . . .

Bilkie barely slept. He was chased by a misty street, black and wet, and harrowing cries that seemed one moment a man's, the next a beast's. He was not given to getting up in the night but he dressed and went outside to walk off the dreariness he'd woke to. A cold and brilliant moon brightened the ground fog which layered the pasture like a fallen cloud. The high ridge of hill behind his fields was ragged with wormshot spruce, wicks of branch against the sky. As a boy he'd walked those high woods with his grandfather who offered him the Gaelic names of things, most of them forgotten now, gone with the good trees. One day he'd told Bilkie about the words for heaven and hell, how they, Druid words, went far back before the time of Christ. *Ifrinn*, the Isle of the Cold Clime, was a dark and frigid region of venomous reptiles and savage wolves. There the wicked were doomed to wander, chilled to their very bones and bereft even of the company of their fellow sinners. And the old heaven, though the Christians kept that name too, was also different: *Flathinnis*, the Isle of the Brave, a paradise full of light which lay far distant, somewhere in the Western Ocean. "I like that some better," his grandfather had said. "Just the going there would be good. As for hell, nothing's worse than cold and loneliness."

As he moved through the fog, it thinned like steam, but gathered again and closed in behind him. Suddenly he heard hoofbeats. Faintly at first, then louder. He turned in a circle, listening. Not a cow of his. They were well-fenced. Maybe the Dunlop's next door. But cow or horse it was coming toward him at a good clip and yet he couldn't make it out, strain as he might. Soon his heart picked up the quick, even thud of the hooves, and when in the pale fog a shape grew and darkened and then burst forth, a head shaggy as seaweed and cruelly horned, he raised his arms wildly in a shout of fear and confusion as the bull shied past him, a dark rush of heat and breath, staggering him like a blow. Aw, that goddamn Highland bull, that ugly bugger. Trembling with anger and surprise, he listened to it crash through thickets off up the hill, the fog eddying in its wake, until Bella called him and he turned back to the house.

On the porch of the manse Bilkie waited for Mrs. MacQueen to answer the door. The porch Rev. MacLean had built, but the white paint and black trim were Bilkie's work, donated last summer when his lobstering was done. He'd enjoyed those few days around the minister. One afternoon when Bilkie was on the ladder he thought he heard Gordon talking to himself, but no, he was looking up, shading his eyes. "It's only a mile from Mull, Iona," Gordon said to him. "Just across the Sound. So it's part of going home, really." Bilkie had said yes, he could see that. But he wasn't sure, even now, that he and the minister meant home in the same way. "Monks lived there, Bilkie. For a long, long time. They had a different view of the world, a different feel for it altogether. God was still *new* there, you see. Their faith was . . . robust."

Mrs. MacQueen, the housekeeper, filled the doorway and Bilkie told her what he would like.

"A book about Iona?" She was looking him up and down. She smelled of Joy, lemon-scented, the same stuff he used on his decks. "I don't read the man's books, dear, I dust them."

"He wouldn't mind me looking. Me and himself are friends." He rapped the trim of the door. "My paint."

"Well, he could have used some friends in Oban."

Mrs. MacQueen showed him into the minister's study, making it clear she would not leave. She turned the television on low, as if this were a sickroom, and sat down on a hassock, craning her ear to the screen.

Wine-colored drapes, half-drawn, gave the room a warm light. Bookshelves lined one wall, floor to ceiling, and Bilkie touched their bindings as he passed. He hadn't a clue where to begin or how to search in this hush: he only wanted to know more about that place, and maybe when the man returned they could talk about what went wrong there. But he felt shy with Mrs. Mac-Queen in the room. A map of Scotland was thumbtacked to the wall. The old clan territories were done in bright colors. Lewis he spotted easily, and Mull. And tiny Iona. On the desktop, under sprigs of lilac in a small vase, he saw a slim red book. In it were notes in Gordon's hand. With a quick glance at the housekeeper, he took it to the leather chair close by the north window, a good bright spot where Gordon must have sat many a time, binoculars propped on the sill. Bilkie put them to his eyes instinctively. Behind the manse a long meadow ran down to the shore. Across the half mile of water his boat rocked gently in the light swells. Strange to see his yellow slicker hanging by the wheel, emptied of him. Moving the glasses slightly he made out Angus standing over his boy, Johnny hunched down into some work or other. Good with engines, was Johnny. Suddenly Angus looked toward Bilkie. Of course his eyes would take in only the white manse on the hill, and the church beside it. Yet Bilkie felt seen in a peculiar way and he put down the binoculars.

Aware of the time, he turned pages, reading what he could grasp. That Iona's founder, St. Columba, had sailed there from Ireland to serve his kinsmen, the Scots of Dalriada. That he and his monks labored with their own hands, tilling and building, and that in their tiny boats they spread the faith into the remote and lesser isles, converting even the heathen Picts. That even before he was born, Columba's glory had been foretold to his mother in a dream:

108

"An angel of the Lord appeared to her, and brought her a beautiful robe—a robe which had all the colors of all the flowers of the world. Immediately it was rapt away from her, and she saw it spread across the heavens, stretched out over plains and woods and mountains. . . ." He read testaments to St. Columba's powers and example, how once in a great storm his ship met swelling waves that rose like mountains, but at his prayer they were stilled. He was a poet and loved singing, and songs praising Columba could keep you from harm. His bed was bare rock and his pillow a stone. During the three days and three nights of his funeral, a great wind blew, without rain, and no boat could reach or leave the island.

Bilkie was deep in the book when Mrs. MacQueen, exclaiming, "That's desperate, just desperate!", turned off the soap opera and came over to him.

"You'll have to go now," she said. "This isn't the public library, dear, and I have cleaning to do."

He would never talk himself past her again, not with Gordon away. He returned the book to the desk and followed her to the front door.

"Did you ever pray to a saint, Mrs. MacQueen?"

She crossed her arms. "I'm no R.C., Mr. Sutherland."

"I don't think that matters, Mrs. MacQueen. The minister has a terrible wound. Say a word to St. Columba."

"He's healing. He's getting better and soon might be coming home, is what I heard."

The next morning the sun glared up from a smooth sea as Bilkie hauled his traps, moving from one swing to another over the grounds his grandfather had claimed. By the time Bilkie was old enough to fish, there was a little money in it. But you had to work. Nobody ever gave it to you, and the season was short. He had started out young hauling by hand, setting out his swings in the old method, the backlines anchored with kellicks, and when he wasn't hauling he was rowing, and damned hard if a wind was on or the tide against you. He had always worked alone, rowed alone. Except when his boy was with him, and that seemed as brief now as a passing bird. He preferred it out here by himself, free of the land for awhile, the ocean at his back.

This season the water was so clear he could see ten fathoms, see

109

the yellow backline snaking down, the traps rising. His grandfather told him about the waters of the West Indies, the clear blue seas with the sun so far down in them it wouldn't seem like drowning at all, for the light there.

He gaffed a buoy and passed the line over the hauler, drawing the trap up to the washboard where he quickly culled the dripping, scurrying collection. He measured the lobsters, threw a berried one back. But after he dropped the trap and moved on, he knew he'd forgotten, for the second time that morning, to put in fresh bait. To hell with it. On the bleak rocks of the Bird Islands shags spread their dark wings to dry. A school of mackerel shimmered near the boat, an expanding and contracting disturbance just beneath the surface as they fed. He cut the engine, letting the boat drift like his mind. He hummed the song of Johnny Carmichael but stopped. Couldn't get the damn tune out of his head. Sick of it. He picked a mackerel out of the bait box and turned it over in his hands, stroking the luminous flow of stripes a kind of sky was named for: a beautiful fish, if you looked at it—the smooth skin, dark yet silvery. Gordon MacLean said from the pulpit that a man should find beauty in what's around him, for that too was God. But for Bilkie everything had been so familiar, everything he knew and saw and felt, until Tormod died. He took out his knife and slid it slowly into the dead fish: now, what might that be like, a piece of steel like that inside you? A feeling you'd carry a long while, there, under the scar.

Astern, the head of the cape rose behind buff-colored cliffs, up into the deep green nap of the mountain. He had no fears here, never in weather like this when the sea was barely breathing. Still, he missed the man, the sound of his voice on Sunday. The last service before he left for Iona, the minister had read Psalm 44, the one, he said, that St. Columba sang to win the Picts away from their magi, the Druids . . . *O God, our fathers have told us, what work thou didst in their days, in the times of old.* . . .

After Bilkie lost his son, he'd stayed away from church, from the mournful looks and explanations, why he should accept God's taking an innocent boy in such a way. His heart was sore, he told Bella, and had to heal up, and nothing in the church then could help it. But a few weeks after Rev. MacLean arrived, Bilkie went to hear him. Damn it, the man could preach. Not like those TV preachers who couldn't put out anything much but their palms and a phone number. A slender string it was that Gordon MacLean couldn't take a tune from. And only once had he mentioned Tormod, in a roundabout way, to show he was aware there'd been a boy, that he knew what a son could mean.

As Bilkie turned in toward the wharf that afternoon, he saw three boats in ahead of him. Above Angus's blue and white Cape Islander the men had gathered in a close circle, talking and nodding. Only Johnny Carmichael was still down below, sitting on the gunnels with his guitar. Bilkie approached the wharf in a wide arc, trying to discern what he saw in the huddled men and the boy off alone bent into his instrument. He brought his boat up into the lee and flung a line to Angus who was waving for it.

"Bilkie, you're late, boy!" he shouted.

"Aw, I was feeling slow today!"

When the lines were secured, Angus called down to him. "Did you hear about it?"

"About what?"

"The minister, Bilkie, for God's sake! He's passed away! It was sudden, you know. Complications. Not expected at all."

Bilkie's hands were pressed against a crate he'd been about to shift. He could feel the lobsters stirring under the wood. He looked up at Angus. "I knew that already," he said.

Instead of going home, Bilkie drove to a tavern fifteen miles away. He sat near a window at one of the many small tables. Complications. Lord. The sun felt warm on his hands and he watched bubbles rise in his glass of beer. The tavern was quiet but tonight it would be roaring. Peering into the dim interior he made out Jimmy Carey alone at a table. Jimmy was Irish and had acted cranky here more than once. But he seemed old and mild now, back there in the afternoon dark, not the hell-raiser he used to be. And wasn't St. Columba an Irishman, after all? Bilkie raised his glass and held it there until Jimmy, who looked as if he'd been hailed from across the world, noticed it and raised his own in return. Bilkie beckoned him over. They drank until well past supper, leaning over the little table and knocking glasses from time to time. Bilkie told him about St. Columba, about the monks in their frail vessels.

"You know about St. Brendan, of course," Jimmy said, his eyes fixing on Bilkie but looking nowhere. "They say he got as far as here even, and clear to Bermuda before he was done."

"Bermuda I know about." Bilkie tried to sing what he remembered. " 'Oh there be flowers in Bermuda, beauty lies on every hand . . . and there be laughter, ease and drink for every man. . . .' " He leaned close to Jimmy's face: " '. . . but there not be joy for *me*.' "

On the highway Bilkie focussed hard on the center line, thinking that Jimmy Carey might have bought one round at least, St. Brendan be damned. To the west the strait ran deep and dark, the sun just gone from it as he turned away toward home. Bad time to meet the mounties. He lurched to a stop by the roadside where a small waterfall lay hidden. He plunged through a line of alders into air immediately cool. The falls stepped gently through mossed granite, down to a wide, clear pool, and he remembered Bella bending her head into it years ago, her hair fanning out red there as she washed the salt away after swimming. He knelt and cupped the water, so cold he groaned, over his face again and again.

As he drove the curves the white church appeared and disappeared above the trees. When he came upon it, it seemed aloof, unattended. Cars were parked carelessly along the driveway to the manse, and Bilkie slowed down long enough to see a man and woman climbing the front steps, Mrs. MacQueen, in her flowered apron, waiting at the door. Oh, there'd be some coming and going today, the sharing of the hard news. When he felt the schoolhouse approaching, he vowed again not to look, not to bother what went on there. But he couldn't miss the blue tent in the front yard, and the life raft filled with water for a wading pool. This time he did not slow down. Too often he had wondered about that blow on the neck, about what his son had felt, and who, in that instant, he had blamed . . . something so simple as a window coming down on his bones. There. In a schoolhouse.

Bella had not seen Bilkie drunk like this in years, but she knew why and said nothing, not even about Rev. MacLean. She could not get him to come inside for supper. He reeled around angrily in the lower pasture, hieing cows away when they trotted toward the fence for handouts of fresh hay. He shouted up at the ridge. Finally he stalked to the back door.

"Gordon was going to Iona," he said to his wife. "He could check the fury of wild animals, that saint they had there. Did Gordon no damn good, eh?"

"You've had some drink, Bilkie, and I've had none. I'm tired now."

He stepped up close to her and took her face in his hands. "Ah, Bella. Your hair was so pretty."

She made him go to bed, but after dark he woke. He smelled of the boat and wanted to wash. Hearing a car, he went over to the window. Near his neighbor's upper pasture headlights bounced and staggered over the rough ground. They halted, backed up, then swept suddenly in another direction until the shaggy bull galloped across the beams. Loose again. A smallish, wild-looking beast they'd imported from Scotland. Could live out on its own in the dead of winter, that animal. You might see it way off in a clearing, quiet, shouldering snow like a monument. The headlights, off again in pursuit, captured the bull briefly but it careened away into the darkness, and the car—a Dunlop boy at the wheel no doubt—raked the field blindly. Complications. A stone for a pillow. His own boy would be a man now. Passed away, like a wave.

It was difficult for Bilkie to get up that day. He had always opened his eyes on the dark side of four a.m. but now Bella had to push and coax him. He sat on the edge of the bed for a long time staring at the half-model of a schooner mounted on the wall. His grandfather had worked her, the *Ocean Rose*, lost on Hogsty Reef in the Bahamas with his Uncle Bill aboard.

"You don't get up anymore. What's the matter with you?" Bella said. He took the cup of coffee she held out to him, nodding vaguely. Squalls had lashed the house all night and now a thick drizzle whispered over the roof. "You know Rev. MacLean is coming home this day, and tonight they'll wake him."

"I can't go," Bilkie said.

"What would he think, you not there at his wake with the others who loved him?"

"He's not thinking at all anymore. That's just a body there, coming back."

"Don't be terrible. Don't be the way you were after Tormod."

"They could have buried him over there. Couldn't they have? Near where he wanted to go?"

"He was born *here*, Bilkie. Nobody asked, I don't suppose, one way or the other."

He could see that she'd been crying. He put the coffee down carefully on the window sill and took her hands in his, still warm

113

from the cup. "Bella, dear," he said. "You washed your hair in that water. It must have hurt, eh? Water so cold as that?"

Gusts rocked the car as Bilkie crossed the bridge that joined the other island. He was determined to take himself out of the fuss, some of it from people who would never bestir themselves were Gordon MacLean here and breathing. Above him the weather moved fast. The sky would whiten in patches but all the while churn with clouds black as the cliffs by the lighthouse. There was a good lop on the water, looking east from the bridge, and when the strait opened out a few miles away the Atlantic flashed white against an ebbing tide.

In the lee of the wharf the lobster boats were surging like tethered horses. No one was around. The waves broke among the pilings beneath him and the timbers creaked. He walked to the seaward end where Angus had stacked his broken traps. Across the roughening water the manse looked small, the cars tiny around it. Every morning his grandfather would say, old as he was, *Dh'iarr am muir a thadhal*. The sea wants to be visited.

He threw off his lines and headed out into the strait, rounding up into the wind, battering the waves until he checked back on the throttle. In the turns of wind he smelled the mackerel in the bait box, the fumes of the engine. But as he drew abreast of Campbell Point, a gust of fragrance came off the land and he strained to see its source in the long, blowing grass of the point. It was quickly gone and there was nothing to account for it but what had been there all along—the thin line of beach, the grass thick as hay all the way back to the woods. To the west, on the New Skye Road, he glimpsed St. David's Church, a small white building behind a veil of rain, set in the dense spruce, no one there now but Bible Camp kids in the summer.

The sea was lively at the mouth of the strait where wind and tide met head to head. He bucked into the whitecaps, slashes of spray cracking over the bow. The waves deepened as the sea widened out but he'd ride better when he reached the deeper water where the breaking crests would cease. He had a notion of the West Indies, of his grandfather under sails, out there over the curve of the world and rolling along in worse weather than this. Hadn't the Irish monks set out in their currachs of wickerwork and hide, just for the love of God? They had survived. They reached those islands

114

they sailed for, only dimly sure where they were. But maybe you could come by miracles easier then, when all of life was harder, and God closer to the sea than he was now. Now with no saints around, saints who could sow a field and sail a boat, you had to find your own miracles. You couldn't travel to them, could you, Gordon, boy?

He would have to go back. He would have to stand at the wake holding his hat like the rest of them, looking at Gordon who'd come dead such a distance. Bilkie watched the rhythm of the waves. He needed a break in them to bring his boat around and run with the sea. But then he wasn't hearing the engine anymore, and the boat was falling away, coming around slowly with no more sound than a sail would make. Columba. A dove. Strange name for a man. *Colmcille. Caoir gheal*, his grandfather called waves like these. A bright flaming of white. The sea had turned darker than the sky, and over the land the boat was swinging toward, clouds lay heavy and thick, eased along like stones, dark as dolmens. "Ah!" was all Bilkie said when the wave rose under him, lifting the boat high like an offering.

nominated by John Daniel

ROSE

fiction by ANDRE DUBUS

from PLOUGHSHARES

In memory of Barbara Loden

Sometimes, when I see people like Rose, I imagine them as babies, as young children. I suppose many of us do. We search the aging skin of the face, the unhappy eyes and mouth. Of course I can never imagine their fat little faces at the breast, or their cheeks flushed and eyes brightened from play. I do not think of them beyond the age of five or six, when they are sent to kindergartens, to school. There, beyond the shadows of their families and neighborhood friends, they enter the world a second time, their eyes blinking in the light of it. They will be loved or liked or disliked, even hated; some will be ignored, others singled out for daily abuse that, with a few adult exceptions, only children have the energy and heart to inflict. Some will be corrupted, many without knowing it, save for that cooling quiver of conscience when they cheat, when they lie to save themselves, when out of fear they side with bullies or teachers, and so forsake loyalty to a friend. Soon they are small men and women, with adult sins and virtues, and by the age of thirteen some have our vices too.

There are also those unforgiveable children who never suffer at all: from the first grade on, they are good at schoolwork, at play and sports, and always they are befriended, and are the leaders of the class. Their teachers love them, and because they are humble and warm, their classmates love them too, or at least respect them, and are not envious because they assume these children will excel at whatever they touch, and have long accepted this truth. They

116

come from all manner of families, from poor and illiterate to wealthy and what passes for literate in America, and no one knows why they are not only athletic and attractive but intelligent too. This is an injustice, and some of us pause for a few moments in our middle-aged lives to remember the pain of childhood, and then we intensely dislike these people we applauded and courted, and we hope some crack of mediocrity we could not see with our young eyes has widened and split open their lives, the homecoming queen's radiance sallowed by tranquilized bitterness, the quarter-back fat at forty wheezing up a flight of stairs, and all of them living in the same small town or city neighborhood, laboring at vacuous work that turns their memories to those halcyon days when the classrooms and halls, the playgrounds and gymnasiums and dance floors were theirs: the last places that so obediently, even lovingly, welcomed the weight of their flesh, and its displacement of air. Then, with a smile, we rid ourselves of that evil wish, let it pass from our bodies to dissipate like smoke in the air around us, and freed from the distraction of blaming some classmate's excellence for our childhood pain, we focus on the boy or girl we were, the small body we occupied, watch it growing through the summers and school years, and we see that, save for some strength gained here, some weaknesses there, we are the same person we first knew as ourselves; or the one memory allows us to see, to think we know.

People like Rose make me imagine them in those few years their memories will never disclose, except through hearsay: *I was born in Austin. We lived in a garage apartment. When I was two we moved to Tuscaloosa . . .* Sometimes, when she is drinking at the bar, and I am standing some distance from her and watch without her noticing, I see her as a baby, on the second or third floor of a tenement, in one of the Massachusetts towns along the Merrimack River. She would not notice, even if she turned and looked at my face; she would know me, she would speak to me, but she would not know I had been watching. Her face, sober or drunk or on the way to it, looks constantly watched, even spoken to, by her own soul. Or by something it has spawned, something that lives always with her, hovering near her face. I see her in a tenement because I cannot imagine her coming from any but a poor family, though I sense this notion comes from my boyhood, from something I learned about America, and that belief has hardened inside me, a

117

stone I cannot dissolve. Snobbishness is too simple a word for it. I have never had much money. Nor do I want it. No: it's an old belief, once a philosophy which I've now outgrown: no one born to a white family with adequate money could end as Rose has.

I know it's not true. I am fifty-one years old, yet I cannot feel I am growing older because I keep repeating the awakening experiences of a child: I watch and I listen, I write in my journal, and each year I discover, with the awe of my boyhood, a part of the human spirit I had perhaps imagined, but had never seen nor heard. When I was a boy, many of these discoveries thrilled me. Once in school the teacher told us of the men who volunteered to help find the cause of yellow fever. This was in the Panama Canal Zone. Some of these men lived in the room where victims of yellow fever had died; they lay on the beds, on sheets with dried black vomit, breathed and slept there. Others sat in a room with mosquitoes and gave their skin to those bites we simply curse and slap, and they waited through the itching and more bites, and then waited to die, in their agony leaving sheets like the ones that spared their comrades living in the room of the dead. This story, with its heroism, its infinite possibilities for human action, delighted me with the pure music of hope. I am afraid now to research it, for I may find that the men were convicts awaiting execution, or some other persons whose lives were so limited by stronger outside forces, that the risk of death to save others could not have, for them, the clarity of a choice made with courage, and in sacrifice, but could be only a weary nod of assent to yet another fated occurrence in their lives. But their story cheered me then, and I shall cling to that. Don't you remember? When first you saw or heard or read about men and women who, in the face of some defiant circumstance, fought against themselves and won, and so achieved love, honor, courage?

I was in the Marine Corps for three years, a lieutenant during a time in our country when there was no war but all the healthy young men had to serve in the armed forces anyway. Many of us, who went to college, sought commissions so our service would be easier, we would have more money, and we could marry our girl friends; in those days, a young man had to provide a roof and all that goes under it before he could make love with his girl; of course there was lovemaking in cars, but the ring and the roof waited somewhere beyond the windshield.

Those of us who chose the Marines went to Quantico, Virginia, for two six-week training sessions in separate summers during college; we were commissioned at graduation from college, and went back to Quantico for eight months of Officers' Basic School; only then would they set us free among the troops, and into the wise care of our platoon sergeants. During the summer training, which was called Platoon Leaders' Class, sergeants led us, harrassed us, and taught us. They also tried to make some of us quit. I'm certain that when they first lined us up and looked at us, their professional eyes saw the ones who would not complete the course: saw in a young boy's stiffened shoulders and staring and blinking eyes the flaw—too much fear, lack of confidence, who knows—that would, in a few weeks, possess him. Just as, on the first day of school, the bully sees his victim and eyes him like a cat whose prey has wandered too far from safety; it is not the boy's puny body that draws the bully, but the way the boy's spirit occupies his small chest, his thin arms.

Soon the sergeants left alone the stronger among us, and focused their energy on breaking the ones they believed would break, and ought to break now, rather than later, in that future war they probably did not want but never forgot. In another platoon, that first summer, a boy from Dartmouth completed the course, though in six weeks his crew cut black hair turned grey. The boy in our platoon was from the University of Chicago, and he should not have come to Quantico. He was physically weak. The sergeants liked the smaller among us, those with short lean bodies. They called them feather merchants, told them You little guys are always tough, and issued them the Browning Automatic Rifle for marches and field exercises, because it weighed twenty pounds and had a cumbersome bulk to it as well: there was no way you could comfortably carry it. But the boy from Chicago was short and thin and weak, and they despised him. Our platoon sergeant was a staff sergeant, his assistant a buck sergeant, and from the first day they worked on making the boy quit. We all knew he would fail the course; we waited only to see whether he would quit and go home before they sent him. He did not quit. He endured five weeks before the company commander summoned him to his office; he was not there long; he came into the squad bay where we lived and changed to civilian clothes, packed the suitcase and seabag, and was gone. In those five weeks he had dropped out of conditioning

119

marches, forcing himself up hills in the Virginia heat, carrying seventy pounds of gear—probably half his weight—until he collapsed on the trail to the sound of shouted derision from our sergeants, whom I doubt he heard.

When he came to Quantico he could not chin himself, nor do ten push-ups. By the time he left he could chin himself five quivering times, his back and shoulders jerking, and he could do twenty push-ups before his shoulders and chest rose while his small flat belly stayed on the ground. I do not remember his name, but I remember those numbers: five and twenty. The sergeants humiliated him daily, gave him long and colorful ass-chewings, but their true weapon was his own body, and they put it to use. They ran him till he fell, then ran him again: a sergeant running alongside the boy, around and around the hot blacktop parade ground. They sent him up and down the rope on the obstacle course. He never climbed it, but they sent him as far up as he could go, perhaps halfway, perhaps less, and when he froze then worked his way down, they sent him up again. That's the phrase: *as far up as he could go*.

He should not have come to Virginia. What was he thinking? Why didn't he get himself in shape during the school year, while he waited in Chicago for what he must have known would be the physical trial of his life? I understand now why the sergeants despised him, this weak college boy who wanted to be one of their officers. Most nights they went out drinking, and once or twice a week came into our squad bay, drunk at three in the morning, to turn on the lights, shout us out of our bunks, and we stood at attention and listened to their cheerful abuse. Three hours later, when we fell out for morning chow, they waited for us: lean and tanned and immaculate in their tailored and starched dungarees, and spit-shined boots. And the boy could only go so far up the rope, up the series of hills we climbed, up toward the chinning bar, up the walls and angled poles of the obstacle course, up from the grass by the strength of his arms as the rest of us reached fifty, seventy, finally a hundred push-ups.

But in truth he could, and that is the reason for this anecdote while I contemplate Rose. One night in our fifth week the boy walked in his sleep. Every night we had fire watch: one of us walked for four hours through the barracks, the three squad bays that each housed a platoon, to alert us of fire. We heard the story the next day, whispered, muttered, or spoken out of the boy's hearing, in the chow hall, during the ten minute break on a march. The fire watch was a boy from the University of Alabama, a football player whose southern accent enriched his story, heightened his surprise, his awe. He came into our squad bay at three-thirty in the morning, looked up and down the rows of bunks, and was about to leave when he heard someone speak. The voice frightened him. He had never heard, except in movies, a voice so pitched by desperation, and so eerie in its insistence. He moved toward it. Behind our bunks, against both walls, were our wall lockers. The voice came from that space between the bunks and lockers, where there was room to stand and dress, and to prepare your locker for inspection. The Alabama boy stepped between the bunks and lockers and moved toward the figure he saw now: someone squatted before a locker, white shorts and white tee shirt in the darkness. Then he heard what the voice was saying: *I can't find it. I can't find it.* He closed the distance between them, squatted, touched the boy's shoulder, and whispered: *Hey, what you looking for?* Then he saw it was the boy from Chicago. He spoke his name, but the boy bent lower and looked under his wall locker. That was when the Alabama boy saw that he was not truly looking: his eyes were shut, the lids in the repose of sleep, while the boy's head shook from side to side, in a short slow arc of exasperation. *I can't find it,* he said. He was kneeling before the wall locker, bending forward to look under it for—what? any of the several small things the sergeants demanded we care for and have with our gear: extra shoelaces, a web strap from a haversack, a metal button for dungarees, any of these things that became for us as precious as talismans. Still on his knees, the boy straightened his back, gripped the bottom of the wall locker, and lifted it from the floor, six inches or more above it and held it there as he tried to lower his head to look under it. The locker was steel, perhaps six feet tall, and filled with his clothes, boots, and shoes, and on its top rested his packed haversack and helmet. No one in the platoon could have lifted it while kneeling, using only his arms. Most of us could have bear-hugged it up from the floor, even held it there. *Gawd damn,* the fire watch said, rising from his squat; *Gawd damn, lemmee help you with it,* and he held its sides; it was tottering, but still raised. Gently he lowered it against the boy's resistance, then crouched again and, whispered to him, *like to a baby,* he told us, he said: *All rot now. It'll be all rot now. We'll find that damn thing in the mawnin';* as he tried to ease the boy's fingers from the bottom edge of the locker. Finally he pried them, one or two at a time. He pulled the boy to his feet, and with an arm around his waist, led him to his bunk. It was a lower bunk. He eased the boy downward to sit on it, then lifted his legs, covered him with the sheet, and sat beside him. He rested a hand on the boy's chest, and spoke soothingly to him as he struggled, trying to rise. Finally the boy lay still, his hands holding the top of the sheet near his chest.

We never told him. He went home believing his body had failed; he was the only failure in our platoon, and the only one in the company who failed because he lacked physical strength and endurance. I've often wondered about him: did he ever learn what he could truly do? Has he ever absolved himself of his failure? His was another of the inspiring stories of my youth. Not *his* story so much as the story of his body. I had heard or read much of the human spirit, indomitable against suffering and death. But this was a story of a pair of thin arms, and narrow shoulders, and weak legs: freed from whatever consciousness did to them, they had lifted an unwieldy weight they could not have moved while the boy's mind was awake. It is a mystery I still do not understand.

Now, more often than not, my discoveries are bad ones, and if they inspire me at all, it is only to try to understand the unhappiness and often evil in the way we live. A friend of mine, a doctor, told me never again to believe that only the poor and uneducated and usually drunk beat their children; or parents who are insane, who hear voices commanding them to their cruelty. He has seen children, sons and daughters of doctors, bruised, their small bones broken, and he knows that the children are repeating their parents' lies: they fell down the stairs, they slipped and struck a table. He can do nothing for them but heal their injuries. The poor are frightened by authority, he said, and they will open their doors to a social worker. A doctor will not. And I have heard stories from young people, college students who come to the bar during the school year. They are rich, or their parents are, and they have about them those characteristics I associate with the rich: they look healthy, as though the power of money had a genetic influence on their very flesh; beneath their laughter and constant talk there lies always a certain poise, not sophistication, but confidence in life and their places in it. Perhaps it comes from the knowledge that they will never be stranded in a bus station with two dollars. But probably its source is more intangible: the ambience they grew up in: that strange paradox of being from birth removed, insulated, from most of the world, and its agony of survival that is, for most of us, a day-to-day life; while, at the same time, these young rich children are exposed through travel and—some of them—culture, to more of the world than most of us will ever see.

Years ago, when the students first found Timmy's and made it their regular drinking place, I did not like them, because their lives were so distant from those of the working men who patronize the bar. Then some of them started talking to me, in pairs, or a lone boy or girl, drinking near my spot at the bar's corner. I began enjoying their warmth, their general cheer, and often I bought them drinks, and always they bought mine in return. They called me by my first name, and each new class knows me, as they know Timmy's before they see either of us. When they were alone, or with a close friend, they talked to me about themselves, revealed beneath that underlying poise deep confusion, and abiding pain their faces belied. So I learned of the cruelties of some of the rich: of children beaten, girls fondled by fathers who were never drunk and certainly did not smoke, healthy men who were either crazy or evil beneath their suits and briefcases, and their punctuality and calm confidence that crossed the line into arrogance. I learned of neglect: children reared by live-in nurses, by housekeepers who cooked; children in summer camps and boarding schools, and I saw the selfishness that wealth allows, a selfishness beyond greed, a desire to have children yet give them nothing, or very little, of oneself. I know one boy, an only child, whose mother left home when he was ten. She no longer wanted to be a mother; she entered the world of business in a city across the country from him, and he saw her for a week-end once a year. His father worked hard at making more money, and the boy left notes on the door of his father's den, asking for a time to see him. An appointment. The father answered with notes on the boy's door, and they met. Then the boy came to college here. He is very serious, very polite, and I have never seen him with a girl, or another boy, and I have never seen him smile.

So I have no reason to imagine Rose on that old stained carpet with places of it worn thin, nearly to the floor; Rose crawling

123

among the legs of older sisters and brothers, looking up at the great
and burdened height of her parents, their capacity, their will, to
love long beaten or drained from them by what they had to do to
keep a dwelling with food in it, and heat in it, and warm and cool
clothes for their children. I have only guessed at this part of her
history. There is one reason, though: Rose's face is bereft of
education, of thought. It is the face of a survivor walking away from
a terrible car accident: without memory or conjecture, only shock,
and the surprise of knowing that she is indeed alive. I think of her
body as shapeless: beneath the large and sagging curve of her
breasts, she has such sparse curvature of hips and waist that she
appears to be an elongated lump beneath her loose dresses in
summer, her old wool overcoat in winter. At the bar she does not
remove her coat; but she unbuttons it and pushes it back from her
breasts, and takes the blue scarf from her head, shakes her greying
brown hair, and lets the scarf hang from her neck.

She appeared in our town last summer. We saw her on the
streets, or slowly walking across the bridge over the Merrimack
River. Then she found Timmy's and, with money from whatever
source, became a regular, along with the rest of us. Sometimes, if
someone drank beside her, she spoke. If no one drank next to her,
she drank alone. Always screwdrivers. Then we started talking
about her and, with that ear for news that impresses me still about
small communities, either towns or city neighborhoods, some of us
told stories about her. Rumors: she had been in prison, or her
husband, or someone else in the family had. She had children but
lost them. Someone had heard of a murder: perhaps she killed her
husband, or one of the children did, or he or Rose or both killed a
child. There was a talk of a fire. And so we talked for months, into
the fall then early winter, when our leaves are gone, the reds and
golds and yellows, and the trees are bare and grey, the evergreens
dark green, and beyond their conical green we have lovely early
sunsets. When the sky is grey, the earth is washed with it, and the
evergreens look black. Then the ponds freeze and snow comes
silently one night, and we wake to a white earth. It was during an
early snowstorm when one of us said that Rose worked in a leather
factory in town, had been there since she appeared last summer.
He knew someone who worked there and saw her. He knew
nothing else.

On a night in January, while a light and pleasant snow dusted the tops of cars, and the shoulders and hats and scarves of people coming into Timmy's, Rose told me her story. I do not know whether, afterward, she was glad or relieved; neither of us has mentioned it since; nor have our eyes, as we greet each other, sometimes chat. And one night I was without money, or enough of it, and she said *I owe you*, and bought the drinks. But that night in January she was in the state when people finally must talk. She was drunk too, or close enough to it, but I know her need to talk was there before vodka released her. I won't try to record our conversation. It was interrupted by one or both of us going to the bathroom, or ordering drinks (I insisted on paying for them all, and after the third round she simply thanked me, and patted my hand); interrupted by people leaning between us for drinks to bring back to booths, by people who came to speak to me, happy people oblivious of Rose, men or women or students who stepped to my side and began talking with that alcoholic lack of manners or awareness of intruding that, in a neighborhood bar, is not impolite but a part of the fabric of conversation. Interrupted too by the radio behind the bar, the speakers at both ends of the room, the loud rock music from an FM station in Boston.

It was a Friday, so the bar closed at two instead of one; we started talking at eleven. Gradually, before that, Rose had pushed her way down the bar toward my corner. I had watched her move to the right to make room for a couple, again to allow a man to squeeze in beside her, and again for some college girls, then the two men to my left went home, and when someone else wedged his arms and shoulders between the standing drinkers at the bar, she stepped to her right again and we faced each other across the corner. We talked about the bartender (we liked him), the crowd (we liked them: loud, but generally peaceful) and she said she always felt safe at Timmy's because everybody knew everybody else, and they didn't allow trouble in here.

"I can't stand fight bars," she said. "Those young punks that have to hit somebody."

We talked about the weather, the seasons. She liked fall. The factory was too hot in summer. So was her apartment. She had bought a large fan, and it was so loud you could hear it from outside, and it blew dust from the floor, ashes from ash trays. She

125

liked winter, the snow, and the way the cold made her feel more alive; but she was afraid of it too: she was getting old, and did not want to be one of those people who slipped on ice and broke a hip.

"The old bones," she said. "They don't mend like young ones."

"You're no older than I am."

"Oh yes I am. And you'd better watch your step too. On that ice," and she nodded at the large front window behind me.

"That's snow," I said. "A light, dry snow."

She smiled at me, her face affectionate, and coquettish with some shared secret, as though we were talking in symbols. Then she finished her drink and I tried to get Steve's attention. He is a large man, and was mixing drinks at the other end of the bar. He did not look our way, so finally I called his name: my voice loud enough to be heard, but softened with courtesy to a tenor. Off and on, through the years, I have tended bar, and I am sensitive about the matter of ordering from a bartender who is making several drinks and, from the people directly in front of him, hearing requests for more. He heard me and glanced at us and I raised two fingers; he nodded. When I looked at Rose again she was gazing down into her glass, as though studying the yellow-filmed ice.

"I worry about fires in winter," she said, still looking down. "Sometimes every night."

"When you're going to sleep? You worry about a fire?"

She looked at me.

"Nearly every night."

"What kind of heat does your building have?"

"Oil furnace."

"Is something wrong with it?"

"No."

"Then—" Steve is very fast; he put my beer and her screwdriver before us, and I paid him; he spun, strode to the cash register, jabbed it, slapped in my ten, and was back with the change. I pushed a dollar toward him, he thanked me, and was gone, repeating an order from the other end of the bar, and a rock group sang above the crowd, a ceiling of sound over the shouts, the laughter, and the crescendo of juxtaposed conversations.

"Then why are you worried?" I said. "Were you in a fire? As a child?"

"I was. Not in winter. And I sure wasn't no child. But you hear them. The sirens. All the time in winter."

"Wood stoves," I said. "Faulty chimneys."

"They remind me. The sirens. Sometimes it isn't even the sirens. I try not to think about them. But sometimes it's like they think about me. They do. You know what I mean?"

"The sirens?"

"*No.*" She grabbed my wrist and squeezed it, hard as a man might; I had not known the strength of her hands. "The flames," she said.

"The flames?"

"I'm not doing anything. Or I'm at work, packing boxes. With leather. Or I'm going to sleep. Or right now, just then, we were talking about winter. I try not to think about them. But here they come, and I can see them. I feel them. Little flames. Big ones. Then—"

She released my wrist, swallowed from her glass, and her face changed: a quick recognition of something forgotten. She patted my hand.

"Thanks for the drink."

"I have money tonight."

"Good. Some night you won't, and I will. You'll drink on me."

"Fine."

"Unless you slip on that ice," nodding her head toward the window, the gentle snow, her eyes brightening again with that shared mystery, their luster near anger, not at me but at what we shared.

"Then what?" I said.

"What?"

"When you see them. When you feel the fire."

"My kids."

"No."

"Three kids."

"No, Rose."

"Two were upstairs. We lived on the third floor."

"Please: no stories like that tonight."

She patted my hand, as though in thanks for a drink, and said: "Did you lose a child?"

"Yes."

"In a fire?"

"A car."

"You poor man. Don't cry."

127

And with her tough thumbs she wiped the beginning of my tears from beneath my eyes, then standing on tiptoe she kissed my cheek, her lips dry, her cheek as it brushed mine feeling no softer than my own, save for her absence of whiskers.

"Mine got out," she said. "I got them out."

I breathed deeply and swallowed beer and wiped my eyes but she had dried them.

"And it's the only thing I ever did. In my whole fucking life. The only thing I ever did that was worth a shit."

"Come on. Nobody's like that."

"No?"

"I hope nobody is."

I looked at the clock on the opposite wall; it was near the speaker that tilted downward, like those mirrors in stores, so cashiers can watch people between shelves. From the speaker came a loud electric guitar, repeating a series of chords, then two or more frenetic saxophones blowing their hoarse tones at the heads of the drinkers, like an indoor storm without rain. On that clock the time was two minutes till midnight, so I knew it was eleven: thirty-eight; at Timmy's they keep the clock twenty minutes fast. This allows them time to give last call and still get the patrons out by closing. Rose was talking. Sometimes I watched her; sometimes I looked away, when I could do that and still hear. For when I listened while watching faces I knew, hearing some of their voices, I did not see everything she told me: I saw, but my vision was dulled, given distance, by watching bearded Steve work, or the blonde student Ande laughing over the mouth of her beer bottle, or old grey-haired Lou, retired as a factory foreman, drinking his shots and drafts, and smoking Camels; or the young owner Timmy, in his mid-thirties, wearing a leather jacket and leaning on the far corner of the bar, drinking club soda and watching the hockey game that was silent under the sounds of rock.

But most of the time, because of the noise, I had to look at her eyes or mouth to hear; and when I did that, I saw everything, without the distractions of sounds and faces and bodies, nor even the softening of distance, of time: I saw the two little girls, and the little boy, their pallid terrified faces; I saw their father's big arm and hand arching down in a slap; in a blow with his fist closed; I saw the five year old boy, the oldest, flung through the air, across the room, to strike the wall and drop screaming to the couch against it. Toward the end, nearly his only sounds were screams; he virtually stopped talking, and lived as a frightened yet recalcitrant prisoner. And in Rose's eyes I saw the embers of death, as if the dying of her spirit had not come with a final yielding sigh, but in a blaze of recognition.

It was long ago, in a Massachusetts town on the Merrimack River. Her husband was a big man, with strongly muscled arms, and the solid rounded belly of a man who drinks much beer at night and works hard, with his body, five days a week. He was handsome too. His face was always reddish-brown from his outdoor work, his hair was thick and black, and curls of it topped his forehead, and when he wore his cap on the back of his head, the visor rested on his curls. He had a thick but narrow moustache, and on Friday and Saturday nights, when they went out to drink and dance, he dressed in brightly colored pants and shirts that his legs and torso and arms filled. His name was Jim Cormier, his grandfather Jacques came from Quebec as a young man, and his father was Jacques Cormier too, and by Jim's generation the last name was pronounced *Cormeer,* and he was James. Jim was a construction worker, but his physical strength and endurance were unequally complemented by his mind, his spirit, whatever that element is that draws the attention of other men. He was best at the simplest work, and would never be a foreman, or tradesman. Other men, when he worked with them, baffled him. He did not have the touch: could not be entrusted to delegate work, to plan, to oversee, and to handle men. Bricks and mortars and trowels and chalk lines baffled him too, as did planes and levels; yet, when he drank at home every night—they seldom went out after the children arrived—he talked about learning to operate heavy equipment.

Rose did not tell me all this at first. She told me the end, the final night, and only in the last forty minutes or so, when I questioned her, did she go farther back, to the beginning. Where I start her story, so I can try to understand how two young people married, with the hope of love, in those days before pandemic divorce ruined the certainty of love, and within six years, when they were still young, still in their twenties, their home had become a horror for their children, for Rose, and yes: for Jim. A place where a boy of five, and girls of four and three, woke, lived, and slept in isolation from the light of a child's life: the curiosity, the questions

129

about birds, appliances, squirrels, and trees and snow and rain, and the first heart-quickening of love for another child, not a sister or brother, but the boy or girl in a sandbox, or on a tricycle at the house down the street. They lived always in darkness, deprived even of childhood fears of ghosts in the shadowed corners of the rooms where they slept, of dreams of vicious and carnivorous monsters. Their young memories and their present consciousness were the tall broad man and his reddening face that shouted and hissed, and his large hands. Rose must have had no place at all, or very little, in their dreams and their wary and apprehensive minds when they were awake. Unless as a wish: I imagine them in their beds, in the moments before sleep, seeing, hoping for Rose to take them in her arms, carry them one by one to the car while the giant slept drunkenly in the bed she shared with him, Rose putting their toys and clothes in the car's trunk, and driving with them far away to a place—What place could they imagine? What place not circumscribed by their apartment's walls whose very colors and hanging pictures and calendar were for them the dark grey of fear and pain? Certainly, too, in those moments before sleep, they must have wished their father gone. Simply gone. The boy must have thought of, wished for, Jim's death. The younger girls, four and three, only that he vanish, leaving no trace of himself in their home in their hearts, not even guilt. Simply to vanish.

Rose was a silent partner. If there is damnation, and a place for the damned, it must be a quiet place, where spirits turn away from each other and stand in solitude and gaze haplessly at eternity. For it must be crowded with the passive: those people whose presence in life was a paradox; for, while occupying space and moving through it and making sounds in it they were obviously present, while in truth they were not: they witnessed evil and lifted neither an arm nor a voice to stop it, as they witnessed joy, and neither sang nor clapped their hands. But so often we understand them too easily, tolerate them too much: they have universality, so we forgive the man who watches injustice, a drowning, a murder, because he reminds us of ourselves, and we share with him the loyal bond of cowardice, whether once or a hundred times we have turned away from another's suffering to save ourselves: our jobs, our public selves, our bones and flesh. And these people are so easy to pity. We know fear as early as we know love, and fear is always with us. I have friends my own age who still cannot say what

130

they believe, except in the most intimate company. Condemning the actively evil man is a simple matter; though we tend not only to forgive but cheer him if he robs banks or Brink's, and outwits authority: those unfortunate policemen, minions whose uniforms and badges and revolvers are, for many of us, a distorted symbol of what we fear: not a fascist state but a Power, a God, who knows all our truths, believes none of our lies, and with that absolute knowledge will both judge, and exact punishment. For we see to it that no one absolutely knows us, so at times the passing blue figure of a policeman walking his beat can stir in us our fear of discovery. We like to see them made into dupes by the outlaw.

But if the outlaw rapes, tortures, gratuitously kills, or if he makes children suffer, we hate him with a purity we seldom feel: our hatred has no roots in prejudice, or self-righteousness, but in horror. He has done something we would never do, something we could not do even if we wished it; our bodies would not obey, would not tear the dress, or lift and swing the axe, pull the trigger, throw the screaming child across the room. So I hate Jim Cormier, and cannot understand him; cannot with my imagination cross the distance between myself and him, enter his soul and know how it felt to live even five minutes of his life. And I forgive Rose, but as I write I resist that compassion, or perhaps merely empathy, and force myself to think instead of the three children, and Rose living there, knowing what she knew. She was young.

She is Irish: A Callahan till marriage, and she and Jim were Catholics. Devout Catholics, she told me. By that, she did not mean they strived to live in imitation of Christ. She meant they did not practice artificial birth control, but rhythm, and after their third year of marriage they had three children. They left the church then. That is, they stopped attending Sunday Mass and receiving Communion. Do you see? I am not a Catholic, but even I know that they were never truly members of that faith, and so could not have left it. There is too much history, too much philosophy involved, for the matter of faith to rest finally and solely on the use of contraceptives. That was long ago, and now my Catholic friends tell me the priests no longer concern themselves with birth control. But we must live in our own time; Thomas More died for an issue that would have no meaning today. Rose and Jim, though, were not Thomas Mores. They could not see a single act as a renunciation or affirmation of a belief, a way of life.

No. They had neither a religion nor a philosophy; like most people I know their philosophies were simply their accumulated reactions to their daily circumstance, their lives as they lived them from one hour to the next. They were not driven, guided, by either passionate belief, nor strong resolve. And for that I pity them both, as I pity the others who move through life like scraps of paper in the wind.

With contraception they had what they believed were two years of freedom. There had been a time when all three of their children wore diapers, and only the boy could walk, and with him holding her coat or pants, moving so slowly beside her, Rose went daily to the laundromat, pushing two strollers, gripping a paper grocery bag of soiled diapers, with a clean bag folded in her purse. Clorox rested beneath one stroller, a box of soap beneath the other. While she waited for the diapers to wash, the boy walked among the machines, touched them, watched them, and watched the other women who waited. The oldest girl crawled about on the floor. The baby slept in Rose's lap, or nursed in those days when mothers did not expose their breasts, and Rose covered the infant's head, and her breast, with her unbuttoned shirt. The children became hungry, or tired, or restless, and they fussed, and cried, as Rose called to the boy to leave the woman alone, to stop playing with the ash tray, the soap, and she put the diapers in the dryer. And each day she felt that the other women, even those with babies, with crawling and barely walking children, with two or three children, and one pregnant with a third, had about them some grace, some calm, that kept their voices soft, their gestures tender; she watched them with shame, and a deep dislike of herself, but no envy, as if she had tried out for a dance company and on the first day had entered a room of slender professionals in leotards, dancing like cats, while she clumsily moved her heavy body clad in grey sweat clothes. Most of the time she changed the diaper of at least one of the children, and dropped it in the bag, the beginning of tomorrow's load. If the baby slept in her stroller, and the oldest girl and the boy played on the floor, Rose folded the diapers on the table in the laundromat, talking and smoking with the other women. But that was rare: the chance that all three small children could at the same time be peaceful and without need, and so give her peace. Imagine: three of them with bladders and bowels, thirst, hunger, fatigue, and none of them synchronized. Most days she put the hot unfolded diapers in the clean bag, and hurried home.

Finally she cried at dinner one night for a washing machine and a dryer, and Jim stared at her, not with anger, or impatience, and not refusal either: but with the resigned look of a man who knew he could neither refuse it nor pay for it. It was the washing machine; he would buy it with monthly payments, and when he had done that, he would get the dryer. He sank posts in the earth and nailed boards across their tops and stretched clotheslines between them. He said in rain or freezing cold she would have to hang the wet diapers over the backs of chairs. It was all he could do. Until he could get her a dryer. And when he came home on those days of rain or cold, he looked surprised, as if rain and cold in New England were as foreign to him as the diapers that seemed to occupy the house. He removed them from the rod for the shower curtain, and when he had cleaned his work from his body, he hung them again. He took them from the arms and back of his chair and lay them on top of others, on a chair, or the edges of the kitchen table. Then he sat in the chair whose purpose he had restored; he drank beer and gazed at the drying diapers, as if they were not cotton at all, but the whitest of white shades of the dead, come to haunt him, to assault him, an inch at a time, a foot, until they won, surrounded him where he stood in some corner of the bedroom, the bathroom, in the last place in his home that was his. His *querençia:* his cool or blood-smelling sand, the only spot in the bull ring where he wanted to stand and defend, to lower his head and wait.

He struck the boy first, before contraception, and the freedom and new life it promised, as money does. Rose was in the kitchen, chopping onions, now and then turning her face to wipe, with the back of her wrist, the tears from her eyes. The youngest girl was asleep; the older one crawled between and around Rose's legs. The boy was three. She had nearly finished the onions and could put them in the skillet and stop crying, when she heard the slap, and knew what it was in that instant before the boy cried: a different cry: in it she heard not only startled fear, but a new sound: a wail of betrayal, of pain from the heart. Wiping her hands on her apron, she went quickly to the living room, into that long and loudening cry, as if the boy, with each moment of deeper recognition, raised his voice until it howled. He stood in front of his seated father.

133

Before she reached him, he looked at her, as though without hearing footsteps or seeing her from the corner of his blurred wet vision, he knew she was there. She was his mother. Yet when he turned his face to her, it was not with appeal: above his small reddened cheeks he looked into her eyes; and in his, as tears ran from them, was that look whose sound she had heard in the kitchen. Betrayal. Accusing her of it, and without anger, but dismay. In her heart she felt something fall between herself and her son, like a glass wall, or a space that spanned only a few paces, yet was infinite, and she could never cross it again. Now his voice had attained the howl, and though his cheeks were wet, his eyes were dry now; or anyway tearless, for they looked wet and bright as pools that could reflect her face. The baby was awake, crying in her crib. Rose looked from her son's eyes to her husband's. They were dark, and simpler than the boy's: in them she saw only the ebb of his fury: anger, and a resolve to preserve and defend it.

"I told him not to," he said.

"Not to what?"

"Climbing on my legs. Look." He pointed to a dark wet spot on the carpet. "He spilled the beer."

She stared at the spot. She could not take her eyes from it. The baby was crying and the muscles of her legs tried to move toward that sound. Then she realized her son was silent. She felt him watching her, and she would not look at him.

"It's nothing to cry about," Jim said.

"You *slapped* him."

"Not *him*. You."

"Me? That's onions."

She wiped her hands on her apron, brushed her eyes with the back of her wrist.

"Jesus," she said. She looked at her son. She had to look away from those eyes. Then she saw the oldest girl: she had come to the doorway, and was standing on the threshold, her thumb in her mouth; above her small closed fist and nose, her frightened eyes stared, and she looked as though she were trying not to cry. But, if she was, there could be only one reason for a child so young: she was afraid for her voice to leave her, to enter the room, where now Rose could feel her children's fear as tangibly as a cold draft blown through a cracked window pane. Her legs, her hips, strained toward the baby's cry for food, a dry diaper, for whatever acts of

134

love they need when they wake, and even more when they wake before they are ready, when screams smash the shell of their sleep. "Jesus," she said, and hurried out of the room where the pain in her son's heart had pierced her own, and her little girl's fearful silence pierced it again; or slashed it, for she felt as she bent over the crib that she was no longer whole, that her height and breadth and depth were in pieces that somehow held together, did not separate and drop to the floor, through it, into the earth itself.

"I should have hit him with the skillet," she said to me, so many years later, after she had told me the end and I had drawn from her the beginning, in the last half hour of talk.

She could not hit him that night. With the heavy iron skillet, with its hot oil waiting for the onions. For by then something had flowed away from Rose, something of her spirit simply wafting willy-nilly out of her body, out of the apartment, and it never came back, not even with the diaphragm. Perhaps it began to leave her at the laundromat, or in bed at night, at the long day's end not too tired for lust, for rutting, but too tired for an evening of desire that began with dinner and crested and fell and crested again through the hours as they lay close and naked in bed, from early in the night until finally they slept. On the car seat of courtship she had dreamed of this, and in the first year of marriage she lived the dream: joined him in the shower and made love with him, still damp, before they went to the dinner kept warm on the stove, then back to the bed's tossed sheets to lie in the dark, smoking, talking, touching, and they made love again; and, later again, until they could only lie side by side waiting for their breathing to slow, before they slept. Now at the tired ends of days they took release from each other, and she anxiously slept, waiting for a baby to cry.

Or perhaps it left her between the shelves of a supermarket. His pay day was Thursday, and by then the refrigerator and cupboard were nearly empty. She shopped on Friday. Unless a neighbor could watch the children. Rose shopped at night, when Jim was home; they ate early and she hurried to the store to shop before it closed. Later, months after he slapped the boy, she believed his rage had started then, alone in the house with them, changing the baby and putting her in the crib while the other girl and boy spat and flung food from their highchairs where she had left them, in her race with time to fill a cart with food Jim could afford: she looked at the price of everything she took from a shelf. She did not

135

believe, later, that he struck them on those nights. But there must have been rage, the frightening voice of it; for he was tired, and confused, and overwhelmed by three small people with wills of their own, and no control over the needs of their bodies and their spirits. Certainly he must have yelled; maybe he squeezed an arm, or slapped a rump. When she returned with the groceries, the apartment was quiet: the children slept, and he sat in the kitchen, with the light out, drinking beer. A light from the living room behind him and around a corner showed her his silhouette: large and silent, a cigarette glowing at his mouth, a beer bottle rising to it. Then he would turn on the light and put down his beer and walk past her, to the old car, to carry in the rest of the groceries.

When finally two of the children could walk, Rose went to the supermarket during the day, the boy and girl walking beside her, behind her, away from her voice whose desperate pitch embarrassed her, as though its sound were a sign to the other women with children that she was incompetent, unworthy to be numbered among them. The boy and girl took from shelves cookies, crackers, cereal boxes, cans of vegetables and fruit, sometimes to play with them, but at other times to bring to her, where holding the cart they pulled themselves up on the balls of their feet and dropped in the box or the can. Still she scolded them, jerked the can or box from the cart, brought it back to its proper place; and when she did this, her heart sank as though pulled by a sigh deeper into her body. For she saw. She saw that when the children played with these things whose colors or shapes drew them, so they wanted to sit on the floor and hold or turn in their hands the box or can, they were simply being children whom she could patiently teach, if patience were still an element in her spirit. And that when they brought things to her, to put into the cart, repeating the motions of their mother, they were joining, without fully knowing it, the struggle of the family, and without knowing the struggle that was their parents' lives. Their hearts, though, must have expected praise; or at least an affectionate voice, a gentle hand, to show that their mother did not need what they had brought her. If only there were time: one extra hour of grocery shopping to spend in this gentle instruction. Or if she had strength to steal the hour anyway, despite the wet and tired and staring baby in the cart. But she could not: she scolded, and jerked from the cart or their hands the things they had brought, and the boy became quiet, the girl

136

sucked her thumb and held Rose's pants as the four of them moved with the cart between the long shelves. The baby fussed, with that unceasing low cry that was not truly crying: only the wordless sounds of fatigue. Rose recognized it, understood it, for by now she had learned the awful lesson of fatigue, which as a young girl she had never felt. She knew that it was worse than the flu, whose enforced rest at least left you the capacity to care for someone else, to mutter words of love; but that, healthy, you could be so tired that all you wanted was to lie down, alone, shut off from everyone. And you would snap at your husband, or your children, if they entered the room, probed the solace of your complete surrender to silence and the mattresss that seductively held your body. So she understood the baby's helpless sounds for *I want to lie in my crib and put my thumb in my mouth and hold Raggedy Ann's dirty old apron and sleep*. The apron was long removed from the doll, and the baby would not sleep without its presence in her hand. Rose understood this, but could not soothe the baby. She could not have soothed her anyway; only sleep could. But Rose could not try, with hugs, with petting, with her softened voice. She was young.

Perhaps her knowledge of her own failures dulled her ears and eyes to Jim after he first struck the boy, and on that night lost for the rest of his life any paternal control he may have exerted in the past over his hands, finally his fists. Because more and more now he spanked them: with a chill Rose tried to deny, a resonant quiver up through her body, she remembered that her parents had spanked her too. That all, or probably all, parents spanked their children. And usually it was the father, the man of the house, the authority and judge, and enforcer of rules and discipline the children would need when they reached their teens. But now, too, he held them by the shoulders, and shook their small bodies, the children sometimes wailing, sometimes frighteningly silent, until it seemed their heads would fly across the room then roll to rest on the floor,while he shook a body whose neck had snapped in two like a dried branch. He slapped their faces, and sometimes he punched the boy, who was four, then five, with his fist. They were not bad children; not disobedient; certainly they were not loud. When Jim yelled and shook them, or slapped or punched, they had done no more than they had in the supermarket, where her voice, her snatching from their hands, betrayed her to the other women. So maybe that kept her silent.

137

But there was more: she could no longer feel love, or what she had believed it to be. On the few nights when she and Jim could afford both a sitter and a night club, they did not dance. They sat drinking, their talk desultory: about household chores, about Jim's work, pushing wheelbarrows, swinging a sledge hammer, thrusting a spade into the earth or a pile of gravel or sand. They listened to the music, watched the band, even drummed their fingers on the table dampened by the bottoms of their glasses they emptied like thirsty people drinking water; but they thirsted for a time they had lost. Or not even that: for respite from their time now, and their knowledge that, from one day to the next, year after year, their lives would not change. Each day would be like the one they had lived before last night's sleep; and tomorrow was a certain and already draining repetition of today. They did not decide to sit rather than dance. They simply did not dance. They sat and drank and watched the band and the dancing couples, as if their reason for dancing had been stolen from them while their eyes had been jointly focused on something else.

She could no longer feel love. She ate too much and smoked too much and drank too much coffee, so all day she felt either lethargic from eating or stimulated by coffee and cigarettes, and she could not recall her body as it had once been, only a few years ago, when she was dating Jim, and had played softball and volleyball, had danced, and had run into the ocean to swim beyond the breakers. The ocean was a half hour away from her home, yet she had not seen it in six years. Rather than love, she felt that she and Jim only worked together, exhausted, toward a nebulous end, as if they were digging a large hole, wide as a house, deeper than a well. Side by side they dug, and threw the dirt up and out of the hole, pausing now and then to look at each other, to wait while their breathing slowed, and to feel in those kindred moments something of why they labored, of why they had begun it so long ago—not in years, not long at all—with their dancing and lovemaking and finally marriage: to pause and look at each other's flushed and sweating faces with as much love as they could feel before they commenced again to dig deeper, away from the light above them.

On a summer night in that last year, Jim threw the boy across the living room. Rose was washing the dishes after dinner. Jim was watching television, and the boy, five now, was playing on the floor between Jim and the set. He was on the floor with his sisters and

wooden blocks and toy cars and trucks. He seldom spoke directly
to his father anymore; seldom spoke at all to anyone but his sisters.
The girls were too young, or hopeful, or were still in love. They
spoke to Jim, sat on his lap, hugged his legs, and when he hugged
them, lifted them in the air, talked with affection and laughter,
their faces showed a happiness without memory. And when he
yelled at them or shook or spanked them, or slapped their faces,
their memory failed them again, and they were startled, frightened, and Rose could sense their spirits weeping beneath the
sounds of their crying. But they kept turning to him, with open
arms, and believing faces.

"Little flowers," she said to me. "They were like little flowers in
the sun. They never could remember the frost."

Not the boy, though. But that night his game with his sisters
absorbed him, and for a short while—nearly an hour—he was a
child in a home. He forgot. Several times his father told him and
the girls to be quiet or play in another room. Then for a while, a
long while for playing children, they were quiet: perhaps five
minutes, perhaps ten. Each time their voices rose, Jim's command
for quiet was abrupt, and each time it was louder. At the kitchen
sink Rose's muscles tensed, told her it was coming, and she must
go to the living room now, take the children and their blocks and
cars and trucks to the boy's bedroom. But she breathed deeply and
rubbed a dish with a sponge. When she finished, she would go
down to the basement of the apartment building, descend past the
two floors of families and single people whose only sounds were
music from radios, voices from television, and sometimes children
loudly playing and once in a while a quarrel between a husband
and wife. She would go into the damp basement and take the
clothes from the washing machine, put them in the dryer that now
Jim was paying for with monthly installments. Then she heard his
voice again, and was certain it was coming, but could not follow the
urging of her muscles. She sponged another dish. Then her hands
came out of the dish water with a glass: it had been a jelly jar,
humanly smiling animals were on it, and flowers, and her children
liked to drink from it, looked for it first when they were thirsty, and
only if it was dirty in the sink would they settle for an ordinary
glass for their water, their juice, or Kool-Aid or milk. She washed it
slowly, and was for those moments removed; she was oblivious of
the living room, the children's voices rising again to the peak that

would bring either Jim's voice or his body from his chair. Her hands moved gently on the glass. She could have been washing one of her babies. Her heart had long ago ceased its signals to her; it lay dormant in despair beyond sorrow; standing at the sink, in a silence of her own making, lightly rubbing the glass with the sponge, and her fingers and palms, she did not know she was crying until the tears reached her lips, salted her tongue.

With their wooden blocks, the children were building a village, and a bridge leading out of it to the country: the open spaces of the living room carpet, and the chairs and couch that were distant mountains. More adept with his hands, and more absorbed too in the work, the boy often stood to adjust a block on a roof, or the bridge. Each time he stood between his father and the television screen, heard the quick command, and moved out of the way. They had no slanted blocks, so the bridge had to end with two sheer walls; the boy wanted to build ramps at either end, for the cars and trucks to use, and he had only rectangles and squares to work with. He stood to look down at the bridge. His father spoke. He heard the voice, but a few seconds passed before it penetrated his concentration, and spread through him. It was too late. What he heard next were not words, or a roar, but a sustained guttural cry, a sound that could be either anguish or rage. Then his father's hands were on him: on him and squeezing his left thigh and left bicep so tightly that he opened his mouth to cry out in pain. But he did not. For then he was above his father's head, above the floor and his sisters, high above the room itself and near the ceiling he glimpsed; and he felt his father's grip and weight shifting and saw the wall across the room, the wall above the couch, so that when finally he made a sound it was of terror, and it came from him in a high scream he heard as he hurtled across the room, seeing always the wall, and hearing his scream, as though his flight were prolonged by the horror of what he saw and heard. Then he struck it. He heard that, and the bone in his right forearm snap, and he fell to the couch. Now he cried with pain, staring at the swollen flesh where the bone tried to protrude, staring with astonishment and grief at this part of his body. Nothing in his body had ever broken before. He touched the flesh, the bone beneath it. He was crying as, in his memory, he had never cried before, and he not only did not try to stop, as he always had, with pride, with anger; but he wanted to cry this deeply, his body shuddering with it, doubling at his waist with it, until he attained oblivion, invisibility, death.

140

Somehow he knew his childhood had ended. In his pain, he felt relief too: now on this couch his life would end.

He saw through tears but more strongly felt his sisters standing before him, touching him, crying. The he heard his mother. She was screaming. And in rage. At his father. He had never heard her do that, but still her scream did not come to him as a saving trumpet. He did not want to live to see revenge. Not even victory. Then he heard his father slap her. Through his crying he listened then for her silence. But her voice grew, its volume filled the world. Still he felt nothing of hope, of vengeance; he had left that world, and lived now for what he hoped and believed would be only a very short time. He was beginning to feel the pain in his head and back and shoulders, his elbows and neck. He knew he would only have to linger a while in this pain, until his heart left him, as though disgorged by tears, and went wherever hearts went. A sister's hand held his, and he squeezed it.

When he was above his father's head, the boy had not seen Rose. But she was there, behind Jim, behind the lifted boy, and she had cried out too, and moved: as Jim regained his balance from throwing the boy, she turned him, her hand jerking his shoulder, and when she could see his face she pounded it with her fists. She was yelling, and the yell was words, but she did not know what they were. She hit him until he pushed her back, hard, so she nearly fell. She looked at his face, the cheeks reddened by her blows, saw a trickle of blood from his lower lip, and charged it; swinging at the blood, the lip. He slapped her so hard that she was sitting on the floor, with no memory of falling, and holding and shaking her stunned and buzzing head. She stood, yelling words again that she could not hear, as if their utterance had been so long coming, from whatever depth in her, that her mind could not even record them as they rushed through her lips. She went past Jim, pushing his belly, and he fell backward into his chair. She paused to look at that. Her breath was deep and fast, and he sat glaring, his breathing hard too, and she neither knew nor cared whether he had desisted or was preparing himself for more. At the bottom of her vision, she saw his beer bottle on the floor beside the chair. She snatched it up, by its neck, beer hissing onto her arm and breast, and in one motion she turned away from Jim and flung the bottle smashing through the television screen. He was up and yelling behind her, but she was crouched over the boy.

She felt again what she felt in the kitchen, in the silence she had made for herself while she bathed the glass. Behind and above her was the sound of Jim's fury; yet she stroked the boy's face: his forehead, the tears beneath his eyes; she touched the girls too, their hair, their wet faces; and she heard her voice: soft and soothing, so soft and soothing that she even believed the peace it promised. Then she saw, beneath the boy's hand, the swollen flesh; gently she lifted his hand, then was on her feet. She stood into Jim's presence again: his voice behind her, the feel of his large body inches from her back. Then he gripped her hair, at the back of her head, and she shook her head but still he held on.

"His *arm's* broken."

She ran from him, felt hair pulling from her scalp, heard it, and ran to her bedroom for her purse but not a blanket, not from the bed where she slept with Jim; for that she went to the boy's, and pulled his thin summer blanket from his bed, and ran back to the living room. Where she stopped. Jim stood at the couch, not looking at the boy, or the girls, but at the doorway where now she stood holding the blanket. He was waiting for her.

"You crazy fucking bitch."

"*What?*"

"The fucking TV. Who's going to buy one? You? You fucking cunt. You've never had a fucking job in your life."

It was madness. She was looking at madness, and it calmed her. She had nothing to say to it. She went to the couch, opening the blanket to wrap around the boy.

"It's the only fucking peace I've *got*."

She heard him, but it was like overhearing someone else, in another apartment, another life. She crouched and was working the blanket under the boy's body when a fist knocked loudly on the door. She did not pause, or look up. More knocking, then a voice in the hall: "Hey! Everybody all right in there?"

"Get the fuck away from my door."

"You tell me everybody's all right."

"Get the fuck *away*."

"I want to hear the woman. And the kid."

"You want me to throw you down the fucking stairs?"

"I'm calling the cops."

"Fuck you."

She had the boy in her arms now. He was crying still, and as she carried him past Jim, she kissed his cheeks, his eyes. Then Jim was beside her. He opened the door, swung it back for them. She did not realize until weeks later that he was frightened. His voice was low: "Tell them he fell."

She did not answer. She went out and down the stairs, past apartments; in one of them someone was phoning the police. At the bottom of the stairs she stopped short of the door, to shift the boy's weight in her arms, to free a hand for the knob. Then an old woman stepped out of her apartment, into the hall, and said: "I'll get it."

An old woman with white hair and a face that knew everything, not only tonight, but the years before this too, yet the face was neither stern nor kind; it looked at Rose with some tolerant recognition of evil, of madness, of despair, like a warrior who has seen and done too much to condemn, or even try to judge; can only nod in assent at what he sees. The woman opened the door and held it, and Rose went out, across the small lawn to the car parked on the road. There were only two other cars at the curb; then she remembered that it was Saturday, and had been hot, and before noon she had heard most of the tenants, separately leaving for beaches or picnic grounds. They would be driving home now, or stopping to eat. The sun had just set, but most windows of the tenements on the street were dark. She stopped at the passenger door, started to shift the weeping boy's weight, then the old woman was beside her, trying the door, asking for the key. Rose's purse hung from her wrist. The woman's hands went into it, moved in there, came out with the ring of keys, held them up toward the streetlight, and found the one for the car. She opened the door, and Rose leaned in and lay the boy on the front seat. She turned to thank the woman but she was already at the front door of the building, a square back and short body topped by hair like cotton.

Rose gently closed the car door, holding it, making certain it did not touch the boy before she pushed it into place. She ran to the driver's side, and got in, and put the key in the ignition slot. But she could not turn it. She sat in the boy's crying, poised in the moment of action the car had become. But she could not start it.

"Jimmy," she said. "Jimmy, listen. Just hang on. I'll be right back. I can't leave the girls. Do you hear me?"

His face, profiled on the seat, nodded.

"I've got to get them."

She pushed open the door, left the car, closed the door, the keys in her hand, not out of habit this time; no, she clung to them as she might to a tiny weapon, her last chance to be saved. She was running to the building when she saw the flames at her windows, a flare of them where an instant before there had been only lamp-light. Her legs now, her body, were weightless as the wind. She heard the girls screaming. Then the door opened and Jim ran out of it, collided with her, and she fell on her back as he stumbled and side-stepped and tried to regain balance and speed and go around her. Her left hand grabbed his left ankle. Then she turned with his pulling, his weight, and on her stomach now, she held his ankle with her right hand too, and pulled it back and up. He fell. She dived onto his back, saw and smelled the gasoline can in his hand, and in her mind she saw him going down to the basement for it, and back up the stairs. She twisted it away from his fingers on the handle, and kneeled with his back between her legs, and as he lifted his head and shoulders and tried to stand, she raised the can high with both hands and brought it down, leaning with it, into it, as it struck his skull. For a moment he was still, his face in the grass. Then he began to struggle again, and said into the earth: "Over now. All over."

She hit him three more times, the sounds hollow, metallic. Then he was still, save for the rise and fall of his back. Beneath his other hand she saw his car keys. She scooped them from the grass and stood and threw them across the lawn, whirling now into the screams of the girls, and windows of fire. She ran up the stairs. The white-haired woman was on the second floor landing. Rose passed her, felt her following, and the others: she did not know how many, nor who they were. She only heard them behind her. No one passed her. She was at the door, trying to turn the knob, while her left arm and hand pressed hot wood.

"I called the fire department," a man said, behind her in the hall.

"So did we," a woman said.

Rose was calling to the girls to open the door.

"They can't," another man said. "That's where the fire is." Then he said: "Fuck this," and pulled her away from the door where she was turning the knob back and forth and calling through the wood to the screams from the rear of the apartment, their bedroom. She was about to spring back to the door but stopped: the man faced it then stepped away. She knew his name, or had known it; she could

144

not say it. He lived on the second floor; it was his wife who had said *So did we*. He stepped twice toward the door, then kicked, his leg horizontal, the bottom of his shoe striking the door, and it swung open, through the flames that filled the threshold and climbed the doorjambs. The man leaped backward, his forearms covering his face, while Rose yelled to the girls: We're coming, we're coming. The man lowered his head and sprinted forward. Or it would have been a sprint. Certainly he believed that, believed he would run through fire to the girls and get them out. But in his third stride his legs stopped, so suddenly and autonomously that he nearly fell forward into the fire. Then he backed up.

"They'll have a net," he said. He was panting. "We'll get them to jump. We'll get them to a window, and get them to jump."

A man behind Rose was holding her. She had not known it till now. Nor did she know she had been straining forward. The man tightly held her biceps. He was talking to her and now she heard that too, and was also aware that people were moving away, slowly but away, down the hall toward the stairs. He was saying: "You can't. All you'll do is get yourself killed."

Then she was out of his hands, as though his fingers were those of a child, and with her breath held and her arms shielding her face, and her head down, she was in motion, through the flames and into the burning living room. She did not feel the fire, but even as she ran through the living room, dodging flames, running through them, she knew that very soon she would. It meant no more to her than knowing that she was getting wet in a sudden rain. The girls were standing on the older one's bed, at the far side of the room, holding each other, screaming, and watching their door and the hall beyond it where the fire would come. She filled the door, their vision, then was at the bed and they were crying: Mommy! Mommy! She did not speak. She did not touch them either. She pulled the blanket from under them, and they fell onto the bed. Running again she grabbed the blanket from the younger girl's bed, and went into the hall where there was smoke but not fire yet, and across it to the bathroom where she turned on the shower and held the blanket under the spray. They soaked heavily in her hands. She held her breath leaving the bathroom and exhaled in the girls' room. They were standing again, holding each other. Now she spoke to them. Again, as when she had crouched with them in front of Jimmy, her voice somehow came softly from

145

her. It was unhurried, calm, soothing: she could have been helping them put on snowsuits. They stopped screaming, even crying; they only sniffled and gasped, as she wound a blanket around each of them, covering their feet and heads too, then lifted them, pressing one to each breast. Then she stopped talking, stopped telling them that very soon, before they even knew it, they would be safe outside. She turned and ran through smoke in the hall, and into the living room. She did not try to dodge flames: if they were in front of her, she spun and ran backward through them, hugging the girls against each other, so nothing of their bodies would protrude past her back, her sides; then spun and ran forward again, fearful of an image that entered her mind though in an instant she expelled it: that she would fall with them, into fire. She ran backward through the door, and her back hit the wall. She bounced off it; there was fire in the hall now, moving at her ankles, and she ran, leaping, and when she reached the stairs she smelled the scorched blankets that steamed around the girls in her arms. She smelled her burned hair, sensed that it was burning still, crackling flames on her head. It could wait. She could wait. She was running down the stairs, and the fire was behind her, above her, and she felt she could run with her girls all night. Then she was on the lawn, and arms took the girls, and a man wrestled her to the ground and rolled with her, rolled over and over on the grass. When she stood someone was telling her an ambulance would—But she picked up her girls, unwrapped now, and looked at their faces: pale with terror, with shock, yes; but no burns. She carried them to the car.

"*No*," she heard. It was a man's voice, but one she did not know. Not for a few moments, as she lay the girls side by side on the back seat. Then she knew it was Jim. She was startled, as though she had not seen him for ten years. She ran around the car, got behind the wheel, reached over Jimmy who was silent now, and she thought unconscious until she saw his eyes staring at the dashboard, his teeth gritting against his pain. Leaning over his face, she pushed down the latch on his side. Then she locked her door. It was a two-door car and they were safe now and they were going to the hospital. She started the engine.

Jim was at her window, a raging face, but a desperate one too, as though standing outside he was locked in a room without air. Then he was motion, on her left, to her front, and he stood at the middle of the car, slapped his hands onto the hood, and pushed. He bulged: his arms and chest and reddened face. With all his strength he pushed, and she felt the car rock backward. She turned on the headlights. The car rocked forward as he eased his pushing, and drew breath. Then he pushed again, leaning, so all she could see of him were his face, his shoulders, his arms. The car rocked back and stopped. She pushed the accelerator pedal to the floor, waited two or three seconds in which she either did not breathe or held what breath she had, and watched his face above the sound of the racing engine. Then, in one quick motion, she lifted her foot from the clutch pedal. He was gone as she felt the bumper and grill leap through his resistance. She stopped and looked in the rear view mirror; she saw the backs of the girls' heads, their long hair; they were kneeling on the seat, looking quietly out the back window. He lay on his back. Rose turned her wheels to the right, as though to back into a parking space, shifted to reverse, and this time without racing the engine, she slowly drove. She did not look through the rear window; she looked straight ahead, at the street, the tenements, the darkening sky. Only the rear tires rolled over him, then struck the curb. She straightened the front wheels and drove forward again. The car bumped over him. She stopped, shifted gears, and backed up; the bump, then the tires hitting the curb. She was still driving back and forth over his body, while beyond her closed windows people shouted or stared, when the sirens broke the summer sky: the higher wail of the police called by the neighbor, and the lower and louder one of the fire engine.

She was in the hospital, and by the time she got out, her three brothers and two sisters had found money for bail. Her parents were dead. Waiting for the trial, she lived with a married sister; there were children in the house, and Rose shied away from them. Her court-appointed lawyer called it justifiable homicide, and the jury agreed. Long before the trial, before she even left the hospital, she had lost the children. The last time she saw them was that night in the car, when finally she took them away: the boy lying on the front seat, his left cheek resting on it as he stared. He did not move while she drove back and forth over his father. She still does not know whether he knew then, or learned it from his sisters. And the two girls kneeling, their breasts leaning on the back of the seat, watching their father appear, then vanish as a bump beneath them. They all went to the same foster home. She did not know where it was.

"Thanks for the drinks," she said, and patted my hand. "Next time you're broke, let me know."

"I will."

She adjusted the blue scarf over her hair, knotted it under her face, buttoned her coat and put on her gloves. She stepped away from the bar, and walked around and between people. I ordered a beer, and watched her go out the door. I paid and tipped Steve, then left the bottle and glass with my coat and hat on the bar, and moved through the crowd. I stepped outside and watched her, a half block away now. She was walking carefully in the lightly falling snow, her head down, watching the sidewalk, and I remembered her eyes when she talked about slipping on ice. But what had she been sharing with me? Age? Death? I don't think so. I believe it was the unexpected: chance, and its indiscriminate testing of the our bodies, our wills, our spirits. She was walking toward the bridge over the Merrimack. It is a long bridge, and crossing it in that open air she would be cold. I was shivering. She was at the bridge now, her silhouette diminishing as she walked on it. I watched until she disappeared.

I had asked her if she had tried to find her children, had tried an appeal to get them back. She did not deserve them, she said. And after the testimony of her neighbors, she knew she had little hope anyway. She should have hit him with the skillet, she said; the first time he slapped the boy. I said nothing. As I have written, we have talked often since then, but we do not mention her history, and she does not ask for mine, though I know she guesses some of it. All of this is blurred; nothing stands out with purity. By talking to social workers, her neighbors condemned her to lose her children; talking in the courtroom they helped save her from conviction.

I imagine again those men long ago, sitting among mosquitoes in a room, or sleeping on the fouled sheets. Certainly each of them hoped that it was not the mosquito biting his arm, or the bed he slept on, that would end his life. So he hoped for the men in the other room to die. Unless he hoped that it was neither sheets nor mosquitoes, but then he would be hoping for the experiment to fail, for yellow fever to flourish. And he had volunteered to stop it. Perhaps though, among those men, there was one, or even more, who hoped that he alone would die, and his death would be a discovery for all.

The boy from Chicago and Rose were volunteers too. I hope that by now the man from Chicago has succeeded at something—love, work—that has allowed him to outgrow the shame of failure. I have often imagined him returning home a week early that summer, to a mother, to a father; and having to watch his father's face as the boy told him he had failed because he was weak. A trifling incident in a whole lifetime, you may say. Not true. It could have changed him forever, his life with other men, with women, with daughters, and especially sons. We like to believe that in this last half of the century, we know and are untouched by everything; yet it takes only a very small jolt, at the right time, to knock us off balance for the rest of our lives. Maybe—and I hope so—the boy learned what his body and will could do: some occurrence he did not have time to consider, something that made him act before he knew he was in action.

Like Rose. Who volunteered to marry; even, to a degree, to practice rhythm, for her Catholic beliefs were not strong and deep, else she could not have so easily turned away from them after the third child, or even early in that pregnancy. So the life she chose slowly turned on her, pressed against her from all sides, invisible, motionless, but with the force of wind she could not breast. She stood at the sink, holding the children's glass. But *then*—and now finally I know why I write this, and what does stand out with purity: she reentered motherhood, and the unity we all must gain against human suffering. This is why I did not answer, at the bar, when she told me she did not deserve the children. For I believe she did, and does. She redeemed herself, with action, and with less than thirty minutes of it. But she could not see that, and still cannot. She sees herself in the laundromat, the supermarket, listlessly drunk in a night club where only her fingers on the table moved to the music. I see her young and strong and swift, wrapping the soaked blankets around her little girls, and hugging them to her, and running and spinning and running through the living room, on that summer night when she was touched and blessed by flames.

nominated by Ploughshares, *Gina Berriault, Daniel Halpern, Elizabeth Inness-Brown, Joyce Carol Oates, and Mary Peterson*

FRIENDS AND FORTUNES

fiction by LINDA HOGAN

from THE THINGS THAT DIVIDE US (Seal Press)

WHERE I LIVE, people do things outdoors. Out in the open air, they do what wealthier and more private people hide inside their homes. Young couples neck beside the broken lilac bushes or in old cars parked along the street. Women knead bread on their steps, and sometimes collapse in a fury of weeping on the sidewalk. Boys break windows in the broad daylight.

We are accustomed to displays, so when Mr. Wrenn across the street has the DT's in front of his house, conversations continue. *What will be, will be, and life goes on*, as my mother is fond of saying. The men who are at home go over to convince Mr. Wrenn that the frogs are not really there. If that tack fails, they kill off the frogs or snakes with imaginary machetes or guns. While they are destroying the terrors that crawl out of the mind, the rest of us talk. We visit while the men lift their arms and swing, aiming at the earth, saying there are no more alligators anywhere.

"Lovely day, isn't it?" someone says. "Did you hear the Beelah girl ran off with the gypsy fellow? The one with long fingernails?"

I lean against the tree on the other side of my mother, like we are holding up the dry elm. "She didn't have fingernails at all," I say. "She is a chewer. Everyone knows that. She even buys hot stuff to put on them to break her out of the habit." My mother jabs me with her elbow.

"Him. He's got long fingernails. He's fancy as a rooster up for the fair." It is Mrs. Bell speaking. She is wearing a pink cardigan buttoned only at the top and her stomach protrudes from the triangular opening.

Mr. Wrenn grows quiet and the men sit beside him on his small front porch, a slab of cement. This day it is my father who is sitting with him. Father has been sick with his heart and he looks pale. Even sick, he is better than a telephone or a newspaper. He's right in the action. He knows everything that happens in the neighbor-hood. When June Kim, the Korean woman who used to live next door, stabbed her enormous husband in his massive stomach, my father was the first to know. He, in fact, surveyed the damage before driving the large, balding man to the hospital. And he is the first man on the scene of any accident. When a Buick drove through Sylvia Smith's bedroom wall, my father was the first man there, catching Mrs. Smith in her nightgrown, her pale chubby hands trying to cover up the rollers in her hair.

He was also the one to speak through the police megaphone to Mr. Douglas who held his wife and kids hostage with a machine gun. "Hey, Doug." My dad called him that for short, like he calls Mr. Smith by the name of Smitty. "Hey Doug," he yelled. "Don't make it any harder on yourself." And so on about how Marge Douglas wouldn't really leave him this time even though Mrs. Martinez had given her spells and charms to help her get away. "Doug. You are a logical man. You know you don't believe in any of that magic crap."

Women sat on the curb, their legs spread like crickets, their dresses great flowered hammocks pushed down between their open thighs. The police did little. They were only interested in how Mr. Douglas got a machine gun and the ammo. They don't really care who shoots each other out here. They don't even answer calls from our neighborhood at night.

I remember the women talking from the curb. "Maybe the crazy loon will shoot himself. I'm going to give Marge some of my grocery money to get away."

"Shoot. You know she won't ever leave that bastard."

"Watch your language. The kids'll hear you."

The women seem to know everything. They know why Mr. Wrenn drinks so much and they are pretty good to him. I like to be with the women. They know, for instance, when a man with a gun will really use it. They can feel it in the air. Maybe the direction of the wind or the vacuum heat of summer. They know Marge is more afraid to leave her husband now than she ever was, that she will instead find ways to get the kids away into early marriages, lives of

151

being orderlies at the hospital, and then she will settle down to old age with Tom Douglas who will become slow and feeble and stupidly sweet. The women know, and have said, that Douglas will be one of those men who spend hours folding handkerchiefs into the shapes of birds and the shapes of women's pointed brassieres, hours tending the few eggplants that will grow in his small plot of garden and when no one even likes eggplant. Children will like him. The women know that. They also know that children will dislike the bitter and grumpy Marge when she is aged and wrinkled and full of anger from living beside Tom who will tell the same stories day and night as if she's never heard them, her scrubbing and sweeping, him story-telling about his wonderful life.

The wide-hipped women know just about everything, including how many books of green stamps it takes to get a bathroom scale or an electric mixer, and they talk about what they will get while my dad returns from Mr. Wrenn's.

But even with all their knowing, the people who are new to the block are still a mystery to the women. The Peñalba family moved into the house next door when June Kim and her husband moved out. The Peñalbas don't do much of their living outside. They seldom come out at all except when the mother and daughter go to church. Then the two females walk solemnly down the street in black old-fashioned looking dresses and black veils on their heads. They walk like a procession, the daughter trailing along behind the mother.

The daughter, Nora, is my age. She speaks with an accent and looks older than us Indian girls in the neighborhood. Her flesh has a gray light around it, like the grayness around the sick. Her house has the odor of burning. There is something feverish about it. Maybe it is the new shabbiness around it, or the way light hits some of the windows now that it is spring. The house is like the great eye of a tornado that the crows have disappeared into.

The streets are brown in the morning light. All the tiny houses fit closely together in the early shadows. They are painted. Some are green, some pink or gold. Occasionally there is a dark brown house as if the tenant wished to make the house invisible, or like a house of the forest. I hear people singing sometimes in the bathrooms, or fighting in the kitchens. I like the sounds.

Last night it rained and now the streets have water rushing in the gutters, climbing the curbs. The water passes over some broken yellow dishes and old leaves that look lovely in the gutter, like something rich and exquisite, like gold in Venice in the history books. I stop to look. There is an earthworm drowning in the water and it is very thin and pale. I take it out and place it on a patch of earth.

Nora Peñalba is suddenly standing beside me, come as silently from the black hole of her house as the quiet air that surrounds it. She is not wearing black. She has changed into a brightly flowered, low-cut dress that makes her look much older and more knowing than anyone else in El Grande county.

Steam is rising off the street in the first sunlight and it surrounds her like fog around a new crop of tulips. Nora has very loose hips. When she walks, it is indecent the way her skirt swings from side to side, her thighs apart and natural, but I like the way she walks and I practice it alone in front of the mirror. She has black curly hair with red highlights. She is lovely, but whenever I look close I notice that grayness, and a secret.

Now she comes outside occasionally at night, but we seldom speak. We walk together to school. She goes with me because the tiny blonde social worker who wears expensive gray dresses has visited Mrs. Peñalba and told her that she is breaking the law if her children do not attend school. Mrs Peñalba hunches over and looks at the floor. Nora translates between Señora Peñalba and Frau Betty, as my father calls her. To the tiny blonde with white nail polish and lipstick, Nora says things like, "Mama says we attend schools. We do not go against none of the legals." She has looked up the words in her dictionary in the presence of Frau Betty. She says such things as, "Yes, we are not citizens. We have been them a long while."

Her English is better than mine and I do not understand why she cannot speak with the little blonde. I imagine it is because she is afraid of her, as we are all afraid of the people from the country. But Nora reads the newspapers, unlike the rest of us, although she does not bother much with school. She understands, though, when I talk about nothing but boys and how I am going to fix hair for a living when I am done with school. She understands my eyes following the two GI's that moved in down the street and that play loud music. She understands when I dress up and sit outside at night looking off in the direction of that house, but she is silent and holds an anger in her blood. "Like a spitfire," my mother says.

"I don't understand," Nora has told me, "why in the North of America you girls do not hold hands and walk the street together. I think we aren't friends."

"Oh yes, we are friends," I tell her. "We are the best of friends. But the people here don't like that kind of touching."

"No, then we are not friends."

Maybe we aren't. She is so burning and deep. Somewhere in my stomach I feel that we can never be close. And also, my mother does not like her. As Nora and I walk to school, I hear my mother's voice in the back of my mind. "She is sneaky, that girl," my mom says to Sylvia Smith across the street. But Sylvia changes the subject. Sylvia says, "I tell him I will even kiss his ass. In fact, I have done it." I listen and make a silent vow to never get married. I can see up Sylvia's skirt which is much too short for a woman her size, see her white ragged underpants.

"Besides," my mother says, "there is something wrong with them, something not right in their house." That's the way they talk, two distinct conversations.

"I would do anything for him. That man. And then he runs off and leaves me all week with his retarded son." Mikey. That is the son's name. And my mother, behind Sylvia's back, says Mikey is retarded because of the way they beat him, and beat him in full view of the neighborhood, right out in front of the house. I feel sorry for Mikey and for his sister, too. Their dad eats steak for supper when he is home and the kids must sit in the other room and have only a bowl of cereal. But Sylvia, herself, is a good woman who goes to confession to tell how poor a wife she is, and she does her penance.

"They put their garbage in the back yard," my mother says. "On the ground. And there are flies all over the place. The old woman doesn't even bother to brush the flies away from her face. She hardly moves at all. She just sits with flies all around her."

"Yes," says Sylvia, shocked into my mother's conversation. "And almost all of their windows are broken and they don't seem to give a darn."

"And with all those flies," Mom says, and then changes her tune.

154

"But that isn't their fault. The local boys asked for protection money and broke their windows to get it."

"Those damn boys. I wish they'd all fall into hell. Where do they get off terrorizing the neighborhood and making us pay them not to wreck our places?"

Today I have some money to see Mrs. Martinez about my future. I walk to her house, making notes in my mind of all I want to ask her. I want to ask her if I will be a beauty operator, if I will get a date with that tall boy in class, Mike Nava. I want to ask if I'll have children or go to someplace exciting. There are small lizards near her house. I frighten them from the sun and they go into hiding beneath the foundation and under the shingles. Mrs. Martinez lets me in.

"Are you happy?" asks Mrs. Martinez. She is robust and wears long gold earrings.

I am surprised. I have seen her three times and she has never asked me about happiness. I have nothing to say. I haven't thought about whether I am happy or not. I had a conversation with Deborah, a girl who used to live a few blocks over. Deborah claimed to have once lived down a street from Marilyn Monroe. I remember saying to Debbie that all I wanted was a nice man and he didn't need to have money because that wasn't the key to happiness. Love was everything, I said. Deborah said she wanted the money and could toss away love because it never lasted anyway, like her mom and dad, for example. In fact, she said she had done away with love already because all the fellows from families around here would never amount to a hill of beans, let alone a house with a swimming pool or a big yard with white plaster statues of swans. She told me about a woman she once knew who even had the cloth for her bedspread imported from Germany, ancient and rich cloth. I didn't believe her. That was last year. I was younger. Then I never believed anyone lived much differently than we did. Now I look at the houses on television and I see what those people live like and it is better than here, even if they don't have much going on outside at all.

Mrs. Martinez heats water for the tea. While it is simmering, she takes out the cards and places them on the green card table where I am sitting. She prepares the tea leaves in the blue china cup. I look at her clean white stucco walls trimmed with enamel red and wonder if she got the money for the red paint from Mrs. Douglas who will never leave her husband.

I drink the tea and Mrs. Martinez looks into the leaves. She says that she sees a dog and a star. I am going to be a star in the world like that very bright one, the morning one, Venus, she says, shining early in the morning when the others have faded. She tells me I will live long, like that star. She asks me if I once had a dog that died. I did, but I don't ever give her too much information about my life because then she will be able to figure me out and my money will be wasted with her.

Mrs. Martinez doesn't even put her hand to her forehead when she says, "No, you won't date that tall boy. You will not have many dates at all because you are going to be following that star alone." Then it is time to look at my palm. It is upturned and a very lovely rich color. I like the lines on it. They are like fish nets cast out upon some river or sea. I have many lines and my palm is almost as cracked as my mom's geographic tongue. Mrs. Martinez touches each fissure and she tells me that I must be patient for three years and that I have a friend who will teach me all about life.

When Mrs. Martinez is finished, I give her two dollars. She looks deep into my eyes like she is reading my soul and she tells me, earnestly, that I have hope and I must find a way to get an education and must study hard at school.

I don't like the solemnity of it, but when I leave I feel lighter and happier. I can tell that my future is full of excitement. When I walk by the preacher's house I remember how I used to get saved every Friday just for something to do, go into the back room with the man and the other children and kneel at the bed and say I believed and beg forgiveness for my sinful thoughts. Now I feel as light and relieved as I did when I used to get saved.

At home, at night, I am sitting on the bed and staring at the gray tile floors. I am not happy. I wonder what has gone wrong with my life. I can think of no living reason on God's green earth for my despair. There is something greatly wrong in the world and something wrong in myself. But I do not know what it is. It's the first time I have thought about happiness and now I know that I have none. Damn Mrs. Martinez, I think, and then feel afraid that, all the way up the street, she will read my thoughts and curse me. I brush the words out of the air before me like they are stolen smoke from a cigarette.

I can hear my mother in her bedroom closing a drawer. I call her and she comes. My father is sitting in the living room in his favorite chair eating peanuts and I imagine his animal warmth and the smell of his shirt. But it is my mother I want.

"What is it?" she asks, and I look up at her with sad eyes. She is wearing her blue robe and a blue hairnet. "What is it? What's wrong?"

"Are you happy?" I ask.

"What kind of question is that?"

"I'm not a happy person."

"Nonsense, Sarah Bernhardt. Of course you are. What's there to be unhappy about?"

I can see that she has never thought about it either, and now it is an even deeper and more troublesome question to me. I wonder if anyone asks themselves if they are happy. Mrs. Martinez has probably ruined my entire life.

My mother says, "It is probably time for your period and so you feel blue." But when she leaves I look in the mirror and see, as if for the first time, my face. It is very pale although I am an Indian and I think perhaps that is what is wrong with me. My eyes are very dark and lonely and they are mysterious in a way I have never noticed, as if Nora's presence were haunting me from the inside out. I put orange lipstick on my hair to see if a tint or a rinse would make me happy but it doesn't look good. I wipe it out with a Kleenex. And then I lift back the covers of my small bed and crawl inside. I stay awake until long after the folks are in bed and I listen to them talking and do not feel comforted.

I think, this morning, that if I wear a yellow dress I will feel happy. As I put on my slip, I look out the window, pull the curtain back to check the weather. Nora and her mother are returning from early mass, dressed like funeral mourners, in black. Nora's younger brother follows them and he is wearing a white shirt. They look tragic and beautiful on the street, walking in the spring light, in the diffuse air that is charged with electric sparks of pollen. Nora's youth is hidden in the black cloth.

I dress and eat some toast and wear a rhinestone barrette in my hair. I leave the house early and go sit on the curb, careful not to dirty my daffodil-colored dress. Nora comes out early also, dressed in red. She sits beside me. It is too early for school but we sit in the sunlight like new flowers.

"Oh Nora," I say. "I am not happy."

She looks at me with her great nocturnal eyes, and says nothing.

"I don't even know when this sadness began."

"Maybe I'll tell you something happy. About the rain in Nicaragua."

"You're from Mexico?"

"No. It is more south than Mexico. And it rains. Warm rain. There are green and blue seas and rain forests of rosewood and balsa and cedar. With vines. In them live tiny, tiny monkeys and birds you call parrots with big eyebrows. It is like a paradise of the bible, the garden called Eden. In the night you hear the monkeys chattering about their boyfriends and the big cats roaring in the jungle out there like this, Grr." She looks fierce. I lean back laughing. "Raar," she yells again, with her hands open like claws. "And sometimes the earth quakes to tell us we have been bad. It roars too."

I try to see it, but I don't. I feel badly that she is giving me some vision of her world and I can't form it in my mind. I wonder what shyness has kept me from asking her about life.

"What color are the houses?" I ask her.

"They are, oh, they are house-colored." She laughs. It is a funny joke. And then she hisses, "Pah!" More a burst of air than a real word. "Of course you are unhappy, being so poor for North Americans." She gestured about in a wide circle and her hand's motion opened my eyes like a camera. For the first time I saw it, the two of us like bright flowers growing out of bulbs, blooming one time only before the winter, surrounded by the oil rags beside cars that did not run, beside the sea-green shards of Coca-Cola bottles that the boys had broken at night, and beer cans, the old yellowed newspapers stuck in fences and trees, saw a few children outside crying, two little boys hitting the earth with sticks that were also used as rifles for playing soldier. I do not think she means it, that we are poor. I think she is making fun of my unhappiness, and I want to be away from her. My body feels tense. I think of Linda at school who announces each week who she loves and I want to be with Linda, want to hear her tell me this week, as she

158

does, "I am in love." I want to see the dreamy look on Linda's innocent face when she tells me she is in love with Rudolph Nureyev and I laugh at the foreign name and laugh even harder when she tells me he is a ballet dancer, laugh until she brings out the magazine picture of him all glorious and almost naked in that stretchy cloth you can see right through.

"It was Mrs. Martinez that caused it," I tell Nora. "When I went to have my fortune, she asked me if I was happy." Some hammering begins in the distance. It is rhythmic.

"I have tried to think when it first began." Nora is silent now and listening to me. "I think it began when the boys on the street were killing the lizards, were throwing them against the walls of houses and breaking them and the lizards would scream like people. And I know I am unhappy when Mr. Smith beats up his son, Mikey. And it all makes me sad. " I feel about to cry.

Nora is quiet a long time and I know she is thinking of something. Then she says, "I think sometimes they are born bad. Men. I wonder too what makes them kill things. My own father, he was a good man and a leader of the people. He hated killings. There were so many killings the whole land was made of bullets and he always said we could rise up."

"What?" I think she is lying. A leader whose family is penniless and living right here in El Grande, next door to us?

"Yes. He was fighting against the government because they were cruel. You know, everywhere in the hot sun there were bodies. My father wanted us to rise up. He got men together to battle the predators." She speaks so slowly now, and words I don't know and have never heard. I try to read the truth on her face. I don't know why she would lie to me. I am her friend.

"How do you speak of the deaths? They hung his head on a pole. When I saw it I began to scream but some old woman put her hand over my face and ran with me away from there."

I don't know how she can say such a thing. She is worse than our history teacher who has scared me half to death of the communists by telling how they will come and cut my brother in half in front of me and will make me choose between my mother and father and then kill them both. It all puts my nerves on edge.

"And they came and took my brothers. I adored my brothers. They were young." She is so matter of fact, as if she is saying nothing.

159

"Stop it." I put my hands over my ears. My face is burning. My dress is moist and my palms are wet. "Stop it. That's a lie. Shut your lying mouth." I stand up and I want to hit her with stones.

Nora stands up too. Breaking as her windows had broken. Her face is pale beneath her rouge and lipstick. She is in a rage, her entire body taut. "No," she screams. "It's true."

Something in her is falling away. It is also falling away in me. "It isn't true! It isn't. Let me alone!"

And she is hitting me in the face and grabbing my hair to pull it. I pull at her dress and we are twisting together on the curb, like flowers in a horrid wind. The people going to work around us are watching and pointing. She hits me again and again and I bend over to protect myself and then grab her to stop the blows while she breaks and screams. She stumbles away and falls, weeping, weeping all the rose colors of makeup over her chest. She falls and then she begins to run away while the children are shouting into the street and the gang of boys are cheering. I don't really hear them, just see Nora racing over the broken glass. Time stops. I have not believed and time stops. I have been pale and American, Gringa, as she calls me now, the screaming girl breaking as the windows of her house have broken, the girl who ran at me in a frenzy hitting me and me with nothing to do but hit her, to hold her and hit her back. As she runs away now, her fingers spread over her face, she is breathing in loud gasps and then she vanishes into the house, her footsteps gone and the door slamming behind her, and the wailing breaking the solitude of that house.

nominated by Michael Dennis Browne

MY LEGACY

by Don Zacharia

from THE KENYON REVIEW

FOR MANY YEARS my father was a communist, an atheist, and a *great* intellectual. When other boys my age were being slipped crisp five dollar bills for bar mitzvah presents, I was out ringing door bells collecting quarters for the Spanish War Relief. My mother and older sister were also communists, atheists, and intellectuals. I was a communist for a while, an atheist for a while, but never, I mean *never*, an intellectual.

More than anything, I liked playing baseball, and none of the boys who were members of my YCL, Young Communist League, knew or cared about baseball.

They all looked alike: very intense, very skinny, with stringy black hair and double thick myopic glasses that looked like wrong-way binoculars perched on their noses. I always had a feeling if I ever threw them a baseball, they would put their hands up and the ball would smack them in the face. My comrades looked upon me with suspicion. My dedication toward the movement was not what it should have been, I was told, and I'm sure, if it hadn't been for my father, I would have been kicked out of the group. We met once a week at night and made plans for America when the revolution took over. The best part of the meetings was when they ended, and we were joined by our sister YCL group for soda, cake, and Chesterfield cigarettes. Everybody, including me, smoked like a fiend in those days. Young communist girls looked a million times better than young communist boys.

I played baseball with a bunch of local Italian kids in Mount Vernon, New York, where I grew up. I never discussed the

U.S.S.R. with any of them. I'm sure if they had known what I was doing one night a week they would have kicked me off the team. One of the boys we played with was Ralph Branca. In those days he pitched and played third base. I played first base. Ralph would whistle the ball to me across the diamond so fast that some nights my left hand would swell up to twice its size, and I would have to soak my hand in warm salt water for hours. I knew my ball playing displeased my father. He never said it in so many words, but I could see the disappointment etched in his face. More than anything, my father wanted me to read. "Not to read," he would say, pausing deep in thought, "is not to have eyesight." I never answered him. What could I possibly say to that? Almost every day my father handed me books—not one book, but six, seven, eight, ten: Faulkner, Hemingway, Steinbeck, Dos Passos, William Carlos Williams, Sandburg, Whitman, Jack Reed. "Here," he would say, "read these and we'll talk about them tomorrow."

I tried. I really did. I would have liked to please my father, but with the exception of Ring Lardner and Jack London, I found them boring.

What My Father Did for a Living

Work interfered with my father's life, so he worked only three hours a day, selling newspapers to the morning commuters in a nearby affluent suburb. Could those people who thrust a nickel at my father for the morning *New York Daily Mirror*, waiting impatiently for their two cents change, possibly know that within the hour this short unshaven man, who some people thought looked like Lenin, would be working on translating a Chekhov story from Russian to Yiddish? My father was fluent in Russian, Polish, French, Italian, German, Hebrew, Yiddish and English. With Mrs. Redka as a Spanish teacher, I failed the only language I ever took, Beginning Spanish, three consecutive years.

Besides his income from his newspaper stand, my father made a modest amount of money translating an author's work from language to language, usually into Yidddish. When I say modest, I mean *modest*. For translating a Kafka novel from German to Yiddish, my father was paid sixty dollars. For translating ten Shalom Aleichem stories from Yiddish to Italian, he was paid forty dollars. I remember that particularly, because he kept complaining

162

that Shalom Aleichem in Italian made as much sense as Baudelaire in Swahili.

Besides selling newspapers, and besides his work as a translator, my father wrote Yiddish poetry. As far as I know, he never received a nickel for his poetry. On the contrary, in a sense he paid for their publication. There were three Yiddish newspapers published in New York in the late thirties and early forties: the *Forward,* which my father and many of his friends considered a right-wing newspaper; the *Day* or *Tog,* a middle-of-the-road newspaper; and the *Freiheit,* a left-wing and, some people thought, communist paper.

My father had two arrangements: one with the *Freiheit* and one with the *Tog*. With the *Freiheit,* for every ten poems they published, he would arrange for three lifetime subscriptions. With the *Tog,* it was a one-on-one basis: for every poem—a lifetime subscription. He published most of his poetry in the *Freiheit*. A lifetime subscription to the *Freiheit* cost twelve dollars and fifty cents. So for thirty-seven dollars and fifty cents, my father published ten poems, or three dollars and fifty cents a poem. I'm sure he never thought of it in this way, but after translating ten Shalom Aleichem stories from Yiddish to Italian, net income forty dollars, and "selling" ten poems to the *Freiheit,* net outlay thirty-seven dollars and fifty cents, he showed a net profit of two dollars and fifty cents.

My House

Culture seeped through my house. It came at you from everywhere. The walls were infused with it; the floors exhaled it; the ceilings inhaled it. Every room looked like a library. Books everywhere: floor to ceiling, wall to wall, sitting on shelves, and, where there were no shelves, vertically stacked from the floor up. There were books in the kitchen, the bathroom, the hallways, and on every windowsill. We had a large oak table in the dining room. I do not recall a single meal served there because the dining room table always had at least a thousand books stacked on it. That was my father's desk: where he worked, read, translated, and wrote his poetry. My mother never had to worry about cleaning the walls, because there were no walls. If they weren't covered by books and bookcases, there were paintings—Picasso, Chagall, Matisse, Weber, Ernst, Walkowitz—paintings everywhere. Using a double-edged razor with black tape on one side, my father would carefully slit his favorite paintings out of the art books, put them in a simple frame, and exchange them for a painting already hanging. A Utrillo went up, a Picasso came down. One week Chagall would replace Matisse, only to be replaced the following week by Mondrian. It was a process without end. Besides the books, besides the art, there was classical music on from the moment he came home until he went to sleep. It was not unusual to see him abruptly stand up and conduct the last portion of Beethoven's Fifth or a Brahms violin concerto.

With the exception of my sister's boyfriends, the only people who came into my house were friends of my father: other intellectuals, poets and writers and would-be poets and would-be writers, communists and almost-communists. Quite often you could hear five languages being spoken simultaneously in my home. But more than anything, there were arguments: loud, shouting fist-thumping arguments. Was Ezra Pound a fascist? Was Leon Trotsky a socialist? What direction should the movement take? Was John Dos Passos truly a greater writer?

In the wintertime our radiators hissed not steam, but Theodore Dreiser. The hum from our refrigerator, the verses of Whitman. The whirr from the washing machine, the voice of Scott Fitzgerald. The sound of running water in the kitchen, the poetry of Sandburg. The way the wind rattled our front screen door, the stories of Shalom Aleichem. And I—I walked about my home from room to room flipping a baseball from hand to hand.

My Older Sister

My sister was twelve years older. Her name was Sarah. I don't know why my parents waited so long to have a second child. I am very grateful to my sister for many reasons, but more than anything else, for my name. When I was born, I was named Ivan Tukhachevshy Roth after the great Russian general. When I was three, Sarah began lobbying my parents to change my name. Her arguments were simple and sound: nobody could spell it, and nobody could pronounce it. Neither argument convinced my parents. "I can spell it," my father said, "and I can pronounce it, and so can my friends. Who else is there?"

The good old Central Committee of the U.S.S.R. saved me from a life of Ivan who? when it had a slight shift of policy (history?) in 1937 and decided that Ivan Tukhachevshy wasn't a hero after all but a neo-Trotskyite, and he was purged. My father, with the weight of this new evidence, relented and a search for a new name began. My father came up with names like Sholem, after Shalom Aleichem or Sholem Asch; Karl or Carl, after Karl Marx or Carl Sandburg; Ezra, after Ezra Pound; and Lincoln, after Lincoln Steffens or Abraham Lincoln. My sister came up with names like Joe, Bill, Bob, and Jim. My mother came up with Chaim, after her grandfather from Smolensk, and they compromised on Noel with three middle names. Don't ask me how Noel came up. A new birth certificate was officially issued, and at the age of three I became Noel Ezra Karl Sholem Roth. One thing you can be sure of, Ivan Tukhachevshy never could have played first base for the Mount Vernon Scarlets—even if he batted left-handed.

My sister Sarah was my go-between. Whenever I had a problem, I went to her, and she went to my father. When I wanted a bike, a radio, a baseball glove, it was Sarah who asked my father. Every request was a storm.

"A bike? A radio? A baseball glove??? For what? What is he going to do? Become a hooligan? Tell him when he reads Chekhov I will consider a *small* radio. A bike is out of the question, and he'll get a baseball thing when Tolstoy sneezes."

Somehow, Sarah arranged for me to get everything I needed.

My sister always had a lot of boyfriends. My father used to say that Sarah had as many boyfriends as he had books, which was an exaggeration. She was tall and attractive and bright and knew how to dress smartly and put on makeup. She was certainly the best-looking communist in Mount Vernon, which confused my father. I think it is safe that my father neither liked nor trusted any of my sister's suitors.

"What they want from her," he said, "has nothing to do with the People's Revolution."

Sarah would occasionally bring her current beau home to meet my father and mother. I never understood why she did it until I was in my late teens.

The tableau was always the same: early 1940s, the young suitor would be sitting nervously in the corner of the couch, Sarah demurely in the other corner, my father in *his* chair, me on the floor squeezing a baseball, and my mother, when not in the kitchen, sitting in *her* chair. My mother would bring in cookies

165

that she made and hot chocolate that Sarah made. My father smoking one Camel cigarette after the other, stared at the young man the way Bob Feller looked at a two-hundred hitter who just got a scratch single off of him. After the brief introductions, there was always an enforced period of silence. If one of the young men ever chanced in a timorous voice, "Nice day today, Mr. Roth," my father would blow smoke in his direction.

Finally, my father would speak. "Do you like my wife's cookies?" he demanded.

"Oh, yes, sir, they're excellent. I'll even have another."

My father nodded. Another long pause. "Do you like my daughter's hot chocolate?" Again the demand.

"Oh, yes, sir. It's truly excellent." A smile toward Sarah.

Another long pause. "I have a slight favor to ask of you." Was that a twinkle I detected in my father's voice? "A very slight favor."

"Anything, Mr. Roth," the boyfriend said, sitting straight up, ready for action. "Anything."

My father handed a book to my sister's soon to be ex-suitor. "I would like you to read *out loud* from Eliot's 'Prufrock,' the first two pages up until the line—'I have measured out my life with coffee spoons'—and when you are finished, tell *me*, what *you* think *Mr. Eliot* was trying to tell *us*."

Well, that always was the end of that. Interestingly enough, everybody (except the boyfriend) got what he or she wanted. My sister got rid of her boyfriend, which pleased her; my mother and my father and I got my mother's cookies, filled with rich pieces of chocolate and pecan nuts, that were delicious.

Songs We Used to Sing

On Sundays we would get into my father's 1938 Dodge truck and drive to the country, to the Kensico Dam in Valhalla, for a picnic lunch. In the picnic hamper there were a foot-long salami, thick chunks of liverwurst, a meat loaf, hard-boiled eggs, rolls of every type, pickles, a bag of fruit, a thermos filled with punch, and beer for my father. He always gave me a couple of swallows despite my mother's admonishings. The drive from Mount Vernon to Kensico Dam took an hour and a half, I think. It's only fourteen miles, and today I have a friend who *jogs* it on Sunday mornings and *he* does it in an *hour and a half*. I know it sounds crazy, but I *swear*, at least in my memory, that's how long it took us to drive fourteen miles. We would leave early in the morning so we would get a good spot for our picnic, and we would sing songs the entire trip.

> Lenin is our Leader
> We shall not be moved
> Lenin is our Leader
>
> We shall not be moved
> Just like a tree
> Standing by the water
> We shall not be moved.
>
> Tell me comrade
> Do you read
> *The Daily Worker*—Yes indeed
> If you do then dance with me
> True comrades—we'll always be.
>
> I dreamed I saw Joe Hill last night
> Alive as you and me
> Says I to Joe
> You're ten years dead
> I never died says he
> I never died says he.
>
> Far and wide as the eye can wander
> Heath and bog are everywhere
> Not a bird sings out to cheer us
> Oaks are standing gaunt and bare
> We are The Peat Bog Soldiers
> We are marching with our spades
> To the bogs.

One Day I Played Catch with the Great Paul Robeson

During World War Two my parents had many fund-raisers for the Russian War Relief. It was a good time to be a communist in America. The U.S.S.R. and America had a common enemy, and you didn't have to hum the Soviet National Anthem under your breath. Little did we know what was to come. My father had somehow managed to get the great Paul Robeson for a brief appearance. There were at least a hundred people crowding our small house beyond capacity. My father said that he wouldn't be surprised if they raised as much as a thousand dollars. I was in the backyard playing catch with myself when Paul Robeson walked out.

"Throw me the ball, son."

I was big for my age, but Paul Robeson was a giant. I couldn't help but stare at him. Nineteen forty-four was before the era of six-foot-six black basketball players, and I had never seen anyone so big or so dark.

"I said 'throw me the ball,' son."

Everyone in the house was staring at us from the porch and windows. "It's a hardball," I said, holding up my taped-over Spaulding for him to see.

"I've caught many a hardball bare-handed." He held his hands up. They looked like they could crush a stone.

I underhanded him the ball and he whistled it back to me. He moved across the yard. "Your father tells me you're quite a ball player."

I was speechless. It was the last thing I would expect my father to talk about to Paul Robeson. The second front, the battle of Stalingrad, the heroic Russian soldier, the Scottsboro boys, the problems of being a Negro in America, *anything* but my ball playing prowess. "My father said that?" I said weakly. I threw him a lazy overhand. He flung it back to me over my head and I caught it gracefully in the web of my mitt.

"I used to play baseball," he said. "I could hit a ball so high it would disappear in the clouds, but the real player in my family was my brother Bill. Bill Robeson hit a ball so hard that if you caught it, your hand would sting for a week."

I wanted to tell him about Ralph Branca, that we were on the same team and he had major league scouts looking at him, but something stopped me. He threw me ground balls—to my left, my right. I handled them easily. He threw me a short hop that I muffed but kept in front of me.

"That's good," he said, "that's good."

He threw me a couple more short hops that I handled cleanly.

All the time I kept on throwing the ball back to him with more and more velocity. I had a feeling he could have caught Dizzy Dean bare-handed. I sensed my father waiting impatiently for our game to stop, but I certainly wasn't going to be the one to quit. After thirty minutes, with a hundred startled American communists watching me and Paul Robeson playing catch on a Sunday afternoon in Mount Vernon, New York, he walked over and handed me the ball.

"You're pretty good," he said.

"Thanks." Should I have said more? Should I have said *at least* that he was pretty good also?

"How long have you had this ball?"

"About a year."

"It's pretty beat-up."

"I play in the street with it a lot. I bang it up against the curb and practice fielding grounders that way."

"It's awfully lumpy."

I shrugged.

"What's your first name?"

"Noel."

"How old are you?"

"Fifteen."

"I have a son. He's fifteen also." Paul Robeson nodded. He seemed deep in thought. I wanted so much to say something, anything, about his son, about how much I admired his singing, but I didn't say a word. To this day I'm sorry for that.

He was studying the ball, turning it around in his gigantic hand, gripping it, squeezing it, still deep in his own thoughts. "Mr. Roth," he finally spoke, calling up to my father who was on the porch. "Comrade Roth," he raised his voice, his bass filling our yard up as if he were in a concert hall, "I would like to make a suggestion, a motion if need be. After our collection today for our Russian brothers, I would like to peel off one dollar and fifty cents from whatever monies we take in and give it to your son for a new Spaulding baseball. Does anyone have any objections?"

I looked up at the dozens of openmouthed faces. My sister was smiling. My father showed no expression. Shapiro, the leader of the local Communist Party who had a head like a pin, was violently shaking his face no, but didn't dare say a word to the great Paul Robeson.

169

"*Do you think we have to get Premier Stalin's permission?*" Robeson's voice thundered out.

"I think it's an excellent idea," I heard my father say, "and I second the motion."

"Well, let's get started." Paul Robeson flipped me the ball and bounded up the stairs.

The next day, with three of my friends, I bought a shiny new Spaulding baseball and promised myself to use it only where, if someone didn't catch it, it would land on grass.

My Father's Favorite Joke

An immigrant is walking down Orchard Street in lower Manhattan and sees a sign in the window of a dry-cleaning store.

> What do you think
> My name is Fink
> I press your pants
> For nothing.

He goes into the store and asks about the sign. The man behind the counter points to the sign and says:

> What do you think
> My name is Fink
> I press your pants
> For nothing.

The immigrant gives him a pair of pants and is told they will be ready on Tuesday. On Tuesday, when he comes back, the man behind the counter tells him that he owes fifty cents for having his pants pressed. "What do you mean?" the immigrant says angrily. He points to the sign in the window and reads out loud:

> What do you think
> My name is Fink
> I press your pants
> For nothing.

"I'm not Fink," the man behind the counter says, "I'm Gold-stein."

I Become a Capitalist—Almost

When I was fourteen, my father put me into business for myself. He opened up another newsstand in Bronxville, about three blocks from his, and put me in charge of it. I didn't get the morning commuters the way he did, but I was on a main street that led to a highway and drivers would stop and buy their papers. My father provided the money to get me started, and I gave him a percentage of the profits and kept everything else for myself. I bought my newspapers from a man my father introduced me to whose name was Al Sharkey. Al got paid every three days and carried a pistol in his glove compartment. I know, because he showed it to me the first time I paid him. Al took a liking to me and would spend time by my stand, sometimes helping me out, and even came to a couple of my baseball games. He had a lot of stories about gangsters, and was always hinting at some close connection of his who could get him, or any friend of his, *anything*. I had no idea what he was talking about. After a while, Al started asking me about girls. He wanted to know if I knew any girls. If I wanted to meet any girls. How far did I ever go with a girl? At the end of every sentence, Al would wink at me. "Remember kid," he had a low husky voice, "if you ever need anything," he winked at me, "ask Big Al." He winked at me. "If Big Al can't do it," he winked again, "nobody can."

I really didn't know what to make of Al. He was different from anyone I had ever met before, but I liked him.

My business flourished. People took kindly to me, many of them going out of their way to buy their morning papers at my stand. I began to develop regular customers whose names I learned. Some of them would buy all four morning papers from me: the *Mirror*, the *News*, the *Tribune*, and the *New York Times*, which was a sixteen cent sale. I had a couple of regulars who gave me a quarter and waved off the change. Not a bad profit.

I started to handle magazines—the *Saturday Evening Post*, *Collier's*, *Look* and *Life*—and my business soared. Many of my customers began to learn *my* name and when picking up their papers would ask how I was doing in baseball. After I had been open for two months, I was taking home twenty dollars a week after all expenses. None of my friends made that kind of money.

My father was proud of my success. He didn't tell me so directly, but he boasted to his friends how well his son the entrepreneur was doing. I began to know him in a different way. He would wake me every morning at four-thirty, and we would have breakfast together at a local diner. He had been eating there for years, and the owners knew him well. My father introduced me to them: three Greeks, all of whom needed shaves. We always ordered exactly the same thing: two scrambled egg sandwiches with bacon on buttered hard rolls. I had milk and my father had tea. On cold mornings, rubbing the sleep from my eyes, blowing into my hands for warmth, sitting next to my father, I could feel his pleasure.

I was doing so well in my stand, I began looking around for other spots to open up. All of the railroad stations were taken, but there were two street corners in Mount Vernon where I thought a stand like mine would succeed. I spoke to my father about it one morning, showed him the location after work, and told him how easy it would be for me to get school friends to run them. "More and more people are driving to work," I said, "and the only place there are newspaper stands are at railroad stations. Look how well I'm doing after being open only a few months."

My father was impressed. We shook hands on it. He told me to speak to Al Sharkey before I did anything. That night I could hardly sleep as fifty dollar bills danced in front of my eyes.

The next day I presented my plan to Al. "It could be a gold mine," I said excitedly. "I got two kids lined up and if these spots work as well as mine, I'm going to start looking in White Plains for spots. In a year I could have ten stands, Al."

When Al didn't like something he had a way of looking at you like you were nuts, and that's the way he was looking at me.

"What's wrong?" I said.

"Let me give it to you straight, kid, forget it."

"Why?"

"Because I said so. You are what we call, very na-ive, kid." He winked at me.

"But you said you could do anything for me. 'Anything, Just ask Big Al.' " I mimicked him angrily.

"I was talking about girls, kid. Girls." He winked at me.

172

"I don't want girls, Al. I want those two corners in Mount Vernon."

Al stared at me. "You're not only na-ive, kid. You're stupid. You can't open a stand in another town. Now let's forget this pipe dream and go over your account—"

"Suppose I just do it, Al. Who's going to stop me?"

"Kid, you're not only na-ive and stupid, but you're dumb besides. If you open up a stand in Mount Vernon, some friend of mine is going to open up a stand next to your father's." Al didn't wink at me.

"Oh," I said, "now I get it."

"I knew you would, kid."

"I thought you were my friend."

"I am, kid."

"If you were my friend, you wouldn't do that."

Al looked hurt. "Boy, you really don't understand. Very na-ive. It's the American way. Someday you'll get it." He winked at me.

The Mount Vernon Scarlets

My baseball team was named the Mount Vernon Scarlets. We were *excellent*. All the boys, except me, were fifteen or sixteen. At fourteen, I was the youngest. I was also the only one who was not Italian. Tony Daniello was our captain, and because of him I was on the team. He pitched and played the outfield. Today he owns a fruit stand. Sal Mosca was our catcher. Sal was a catcher because he looked like a catcher; short and squat, he could fire a ball to second base from the kneeling position. Very few people could steal against him. He reads meters for Con Edison now. Jackie Campanella played second base. No relation. A wonderful fielder but couldn't hit the ball out of the infield. He batted ninth, and was killed in Korea. Fishman played shortstop. I don't remember his real name. His father owned a fish store, so everybody called him Fishman. Fishman and I didn't get along. He always called me Rothman, instead of Roth, made snide cracks about me being Jewish, and—even worse—would purposely throw me short hops to make me look bad. We got into a fist fight once that Sal Mosca broke up, but not until Fishman broke my nose with a left hook I never saw. Today, Fishman owns a fish store, and I occasionally see him. The Rico Brothers, Frank and Anthony, played left and right

173

field. Anthony had the better arm, but Frank was our clean-up hitter. Today they are both electricians. Anthony Pelligrino was our center fielder. He was the fastest boy on the team. I never recall a fly ball being hit over his head. Anthony works in Tony Daniello's fruit stand.

Ralph Branca pitched and played third base. We all knew that Ralph was going to make it in the major leagues. We just knew it. It was the kind of thing we just knew. I played first base. I batted second. I was tall and rangy for my age and had a natural, whippy swing that produced a lot of line drives. One of the scouts for the Philadelphia Athletics who came to watch Ralph Branca pitch once told me that it was too bad I wasn't left-handed. I own a men's clothing store.

I played for the Scarlets for two year until the team broke up. In that time we never lost a game. We played other sandlot teams from surrounding towns, and we scrimmaged the local high school team, kids that were three and four years older, and we always beat them. We were—great. But, with the exception of Ralph Branca, not one of us ever played high school baseball.

My Father Has a Crisis and I Come to His Aid

One day my father stopped writing poetry because he ran out of friends. Everybody he knew, every single person he could think of, was now receiving a lifetime subscription to the *Freiheit* or the *Tog*. It didn't make sense to me, but no more friends to offer free subscriptions, no more poetry. He became despondent and depressed. I tried talking to him about it in the mornings when we were having breakfast at the Greeks', usually a good time for us, but he looked upon me with a combination of disdain and compassion. I pressed the issue.

"Couldn't you continue to write poetry?" I asked him one morning.

"And do what with it?"

"Give the *Freiheit* whatever you normally give them and let them do with the money what they want. Make a contribution. What difference does it make?"

He slammed his fist on the table. "You mean I should pay to have my poetry published?" he shouted. "Is that what you are telling me? Is that my son's *great* advice? I should pay to have my poetry published. Where is your sensitivity? How can you tell me about my poetry? That kind of advice is like a blob of snot. My poetry is everything to me. Do you think I obtain pleasure from selling Mr. Big Shot the *New York Times*, with his gloved hand waiting for pennies change? Do you think this is my pleasure? Or perhaps you think your ability to throw a ball is my pleasure? Or even better, perhaps you think that one day I will come to one of your games and cheer, and afterward you imagine the two of us playing catch?"

My father never hit me, but each word he said to me that morning was like a slap in the face. I fought back the tears. I wanted to tell him that just because I didn't read poetry didn't mean I couldn't understand his pain, and yes, very much, I would like to play catch with him. Would that be so terrible? To throw a ball with your son? But I was fourteen, and sentences like that did not form in my mouth.

My father's depression got worse. He stopped reading. He stopped translating and he stopped talking to me except for an occasional monosyllable.

"Look," I said one morning, "I have a way that you can start writing your poetry again."

"I'm not interested. Let it rest. I'm not interested. When the day comes that I need advice from my son who can't read past the sports pages, I'm in trouble."

"I think I can help you," I persisted.

"You cannot help me. Now stop talking. That would help me."

"Will you do me a favor?"

"No."

"Will you go to the library with me after work?"

"The library?" My father showed some emotion. "I didn't know you knew where it was."

"Will you?"

"Why? What are we going to do there?"

"I'm not going to tell you." I knew if I told him my idea he wouldn't go. "Will you do it?"

"All right. My son wants to take me to the library? In America, wonders never cease."

That morning, after work, we went to the Mount Vernon library. "Sit here," I told my father. "I'll be right back." I returned in a moment with my arms loaded down with twenty or so phone books from Montana, Idaho, and Wyoming.

175

"What are those?"

"They're phone books."

My father closed his eyes. "We are in a library," he took a deep breath, "I am in a library with my son, a library where the shelves are filled with Stendhal and Proust and Dostoyevsky and Tolstoy and my son, my son brings me a phone book."

Paying no attention to him I opened the Idaho book at random. "Look at this."

"What am I looking at?"

"In Idaho there is a town called Kimberly. It can't be very big. There are only two pages of phone numbers. Here." I pointed to a name in the middle of a page and wrote it down on a pad. "Ralph Sanders, that's a nice name, County Road 16, Kimberly, Idaho." I skipped a few pages to another town. "Tremont. This is bigger. There are six pages. How's this one? Frank Mace. County road 21, Tremont, Idaho." I wrote it down.

"What are you doing?" My father said. "Why did you shlep me here? Is this funny? Am I to laugh?"

"These names, Pop, names of people you can send lifetime subscriptions to the *Freiheit*."

"Are you mad?"

"Why? What's wrong with it? Why not?"

There was a half a minute of silence. My father nodded.

"Let me help you pick the names," he said.

My father started writing poetry again. To this day there is a vision that slips in front of my eyes of Farmer Sanders riding to his mailbox on his tractor, opening it, and there is the morning *Freiheit*, every morning, forever.

My Son

Much has happened. The world has changed. My days as a young man are shadows. When I tell my wife and son that once I was a member of the Communist Party they look at me with skepticism.

My father died a few years ago. He was eighty-six. Although I was angry at him for many years, my anger has dissipated since his death, and now I remember most of all this tough little man who wanted more than anything in the world for his son to read a book.

I have been trying in vain to find some of his poetry with the idea of publishing a collection with a vanity press. (I'm sure it would cost me more than three dollars and fifty cents a poem.) It is inconceivable, but he never kept copies of his work. I suppose my father thought the *Tog* and especially the *Freiheit* were as immortal as the *New York Times*. The *Tog* has long since stopped publishing, and the *Freiheit* publishes a tabloid once a week that bears little resemblance to the paper I knew. Almost everybody from that world is gone, and I have not been able to uncover a single poem that my father wrote. I have asked everyone there is to ask, but in 1982 no one has copies of Yiddish newspapers from forty-five years ago.

When my father died, his entire estate consisted of books: thousands and thousands of books. On a rainy Sunday afternoon my sister and I divided them up. Half of them sit in my house now, and my son, who is sixteen, reads them. I don't think my son has ever held a baseball in his hand, but he reads books with a passion and voracity that is astonishing. "I want," he told me, "to read every book ever written."

Besides the books, my father had bound all of the literary magazines that were being published in the twenties and thirties: *Dial, Poetry, Hound and Horn, Pagany, Exile, Quarterly* and *Transition*, to mention just a few. When my son first discovered them in dusty cartons, he acted a little bit like a young man in love. A few days later, he came to me with a copy of a 1928 issue of *Dial*. "Look what I found," he said. In the middle of the magazine, in a William Carlos Williams poem, was a yellowed piece of paper folded over twice. It was an eight-line poem of my father's, written in Yiddish. I don't know why it was there.

"What is it?" my son asked.

"It's your legacy," I answered.

nominated by The Kenyon Review

IN A POLISH HOME FOR THE AGED (CHICAGO, 1983)

by EDWARD HIRSCH

from GRAND STREET

It's sweet to lie awake in the early morning
Remembering the sound of five huge bells
Ringing in the village at dawn, the iron
Notes turning to music in the pink clouds.

It's nice to remember the flavor of groats
Mixed with horse's blood, the sour tang
Of unripe peppers, the smell of garlic
Growing wildly in Aunt Stefania's garden.

I can remember my grandmother's odd claim
That her younger brother was a mule
Pulling an ox-cart across a lapsed meadow
In the first thin light of a summer morning;

Her cousin, Irka, was a poorly-planted tree
Wrapping itself in a dress of white blossoms.
I could imagine an ox-cart covered with flowers,
The sound of laughter rising from damp branches.

178

Some nights I dream that I'm a child again
Flying through the barnyard at six a.m.:
My mother milks the cows in the warm barn
And thinks about her father, who died long ago,

And daydreams about my future in a large city.
I want to throw my arms around her neck
And touch the sweating blue pails of milk
And talk about my strange, childish nightmares.

God, you've got to see us to know how happy
We were then, two dark caresses of sunlight.
Now I wake up to the same four walls staring
At me blankly, and the same bare ceiling.

Somehow the morning starts over in the home:
Someone coughs in the hall; someone calls out
An unfamiliar name, a name I don't remember;
Someone slams a car door in the distance.

I touch my feet to the cold tile floor
And listen to my neighbor stirring in his room
And think about my mother's peculiar words
After my grandmother died during the war:

"One day the light will be as thick as a pail
Of fresh milk, but the pail will seem heavy.
You won't know if you can lift it anymore,
But lift it anyway. Drink the day slowly."

nominated by Michael Ryan, Sherod Santos and Maura Stanton

MORRO ROCK

by GARRETT KAORU HONGO

from FIELD

       —a Thirties blue fedora
slouching through thick China fog off the Pacific;
or, in the bright sun, the grey colt
romping in curls of surf, the wash
at its heels, foam breaking against the slate chest;
Duchamp-Villon's horse stolen from its museum
and spray-painted camouflage green,
sliding from the junker pickup
speeding along Highway One, bouncing from its crate
as it slams across asphalt and the gravel shoulder,
at rest, finally, in the cold sand,
nose awash in running tide,
some huge and abandoned engine
stripped from its hot car,
salvage in the sea's green oil,
churning still in the vicious pistons of surf.

I remember best stories in which it figures
as centerpiece or sublime backdrop:
the great albacore run of the Sixties,
men in fraying mackinaws stained with blood
crammed thick as D-Day on the decks
of an excursion or half-day boat
chugging slowly through light fog,
slicks belowdecks, poles high-masted,
a small denuded forest on the sea's false winter,

180

maybe a thousand fish iced in the hold,
the coast in sight, harbor invisible
except for the black bead of the Rock,
a notched landfall, eloquent on the horizon.

Or the time I played Weston with it,
forcing my father to drive north one day,
up the coast through patchy fog to the Bay.
We stopped at an overlook
snarling with brush and bunches of iceplant,
and he chose the shot, setting the tripod,
while I fiddled with filmpacks
and tested the cloth shutter in the car.
We waited an hour for the fog to be right—
the Rock emerging from it, finally,
a black clipper from the sea.

And I knew a girl once
who lived near there,
and whom I'd visit,
hitching north, needing her still.
She was the first I'd known
who could sit, oblivious,
still in her long shift,
pull both knees to her arms,
and rock gently in the sand
while a thin film of sea washed around her.
I'd stand barefoot in the foam
while the ocean percolated around us,
and toss wet handfulls of sand
towards the combers, empty of feeling.
The Rock filled the space behind us.

Sometimes though,
it's successful lovers I recall,
the battered myth of my teens,
a cheap tale told over bonfires
snapping with kelp and whistling driftwood.
They were young too,
or old beyond counting,

181

a bachelor Abraham and maidenly Sarah
working their poor farms
on opposite ends of the cove.
They saw each other Sundays at church,
sold raffle tickets and donated specialties
to the annual charity auction—
he volunteered lessons in pier fishing,
she, a picnic lunch in the park by the dunes.
Shyly at first, then with humor and verve,
they bid for each other, waving off competitors.
There was a season of courtship—
football games, holiday dinners together,
a New Year's Eve with foreign champagne
and Glenn Miller records on the hi-fi.
By the next spring, they were making love,
discreetly at first, then, finding the gods
in each other, fierce as teenagers
parked by the Rock, they'd kiss openly,
sprawl over each other on blankets at the Esplanade,
ignoring first the whispers, then the minister's call
and letters of petition from the neighbors.
Before the police could come,
after indecent afternoons under the pier,
riders in pickups came,
hooded like hanged men or cowled in ski masks.
There were women too, undisguised
in their housedresses but keening in the night
as they assembled, crowlike, by the farmshack.
No gunfire, the lovers were killed with stones,
with the snapped limbs of beach oak
and a quick, purging fire of hate.

Before death, smeared with bruises
and the beach tar and twigs of ritual,
the couple spoke through their wounds
and fear of death, mumbling an exchange
of pledges and a curse for the Bay.
The following day, the charcoaled pillars
and collapsed floor still hissing,
a pair of cranes landed, loonlike,

from the overcast, snow-flurried skies.
A runaway chill spreading south from the Sierras
had brought them, and the steaming ruins
made their haven from the cold.
They danced a curious rite of celebration,
blue and grey-tipped wings furling,
red dandelion crests erect,
lifting from ground to air like curling smoke,
until, finally, by early evening,
they drifted downwind past the town
and landed cloudlike, small white floats,
plumed gardenias on the Rock's dark brow.

Love is always violent *and* sacred, and though death
might be peace, dying often seems love's own act,
a strong taking and the murder of reason.

All is true, a story sanded by several tellings
until it shines, jewel in the soft fingers of tide,
the constellated image high in its heaven of likenesses.

It doesn't matter how I think of it,
it continues to define itself,
this chunk of continent equal to nothing.

nominated by Field, *Stuart Dybek, Sherod Santos,*
Elizabeth Spires and Vern Rutsala

DELFINA FLORES AND HER NIECE MODESTA

by HERBERT MORRIS

from SHENANDOAH

Delfina Flores, named for flowers, poses
through the afternoon with the child, Modesta,
named for modesty, squirming in her lap.
Why the painter should want them to pose for him
eludes her, will, it seems, always elude her,
but she will not dwell too long on that aspect.
She does what she is told now, will attempt to
have the child do the same, or very nearly.
Santiago is beautiful, she thinks.
It is he she would paint, if she could paint,
his face and body, if she were a painter
and knew where to make a mark on the canvas,
where, in that field of absence, to begin.

How could anyone think her more than plain?,
she wonders, with these braids (too coarse, too black),
a nose and mouth not small or fine, a look
with too much of the Indian, perhaps
and little enough of the Mexican.
The child, she thinks, is worthy of a portrait,
will be a beauty when she is fourteen.
With those eyes, with such dainty hands and feet
(Señor Rivera asked that they sit shoeless;

184

dressed in their Sunday church frocks, it seemed fitting
that they wear shoes, as well, but he assured them
his instincts could be trusted in such matters),
she will have any young man that she chooses.
Tía Dolores sewed these blouses for them,
hers and the child's, awoke, these last two mornings,
long before dawn, to baste the final stitches,
the appliqué embroidered at the neckline,
and have them done by the time they would sit.
Let the painter see you both at your best,
she told Delfina Flores; we must show him
those who have little still retain their pride.
It is an honor that this man, Rivera,
has you to sit for him and paints your portrait.
You will become, if you are not already,
the envy of the young girls of this village.

She thinks she would prefer, given the choice,
that Santiago, once, tell her he loves her
to the honor the sitting represents.
Santiago has never told her that,
though he has told her other things, things young men
always, so she has heard, tell those they court,
or hope to court, or dream one day of courting.
Wait, Modesta, wait for a boy to want you
who never brings himself to say he loves you.
But I expect you will know nothing of that;
with such fine hair, and with those hands and feet
as delicate as flowers, what young man
will not feel love for you, when it is time,
will not need to tell you of it himself,
the pain is so intense, so overwhelming.
Be still, Modesta; in this straight-back chair
he has posed us in, how do you expect me
to hold you in my arms if you keep twisting?
It cannot be much longer; we have been here
all afternoon, the sun has set, and Señor
Rivera seems himself ready to quit—
see the sweat on his forehead, see him squint,
see how he rubs his fingers? If, tomorrow,

185

you behave for the length of the whole sitting,
I will give you a toffee, cinnamon,
your favorite, or almond. Would you like that?
Tía Dolores made these blouses for us;
try not to wrinkle yours. Señor Rivera
says this picture he paints will be a mirror
where we will see our images exactly,
even these cross-stitches Tía Dolores
embroidered here in front, wanting to please us.

Here, take my chain and locket. See the light
catch in the links? See the medallion spinning
in the wind when I breathe on it, like this?
That's Our Lady of Guadeloupe, remember?,
Our Lady of the Sorrows. Every Sunday
the candle which we light we light for her.
We leave it at her feet so that she knows
we have been there and we have not forgotten.
You'll show your nieces how, when it is time;
you'll tell them not to lean into the flame
when you stand at the altar, as I tell you;
you'll hold their hand, as I hold yours, you'll touch
your candle to their candle, as I do;
you'll teach them what the words are, what they mean;
you'll sew their blouses, as our aunts sew ours.
When I was nine I asked Tía Dolores
what sorrow is, or what the sorrows are.
She took a long, deep breath before she spoke
and, when the words came, they came with such passion,
such heat, I looked to see whether her teeth
had split beneath the hammer of her answer:
Another name for Mexico, she whispered.
It seemed she'd always known how she'd respond,
known precisely what she would say, if asked,
and had been waiting only to be asked.

It may be best not to expect too much,
Tía Dolores tells me in the evening,
when she brushes my hair, or mends my skirt.
It is better not to be disappointed.

186

When I speak to her about Santiago,
what I feel for him, what I wish he felt,
she says it may be unwise to entrust
hope for one's future to another person.
God and the earth are all one can depend on,
and not always even the earth, she says.
I know how hard it is, and has been, for her;
yet, when the time comes that you understand
such things, little Modesta, when, at evening,
I let down your black hair, undo the braids,
begin slowly to brush it, I could never
bring myself to tell you what she tells me.
(Love, I might tell you, if you can; if not,
if, for some reason, feeling is closed to you,
hope in time your life opens you to that,
hope one day for the courage necessary).

Señor Rivera has, in fact, grown weary.
The light begins to go and the wrists ache.
It may be the heat or a combination
of factors: heat, exhaustion, the toll beauty
exacts of vision, darkness slowly falling.
It may be time to stop now, to resume
tomorrow, should the family agree.
The older child (fourteen?), Delfina Flores,
has a look which wholly intrigues him, not quite
Mexican and yet not quite Indian;
Oriental, perhaps, chiseled from marble,
some great, dark marble, veined and streaked with light.
Part of her beauty, too, he thinks, must be
that she does not know she is beautiful,
thinks the reverse, in fact, and so her features
have not had time to recognize themselves,
to settle into mere self-satisfaction.
Her niece, Modesta, is, like any child
her age, two, he would guess, possibly three,
available to what the future stamps
across her face, available, no more.
All of it, all, remains to be decided
and, though conclusions are impossible

at this point, one at least can say the makings
of a woman of splendor (hands, feet, eyes)
are already in evidence, it seems.
Nothing more can be said of her than that.

Delfina Flores is another matter.
What she might have become she has become.
Her years already tell us who she is.
Nothing remains to be decided, nothing.
Oh, there will be a wedding one day, children
of her own, hair to brush at evening, births
and deaths, the rituals, time passing, nights,
labor in sun-bleached fields, but the essentials,
that on which it all lies, stands now in place.
Looking into her face, he thinks, is like
looking, for the first time, at Mexico
directly, all at once, face to full light.
Though the artist is not quite brash enough
to make such claims, he would not be displeased
if the viewer, seeing the finished portrait,
Delfina Flores and Her Niece Modesta,
might be moved to cry out one word, just one,
standing before it, one word: Mexico!,
Mexico!, with that sense of recognition
overtaking us when we know the name
of something but not how we come to know it.

The girl, Delfina Flores, at the outset
confided to him her uncertainty,
if she were painting pictures, where to start,
where, in that "field of absence", to begin,
to make one's presence known, and with what stroke.
Though, each day, he confronts the canvas, he knows
no more about the process than Delfina.
Some mornings, entering the studio,
he will not know what first move he might make
(and he thinks it shall all lie with first moves);
the canvas on the easel will assail him
with the burden of emptiness it bears,
with the depth of the silences it shrieks with,

the possibilities it opens to,
could open to, given the gift, luck, or technique
that knows what can be done with emptiness,
that understands what can be worked with silence.
Then, too, one's subject rises, if it rises,
to meet you, singles you as its accomplice,
leaps out at you, seems to insist, *insist*,
everything must be laid aside for this,
implying that this moment, this grand courtship,
if you will, this romance, this pure seduction
of painter by his subject, at first sight,
presents itself, and this intensely, once.
Returning "later" will, of course, be futile.
"Tomorrow", in this case, is unavailing.
You have only to be accessible,
now, at this moment, here, rapt, undivided,
only to learn to resist not at all,
should the moment be at hand and resistance
seems to you the most logical defense
by one who stands there silent, overwhelmed,
besieged, so taken by surprise, so taken
off guard, late, unprepared, now touched beyond
any formerly adequate, if useless,
definition of touched, made obsolete
by these two girls who, Mexican and shoeless,
sit in a straight-back chair where he has placed them,
faces to light, to what remains of light,
patient, obedient, doing as asked,
like Mexico itself ready to please
(how many hours have they been sitting?; evening
already moves down from the hills, the stars rise,
the dogs begin their barking, the wrists ache),
the one whom someone thought to name for flowers,
whom Santiago will not tell he loves
(Santiago of the dark brows and head,
whose darkness she would paint, if she could paint,
bending shirtless in fields beneath those suns
too punishing not to be Mexican),
thinking all afternoon of games, distractions,
both for herself and for her niece, Modesta

(chain and medallion, riddles, revelations
wholly lost on the child, all in a Spanish
equal to music as she hums it, croons it,
the Spanish one is born to and will die with),
so that the child be still, not lose the look
Señor Rivera claims to want, or finds,
or holds to through the afternoon; the other,
the one who has been named for modesty,
delicate even to her feet and hands,
a beauty in the making, for the moment
fascinated by the tears of Our Lady
of the Sorrows (gold leaf staining tin cheeks),
enchanted by the spinning of that figure
dangling before her from thin, beaten links,
turning slowly, slowly now, in the wind
Tía Delfina, out of tenderness,
has devised for her, turning in a way
not unlike the way the continent turns
beneath them, as they sit there (all of it,
forest, lagoon, swamp, cordillera, salt flat,
pasture, scrub, mesa), turning in the only
direction it can turn, downward to evening,
the mountains plunging fiercely to the sea
and the sea slipping underneath the mountains
where the darkness accumulates, or blindness,
or the thing, not yet named, Tía Dolores
calls Mexico, our Mexico, our sorrow.

nominated by Shenandoah

DON'T GO TO THE BARN

by TOM SLEIGH

from ANTAEUS

for Rosamund Sleigh

The brick of the asylum shimmered in the sun
As I watched the black hood of your depression
Lower down across your face immobile
But for the eyes staring off into the crystal

Blue bracing the scorched mountain.
Fire like a razor had swept the rock face clean. . . .
Cut off from your despair, I stared across the lawn
To your drug-blinkered gaze staring down

The shivering, flashing eyes of the aspen:
Blinking back that glare, I saw your heart eaten
By the gloom of the weather-warped barn
Off behind the orchard alleys convulsing

Into bloom, saw you walk into the shudder
Of blossoms rippling down in spasms
Of cool wind, the weeds you tread under
Springing back bristling, the tough, fibrous green

Closing in behind you, the chill brushings
Of the leaves feathering dew across your skin.
The barn like a grey flame burns above the bloom,
The hoof-cratered mud, glistening in the sun,

Squelching as you slog across the yard.
And now you enter into the raftered
Damp of lofty spaces cut by the veer
And slice of scaly wings, knot the knot hard,

Loop the rope around the beam, the zero
Of the noose dangling down: Your gaze swings
To mine, and I see your chances narrow:
Sprawled on the table, the volts axing

Through your skull, you jerk and shake,
Your body drugged to flab trembling and trembling,
Your teeth clenching jolt after jolt until crackling
In your brain a voice of fire speaks,

Divinely disapproving: "Don't go to the barn
And try to hang yourself. Don't go to the barn
And try to hang yourself. Don't go to the barn
And try to hang yourself. Rose, don't go to the barn."

nominated by Cleopatra Mathis, Sandra McPherson, and David St. John

THE ISLAND OF VEN

fiction by GINA BERRIAULT

from PLOUGHSHARES

"ELLIE, LISTEN TO THIS: *In the evening after sunset, when according to my habit I was contemplating the stars in a clear sky, I noticed that a new and unusual star, surpassing all others in brilliancy, was shining almost directly above my head, and since I had, almost from boyhood, known all the stars in the heavens perfectly, it was quite evident to me that there had never before been any star in that place in the sky. I was so astonished at this sight that I was not ashamed to doubt the trustworthiness of my own eyes. A miracle indeed!* Ellie, you know what it was? A colossal stellar explosion, a supernova. But back then they thought the heavens were changeless, and so there's young Brahe gazing up at the new star one calm evening and he figures it's a miracle. No telescopes yet and he didn't need one. Even when the sun came up he could see it."

Noel read quietly, a lodger respectful of the hour of midnight in this foreign city and of the little family who had rented out a room on this night of the tourist season when all hotels were filled and who were asleep somewhere in the dark apartment. Like a tour guide whose memory isn't equal to the task and who reads over salient points each night before sleep, he was sitting up in bed, reading from the concise but colorful book on early European astronomers. A tour guide, but hers alone.

The beds were single, and he had pushed them together so he could take her in his arms and comfort her in the night, though she never asked for comforting. She lay with her hands under her cheek, palms together, watching his profile and loving him almost

193

reverently, yet at an errant distance from him, as if she loved him only in memory; and at a distance from their son beyond the actual miles, wherever he was on his own journey; and at the farthest distance from their daughter, *Nana*, a distance never to be comprehended, even as the child's sixteen years of life had become only a mystification of the mother.

"Listen, sounds like he went around the bend: *The star was at first like Venus and Jupiter, giving pleasing effects, but as it then became like Mars, there will next come a period of wars, seditions, captivity and death of princes, and destruction of cities, together with dryness and fiery meteors in the air, pestilence and venomous snakes. Lastly, the star became like Saturn, and there will finally come a time of want, death, imprisonment and all sorts of sad things.* Sounds like he freaked out. Imagine Einstein writing that in his journal?"

She saw him as he must have been when he was a boy—six, seven—adjusting the telescope an uncle had given him, bringing a star down close to his backyard for the first time, convinced then, he had told her, that the silvery music of crickets all around in the summer night was really the sound the stars were making. On so many nights of their years together, when he sat late over his work and she heard him go out into the garden to gaze at the stars, she wondered if he were seeing all things again as indivisible, or trying to, or not trying. The measuring of vast distances, incredible velocities—it was this that enthralled him. At parties, when the other guests wandered out into a patio, a garden, lifting their faces to a placid moon, he would gently remind them of something they may have neglected to remember, that those far lights and all the galaxies were racing away from the earth and from one another. *The farther the distance from us, the faster they're leaving us behind. Imagine four hundred million miles an hour?* And they would smile obligingly as over a joke on them all.

His face was softened by the lamplight, and she saw again how Nana had resembled him, and felt again the same mute alarm that, back home, drew her up from the bed in the middle of the night, alone as if she had no husband, nor ever had children, nor even parents to begin. She closed her eyes. This journey was his offering of love, a ritual of healing. By visiting together the places where the early astronomers had lived, the narrow Golden Street in Prague where they had strolled, a castle in Italy from where one had viewed the heavens, he hoped to humanize them for her.

194

They, too, had suffered afflictions of the soul, yet despite their earthly trials they had never turned their eyes away from all that marvelous beckoning up there.

The lamp was switched off. Darkness now in this room in a stranger's house. This night and one more night when they returned from their day's trip to the Island. Noel bent over her and kissed her face imperceptibly as you kiss a sleeping person lost in the self. She said "I'm awake" and he took her in his arms. A street of trees. Branches stirred close to the small, high window, and distant sounds from the Tivoli Gardens—fireworks and music—trembled against the glass. She lay very still. Any movement, no matter how small, might wake the little family like incoherent words spoken out from her sleep.

By boat from Copenhagen to the town of Landskrona on the Swedish Coast. Old brick buildings with corby steps, factories blowing out sulphurous smoke. And now by a tough little boat, its yellow smokestack the only touch of color on the heavy gray Baltic Sea or a slender finger of that sea but so wide both shores were lost to view. A sea she had never thought about or ever wished to cross. They had climbed up from the hold to stand on deck. She had felt confined, deprived of the sight of the wind-driven swells the boat was striking against. The other passengers, Swedes, Danes, seemed content down there on hard benches in company of their bicycles and cases of beer and fruit. Like a compliant patient wanting to believe in a cure, she kept her gaze straight ahead to see the island the moment it came in sight. She must have glanced away. The island had risen the moment her head was turned.

The iron, stark look of it gave her an imagined view of immense rocks under the water. An island so precariously small, leveled down eons ago by fierce winds and sweeping torrents and monstrous waves, until water and wind calmed down and lay back. The inhabitants now, how did they feel about it? Stay calm. They must tell themselves to stay calm, and if the waters begin to rise again and the winds to stir again, some exquisite instrument, designed by a mind like Noel's, will detect the slightest threat in the depths of the sea, in the atmosphere, and everyone will be warned in ample time to hop onto their bicycles and peddle away to the nearest church, which, since it was four, five hundred years old, was to last forever.

A harbor town for those who trusted in fair weather always.

Houses, gardens, low fences, trees, all on the very edge of deep gray water, little sailboats pleasantly rocking as if upon a transparent azure sea. The boat was moored, the passengers walked their bicycles up the rise and rode off past an approaching wagon drawn by two tawny horses and followed by two men walking leisurely. The horses stopped, the passengers climbed down. Except a little boy and his mother, the boy asleep on the blue wooden bench, his head in his mother's lap. The visor of his cap was tipped back, baring his face to the sky. Tiny purple flowers clung to the edge of his jacket pocket. The boy opened his eyes and, surprised by the sky, closed them again, and Ellie, watching, pictured his face growing older, his eyes less surprised day by day, night by night. Carefully the mother and child climbed down.

"Tycho Brahe's museum?" Noel's voice always sharply friendly in a foreign land. The driver, up on his high seat, appeared to nod.

The wagon joggled along the road that must be in the very center of the island, like a spine, and Noel sat very erect. The pale sun was turning his light hair to silver, a swift aging he didn't know about. Some of the gray of the sea was taken up and spread in a high, flat film over the sky, and the shadow of it, or the reflection, crept over the land, over the fields the tawny color of the horses and over the green meadows and the black cattle and over the thatched roofs of barns and cottages. Roofs thick as those in pictures she had painted for a children's book. Nana in her small chair by her mother's chair had watched everything come to life, sooner for her than for all the other children in the world: Squat cottages under an indigo sky dotted with white stars, and in the nightgreen stalks of grass, a cricket. Unlike those cozy roofs, unlike that painting years ago, these thatched roofs they were passing could be overrun by rivers of fire.

The horses were halted, the driver waited for somebody to climb down. Nobody did. "Tycho Brahe," he said to the air.

Noel leaped down, helped her down, and the horses clopped on. No bicycle, no wagon appeared along the road from either horizon. The silence must be the presence of the sea, unseen but all around, a silence not to be trusted. Across the road—a Turistgarden, deserted, white slat tables and chairs under trees, and far back a yellow-brick hotel strung with colored lightbulbs. On their side of the road—a church, red-brick with slate roof, pink roses in the yard; the Tycho Brahe Museet, closed, so small it must contain only a few precious books, a few drawings. Far back, a row of giant mulberry trees, and by the trees a tall stone statue. The Astronomer.

"It's him!"

Noel hurried toward it, as if the statue were the man himself about to flee, and, following, she found him roaming around the statue, gazing up with scholarly respect, gazing down at the indecipherable inscription carved along the sides of the base. Twice as tall as any man on earth, the astronomer wore a cloak that hung down to the soles of his boots, knickers of many stony folds, a ruff around his neck. His head thrown back, he scanned the heavens, his goatee pointing at the great shallow bowl of earth where his observatory had stood. Out in the fields behind him a farmer was burning chaff and the smoke passed close to the ground, a long, long, ribbon, and farther away a tractor started up and a rabbit bounded along before it. A lone seagull was soaring high over all, just under the layer of gray clouds.

They stepped down the slope of the wide grassy bowl, so shallow it was almost imperceivable, and stood within the lost observatory, within the Castle of the Heavens, as fancifully, as airily beautiful as castles that are only imagined. Every stone gone, carted away by the peasants, and all its coveted carvings taken away by a king's mistress to decorate her own small castle. Nothing left, and where the foundation had been now filled with five centuries of earth. A toad at their feet stayed where it was, unafraid of large, slow animals. Up there at the top of his castle in the night, how did the astronomer look to a boy straining his neck to see from the highest branch? Was he plotting an invasion of the heavens? Was he a nocturnal predator on the trail of a celestial creature? The peasants must have lain awake, afraid that each night was the night the avenging angels would swoop down to destroy the island in an unearthly fire.

"Ellie, are you hungry? Are you thirsty?"

They sat down by the road, and Noel brought up from his knapsack a bottle of mineral water, raisins, cheese, sweet crackers.

"If you eat this raisin, all my wishes will come true." He kissed her temple.

She took the raisin on her lip, swallowed it. All his wishes, she knew, were for her recovery, and hers were not. The tricks, the jokes, the conundrums—he hoped to take them back to that

197

spirited time at the beginning of their future together, a young couple again, picnicking on the spot from where a universe had flowered.

Along the road now in search of the astronomer's underground observatory, Noel consulting a map given him by the tourist office in Copenhagen. His light boots stirred up puffs of dust, her sandals stirred up none. She had got so thin, her legs, though bare and tan, were a warning to her. The winds—Noel was saying—buffeted the castle, interfering with the precision of observations, and so the astronomer had taken his instruments underground. What did they think *then*? she wondered. Up so high and then so deep? What did they think when they saw him walking along this same road at night, wrapped in his cloak, his gleamy, gloomy eyes always upward, at his side a servant with a lantern, cautioning him about his step. That he was hiding from the wrath of God? That everyone else would perish? That when he poked his silver nose out from his underground refuge, the silver nose affixed with wax to replace his own lost in a duel, it would not melt, it would only turn gold, reflecting that unearthly fire.

By the side of the road, a girl and two boys were running about within a fantasy place no larger than their own yard. Strange copper shapes rose up from a carpet of short dry grass. Geometrical shapes, like a dome, a tent, a cone. The little girl slid down the slanting copper roof of the closed-up entrance, like the entrance to a cellar, and the boys followed, all shouting dares, their voices ringing back on the still air to the church and the mulberry trees. Skylights—they were the astronomer's skylights that segment by segment were opened to the night's panorama. Scales of green-blue patina covered them, and hinges hung loose.

"Come look."

Noel opened a section of the dome, and the children came up beside them, the little girl pressing close to her. Almost twelve feet down to rocks and bottles, earth and rainwater. While Noel and the children looked down into the lost interior, waiting for something to come into view, while the children shuffled their black leather sabots and a rooster crowed close by, she gazed down at the girl's blond hair—how silky, how shiningly new under the sun. The little girl was the first to laugh, a mocking titter, and the boys took it up, roughly. They already knew there was nothing down there.

Out on the sea again, the waters darker, films of rain in the distance, the harbor shrinking, its cottages, low walls, trees, masts, all sliding under the sea. It was night when the boat slowed into the harbor at Landskrona. From far in the heavy dusk, she had mistaken the trees of the town for piles of iron ore or coal. They sat in the dimly-lit small waiting station, on a bench against the wall, until yellow lights, white lights moved through the murky night with the hushing presence of a large boat bound for Copenhagen.

Noel led her down into the salon, into the rousing noise of drinkers at every table and the portable organ's music, pounded out by a young man in suit and tie. Glasses everywhere on red tablecloths, gliding on spilled beer. An elderly woman danced alone among the few dancing couples, eyes closed, the flesh of her lifted arms swaying. Next to Ellie at the table, a handsome old man in a dark suit. Noel, leaning across her, asked him where the boat was from. An excursion boat, leaving Copenhagen in the morning and returning at night—and the whole day's pleasure was evident on his rosy face, a look that might have been there the first day of his life.

"American?"

"Yes," said Noel.

"Did you come by flying machine?"

Ellie nodded, looking into his face, seeing a boy out in the night, his eyes lifted to a moving light lower than the stars, an amazing machine that flew and filled the dome of the sky with an echoing roar. As much of a miracle, as much of a portent as Brahe's star.

"We went to Tycho Brahe's island," she said.

"Ah. A tourist garden is there. My sister was there for the honeymoon."

"One night," she said, "he saw an immense star that wasn't there before. He said it meant the death of princes, all sorts of sad things. He believed our destiny is in the stars. Yourself, do you believe that?"

She could see he was amused by her. He must hear this kind of talk from strangers in taverns, fellow passengers on excursion boats out for a day of revelry, their need to be intimately serious rising fast like the foam on their beers.

"Ah yes." Agreeable. A kind man, strongly old, how many faces had he gazed into as he was gazing into hers? Beloved faces, the others, each one gone while he lived on and on. A time to be born and a time to die. It was the only way to accept their going, the only way to ease the alarm.

Spaced green lights in the night, out there: the shore of somewhere moving slowly past. In the taxi to their tranquil street of trees, Noel was silent, wondering, she knew, if she had gone over the edge, if she had given up her mind to the astronomer's supersititious one. A lamp was on in the hall, for them. The little family was asleep.

When he lay down on his separate bed he leaned over her and brushed the wisps of hair from her brow, hoping, she knew, to clear her mind by clearing her brow. She lifted her arms and brought his head down upon her breasts, an embrace alive again, and, holding him, a picture of the astronomer composed itself for her mind's eye, for her hand someday. Out in his garden, the young Brahe, his face lifted to that strange brilliance, to that inescapable portent, its reflection floating in his eyes and in the gems on his plump fingers and on every leaf turned toward the heavens and in the dark waters of the fountain.

nominated by Ploughshares,
Andre Dubus, and Joyce Carol Oates

LEVIATHAN

fiction by TOBIAS WOLFF

from TRIQUARTERLY

On her thirtieth birthday Ted threw a surprise party for Helen. It was a small party—Mitch and Bliss were the only guests. They'd chipped in with Ted and bought Helen two grams of white-out blizzard that lasted the whole night and on into the next morning. When it got light enough everyone went for a swim in the courtyard pool. Then Ted took Mitch up to the sauna on the fifth floor while Helen and Bliss put together a monster omelet.

"So how does it feel," Bliss asked, "being thirty?" The ash fell off her cigarette into the eggs. She stared at the ash for a moment, then stirred it in. "Mitch had his fortieth last month and totally freaked. He did so much Maalox he started to taste like chalk. I thought he was going to start freebasing it or something."

"Mitch is *forty?*" Helen said.

Bliss looked over at her. "That's classified information, O.K.?"

Helen shook her head. "Incredible. He looks about thirty-five, maybe twenty-seven at the absolute most." She watched Bliss crumble bacon into the bowl. "Oh God," she said, "I don't believe it. He had a face-lift."

Bliss closed her eyes and leaned against the counter. "I shouldn't have told you. Please don't say anything," she murmured hopelessly.

When Mitch and Ted came back from the sauna they all had another toot, and Ted gave Helen the mirror to lick. He said he'd never seen two grams disappear so fast. Afterwards Helen served up the omelet while Ted tried to find something on the TV. He kept flipping the dial until it drove everyone crazy, looking for

201

Roadrunner cartoons, then he gave up and tuned in on the last part of a movie about the Bataan Death March. They didn't watch it for very long though because Bliss started to cry. Ted switched over to an inspirational program but Bliss kept crying and began to hyperventilate. "Come on, everyone," said Mitch. "Love circle." Ted and Mitch went over to Bliss and put their arms around her while Helen watched them from the sofa, sipping espresso from a cup as blue and dainty as a robin's egg—the last of a set her grandmother had brought from the old country. Helen would have hugged Bliss too but there wasn't really any point; Bliss pulled this stunt almost every time she got herself a noseful, and it just had to run its course.

When Helen finished her espresso she gathered the plates and carried them out to the kitchen. She scattered leftover toast into the courtyard below, and watched the squirrels carry it away as she scoured the dishes and listened to the proceedings in the next room. This time it was Ted who talked Bliss down. "You're beautiful," he kept telling her. It was the same thing he always said to Helen when she felt depressed, and she was beginning to feel depressed right now.

I need more fuel, Helen thought. She ducked into the bedroom and did a couple of lines from Ted's private stash, which she had discovered while searching for matches in the closet. Afterwards she looked at herself in the mirror. Her eyes were bright. They seemed lit from within and that was how Helen felt, as if there were a column of cool white light pouring from her head to her feet like a waterfall. She put on a pair of sunglasses so nobody would notice and went back to the kitchen.

Mitch was standing at the counter, rolling a bone. "How's the birthday girl?" he asked without looking up.

"Ready for the next one," Helen said. "How about you?"

"Hey, bring it on," Mitch answered.

Helen smiled at him. At that moment she came close to letting him know she knew, but she held back. Mitch was good people and so was Bliss when you could get her off the subject of Mary Kay. Helen didn't want to make trouble between them. All the same, Helen knew that someday she wasn't going to be able to stop herself from giving Mitch the business. It just had to happen. And Helen knew that Bliss knew. But she hadn't done it this morning and she felt good about that.

Mitch held up the joint. "Taste?"

Helen shook her head. She glanced over her shoulder toward the living room. "What's the story on Bliss?" she asked. "All bummed out over World War II? Ted should have known that movie would set her off."

Mitch picked a sliver of weed from his lower lip. "Her ex is threatening to move back to Boston. Which means she won't get to see her kids except during summer, and that's only if we can put together the scratch to fly them here and back. It's tough. Really tough."

"I guess," Helen said. She dried her hands and hung the towel on the refrigerator door. "Still, Bliss should have thought about that when she took a walk on them, right?"

Mitch turned and started out of the kitchen.

"Sorry," Helen called after him. "I wasn't thinking."

"Yes you were," Mitch said, and left her there.

Oh, hell, she thought. She decided she needed another line but made no move to get it. Helen stood where she was, looking down at the pool through the window above the sink. The manager's afghan dog was lapping water from the shallow end, legs braced in the trough that ran around the pool. The two British Air stewards from down the hall were bathing their white bodies in the morning sunshine, both wearing blue swimsuits. The redheaded girl from upstairs was floating on an air mattress. Helen could see the long shadow of the air mattress glide along the bottom of the pool like something stalking her.

Helen heard Ted say, "Jesus, Bliss, I can understand that. Everybody has those feelings. You can't always beat them down." Bliss answered him in a voice so soft that Helen gave up trying to hear; it was hardly more than a sigh. She poured herself a glass of Chablis and joined the others in the living room. They were all sitting cross-legged on the floor. Helen caught Mitch's eye and mouthed the word *Sorry*. He stared at her, then nodded.

"I've done worse things than that," Ted was saying, "I'll bet Mitch has, too."

"Plenty worse," Mitch said.

"Worse than what?" Helen asked.

"It's awful." Bliss looked down at her hands. "I'd be embarrassed to tell you." She was all cried out now, Helen could see that. Her eyes were heavy-lidded and serene, her cheeks flushed, and a little smile played over her swollen lips.

"It couldn't be that bad," Helen said.

Ted leaned forward. He still had on the bathrobe he'd worn to the sauna and it fell open almost to his waist, as Helen knew he intended it to do. His chest was hard-looking from the Nautilus machine in the basement, and dark from their trip to Mazatlán. Helen had to admit it, he looked great. She didn't understand why he had to be so obvious and crass, but he got what he wanted: she looked at him and so did Bliss.

"Bliss, it *isn't* that bad," Ted went on. "It's just one of those things." He turned to Helen. "Bliss' little girl came down with tonsillitis last month and Bliss never got it together to go see her in the hospital."

"I can't deal with hospitals," Bliss said. "The minute I set foot inside of one my stomach starts doing flips. But still. When I think of her all alone in there."

Mitch took Bliss' hands in his and looked right at her until she met his gaze. "It's over," he said. "The operation's over and Lisa's out of the hospital and she's all right. Say it, Bliss. *She's all right.*"

"She's all right," Bliss said.

"Again."

"She's all right," Bliss repeated.

"O.K. Now believe it." Mitch put her hands together and rubbed them gently between his palms. "We've built up this big myth about kids being helpless and vulnerable and so on because it makes us feel important. We think we're playing some heavy role just because we're parents. We don't give kids any credit at all. Kids are tough little monkeys. Kids are survivors."

Bliss smiled.

"But I don't know," Mitch said. He let go of Bliss' hands and leaned back. "What I said just then is probably complete bullshit. Everything I say these days sounds like bullshit."

"We've all done worse things," Ted told Bliss. He looked over at Helen. When Helen saw that he was waiting for her to agree with him she tried to think of something to say, but finally just nodded. Ted kept looking at her. "What have you got those things on for?" he asked.

"The light hurts my eyes."

"Then close the curtains." He reached across to Helen and lifted the sunglasses away from her face. "There," he said. He cupped her chin in one hand and with the other brushed her hair back from her forehead. "Isn't she something?"

"She'll do," Mitch said.

Ted stroked Helen's cheek with the back of his hand. "I'd kill for that face."

Bliss was studying Helen. "So lovely," she said in a solemn, wistful voice.

Helen laughed. She got up and drew the curtains shut. Little spangles of light glittered in the fabric. She moved across the dim room to the dining nook and brought back a candle from the table there. Ted lit the candle and for a few moments they silently watched the flame. Then, in a thoughtful tone that seemed part of the silence, Mitch began to speak.

"It's true that we've all done things we're ashamed of. I just wish I'd done more of them. I'm serious," he said when Ted laughed. "I wish I'd raised more hell and made more mistakes, real mistakes, where you actually do something wrong instead of just let yourself drift into things you don't like. Sometimes I look around and I think, *Hey—what happened?* No reflection on you," he said to Bliss.

She seemed puzzled.

"Forget it," Mitch told her. "All I'm saying is that looking out for the other fellow and being nice all the time is a bunch of crap."

"But you *are* nice," Bliss said.

Mitch nodded. "I know," he said bitterly. "I'm working on it. It gets you exactly nowhere."

"Amen," said Ted.

"Case in point," Mitch went on. "I used to paralegal with this guy in the city and he decided that he couldn't live without some girl he was seeing. So he told his wife and of course she threw him out. Then the girl changed her mind. She didn't even tell him why. We used to eat lunch together and he would give me the latest installment and I swear to God it was enough to break your heart. He wanted to get back together with his family but his wife couldn't make up her mind whether to take him. One minute she'd say yes, the next minute she'd say no. Meanwhile he was living in this ratbag on Post Street. All he had in there was lawn furniture. I don't know, I just felt sorry for him. So I told him he could move in with us until things got straightened out."

"I can feel this one coming," Helen said.

Mitch stared at the candle. "His name was Raphael. Like the

angel. He was creative and good-looking and there was a nice aura around him. I guess I wanted to be his friend. But he turned out to be completely bad news. In the nine months he stayed with us he never once washed a glass or emptied an ashtray. He ran up hundreds of dollars worth of calls on our phone bill and didn't pay for them. He wrecked my car. He stole things from me. He even put the moves on my wife."

"Classic," Helen said.

"You know what I did about it?" Mitch asked. "I'll tell you. Nothing. I never said a word to him about any of it. By the time he left, my wife couldn't stand the sight of me. Beginning of the end."

"What a depressing story," Helen said.

"I should have killed him," Mitch said. "I might have regretted it later on but at least I could say I *did* something."

"You're too sweet," Bliss told him.

"I know," Mitch said. "But I wish I had, anyway. Sometimes it's better to do something really horrendous than to let things slide."

Ted clapped his hands. "Hear, hear. You're on the right track, Mitch. All you need is a few pointers, and old Ted is just the man to give them to you. Because where horrendous is concerned I'm the expert. You might say that I'm the king of horrendous."

Helen held up her empty glass. "Anybody want anything?"

"Put on your crash helmets," Ted went on. "You are about to hear my absolute bottom-line confession. The Worst Story Ever Told."

"No thanks," said Helen.

He peered at her. "What do you mean, 'No thanks'? Who's asking permission?"

"I wouldn't mind hearing it," Mitch said.

"Well, I would." Helen stood and looked down at Ted. "It's my birthday party, remember? I just don't feel like sitting around and listening to you talk about what a crud you are. It's a downer."

"That's right," Bliss said. "Helen's the birthday girl. She gets to choose. Right, Ted?"

"I know what," Helen said. "Why don't you tell us something good you did? The thing you're most proud of."

Mitch burst out laughing. Ted grinned and punched him in the arm.

"I mean it," Helen said.

"Helen gets to choose," Bliss repeated. She patted the floor

206

beside her and Helen sat down again. "All right," Bliss said. "We're listening."

Ted looked from Bliss to Helen. "I'll do it if you will," he said. "But you have to go first."

"That's not fair," Helen said.

"Sounds fair to me," said Mitch. "It was your idea."

Bliss smiled at Helen. "This is fun."

Before Helen began, she sent Ted out to the kitchen for more wine. Mitch did some sit-ups to get his blood moving again. Bliss sat behind Helen and let down Helen's hair. "I could show you something for this dryness," she said. She combed Helen's hair with her fingers, then started to brush it, counting off the strokes in a breathy whisper until Ted came back with the jug.

They all had a drink.

"Ready and waiting," Ted told Helen. He lay back on the sofa and clasped his hands behind his head.

"One of my mother's friends had a boy with Down's syndrome," Helen began. "Actually, three or four of her friends had kids with problems like that. One of my aunts, too. They were all good Catholics and they didn't think anything about having babies right into their forties. This was before Vatican II and the pill and all that—before everything got watered down.

"Anyway, Tom wasn't really a boy. He was older than me by a couple of years, and a lot bigger. But he seemed like a boy—very sweet, very gentle, very happy."

Bliss stopped the brush in mid-stroke and said, "You're going to make me cry again."

"I used to take care of Tom sometimes when I was in high school. I was into a serious good-works routine back then. I wanted to be a saint: honestly, I really did. At night, before I went to sleep, I used to put my fingers under my chin like I was praying and smile in this really holy way that I practiced all the time in front of the mirror. Then if they found me dead in the morning they would think that I'd gone straight to heaven—that I was smiling at the angels coming to get me. At one point I even thought of becoming a nun."

Bliss laughed. "I can just see you in a habit—Sister Morphine. You'd have lasted about two hours."

Helen turned and looked at Bliss in a speculative way. "It's not something I expect you to understand," she said, "but if I had gone

207

in I would have stayed in. To me, a vow is a vow." She turned away again. "Like I said, I started out taking care of Tom as a kind of beatitude number, but after a while I got to look forward to it. Tom was fun to be with. And he really loved me. He even named one of his hamsters after me. We were both crazy about animals so we would usually go to the zoo, or I would take him to this stable out in Marin that had free riding lessons for special kids. That was what they called them, instead of handicapped or retarded—'special.' "

"Beautiful," Mitch said.

"Don't get too choked up," Helen told him. "The story isn't over yet." She took a sip of her wine. "So. After I started college I didn't get home all that much, but whenever I did I'd stop by and get Tom and we'd go somewhere. Over to the Cliff House to look at the sea lions, something like that. Then this one day I got a real brainstorm. I thought, Hey, why not go whale-watching? Tom had whale posters all over his bedroom but he'd never seen a real one, and neither had I. So I called up this outfit in Half Moon Bay and they said that it was getting toward the end of the season, but still worth a try. They were pretty sure we'd see something.

"Tom's mother wasn't too hot about the idea. She kept going on about the fact that he couldn't swim. But I brought her around, and the next morning Tom and I drove down and got on board the boat. It wasn't all that big. In fact it was a lot smaller than I thought it would be, and that made me a little nervous at first, but after we got under way I figured hell with it—they must know what they're doing. The boat rocked a little, but not dangerously. Tom loved it.

"We cruised around all morning and didn't see a thing. They would take us to different places and cut the engine and we would sit there, waiting for a whale to come along. It was nice out on the water. We were with a good bunch of people and one of them fixed up a sort of fishing line for Tom to hang over the side while we waited. I just leaned back and got some sun. Smelled the good smells. Watched the seagulls. After an hour or so they would start the engine up again and go somewhere else and do the same thing. This happened three or four times. Everybody was kidding the guide about it, threatening to make him walk the plank and so on. Then, right out of nowhere, this whale came up beside us.

"He was just suddenly *there*. All this water running off his back. This unbelievably rancid smell all around him. Covered with barnacles and shells and long strings of seaweed trailing off him.

Big. Maybe half again as long as the boat we were in." Helen shook her head. "You just can't imagine how big he was. He started making passes at the boat, and every time he did it we'd pitch and roll and take on about five hundred gallons of water. We were falling all over each other. At first everyone laughed and whooped it up but after a while it started to get heavy."

"He was probably playing with you," Mitch said.

"That's what the guide told us the first couple of times it happened. Then he got scared too. I mean he went white as a sheet. You could tell he didn't know what was happening any better than the rest of us did. We have this idea that whales are supposed to be more civilized than people, smarter and friendlier and more together. Cute, even. But it wasn't like that. It was hostile."

"You probably got a bad one," Mitch said. "It sounds like he was bent out of shape about something. Maybe the Russians harpooned his mate."

"He was a monster," Helen said. "I mean that. He was hostile and huge and he stank. He was hideous, too. There were so many shells and barnacles on him that you could hardly see his skin. It looked as if he had armor on. He scraped the boat a couple of times and it made the most terrible sound, like people moaning under water. He'd swim ahead a ways and go under and you'd think, 'Please God don't let him come back,' and then the water would start to churn alongside the boat and there he'd be again. It was just terrifying. I've never been so afraid in my life. And then Tom started to lose it."

Bliss put the brush on the floor. Helen could feel her stillness and hear the sound of her breathing.

"He started to make these little noises," Helen said. "I'd never heard him do that before. Little mewing noises. The strange thing was, I hadn't even thought of Tom up to then. I'd completely forgotten about him. So it gave me a shock when I realized that he was sitting right next to me, scared half to death. At first I thought, 'Oh no, what if he goes berserk!' He was so much bigger than me I wouldn't have been able to control him. Neither would anyone else. He was incredibly strong. If anyone had tried to hold him down he'd have thrown them off like a dog shakes off water. And then what?

"But the thing that worried me most was that Tom would get so confused and panicky that he'd jump overboard. In my mind I had a completely clear picture of him doing it."

"Me too," Mitch said. "I have the same picture. He did it, didn't he? He jumped in and you went after him and pulled him out."

Bliss said "Ssshhh. Just listen, O.K.?"

"He didn't jump," Helen said. "He didn't go berserk, either. Here we come to the point of the story—Helen's Finest Hour. How did I get started on this, anyway? It's disgusting."

The candle hissed and flared. The flame was burning in a pool of wax. Helen watched it flare up twice more, and then it died. The room went gray.

Bliss began to rub Helen's back. "Go on," she said.

"I just talked him down," Helen said. "You know, I put my arm around his shoulder and said, 'Hey, Tom, isn't this something! Look at that big old whale! Wow! Here he comes again, Tom, hold on!' And then I'd laugh like crazy. I made like I was having the time of my life, and Tom fell for it. He calmed right down. Pretty soon after that the whale took off and we went back to shore. I don't know why I brought it up. It was just that even though I felt really afraid, I went ahead and acted as if I was flying high. I guess that's the thing I'm most proud of."

Helen rose up on her knees and stretched. "This happened nine years ago," she added.

"Thank you, Helen," Mitch said. "Thank you for sharing that with us. I know I sound phony but I mean it."

"You don't talk about yourself enough," Bliss said. Then she called, "O.K., Ted—it's your turn."

Ted did not answer.

Bliss called his name again.

"I think he's asleep," Mitch said. He moved closer to the sofa and looked at Ted. He nodded. "Dead to the world."

"Asleep," Helen said. "Oh, God."

Bliss hugged Helen from behind. "Mitch, come here," she said. "Love circle."

Helen pulled away. "No," she said.

"Why don't we wake him up?" Mitch suggested.

"Forget it," Helen told him. "Once Ted goes under he stays under. Nothing can bring him up. Watch." She went to the sofa, raised her hand, and slapped Ted across the face.

He groaned softly and turned over.

"See?" Helen said.

"What a slug," Bliss said.

"Don't you dare call him names," Helen told her. "Not in front of me anyway. Ted is my husband. Forever and ever. I only did that to make a point."

Mitch said, "Helen, do you want to talk about this?"

"There's nothing to talk about," Helen answered. "I made my own bed." She hefted the jug of wine. "Who needs a refill?"

Mitch and Bliss looked at each other. "My energy level isn't too high," Bliss said.

Mitch nodded. "Mine's pretty low, too."

"Then we'll just have to bring it up," Helen said. She left the room and came back with three candles and a mirror. She screwed one of the candles into the holder and held a match to the wick. It sputtered, then caught. Helen felt the heat of the flame on her cheek. "There," she said, "that's more like it." Mitch and Bliss drew closer as Helen took a glass vial from her pocket and spilled the contents onto the mirror. She looked up at them and grinned.

"I don't believe this," Bliss said. "Where did you get it?"

Helen shrugged.

"That's a lot of toot," Mitch said.

"We'll just have to do our best," Helen said. "We've got all day."

Bliss looked at the mirror. "I really should go to work."

"Me too," Mitch said. He laughed, and Bliss laughed with him. They watched over Helen's shoulders as Helen bent down to sift the gleaming crystal. First she chopped it with a razor. Then she began to spread it out. Mitch and Bliss smiled up at her from the mirror, and Helen smiled back between them. Their faces were rosy with candlelight. They were the faces of three well-wishers, carolers, looking in at Helen through a window filling up with snow.

nominated by Sara Vogan

TODAY WILL BE A QUIET DAY

fiction by AMY HEMPEL

from THE MISSOURI REVIEW

"I THINK IT's the other way around," the boy said. "I think if the quake hit now the *bridge* would collapse and the *ramps* would be left."

He looked at his sister with satisfaction.

"You are just trying to scare your sister," the father said. "You know that is not true."

"No, really," the boy insisted, "and I heard birds in the middle of the night. Isn't that a warning?"

The girl gave her brother a toxic look and ate a handful of Raisinets. The three of them were stalled in traffic on the Golden Gate Bridge.

That morning, before waking his children, the father had canceled their music lessons and decided to make a day of it. He wanted to know how they were, is all. Just—how were they. He thought his kids were as self-contained as one of those dogs you sometimes see carrying home its own leash. But you could read things wrong.

Could you ever.

The boy had a friend who jumped from a floor of Langley Porter. The friend had been there for two weeks, mostly playing ping-pong. All the friend said the day the boy visited and lost every game was never play ping-pong with a mental patient because it's all we do and we'll kill you. That night the friend had cut the red

212

belt he wore in two and left the other half on his bed. That was this time last year when the boy was twelve years old.

You think you're safe, the father thought, but it's thinking you're invisible because you closed your eyes.

This day they were headed for Petaluma—the chicken, egg, and arm-wrestling capitol of the nation—for lunch. The father had offered to take them to the men's arm-wrestling semi-finals. But it was said that arm-wrestling wasn't so interesting since the new safety precautions, that hardly anyone broke an arm or a wrist any more. The best anyone could hope to see would be dislocation, so they said they would rather go to Pete's. Pete's was a gas station turned into a place to eat. The hamburgers there were named after cars, and the gas pumps in front still pumped gas.

"Can I have one?" the boy asked, meaning the Raisinets.

"No," his sister said.

"Can I have two?"

"Neither of you should be eating candy before lunch," the father said. He said it with the good sport of a father who enjoys his kids and gets a kick out of saying Dad things.

"You mean dinner," said the girl. "It will be dinner before we get to Pete's."

Only the northbound lanes were stopped. Southbound traffic flashed past at the normal speed.

"Check it out," the boy said from the back seat. "Did you see the bumper sticker on that Porsche? 'If you don't like the way I drive, stay off the sidewalk.' "

He spoke directly to his sister. "I've just solved my Christmas shopping."

"I got the highest score in my class in Driver's Ed," she said.

"I thought I would let your sister drive home today," the father said.

From the back seat came sirens, screams for help, and then a dirge.

The girl spoke to her father in a voice rich with complicity. "Don't people make you want to give up?"

"Don't the two of you know any jokes? I haven't laughed all day," the father said.

"Did I tell you the guillotine joke?" the girl said.

213

"He hasn't laughed all day, so you must've," her brother said.

The girl gave her brother a look you could iron clothes with. Then her gaze dropped down. "Oh-oh," she said, "Johnny's out of jail."

Her brother zipped his pants back up. He said, "Tell the joke."

"Two Frenchmen and a Belgian were about to be beheaded," the girl began. "The first Frenchman was led to the block and blindfolded. The executioner let the blade go. But it stopped a quarter inch above the Frenchman's neck. So he was allowed to go free, and ran off shouting, 'C'est un miracle! C'est un miracle!'"

"What does that mean?" her brother asked.

"It's a miracle," the father said.

"Then the second Frenchman was led to the block, and the same thing—the blade stopped just before cutting off his head. So *he* got to go free, and ran off shouting, 'C'est un miracle!'

"Finally the Belgian was led to the block. But before they could blindfold him, he looked up, pointed to the top of the guillotine, and cried, 'Voilá la difficulté!' "

She doubled over.

"Maybe *I* would be wetting *my* pants if I knew what that meant," the boy said.

"You can't explain after the punchline," the girl said, "and have it still be funny."

"There's the problem," said the father.

The waitress handed out menus to the party of three seated in the corner booth of what used to be the lube bay. She told them the specialty of the day was Moroccan chicken.

"That's what I want," the boy said. "Morerotten chicken."

But he changed his order to a Studeburger and fries after his father and sister had ordered.

"So," the father said, "who misses music lessons?"

"I'm serious about what I asked you last week," the girl said. "About switching to piano? My teacher says a real flutist only breathes with the stomach, and I can't."

"The real reason she wants to change," said the boy, "is her waist will get two inches bigger when she learns to stomach-breathe. That's what *else* her teacher said."

The boy buttered a piece of sourdough bread and flipped a chunk of cold butter onto his sister's sleeve.

"Jeezo-beezo," the girl said, "why don't they skip the knife and fork and just set his place with a slingshot!"

"Who will ever adopt you if you don't mind your manners?" the father said. "Maybe we could try a little quiet today."

"You sound like your tombstone," the girl said. "Remember what you wanted it to say?"

Her brother joined in with his mouth full: "Today will be a quiet day."

"Because it never is with us around," the boy said.

"You guys," said the father.

The waitress brought plates. The father passed sugar to the boy and salt to the girl without being asked. He watched the girl shake out salt onto the fries.

"If I had a sore throat, I would gargle with those," he said.

"Looks like she's trying to melt a driveway," the boy offered.

The father watched his children eat. They ate fast. They called it Hoovering. He finished while they sucked at straws in empty drinks.

"Funny," he said thoughtfully, "I'm not hungry any more."

Every meal ended this way. It was his benediction, one of the Dad things they expected him to say.

"That reminds me," the girl said. "Did you feed Rocky before we left?"

"Uh-uh," her brother said. "I fed him yesterday."

"*I* fed him yesterday!" the girl said.

"Okay, we'll compromise," the boy said. "We won't feed the cat today."

"I'd say you are out of bounds on that one," the father said.

He meant you could not tease her about animals. Once, during dinner, that cat ran into the dining room shot from guns. He ran around the table at top speed, then spun out on the parquet floor into a leg of the table. He fell over onto his side and made short coughing sounds. "Isn't he smart?" the girl had crooned, kneeling beside him. "He knows he's hurt."

For years, her father had to say that the animals seen on shoulders of roads were napping.

"He never would have not fed Homer," she said to her father.

215

"Homer was a dog," the boy said. "If I forgot to feed him, he could just go into the hills and bite a deer."

"Or a Campfire Girl selling mints at the front door," their father reminded them.

"Homer," the girl sighed. "I hope he likes chasing sheep on that ranch in the mountains."

The boy looked at her, incredulous.

"You *believed* that? You actually *believed* that?"

In her head, a clumsy magician yanked the cloth and the dishes all crashed to the floor. She took air into her lungs until they filled, and then she filled her stomach, too.

"I thought she knew," the boy said.

The dog was five years ago.

"The girl's parents insisted," the father said. "It's the law in California."

"Then I hate California," she said. "I hate its guts."

The boy said he would wait for them in the car, and left the table.

"What would help?" the father asked.

"For Homer to be alive," she said.

"What would help?"

"Nothing."

"Help."

She pinched a trail of salt on her plate.

"A ride," she said. "I'll drive."

The girl started the car and screamed, "Goddammit."

With the power off, the boy had tuned in the Spanish station. Mariachis exploded on ignition.

"Dammit isn't God's last name," the boy said, quoting another bumper sticker.

"Don't people make you want to give up?" the father said.

"No talking," the girl said to the rear-view mirror, and put the car in gear.

She drove for hours. Through groves of eucalyptus with their damp peeling bark, past acacia bushes with yellow flowers pulsing off their stems. She cut over to the coast route and the stony grey-green tones of Inverness.

"What you'd call scenic," the boy tried.

Otherwise they were quiet.

216

No one said anything until the sky started to close, and then it was the boy again, asking shouldn't they be going home.

"No, no," the father said, and made a show of looking out the window, up at the sky and back at his watch. "No," he said, "keep driving—it's getting earlier."

But the sky spilled rain, and the girl headed south towards the bridge. She turned on the headlights and the dashboard lit up green. She read off the odometer on the way home: "Twenty-six thousand, three hundred eighty three and eight-tenths miles."

"Today?" the boy said.

The boy got to Rocky first. "Let's play the cat," he said, and carried the Siamese to the upright piano. He sat on the bench holding the cat in his lap and pressed its paws to the keys. Rocky played "Born Free." He tried to twist away.

"Come on, Rocky, ten more minutes and we'll break."

"Give him to me," the girl said.

She puckered up and gave the cat a five-lipper.

"Bring the Rock upstairs," the father called. "Bring sleeping bags, too."

Pretty soon three sleeping bags formed a triangle in the master bedroom. The father was the hypotenuse. The girl asked him to brush out her hair, which he did while the boy ate a tangerine, peeling it up close to his face, inhaling the mist. Then he held each segment to the light to find seeds. In his lap, cat paws fluttered like dreaming eyes.

"What are you thinking?" the father asked.

"Me?" the girl said. "Fifty-seven T-bird, white with red interior, convertible. I drive it to Texas and wear skirts with rick-rack. I'm changing my name to Ruby," she said, "or else Easy."

The father considered her dream of a checkered future.

"Early ripe, early rot," he warned.

A wet wind slammed the window in its warped sash, and the boy jumped.

"I hate rain," he said. "I hate its guts."

The father got up and closed the window tighter against the storm. "It's a real frog-choker," he said.

In darkness, lying still, it was no less camp-like than if they had been under the stars singing to a stone-ringed fire burned down to embers.

217

They had already said good-night some minutes earlier when the boy and girl heard their father's voice in the dark.

"Kids, I just remembered—I have some good news and some bad news. Which do you want first?"

It was his daughter who spoke. "Let's get it over with," she said. "Let's get the bad news over with."

The father smiled. They are all right, he decided. My kids are as right as this rain. He smiled at the exact spots he knew their heads were turned to his, and doubted he would ever feel—not better, but *more* than he did now.

"I lied," he said. "There is no bad news."

nominated by Missouri Review, *Joyce Carol Oates, Bob Shacochis and Sara Vogan*

QUARTER TO SIX

by DORIANNE LAUX

from FIVE FINGERS REVIEW

And the house swept with the color of dusk
I set the table with lace and plates.
In these minutes left to myself, before
the man and child scuff at the doorstep
and come in, I think of you and wonder
what I would say if I could write.
Would I tell you how I avoid his eyes,
this man I've learned to live with, afraid
of what he doesn't know about me.
That I've finished a pack of cigarettes
in one sitting, to ready myself for dinner,
when my hands will waver over a plate of fish
as the bones of my daughter grow normal
in the chair beside me.

Missy, this is what's become of the wedding
you swore you'd come to wearing black.
That was in 1970 as we sat on the bleached
floor of the sanitarium sharing a cigarette
you'd won in a game of pool.
You said even school was better than this ward
where they placed the old men in their draped
pants, the housewives screaming in loud flowered
shifts as they clung to the doors that lined the halls.
When we ate our dinner of boiled fish and potatoes
it was you who nudged me under the table

when the thin man in striped pajamas climbed
the chair beside me in his bare feet, his pink
tinged urine making soup of my leftovers.
With my eyes locked on yours I watched you
continue to eat. So I lifted my fork to my open
mouth, jello quivering green against the tines,
and while I trusted you and chewed on nothing
he leapt into the arms of the night nurse
and bit open the side of her face.

You had been there longer, knew the ropes, how to take
the sugar coated pill and slip it into the side
pocket of your mouth, pretend to swallow it down
in drowsy gulps while the white frocked nurse
eyed the clockface above our heads.
You tapped messages into the wall while I wept,
struggling to remember the code, snuck in
after bedcount with cigarettes, blew the blue smoke
through barred windows. We traded stories,
our military fathers, yours locking you in a closet
for the days it took to chew ribbons of flesh
from your fingers, a coat pulled over your head—
then mine, who worked his ringed fingers inside me
while the house slept, my face pressed to the pillow,
my fists knotted into the sheets. Some nights,
I can't eat. The dining room fills with their chatter,
my hand stuffed with the glint of a fork
and the safety of butter knives quiet at the sides
of our plates. If I could write you now
I'd tell you I wonder how long I can go on
with this careful pouring of the wine from its bottle,
straining to catch it in the fragile glass.

Tearing open my bread I see the scars, stitches
laced up the root of your arm, the flesh messy
where you grabbed at it with the broken glass
of an ashtray. That was the third time.
And later you laughed when they twisted you into
the white strapped jacket, demanding you vomit the pills.
I imagined you in the harsh light of a bare bulb

where you took the needle, without flinching, retched
when the Ipecac hit you, your body shelved over the toilet
and no one to hold the hair from your face.

I don't know where your hands are now, the fingers
that filled my mouth those nights you tongued me open
in the broken light that fell through chicken wired windows.
The intern found us and wrenched us apart, the half moon
of your breast exposed as you spit on him.
"Now you're going to get it." he hissed through his teeth
and you screamed, "Get what?" as if there was anything
anyone could give you.

If I could write you now I'd tell you I still see
your face, bone white as my china above the black
velvet cape you wore to my wedding twelve years ago,
the hem of your black crepe skirt brushing up the dirty
rice in swirls as you swept down the reception line
to kiss me. "Now you're going to get it." you whispered,
cupping my cheek in your hand.

nominated by Five Fingers Review
and Sandra McPherson

I SEND MAMA HOME

by MARILYN WANIEK

from THE SOUTHERN REVIEW

I send you down the road from Paden
scaring bobwhites and pheasants
back into the weeds;
a jackrabbit keeps pace
in front of your headlights
if you drive there at night.
I send you to Boley
past a stand of post oaks
and the rolling blackjack hills.

On Pecan Street
a brown rectangle outlines the spot
where King's Ice House used to be.
The Farmer's and Merchant's Bank
is closed, grizzled boards
blind its windows.
The ghosts of Mister Turner,
the murdered banker,
and Floyd Birdwell,
the right hand of Pretty Boy Floyd,
spill like shadows
over the splintering floor.

This was the city of promise,
the town where no white man
showed his face after dark.

The *Progress* extolled it
in twice weekly headlines
as "Boley, the Negro's Dream."

Mama, I give you this poem
so you can drive past
Hazel's Department Store,
Bragg's Barber Shop,
the Truelove Cafe,
the Antioch Baptist Church,
the C.M.E. church and school,
the Creek-Seminole college.

I deliver you again
to your parents' bedroom
where the piano gleamed
like a black pegasus,
to the three-room farmhouse,
to the Oklahoma plains.
I give you the horses, Prince and Lady,
and the mules. I give you your father's car,
a Whippet, which you learned to drive
at a slow bounce through the pasture.
I give you the cows and calves
you and your brother played rodeo on,
the full smokehouse, the garden,
the fields of peanuts and cotton.

I send you back
to the black town you missed
when you were at college
and on the great white way.
I let you see
behind the mask you've worn
since the fifty-year-ago morning
when you waved goodbye from the train.

nominated by Philip Schultz

PLAIN SONG

by HAYDEN CARRUTH

from THE GREENFIELD REVIEW

After the storm a peculiar
　　calm crept over us, a
hush. Everything was white, the roads
　　were vanished. Superla-

tives upon superlatives of
　　snow transcended any-
thing anyone could say. The roof
　　of T.J.'s Family

Restaurant that had lifted and
　　turned and sailed a hundred
feet onto my patio, in-
　　to my glass doors, was bed-

ded against my sofa, now un-
　　der a blanket of snow.
It's no rarity here; we have
　　big storms that come and go

all winter, and some are true bliz-
　　zards. But hell this one ex-
ceeded all records, all measure-
　　ments. It was huge, complex,

unbelievable. It was Su-
    perbliz. Then it was si-
lence, at least at first, a force as
    awesome and broad and high

as the roaring and wreckage of
    the storm itself, nature's
two utterly opposite as-
    pects, between which adverse-

ly we human creatures shrank to
    nothing. No voice, no mach-
ine. Only the snow. Where we had
    become used to the trash

of the strip, all the gaudy plas-
    tic of the fast food chains
and filling stations, the dete-
    rioration, dirt, stains

of rust and corruption, brok-
    en glass, now the snow spread
smooth and swirling over every-
    thing: from our upper bed-

room windows we saw it. Silence
    and snow. Sleekly soft, fan-
ciful as dunes. "Who killed Cock Rob-
    in?" "Who knows?" "Who cares?" Can-

cer is the answer, like every-
    body. And the snow got
holes in it very quickly, the
'   bridal gown was forgot-

ten, lying motheaten, and so
    was the bride, her bones show-
ing through. The children gave up their
    prayers and began to crow

in welcome of noise again, the
    great machinemaking fount-
ains of dirty, slushy, slimy
    snow. Somewhere the account-

ants got busy with new figures.
    "Even steven, all is
less." So it took three days to get
    all the cars dug out, this

being what mattered, of course. For
    those three days people laughed
and joked, spoke of the Donner Pass
    and Admiral Byrd. Aft-

er that the old anxiety
    and greed settled back on,
grimace and pain. The TV came
    back. We were not aston-

ished to find it was Christmas. The
    kids danced to see the lights
of the shrieking ambulances
    again, filling the nights

with comfortable nips of hor-
    ror. I paid, myself, to
have the patio and doors re-
    paired. Who wants to go through

all the red tape for a disas-
    ter loan? There's where they spliced
the railing, hardly noticea-
    ble now under the Christ-

ly multiplications of clem-
    atis, though that's what turned
my thoughts back now on this hot night
    to Superbliz. Who learned

anything from it? Ten feet of
    snow in 24 hours,
December 1983—
    the biggest, and all ours.

But nobody remembers. All
    days are records. I won-
der what it would really take to
    grab people's attention?

nominated by Joe-Anne McLaughlin and Joyce Carol Oates

WRITING IN THE COLD

by TED SOLOTAROFF

from GRANTA

DURING THE DECADE of editing *New American Review*, I was often struck by how many gifted young writers there were in America. They would arrive every month, three or four of them, accomplished or close to it, full of wit and panache or a steady power or a fine, quiet complexity. We tried to devote twenty-five percent of each issue to these new voices and seldom failed to meet the quota. Where were they all coming from? They seemed to come from everywhere: Dixon, New Mexico, and Seal Rock, Oregon, as well as Chicago and San Francisco, from English departments in community colleges as well as the big creative writing centers. They also came amid the 1,200 or so manuscripts we received each month. Eugenics alone would seem to dictate that half of one percent of the writing population would be brilliant.

What has happened to all of that bright promise? When I look through the cumulative index of the *New American Review*, I see that perhaps one-quarter of our discoveries have gone on to have reasonably successful careers; about the same number still have marginal ones, part of the alternative literary community of the little magazines and small presses. And about half have disappeared. It's as though some sinister force were at work, a kind of literary population control mechanism that kills off the surplus talent we have been developing or causes it to wither slowly away.

Literary careers are difficult to speculate about. They are so individual, so subject to personal circumstances that are often hidden to the writer himself. What is not hidden is likely to be held so secretly that even the editor who works closely with a writer knows little more about his or her sources of fertility and potency than anyone else, and the writers who fail are even more inclined to draw a cover of silence over the reasons. Still, it's worth considering why some gifted writers have careers and others don't. It doesn't appear to be a matter of the talent itself—some of the most natural writers, the ones who seemed to shake their prose or poetry out of their sleeves, are among the disappeared. As far as I can tell, the decisive factor is durability. For the gifted writer, durability seems to be directly connected to how one deals with uncertainty, rejection, and disappointment, from within as well as from without, and how effectively one incorporates them into the creative process itself, particularly in the prolonged first stage of a career. In what follows, I'll be writing about fiction writers, the group I know best. But I don't imagine that poets, playwrights, and essayists will find much that is different.

Thirty years ago when I came out of college and went off to become a writer I expected to remain unknown and unrewarded for ten years or so. So did my few associates in this precarious enterprise. Indeed, our low expectations were, we felt, a measure of our high seriousness. We were hardly going to give ourselves less time and difficulty than our heroes—Joyce and Flaubert, say—gave themselves. It was a dubious career, and none of our families understood, much less supported, us. Nor were there any universities—except for Iowa and Stanford—that wanted us around once we'd got a degree, except as prospective scholars. Not that we knew how to cope with the prolonged isolation and likely poverty that faced us—who does until he has been through them?—but at least we expected them and even understood something of their necessity.

I don't find that our counterparts in the present generation are as aware of the struggle to come. As the products of American postwar affluence and an undemanding literary education, most of them have very little experience with struggle of any kind. Their expectations of a writer's life have been formed by the mass-marketing and subsidization of culture and by the creative writing industry, and their career models are not, say, William Faulkner or Henry Miller but John Irving or Ann Beattie. Instead of the jazz musicians and painters of thirty years ago somehow making do, the other arts provide them with the model life-styles of rock stars and

229

the young princes of New York's Soho. There is not a Guggenheim or Yaddo writers' residency far up the road, but a whole array of public and private grants, colonies and fellowships that seem just around the corner. Most of all, there is the prospect—not immediate but still only a few significant publications away—of teaching, with its comfortable life and free time. As the poet William Matthews recently remarked, 'What our students seem mainly to want to do is to become us, though they have no idea of what we've gone through.'

I don't think one can understand the literary situation today without dealing with the one genuine revolutionary development in American letters during the second half of the century: the rise of the creative writing programs. At virtually one stroke we have solved the age-old problem of how literary men and women are to support themselves: today they teach writing. They place themselves in an environment, mild and relatively static, whose main population is always growing a year younger and whose beliefs and attitudes become the writer's principal reflection of the society-at-large. Because of the peculiar institution of tenure, the younger writer tends to publish too quickly and the older one too little. It's no wonder that steady academic employment has done strange things to a number of literary careers and, to my mind, has devitalized the relationship between literature, particularly fiction, and society.

For a young writer, the graduate writing program is a mixed blessing: while it starts him out under conditions that are extremely favourable, they are also extremely unreal. At a university or college like Johns Hopkins or Houston or Sarah Lawrence or the twenty or thirty others with prestigious programs, the chances are that several highly accomplished, even famous, writers will be reading one's work—John Barth, perhaps, or Donald Barthelme, or Grace Paley. His work will be taken very seriously, and also read by a responsive and usually supportive audience—the other writers in the program: a small, intense milieu that envisages the good life as a literary career. And, of course, he will have a structure of work habits provided by the workshops, degree requirements, and deadlines.

While I think graduate writing programs are mostly wasted on the young, I can also see these programs as a kind of greenhouse than enables certain talents to bloom, particularly those that produce straightforward well-made stories, the kind that teach well in class, and, depending on the teacher, even certain eccentric ones, particularly those patterned on a prevailing fashion of post-modernism. Nevertheless, the graduate writing program makes the next stage—being out there by oneself in the cold— particularly chilling. Here, she receives not personal and enlightened responses to her writing, but mostly rejection slips. Instead of standing out, she is among the anonymous masses. Without a literary community, she now has to rely on herself for stimulation, support, and discipline. And writing itself has to be fitted into the interstices left by a full-time job or parenthood. In short, her character as a writer will now be tested—and not for a year or two but much more likely for five or ten.

That's how long it generally takes for the gifted young fiction writer to find his way, to come into her own. The two fiction writers whose work appears to be the most admired and influential in the graduate writing programs just now are Bobbie Ann Mason and Raymond Carver. Mason spent some seven years writing an unpublished novel, and then story after story, sending each one to Roger Angell, an editor at the *New Yorker*, getting it back, writing another until finally the twentieth one was accepted. In his essay 'Fires', Carver tells about the decade of struggle to write the stories that grew out of his heavily burdened life of 'working at crap jobs' and raising two children until an editor, Gordon Lish, began to beckon from the tower of *Esquire*. It would be another seven years before Carver's first book appeared. Three novelists whose recent 'arrival' I attended—Lynne Sharon Schwartz, Joan Chase and Douglas Unger—were by then in their thirties and each had already written at least one unpublished novel. My most recent find, Alan Hewat, whose novel *Lady's Time* will be published this summer, is in his early forties and has written two unpublished novels.

Why this long delay? These writers no longer regard it as one. All of them say that the unpublished novels shouldn't have been published, and that they were mainly part of a protracted effort to find a voice, a more or less individual and stable style that best uncovers and delivers the writer's material. And this effort simply requires time. The writer in his middle twenties is not that far removed from adolescence and its insecurities; indeed, the high level sensitivity he is trying to develop comes precisely from that side of himself that he probably tried to deny only a few years ago as freakish, unmanly and unpopular. Hence the painful paradoxes of his new vocation: that his most vulnerable side is now his working one—the one that goes forth into the world and represents him; and that through this vulnerable side he must now find his subject: *his* understanding about how and why he and others live, and *his* conviction about what is morally significant in their lives as well as his own. And all of this from a self that is likely to be rejected each time it looks for confirmation by sending out a manuscript.

The typical student in creative writing has spent eighteen of his, say, twenty-five years in school and university. His grasp of how people live and feel and look at things is still fairly limited to books and films—sources he still needs to sift out—and to his family and its particular culture, from which he is probably rebelling in predictable ways. Throw in a few love-affairs and friendships, a year or two of scattered work experience, perhaps a trip abroad, and his consciousness is still playing a very limited hand. (There appears to be a long term psycho-social trend over the past fifty years or so in which each generation takes several years longer to mature than the preceding one: many of the post-war generation of fiction writers such as Mailer, Bellow, Styron, Baldwin, Bowles, Flannery O'Connor, Truman Capote, Updike, Roth, Reynolds Prices were highly developed by their mid- to late twenties.) The writer's gift itself may keep him from understanding his true situation by producing a few exceptional stories, or even a novel from the most deeply held experiences of his life. But except for these he has only his share of the common life of his age that he must learn to see and write about in a complex and uncommon way.

A young writer I know won a national award a few years ago for the best short story submitted by the various writing programs. It was one of a group of several remarkable stories that she published, almost all of them about members of her family, grey-collar people finely viewed in their contemporary perplexities by her as the kid sister and the one who would leave. But almost nothing she wrote later came near their standard; the new fiction was mostly about a difficult love affair to which she was still too close to write about with the same circumspection and touch as her family stories. After they were turned down, she went to work reading for a film company. Recently she sold an adaptation of one of her early

232

stories, is now writing another script, and is looking to take up fiction again. By the time she publishes her first collection, if she does, she'll be well into her thirties.

What she has been going through as a fiction writer is the crisis of rejection from without and, more importantly, from within. All writers are always sending themselves rejection letters, as the late George P. Elliot observed, to this sentence and paragraph and turn of the story, or—heartbreak time—to the story that has eluded months of tracking, or the hundred pages of a novel that has come to a dead stop. Through adversity the writer learns to separate rejection of her work from self-rejection, and self-criticism from self-distrust. For the inexperienced writer a year or two of rejection or a major rejection of, say, a novel, can lead all too easily to self-distrust, and from there to a disabling distrust of the writing process itself. Anxious, depressed, defensive, the writer gives up her most fundamental and enabling right: the right to write uncertainly, roughly, even badly. A garden in the early stage is not a compelling place: it's a lot of arduous, messy, noisome work— digging up the hard ground, putting in the fertilizer, then the seeds and seedlings. So with beginning a story or novel. But the self-rejecting writer goes not from task to task, as in a garden, but from creating to judging: from her mind to the typewriter to the waste-paper basket, and in time, her mind becomes a ruthless system of self-cancellation.

The longer this goes on, the more writing becomes not a process but an issue of entitlement and prohibition. Even if she hits upon an exciting first sentence or paragraph or even a whole opening development, the dull stuff returns, her uncertainty follows, and soon she is back in court again, testifying against herself. To stay in this state too long is to reach the dead-end of narcissistic despair known as writer's block in which vanity and guilt have so perse- cuted craft and imagination and so deprived them of their allies— heart, curiosity, will—that they have gone into exile and into the sanctuary of silence.

It is not too much to say that how well a writer copes with rejection determines whether he has a genuine literary vocation or just a literary flair. Rejection along with uncertainty are as much a part of a writer's life as snow and cold are of an Eskimo's: they are conditions one has not only to learn to live with but also learn to make use of.

Most youthful first novels lack complexity, the evidence of

prolonged struggle with uncertainty. They typically keep as much as possible to the lived lines of the author's life, providing the security of a certain factuality but at the expense of depriving the imagination of its authority. Too insistent here, too vague there, the novel is often overstuffed and overwritten: the doubt of what belongs and what doesn't being too easily resolved by leaving it in. If he has some literary sophistication, the writer may try to quell uncertainty by allying himself with some current literary fashion. Of course, the struggle with uncertainty may intermittently be strongly engaged and won: the material rings true, the narrative grows intense and unpredictable. If there is enough earned truth and power the manuscript is viable and its deadnesses are relatively detectable. The rest is mostly a matter of the writer's willingness to persist in his gift and its process and to put his ego aside.

Douglas Unger, whose first novel, *Leaving the Land*, was received with considerable acclaim last year, began writing it in 1976. He had already had a previous novel optioned by a major publisher, had rewritten it three times to meet his editor's reservations, only to have it finally rejected. 'He literally threw the manuscript at me and told me to get out of his office. Since I didn't know what to do next—I didn't have an agent or anything—I enrolled at the Iowa Writers' Workshop.' I met him there the following year when I used the opening section of his next novel to teach a workshop. It begins with a young woman, Marge, walking along the street of a farm town in the Dakotas, on her way to be fitted for a wedding dress by her prospective mother-in-law. It is just after World War II, in which her two brothers have been killed, and she has chosen the best of a bad lot. The writing was remarkably sensitive to the coarse and delicate weave of a farm girl's childhood and adolescence and to the pathos of her love life. At the same time, Unger wrote vividly about crops and farm machinery and the plight of farmers, driven by wartime policy into the clutches of a giant food trust that had driven down the farmers' prices and wanted their land. Marge's thoughts are interrupted when a convoy of trucks transporting factory equipment rolls into town, in the midst of which is an attractive man in a snappy roadster. She senses that her luck may have suddenly changed, and she sets out to pick him up. All in all, it was a terrific beginning.

About eighteen months later Unger sent me the final manu-script. It was some 700 pages long. About a fifth was taken up by a separate story of German prisoners-of-war working for the food trust; the final third jumped ahead thirty years to tell of the return of Marge's son to Nowell, now a ghost town. Along with its disconnected narrative, the writing had grown strangely mock-allegorical and surreal in places, as though Unger's imagination had been invaded by an alien force, perhaps Thomas Pynchon's. Most disappointing of all, he seemed to have turned away from a story with a great deal of prospective meaning—the eradication of farmers and agrarian values by agribusiness—to make instead the post-modernist point of pointlessness. I wrote him a long letter along these lines, and ended by saying that I still sensed there was a genuine novel buried inside this swollen one and hoped he would have the courage to find it. When he read the letter, Unger was so enraged he threw down the manuscript and began to jump on it, shouting, 'But I've spent so much time on it already.'

He didn't write anything for a year and a half. By then he was living on an unworked farm and had become a commercial fisher-man. One night he woke up with the people he had written about on his mind, pulled out the manuscript and began to reread it. He was struck by the distortions: 'I was running up against people every day who gave the lie to what I'd done to my characters. Then one day my wife's older sister turned up with one of her sons to try to get the farm going again: he wanted nothing to do with it. Their struggle made me see that the original version was wrong. It should have been about Marge all along and her efforts—by staying in that forsaken community—to hold on to the land with the same tenacity her father had shown and pass it on to her son. Much of this material was already there. In order to feel easy again, I had to rework it.'

It took another three years. After he had left Iowa City, Unger spent some time with Raymond Carver. 'Anyone who knows Ray knows that you have to believe that if you write well you'll eventually get published. Ray kept saying that "a good book is an honest one." I knew that his whole career had been an effort to write honestly, so those words really sunk in. At Iowa I was desperate to get published, and I thought it would help if I put in a lot of post-modernist effects. Barth and Barthelme and Pynchon were all the rage.'

235

Unger ended up with three novellas: Marge's early life culminating in her affair and marriage to the man in the roadster, a lawyer for the food trust; the prisoners-of-war story; Marge and her son twenty-five years later, her marriage long over, the farm and most of the area abandoned. A brave, sad, increasingly bleak wind of feeling blew through the final novella, joining it tonally as well as narratively to the first. Were they the buried novel? The prose of all three maintained the straightforward realism of the original opening but Unger's style had grown diamond-hard, with glints of light whichever way it turned. The three were eminently publishable as they were. Unger decided to go for the novel and set to work revising the first and last to join them more securely together.

What enabled him to persist through all of his rewriting and also to let 150 pages of very good writing go by the board? 'By now I'd lost any egotistical involvement in the work, and was watching—almost impersonally—a process occurring. The book wanted to come together and I was the last person to stand in its way.'

Unger needed a period of adversity and silence not only to recover from 'my litany of flaws', as he put it, but also to reorient himself as a writer and to undo the damage that the fashionable and false writer, wanting to be published as soon as possible, had done to the uncertain true one who had started the project. Then the characters, like rejected family or abused friends, began to return.

It is precisely this struggle with rejection that helps the young writer develop his main defence against the narcissism that prompts him to speak out in the first place. Writing to a friend, Pushkin tells of reading a canto of *Eugene Onegin* which he had just composed, jumping from his chair, and proudly shouting, 'Hey you, Pushkin! Hey you, son of a bitch!' Every writer knows that feeling, but every writer also knows how easily it can turn over into self-hatred, when the writing or the blank page reflects back one's limitations, failure, deadness. The writer's defence is his power of self-objectivity, his interest in otherness, and his faith in the process itself which enables him to write on into the teeth of his doubts and then to improve it. In the scars of the struggle between the odd, sensitive side of the self that wants to write and the practical, socialized one that wants results, the gifted young writer is likely to find his signature. Writing itself, if not misunderstood and abused, becomes a way of empowering the writing self. It converts diffuse anger and disappointment into deliberate and durable aggression, the writer's main source of energy. It converts sorrow and self-pity into empathy, the writer's main means of relating to otherness. His wounded innocence turns into irony, his silliness into wit, his guilt into judgement, his oddness into originality, his perverseness into his stinger.

Because all of this takes time, indeed most of a lifetime to complete itself, the gifted young writer has to learn that his main task is to persist. This means he must be tough-minded about his fantasies of wealth, fame and the love of beautiful men or women. However stimulating these may be for the social self, for the writing one who perforce needs to stay home and be alone, they are enacted mostly as fantasies that maintain the adolescent romance of the magically empowered ego that the writer must outgrow if he is to survive. And this is so even if the fantasies come true, and often enough, particularly if they come true. No writer rode these fantasies further or more damagingly than Scott Fitzgerald, but it was Fitzgerald who said that inside a novelist there has to be a lot of the peasant.

Rejection and uncertainty teach the writer the value and fragility of his gift—a gift that is both a skill, better at some tasks than others, and a power that comes and goes. Even when it comes, it is often only partly functioning and its directives are only partly understood. Writing a first draft is like groping one's way into a pitch dark room, or overhearing a faint conversation, or telling a joke whose punchline you've forgotten. As someone said, one writes mainly to rewrite, for rewriting and revising are how one's mind comes to inhabit the material fully.

In its benign form, rewriting is a second, third, and nth chance to make something come right, to 'fall graciously into place', in Lewis Hyde's phrase. But it is also the test: one has to learn to respect the misgiving that says, This still doesn't ring true, still hasn't touched bottom. And this means to go back down into the mine again and poke around for the missing ore and find a place for it and let it work its will. Revision is another process: turning loose the editor in oneself, a caretaker who straightens out and tidies up. At the same time, one must come to the truth of Conrad's remark that no work is ever finished, only at a certain point abandoned.

Beyond that point, rewriting and revising can turn compulsive and malignant, devouring the vitality and integrity of what one has to tell.

There appear to be better and worse ways to get through this long period of self-apprenticeship. Of the first novelists and story writers I've recently been involved with, virtually none of them were teaching writing, at least not full-time. Teaching offers the lure of relatively pleasant work and significant free time, but it comes with the snare of using and distorting much of the same energy that goes into writing and tends to fill the mind with the high examples of the models one teaches and the low ones of student work. It is insulating and predictable during the period when the young fiction writer should be as open as possible to a range of experience, for the sake of his characters as well as his material. A job that makes use of another skill or talent and doesn't come home with one seems to work best over the long haul. It's also well, of course, to give as few hostages as possible to fortune.

What the young writer most needs is 'patient time'. Bobbie Ann Mason says that, when asked by students how to get published, she feels like saying, 'Don't worry about it for twenty years or so. It takes that long before you really know what you're doing.' She began writing fiction in 1971 after she got out of graduate school, and for the next five years or so wrote in a desultory way, finding it hard to get focused—until 1976, when she finished a novel about a girl, like herself addicted to Nancy Drew novels. 'It took another two years before I began to find my true subject, which was to write about my roots and the kinds of people I'd known, but from my own point of view. It mainly took a lot of living to get to that point. I'd come from such a sheltered and isolated background that I had to go through culture-shock by living for years in the North to see the world of Mayfield, Kentucky, in a way I could write about as I was now—as an exile of sorts. It wasn't until I was in my thirties that I got enough detachment and objectivity to see that many of those people back home were going through culture-shock too.'

My own sense is that young fiction writers should separate the necessity to write fiction from what it is often confused with, the desire to publish it. This helps to keep the writer's mind where it belongs—on his own work—and where it doesn't—on the market, which is next to useless, and on writers who are succeeding, which is discouraging. Comparisons with other writers should be inspiring; otherwise they're invidious. Bobbie Ann Mason says that 'the writer I was most involved with was Nabokov. It was because he was a stylist and had a peculiar sensibility. In some ways, comparing myself to him is like comparing Willy Nelson to an opera singer, but I felt connected to him because he had the sensibility of an exile, was working with two opposing cultures which made him peculiar, the same way I felt myself.'

Thirty years ago there was a great fear of 'selling out', and 'prostituting your talent'. Literary mores no longer place as much stock in the hieratic model of the writer, which is just as well. Unless one is good at self-sacrifice, endowed with an iron will and a genius-sized gift, it's likely to be a defeating thing to insist on producing Art or nothing.

If one of the primary projects of the gifted young writer is to begin to create a 'demilitarized zone' between his social side and his literary one, so that the latter can live in peace for a while, it is also true that both need exercise and some degree of satisfaction and toughening. Many novelists-in-progress find it helpful to take their talent, at least some of the time, out of the rarefied and tenuous realm of literature and put it to work in the market-place to try to earn part of its keep. Even hackwriting has the benefit of putting serious writing into its proper perspective as a privilege rather than a burden. At a respectable professional level, writing for publication makes one into someone who writes rather than, in Robert Louis Stevenson's distinction, someone who wants to have written. Writing without publishing gets to be like loving someone from afar—delicious for fantasies but thin gruel for living. That is why, to my mind, a strongly written review, profile, piece of reportage in a regional magazine—the *Village Voice,* or the *Texas Monthly* or *Seattle Magazine*—is worth three 'Try us again's' from the *New Yorker*.

The first years on your own are a good time to let the imagination off the leash and let it sniff and paw into other fields of writing. From journal writing it's only a small Kierkegaardian leap into the personal essay. There is also the possibility of discovering that criticism or reportage or some other mode is for the time being more congenial than fiction. A young fiction writer I'd been working with for years had about come to the end of his line when he had the wit to turn one of his stories into a one-act play, and has been writing as a playwright ever since. One of the most deforming aspects of American literary culture is the cult of the novel and—with it—the decline of the concept of the man of letters, which less specialized times and less academicized literary cultures than ours took for granted. And still do in Europe, where a Graham Greene, a Robbe-Grillet, a Grass, a Kundera write in three or four modes, depending upon the subject, occasion and the disposition of his well-balanced Muse. Experimenting with other modes, in any case, releases energy and helps to demystify the writer's vocation which, like any other, is an ongoing practice rather than a higher state of being. This is particularly so for a prospective novelist. Auden puts it very well when he says that the novelist

> Must struggle out of his boyish gift and learn
> How to be plain and awkward, how to be
> One after whom none think it worth to turn.
>
> For to achieve his lightest wish, he must
> Become the whole of boredom, subject to
> Vulgar complaints like love, among the Just
> Be just, among the Filthy filthy too.

Virtually all of the fiction writers I've mentioned fix the turning point in their writing lives at the stage when the intrinsic interest of what they were doing began to take over and generate a sense of necessity. This seems to be particularly true of women writers. As Lynne Sharon Schwartz explained, 'Most women don't give themselves the freedom to pursue their dream. Being brought up a girl has meant just that.' She began to write stories when she was seven and did so again during and after college, but without taking the enterprise very seriously. 'I'd get a letter from the *Paris Review* inviting me to submit other work and I'd think, "That's nice," and then put it away in a drawer. Writing fiction was one of several dreams that probably wouldn't be realized.' She married, had children, went back to graduate school which somehow seemed okay to do, perhaps because no one does much dreaming in graduate school. 'I found, though, that I didn't want to write a dissertation when I got to that point. I just couldn't face the library part of it. Going down into the stacks seemed so alien to my real sources. About that time a childhood friend who also was married and had children told me she had resolved to give herself five years to become a dance critic. It was the way she did it, putting everything else to the side. It was her fierce tenacity that inspired me. I gave up graduate school and started to write fiction again.'

Over the next few years she worked on a first novel which went unpublished. 'Just as well, but it got me an agent and some nice rejection letters, which was encouraging.' In time she developed a small network of women fiction writers, published two stories in little magazines, and then a satire on Watergate in the *New Republic*. 'Doris Grumbach, then the literary editor, called me up to tell me and asked me who I was, where I'd been all this time. I realized I might be someone after all.'

Shortly after that, she received a rejection letter from me which so offended her that she burned it in a little ceremony of exorcism. A year or two later I chose another of her stoires, about a professional couple trying to have a baby and then to cope with the changes it brings, for the *Best American Short Stories of 1977*. I sent her a blithe letter asking if she had anything else I could see or talk with her about. Her outrage was still on tap. 'I had been learning from my husband how one went about developing a career, and when I told him I'd be damned if I'd have lunch with you, he told me to be sensible and see what you had to say—"He probably doesn't even remember writing to you." So I decided to be very professional about it.' Which she was. One meeting led to another in which we began to plan a collection of stories about the professional couple, which instead turned into the novel *Rough Strife*.

Now, four books later, Lynne Schwartz looks back at these years and sees mainly herself at work. 'I had to learn to write completely alone. There was no help, no other writer to emulate, no one's influence. It was too private for that. Once I got started I wanted the life of a writer so fiercely that nothing could stop me. I wanted the intensity, the sense of aliveness that came from writing fiction. I'm still that way. My life is worth living when I've completed a good paragraph.'

The development of this sense of necessity seems to be the rock bottom basis for a career as a novelist. Whatever may feed it, whatever may impede it finally comes to be subsidiary to the simple imperative of being at work. At this point, writing fiction has become one's way, in the religious sense of the term. Not that there are any guarantees that it will continue to be for good or that it will make your inner life easier to bear. The life of published fiction writers is most often the exchange of one level of rejection, uncertainty and disappointment for another, and throughout, they need the same durable, patient conviction that got them published in the first place.

Nominated by
Frederick Busch

ELEGY ON INDEPENDENCE DAY

by ARTHUR SMITH

from *Elegy on Independence Day* (University of Pittsburgh Press)

Over the balcony eave, seaside,
One after another, the rockets arc
Barely into view, each sudden thud
Rolling from behind the brickface.
We used to say the rockets "burst,"
As though speaking of someone's heart—
Star-beam, dream-light, bright spokes
Wheeling, falling in a sort of glory.

One summer, in an orchard in Manteca,
The scent of peaches was like fog,
The dust rose and settled like fog,
And both of us went waving sparklers.
You ran on, out farther, tracing
Spirals high in the air. They stayed
Long after the light went, after you
And the heavy, sweet trees were one.

Now I close my eyes and find only
Traces of those wiry figures burned
Into the night. They are fading as
They must, and as they always do.
Whatever shines, however briefly,
We tend toward and love perhaps,
Grounded as we are in the literal—
The powder, the ashes, the earth.

Nominated by Jim Simmerman

THE BIBLICAL GARDEN

by JOHN DRURY

from THE MISSOURI REVIEW

Naturally, it's plotted like a cross.
At the intersection, a worker lifts pots
of date palm and oleander
from a wheel barrow. Later, he saws
a dead apricot—said to be
the real tree of knowledge—to a stump.

I latch the picket gate behind me,
warned about the peacock
who likes to rampage through the mustard seeds,
still hearing trucks grind
on Cathedral Parkway, bottles smashed
in the new recycling center.

On a bench, I open
a second-hand Bible, once used on a ship—
with a name on the death page
and coordinates where they lowered his body
in the North Pacific—and locate
the verses listed on plaques.

At the far end, a goldfish pond
serves as the Nile. Papyrus
clusters in the water, reeds on the bank
stiffen. As it points out in Kings,
if you leaned on a stalk
it would pierce you, like misplaced trust.

I look for "dove's dung,"
the Stars of Bethlehem, whose bulbs
were once ground for flour,
but the dirt patch is bare and raked.
I hear the squeals
of day campers running in the parking lot.

I hear the cedars of Lebanon
brushing against the cathedral wall,
the clicking sound
of squirrels as they dig near the roots,
a peacock's cry
and the squawking of chickens.

In the weeds below where I'm sitting
there's a hint of pink.
I reach and pull up
a flimsy letter, postmarked in Asia
a decade ago. I open it and read
the goodbyes and excuses of a lover in the Peace Corps.

I think of the woman who read it
and tucked it away, under the stone bench,
looking, perhaps, at the flax
that exploded in a blue cloud,
miffed by the sight
of the Judas tree in blossom.

Love has led someone to rip off
the Madonna lilies, leaving a bed of cut stems,
shunning the narcissus, the "rose"
for which the desert rejoiced—
flattened by cloudbursts, wilted by the heat.
A crowd has gathered. A guide pipes up.

She explains that cumin and dill
were used to pay taxes, that judges carried
sprigs of rue into courtrooms because of the stench,
that olives were grown for lamp oil
since candles belonged to the Middle Ages,
that Russians, on Palm Sunday, wave pussy willows.

A faith in living things,
their flourishing, could grow here,
along the paths of baked earth, where bees land
on the purple flowers of the hyssop,
where aloe leaves, rubbed on burns, are soothing,
where cinnamon leaves reek of camphor.

To whom can these blessings speak?
The bitter herbs and tamarisks
are so full of themselves, so complete,
they spring from the tended earth
of testaments, emerging like the willow to say
"I cover you with shadow, I compass you about."

To my mother, who taught me in Sunday School,
who gardened so aimlessly
her tomatoes, once halved,
had the seeds of zinnias inside,
the rye says, "I was not smitten
because I was not grown up."

To the children on the blacktop
struggling at volleyball,
urged on by counselors who shout *Rotate
and serve* and blow whistles,
the bay tree says, "I spread
like the wicked in great power."

To the woman who wept
when she folded her letter
and slipped it in the envelope and hid it,
the mustard says "I am the least
of seeds, but the birds of the air
will lodge in my branches."

nominated by Andrew Hudgins

AMARYLLIS

by DANIEL HALPERN

from THE BENNINGTON REVIEW

Far out beyond the forest I could hear
the calling of loud progress . . .
            —Edwin Arlington Robinson

Through the city the flocks are led
to their last standing, and we look to John
not Luke, to understand the other life.
Our lessons begin with what is less beautiful.

As I knelt by the grave of our mother
a storm passed over us, and harsh rain
snapped the necks of the long-stemmed tuberoses
we brought to honor memory. The rain

passed and left the day without a breeze,
left the humid heat that follows summer rain.
One by one those attending the dead
filed through the mud of the cemetery

until I was left alone, standing there
in the place of stillness. And soon the light
began to fade and there was only
the loneliness of the afterlife that hung

just beyond the sickening scent of unrooted
flowers tightening on their last day.
Around so many dead the ante is one
more indispensable member of the living—

we are to imagine that person here on another day
and to understand how the women and men
who lie here have each been the imagined.
As I stood by this graveside, giving over

one of the beloved to the sanctified earth,
a man I didn't know was there touched my arm
and motioned for me to follow him.
Distraught, as he must have been each time here,

he brought me to the one unflowered grave
and placed my hand on the stone with his
wife's name cut into it. And then he dropped
to his knees in the mud and began to rock.

There must have been a brief song to accompany
the palsied hand and opaque eye,
but I heard only the whine of tires
pursuing the expressway,

the water dropping through the trees. I watched him there
as he rocked in the mud and spoke to her without a sound—
with witness he appeared lonely no longer under this
seasonable summer weather. I touched

his little shoulder and he stood up.
His loss meant nothing to me—and mine
nothing to him, not this loss or my losses to come,
not yet finished with this enclosed landscape.

I remember thinking the man too old
to stand here like this. He brought no flowers,
didn't dress up, didn't know what to say
as we stood there, the knees of his pants

baggy with mud. He hadn't said a word,
but it was his loss that seemed at that moment
the one attended. Small birds
clouded the air, the hum of evening traffic grew.

nominated by Joyce Carol Oates

THE PAPERBOYS

by JOHN LOGAN

from AMERICAN POETRY REVIEW

In the thin cold town where I was born, I hauled and groaned
my red wooden wagon up hill, its wheels squeaking in the still
   blowing snow,
wound by my fond brother's long blue scarf clear up to here,
my nearsighted eyes peering out—
like the filmed Invisible Man—
I headed for Cozad's station, which wanted at six
o'clock two miles out the first newspaper on my route:
and I must have been quite a sight,
blind in my short pants and laced legs,
my corduroys open at the knees (which chilled my thighs)
and my blank face destroyed by snow
like the boy's bleak look on the antique candy box at home.

2.

   There was no place to get warm (Cozad's not open yet)
so I headed for the hotel, its pillars swept white.
First I bought a jelly donut at the shop inside.
It was warm and good going down.
I was always spending my money here when they paid
my newspaper fee in advance,
and then I was broke till next time.
It was nearly dawn in the long halls of the hotel;
it seemed every body was asleep, husbands and wives

snoring together over the transoms and *breathing!*
and you could see the messed up beds
when the thick doors weren't tightly hitched
and had the chains on. Once at dawn
I took a newspaper up there and I saw a woman
with big shadowy tits and only her night gown on.
I saw somebody else also
under the covers. I wished they would not leave their doors
open like that or that at least I wouldn't look in.
I was glad that my dead mother didn't sleep in bed,
her hair stringy like my stepmom's
and I hoped she didn't see me
when I sat on that hid corner of the hall on my
big bag and did it to myself.
My young cousin John and I had practiced in the barn—
we couldn't get it right at first
(I whirled it like a crank, but I was getting better).
I knew that I shouldn't do it, and I was afraid
my mother saw me from heaven.
I was ashamed the rest of the way around my route
and threw my handkerchief away before I got home.

3.

   Then once when I was grown I saw a young paperboy
going about his rounds near my home. He was thinly dressed
and I guessed he was shivering in the winter cold;
He pulled a red metal wagon behind and my mind
simply fled at once back to me.
I feel that this young boy was a double for myself.
I invited him (whose name was Jim like my brother)
to come with me into my house
and get warmed up before he had to finish his route.
Jim came in so I excused myself to make cocoa.
He sat on the brown couch and admired my pictures,
which are all by Northwest painters who are friends of mine.
I came back carrying the cups
and he was standing by my favorite thing—a drawing
by Morris Graves: it is pencil on yellow paper

with the revision lines left in
lightly, so that the deer seems to leap out of its frame
beautifully. I felt quite moved by the boy named Jim
standing amid the pictures I had loved for so long,
and then quite simply I turned toward him and hugged him.
I was surprised when Jim hugged back:
I thought that perhaps in my eyes he had recognized
the boy whom I had for fifty years thought dead
and I knew then that my kid spirit lives on in me.
And I saw in Jim his vision of the man to be,
which made him seem so vulnerable to a father,
for Jim still must pass through pain and loss to find himself.
Our exchange of touch like art returned the world to us.

4.

Pablo Neruda tells the tale of the boy next door,
a neighbor he had never seen:
one day the boy pushed a toy lamb (awkward on its wheels)
into the small hole in the wall.
Neruda took it in his hand
and ran into the house to find his prized old pine cone.
He placed it in the hole and saw the neighbor boy's hand
snatch it up quick, and disappear behind the stone wall.
Neruda said poetry was like this: an exchange
between strangers, and when Jim left
he was warmed and asked to return
for a respite from his hard route.
I hoped that we could become friends,
the old and the young paperboys.
But with Jim's extreme youth it seemed
Neruda's wall stood between us.
So we'll grow and be satisfied in our chaste exchange.

nominated by Robert Phillips and Pamela Stewart

SOMEWHERE GEESE ARE FLYING

fiction by GARY GILDNER

from THE GEORGIA REVIEW

AT A CAFÉ near the Métro St. Michel, sitting outside, Thrasher watches the evening show going by. The Africans hawking their leather goods, moving from café to café as if sleepwalking, bewitched, their faces revealing nothing, their beckoning black arms offering the same string of purses, the same possums hinging from the same black branch—the backpackers among them weaving in and out, Americans, pioneers, eating Italian heroes, ices, their eyes wide open, eager to discover something—the couples close together, a hand casually in the partner's rear pocket, palming a cheek, keeping the hand warm, the other hand a fist at the mouth, warm breath being blown into it—the street wet, glistening, reflecting hot colors—the odors of perfume and tobacco and cooked meat gathering . . .

Thrasher blows breath into his own hands, finishes his cognac, and leaves. He crosses the Quai St. Michel in the middle, a taxi shrieking its horn at him, and walks along the river toward Notre Dame.

In a corner of his brain he can hear something good. Ducks, geese. This time of year? This late? Stopping, leaning on the parapet, he looks at the Seine. After a while he sees himself running across a golf course behind his daughter's retriever. Sweet, blessed fresh air! He gulps it, hogs it down. His brain spins and his legs tremble. What is he doing? Suddenly the dog stops—it whirls around, foam flying from its lips, and gives Thrasher a look that says the same thing, or worse, "Who are you?" It is thirty degrees, more snow is promised, and a lone figure far out on the fairway—a crazy—approaches his ball. It is four o'clock on a gray, brittle afternoon on the prairie, dusk is gathering, and the figure swings his club. The sound to Thrasher is that of a slap against flesh . . .

Barbara is standing in the driveway, home from the office, when he returns the dog. They look at each other a long time. She seems smaller, more precise. She has dyed the delicate gray wings out of her hair, and he wants to rub there, rub them visible again.

"Why are you here, Thrasher?"

Her voice is more precise too. It almost has corners, a frame around it.

"Because I couldn't answer your question . . ."

So he is back in the States. In a motel with a pink heron perched on the roof. And a record cold is predicted for the prairie. He pours a shot of Jack Daniels. He exchanges stares with the white-faced cattle on the motel's calendar, the prize feeders. Then he goes out, to wait for his daughter on the path that Barbara has directed him to, down a slope behind the school, a pasture beyond. Two horses nose each other, exhaling doilies of breath in their manes. What will she say? What will *he* say? His mind can produce nothing. I've got a pink heron on my roof, Francine. Or is it a flamingo? No jokes, Dad, please. How would you like to come to Scotland with me? We could climb in the Cuillins, the sky's the color of apricots there—

Then he saw her. Tall, slim, dragging her bookbag down the slope as if she were pulling a sled. Coat unbuttoned, whistling, glancing back at the bookbag—yes, she *was* pretending to pull a sled! Thrasher's throat tried to close up on him.

He coughed.

She cocked her head, squinting. Then she stopped.

"Francine," he said.

She didn't move. Her eyes were bright blue startled things rimmed with black. Mascara?

"Guess who?" he said. "The monster from the deep lagoon."

"Dad!"

They were hugging and Thrasher was thinking he wasn't there, he was up in a tree, that tree over there, holding on, tired, any

255

second now he'd let go, have to—his throat was closed up good now, no hope for it—she was so big . . .

He held her hand. They were walking. What did they *say?*

Sociology, she was just in sociology thinking, God this is so boring.

You've got winter here, Francine, winter, lord.

Have you seen Ralph?

Yes, we ran, I jogged, he's . . .

I got him a cat. Stanley. Stanley's a girl, we didn't know.

You're so big. You're—you're going to catch cold. Is school . . .?

I hate it, except for—so, you're back.

So he was back. For Christmas, yes. And one night, wrapping presents on the dining-room table, Francine ordered them not to come in, to go make themselves scarce. Barbara took him downstairs to the basement room she'd fixed up—carpeting, sofa, a TV—yes, it is nice, he said. She pointed to a clock on the wall between two mirrors.

"The last time my parents were here," she said, "Dad built that for me. You can hear the second hand click off the seconds if you sit quietly."

They sat on the sofa and listened.

"Yes," he said, "I can hear it."

"It runs on a common flashlight battery. For a year."

"Your father always was good at, you know . . ." He trailed off.

A long silence gathered between them, pricked by the clock.

"It's supposed to be a sunflower," Barbara said.

"Yes . . . yes, I can see that. It's very good."

"He worked on it all one afternoon. He was so proud of the petals."

"The petals?"

"Those sticks." Barbara pointed to the clock.

"Yes," he said, "I see, they were a delicate job."

"It's balsa wood. He gave it two coats of stain."

They watched the second hand and listened to it click.

"Whenever he visits relatives these days," Barbara said, "he builds them a clock."

Thrasher reached back to remember his former father-in-law, the bald suntanned head, thin white mustache. He knew where the fish were, said he could smell a trout, proved it, never came home empty-handed. Clocks?

"We thought about joining them in Arizona for the holidays. But I can't get away," Barbara said.

"Arizona?" Thrasher said.

"They've left Michigan. They're old. The Arizona weather is kinder to them."

"How are they?"

"Mother still yells at him like she did. She just doesn't realize what she sounds like. He teases her about it—I do too—but she doesn't get what we're trying to tell her. Of course if we told her how really awful she sounds, and how it hurts Dad, it would crush her."

And one night he and Barbara drove into town for a drink after Francine and her date went off to the school dance. They talked about how she'd grown, how grown-*up* she looked in high heels, her new dress—how her laugh made the room warmer, lighter, how it promised to return, Thrasher said, after circling a few stars in the sky.

They were excited, talked easily, at times quickly, together, and smiled remembering how self-conscious her date was, Kenny—tall, skinny, couldn't get his tie right and Barbara fixed it for him.

Thrasher said, "Those hands and feet! Kid'll grow another foot, two—that's how you tell, like with a pup, the hands and feet."

Barbara said, "He's a nice boy, not a dog, Thrasher. And he rides a bike. Races, you wouldn't think so, thin as he is. Francine rides too, we both do. Did she tell you she's planning to *build* a bike next summer?"

"She's something," Thrasher said.

"She's a very confident young woman. Much more than I was at her age. Gee, when I was sixteen," Barbara shook her head, smiling, "I think I ruined every sweater I owned."

"Fighting?"

"No, Thrasher," she said with mock patience, "perspiration. The nervous kind, the worst kind."

"The sweet sweat of youth."

"Shall we have another?" She held up her glass. "Another drink, I mean?"

The chubby waitress brought their drinks over.

"You folks got all your Christmas shopping done yet?" the waitress said.

"Yes," they said.

"*I* want Santa to bring me a set of snow tires!" she said and burst out with a raw throaty laugh that followed her all the way back to the bar.

"Cheers," Barbara whispered, touching his glass with hers.

"*Na zdrowie*," Thrasher said.

"I know what!" she said suddenly. "Let's take Ralph for a walk on the golf course. He'll love it."

They crossed a field where pumpkins had grown—here and there one rolled up in the moonlight, frosty, mottled white, a clown lifting his head from a nap—and entered the golf course. They let Ralph go free. The turf was frozen, spiky, and their boots made a sound like a small fire starting. They walked without speaking. From time to time Ralph came racing back, brushed one or the other's legs, and sped off again. Climbing a knoll struck white with moonlight and weather, Thrasher fancied he was stepping on a mammoth eyeball and stepped softly. In the distance, all around them, timber reached for the sky.

"I'm finished with guilt," Barbara said, and her voice made him whirl around, not what she said but the sweet noise of it—for a second or two he thought she was singing a song. Then her meaning, like an echo, came through and he thought, Yes . . . of course . . . you should be. And he felt happy for her. For both of them.

But as they walked along and he thought more about it, he wanted to see guilt, see it all by itself, a thing you *could* be finished with like a dirty rag, a rag stained with human grease. The best he could do was imagine a pile of sharp stones in the road, boulders, a huge pile, a mountain, bearing a crude hand-lettered sign on top: GUILT. You couldn't go around the mountain of course, that wouldn't be earning your freedom. You had to climb over it, over all the sharp edges. Years and years it might take, but finally you're over it. Now what? Do you fall down on your hands and knees in gratitude, thanksgiving? Hell yes. And while you're down there, catching your breath, maybe starting to hum a little, smiling to yourself—

I mean, you did it!—might you also be tempted to pick up that small pebble over there, yes that one, just to take along for a souvenir?   I mean—if you can shrug off a sense of guilt at will—

Thrasher broke into a jog. "Come on, Barbara!" He didn't want to think about guilt, not even play with it, he wanted to hog air, move, feel the heart earn its keep!

"How do you feel?"

"Fine!" she said.

They jogged side by side around a sand trap and up to a snow-covered green—a gorgeous piece of china, a giant discus—over the green, down around another sand trap, and out on the fairway.

"I saw a guy out here the other day whacking a ball! Can you believe it?"

"Yes! It's the curse of the prairie . . . people go mad . . . perfectly normal one minute . . . playing golf on ice and snow the next. Whew! I've got to take a break."

"You know," he said, winded himself, "you're not bad for a middle-aged lady."

"I'm not, am I." She looked around. "Now where's Ralph?"

Thrasher whistled.

"Here, Ralph!" she called.

"He'll come."

"Little devil better. He's been known—"

"There he is."

Ralph came running up and Barbara tried to put the leash on him, but when she commanded him to sit he'd bow down on his front legs, then leap away as she approached.

"Rascal wants to play," she said. "Now behave, you! He's been to the pound twice since Thanksgiving."

"You don't sound like you mean it when you give a command."

"Ralph!" she said, stern.

But the dog only played harder to get.

"He got hit by a car, too. Not hurt though. Ralph, *please*."

Thrasher said, "Sit!" and the dog, after hesitating, sat. Barbara put the leash on.

"We'll walk now," she told him, "nicely."

Thrasher had to laugh.

"What's so funny?"

"Oh, nothing. I just feel good."

"You were laughing at me."

"Because you're so sweet."

"You think I can't be tough?"

"I *know* you can be tough."

259

"I can be tough about other things, than a divorce, if that's what—" She stopped. They'd reached another green and were standing in the middle of it. They stood there a while without speaking. The divorce, Thrasher thought. Let it die and leave nothing behind, no will, no rags . . .

"How about that way?" he finally suggested. "Toward that bridge?"

"I'd rather go home. Come home with me, Thrasher."

Home, Thrasher thinks, crossing the Seine toward the cathedral. You know what Frost said: home was where, when you had to go there, they had to take you in. Home rimes with poem and poem with apple, or close enough. A pomme a day, you're the pomme of my eye, the forbidden fruit. He is approaching the Place du Parvis now and parvis, he thinks, comes to us from the word paradise. Of course. And there's the great façade of Our Lady and I am in paradise among the late tourists popping their flashbulbs. Is there presently a janitor with a rural eye in one of the great twin towers, seeing us as the first fireflies of the season? Or the last? Or maybe they don't have fireflies in France, only us poppers standing in paradise. To my left is the Hôtel-Dieu for the lame, behind me is the Préfecture de Police for the blame, to my right a little green we can call the Garden, and straight ahead, fixed in stone, balanced, cast with kings, angels, saints, birds, monsters, and flowers, with the wise and foolish, the good and the damned, with a God-child and His Virgin Mother, sure of its beginning, middle, and end, straight ahead, no joke, no playing around, no money down, no easy payments, straight ahead on the main concourse is The Story.

—I mean, if you can shrug off a sense of guilt at will, what in the world else will be true?

Her room had a bed he didn't know and a bookcase and chest of drawers he did. He sat on the strange bed, at the foot, and gazed toward the books, waiting for her. She had told him to go on in, she'd be just a minute. They had come back from the golf course and, in the kitchen, still in their coats, she leaning against the counter, he against the door (the dog lapping noisily at his water dish between them), they looked at each other. Finally she said, "Well?" Then she took off her coat and went in the next room and he could hear her climbing the stairs. "Ralph can come up too," she called back.

Thrasher now turned from the books to the dog who lay flat out, panting quietly across the threshold—and then she stepped over him.

"You're still dressed," she said, rubbing lotion on her hands, the stretch marks from Francine the same delicate, pearly trails running above and below her tan line.

She tossed the extra pillows off the bed and got under the quilt. "Thrasher?"

He turned. She was looking at the ceiling.

"I'm pretty nervous, Thrasher, I wish you'd hurry up."

He undressed and got in beside her, close, closer, slid one arm under her shoulders, the other around the backs of her cool legs, pulling her tight to him. He moved his nose back and forth in her cowlick.

She said, "I'm going to kiss you now, Thrasher. Hold still."

"I can't."

"Sure you can. One, two, three—stop."

She kissed him a quick peck on the lips.

"You still wiggle around like a big fish, you know that?"

He moved his nose to one of her ears.

"Can you feel my heartbeat?" she said.

He gave her a sudden big hug.

"Oh God—whew!—I'm not a tackling dummy!"

"Just getting warm," he said. "I'm nervous too."

"I think you cracked a rib."

"Ribs don't do much."

"Thrasher?"

"What?"

"I'm ready."

So he was back in the States, in a strange but good bed, his palm smeared with blood, afraid. He'd been dreaming of running with the dog again, cleaning out his lungs, getting in shape, real shape, eight or ten miles worth at a clip. But first, in the dream, he was lying in a vast field of timothy, thinking about the run, savoring it, and also regarding the sky, for the sky had said—a voice up there had said—*You are almost home.* Then he was waking up, could

261

hear someone in the distance preparing a tub, could hear Barbara call to Francine, "It's time, Sunshine . . . it's time . . ."—and Thrasher, leaving the field of timothy, about to go run, felt warm, felt ready. Then the thing happened on his face—struck his face, clawed it once quickly and was gone. His eye burst into flame. He covered the fire with his hands and cried out, "The cat! Take it away!"

Leaving the Place du Parvis, Thrasher walks up the dark Rue du Cloître-Notre Dame toward the Pont St. Louis. It's not a street he likes. Though it's deserted now, big buses are often parked there, the customers collected in knots on the sidewalk, the guides switching from German to Spanish to English to explain the symbolism of the serpent under the Virgin's foot or what time lunch is. But the other way around the cathedral to the bridge, through the pretty Square Jean XXIII, is closed at this hour. Thrasher goes to the square to read sometimes. In the afternoon babies and small children are brought there by mothers and grandmothers. He's gotten to know a few by sight—in particular a chunky little girl and her grandmother who always take the same bench and discuss the grandmother's dreams. Because they speak slowly Thrasher can follow them well enough to know that the woman has a recurring dream in which, like an angel, she flies a lot, around the Eiffel Tower, up and down the Seine, and somewhere in the suburbs where, during the war, she raised chickens for German officers. Telling her granddaughter about it, she shakes her head no, no, no, she doesn't want to, but what can she do? She lights a cigarette and sits back wearily on the bench. "I am fatigued from it!" she says in French. The three or four times that Thrasher has witnessed this scene, the little girl has responded that these adventures are good for her grandmother's appetite and complexion. The chunky girl reminds him of Orson Welles. The woman on the other hand is slim, fine-boned, and certainly must have been beautiful forty years ago.

Standing on the Pont St. Louis now, gazing down at the Seine, Thrasher remembers that one time she covered her face with her scarf and held it there until her cigarette burned her fingers.

"Anyway, what do you *do?*"

They were all three at the kitchen table. He was sipping coffee with one hand, holding an ice cube in a washrag under his eye with the other. And his daughter, who was so much older than the daughter he saw the last time, whose position in the universe—she had let him see—she was learning to protect with sudden laughter and could do all right with it, was now giving him another view of her: regarding him as hard as she could, as hard as those fragile eyes could bear to look at anyone who might hurt her. She wanted to know some things he owed her, no joking around.

"Well," he began, "I travel to names on the map to see what they look like. I try to go by bicycle if I can. Once I rode across Montana on a bike and slept in Deadman's Basin, which looked like a place plenty of men and women had died in, although I didn't see any that night, dead or alive. The sky, Francine, was wide open and full of stars, and you could smell sage everywhere. Made me hungry for a pork roast."

Thrasher looked at his daughter hoping she would smile.

"What else do you do?" she said, cool as a cop with a clipboard.

"Well, I do a lot of that, camping out and getting hungry. Except up in Canada. I didn't have the right gear and it was very cold. Had to abandon my bike up there too. But I caught some nice fish in Alberta, near a place called Henry House, not far from Pocahontas. Henry House—sounds like something from a kid's book, doesn't it?"

"All by yourself you do this?" Still cool.

"Pretty much."

"But don't you have friends?" Ah, she was warming up a little.

"You meet people, sure."

"I mean *friends*."

"No."

"I can't believe it," she said.

Was he lying to her? "Can't believe what?"

"Everything."

"Hold on now."

"You do next to nothing and have no friends. You enjoy that?" That foolishness, did she mean?

"I work when I can—seasonal jobs, canning, farming. I'm learning things, Francine."

"Like what, though?"

"Oh, that I might like to start a fish farm. Raise trout from fry. I know how to do it, from working in hatcheries out West."

263

"Where would you do it?"

"Maybe"—he glanced at her sidelong over the washrag—"around here someplace, the great prairie."

Her eyes narrowed a notch.

He said, "It would be fun, don't you think, raising fish?"

Barbara said, "Don't rub your eye. Here, let me see it again. Oh, it's much better. But another dab of this cream, I think. Hold still."

"He can't," Francine said as if to herself.

"There," Barbara said, "you'll live."

Thrasher looked at his daughter. What *could* he tell her about his—his time away? That he'd been trying to understand a few simple things. What would that mean to her? *She* was trying to understand a few complicated things. He shook his head. Look, baby, I'm stuck for words—can't you see that? Your old man's tongue-tied. The cat just missed his eye but got his tongue. Stanley, you ugly bastard. But I'm here, I love you, and I want to see more of you before . . . before you grow up. Grow up? Before you *leave* us, Francine, the three of us. I want to come back!

But Thrasher could say none of this. Instead, his armpits wet, he said, "Would you tell me more about school?"

"School?" she said with contempt.

"Is it really so bad?"

Rolling her eyes, "Yes."

"Yes," he agreed, suddenly tired, "I suppose it is . . ."

"You got out," she said, looking at him hard.

He knew that was coming. If the teacher hates school, why can't the student? He nodded. "But—" But what?

She sighed heavily, and said, as if reciting a prepared speech, "Sociology is boring, a waste. I do not believe in judging people as groups despite what Mr. Phipps says. I believe in brotherhood but that's another story. Composition for the College Bound, no comment, just ugh. Spanish is fine. Of course you can put up with a lot when you love the language. Modern Dance is good for my body and American Literary Masterpieces, you'll be glad to hear, has helped me to like Robert Frost. I'm the only one in the class who does."

They were quiet for a while. Then Francine said to her mother, "Tell him our favorite sentence from Dr. Marty."

Barbara said, "Dr. Marty is the principal. He writes a monthly newsletter for parents. In one of them, under something called Parent Support Group,' he wrote: 'Besides sharing concerns, parents will have an opportunity to practice facilitative communications and to use a decision-making model for problem situations.' "

"Basically though," Francine looked her father in the eye, "I hate school and can't wait to get out and start living my life. You can understand that."

Thrasher's not alone on the bridge, he now sees. A nun—a nun?—no, a man in a long coat, a small tent, stands near the far end, almost on the Île itself. He lifts a bottle to his mouth. Mr. Flood? Having a nightcap under the stars, sir?

It's late. Though Thrasher is tired, whipped, he doesn't want to go back to his hotel. He wishes he had a bottle too. One sits in his room ten minutes away, a nice Margaux, but he wants one here, now, on the Pont St. Louis, between La Cité and the Île St. Louis, in February or March of this year, this unusually warm season. A bottle, if he could choose, of Polish vodka, yes, the bull on the label, the golden straw inside, cheers, *salud*, health, *na zdrowie!*

He's walking toward the man now. The man hugging his bottle looks up slowly, suspicious, an old man—Lord no, a man about his own age—a man wrapped in three or four coats, furry brownish weasel face, eyes floating in egg white, runny, mouth sinking into his head, no luck, no tit, the man's had nothing, no sunny childhood, kicked from the womb by a startled mad hag who crawled off and never looked back. A bum. A clochard. Thrasher can smell the river water that's lapped at his skin without washing away anything.

He holds out a ten-franc piece. The man's eyes fry, congeal, and his collapsed lips separate, the hole smiles. The man takes the money. Thrasher points to the bottle.

So he was back without being back, splitting wood for their Christmas Eve fire, moved in without being in, out from under the heron anyway, the staring beef, in the yard with Ralph watching, snow on the ground and more falling, big sudden stars of it, Barbara and Francine off in the car, dropping off presents here and there for friends they'd made, a white yule, Bing, Rudolph, and Barbara said he could stay a while, let's not plan anything now,

265

they shook hands (shook hands!) after coming apart, I did miss fucking you Thrasher, straight from the shoulder, no theatrics, sweet but not soppy, Francine knocking on their door after the dance, I'm home, I'm sober, the light laughter (protection? because he was there? careful Thrasher), a match being struck, a slight odor of tobacco smoke, her own door closing, she has one a day Barbara told him, a Camel, your brand Thrasher, she's a lot like you, likes you too, you can see that can't you, can see I can't do anything that's not in our best interests, we've become—I hate to say—like sisters, but I like our life, my life, still we had all those years, good years, tender, corny, they get in your bones, mine anyway (mine too!), that's why I wrote, my bones wrote, curious, middle-aged, don't you think about getting older, getting a few things straight?

Yes!

Bringing the axe down hard, clean, a good split, smell that. Red oak.

He'll build a splendid fire, ice the champagne—no, first take a walk, come on Ralph, put one foot in front of the other, stick out his tongue and snare a few snowflakes, eat the stars, those intricate feathers, tail feathers Ralph, pay attention, from a rare bird that flies only once in a blue arctic moon, during the mating season when his quickened heart, and hers, beat so rapidly the results can be seen as far away as your little plot on the prairie.

The bum on the bridge, mumbling, wiggling shit-colored fingers, wants a cigarette. Thrasher gives him one and takes another pull on the sour bottle—the skin housing his mouth drawing tight, puckering. Rhubarb juice in there? Or some exotic disease that will claim all his teeth?

It's starting to blow a bit, witch tails on the Seine, and here comes the rain. Be gentle.

"You know," he says to the bum, "I've often wondered about you fellows."

The bum puts up his collars, grunts for the bottle. Opens his hole, pours, ahhh, belches *baarawwk!*

"We all wonder, sir. We see you sleeping on a hot-air vent in the sidewalk, broad daylight, having a steam and a sprawl, relaxed, oblivious to the daily bump and grind, rosy-nosed, snoring perhaps, and we wonder."

Thrasher accepts the bottle for his turn at it. He remembers sharing a bottle of beer with his father, at lunch on the job site, a swig or two before biting into those thick roast-beef sandwiches his mother packed, the apple pie, good wholesome fare, coffee with Pet milk afterwards, maybe a snooze in the back of the truck, head resting on a stack of sweet, white-pine two-by-fours . . .

He pulls at the sour wine and wipes his mouth. "Yes sir, my man, we wonder. And what we wonder—some of us—is this: what do you think of us as we hustle past in our clean cottons and polyesters, underarms protected, unsightly nostril hairs removed?"

He hands the bottle back, or starts to—his companion wants him to hold it a minute while he unbuttons and has a pee. Not so easy, two or three pairs of pants. There. Ahh . . . throat graveling satisfaction, steam rising, laughing as he sprays the bridge, one hand pointing up in the rain, "Dieu . . ."

"Yes, I see. You're both having a leak, you and the Almighty. So *that's* what you think of us, is it? Wonderful!"

Baarawwk!

"Excellent!"

His companion is ready for a drink now, the job's done, a thirst created. But what's this, the bottle's almost empty! The man shakes his head sadly, drinks, measures the level, regards Thrasher (wants an opinion? sympathy?), quickly takes another drink, then offers Thrasher what's left. The sludge.

"You are too kind, sir." Thrasher lifts the bottle above his head, "A toast. To God's kidneys!" He downs the stuff—rhubarb leavings, stringy, awful. He spits.

The bum, appraising the empty bottle, broods. Gives it a final, fruitless suck. Bah! Seems to be sinking farther into his tent, mouth first. Hunched. Mumbling. No luck, no tit.

Thrasher lights a cigarette.

"My good fellow," he says at last, his shriveled mouth-skin making speech difficult, "I have an idea! Not far from here"—he points—"lies a surprise that"—he spits again—"that I suspect will follow your noble number admirably. Come."

His companion isn't sure. The eyes floating forlorn.

"But of course," Thrasher urges him, pointing, lifting a phantom bottle to his lips, smacking them, "of course!"

Back from his walk with Ralph, Thrasher laid wood in the fireplace and then went to work in the kitchen—celery, carrots, onions, garlic, bread crumbs for the stuffing. Barbara and Francine weren't home yet. Mincing, chopping, I should call my mother, he thought. But what would I say? She'll cry and ask me why and I won't want to talk about it, and what kind of a Christmas is that for her? She'll say Barbara is so sweet. I'll say I know. No, first she'll say where *are* you? At Barbara's I'll say. At Barbara's?! She'll be confused . . . she'll be having a drink . . . my brother and his family just came in . . . everyone ebullient . . . her stuffing, her bread smell wonderful. . . . Are you *living* there? Are you getting back together? Oh Son. *Then* she'll start to cry. And that sweet Francine, she'll say, I feel so sorry for her. The truth is, Mom, I came home to ask Barbara to take me back. We've decided for now not to decide anything. We shook hands on it. Meantime I'm careful, watching my step, the old temper, the Polish half. Meantime I run with the dog and help in the kitchen. Meantime I've slept in her bed and you're right, she is sweet, sweet as ever. Meantime, ah meantime . . .

No, he'll go see her after the holidays, not so much pressure then.

Thrasher's companion, they discover, has a name, Claude, and as they approach the Hôtel Jeanne d'Arc on the Rue Jarente—dark now, even the little café closed up—Claude begins to sing in the rain, or croak, or croak-and-wheeze; in any case he smells the bottle that Thrasher has promised and repromised half a dozen times during their journey, and his spirits are high, the weasel face and the runny eyes almost shine with health and adventure. A couple of times he's tried to throw a friendly arm around Thrasher's shoulders, but he stands a good foot shorter and, wrapped in all those bulky clothes, his arm only bounced off Thrasher's back.

At the hotel door his *beeg Anglais* friend quiets him down. "My concierge, sir, who is also the owner of this establishment, is a Yugoslav lady with very white skin and flaming red hair piled up in a tidy cone. Moreover she comes from a fine family in Ljubljana. She would get a pimple if she saw you."

Inside, however, the coast is clear and Thrasher leads him up the stairs. It's warm in the hotel. The madame does not like *zima*, the cold. On the third floor, halfway, Claude's furry face, Thrasher sees, begins to pale where it can and the flaps of skin around his mouth-hole flutter in and out for air. Thrasher takes off his coat and indicates that Claude should do the same; but when Claude does—

reluctantly, and only one of his valuable coats—Thrasher is sorry. A rich new odor assaults the warm Yugoslav keep, an animal days-ripe in the hateful trap, a stink to make the duke think twice about crossing the swamp and taking his rightful castle.

They stop for Claude again on the fifth floor, his runny eyes at the brink of losing their yolks. Thrasher whispers, "Don't die here, sir, please, the maids in the morning, their sensibilities, you understand. Yes, that's it, breathe slowly, accept the fear, go with it . . ."

On the sixth floor finally, Thrasher shakes his companion's clammy hand. "We're home, boy!" In the room he decides against suggesting that Claude remove another coat, settles him in a chair, opens the window. At the closet he gets the Bordeaux he's promised.

"A gift from an angel," he says, bringing it to Claude, showing him the label. "Chateau-Margaux, '74. A decent year, I think. You agree?"

Claude's eyes achieve a confused light, his tongue appears at the hole like a freshly skinned mouse. He really hasn't recovered from the climb yet, but he's working at it, working at it.

"Ah, a respectable pop," Thrasher says, pulling the cork. "I suppose we should let it breathe a bit, all that loving care inside . . . then again—" He takes a slug. "Umm, not quite up to the sass yours had, but it'll do. Have at it, pal."

Claude receives the bottle with trembling hands as if it were a brand new thing—no, much more: a brand new life, bright and shiny with good teeth, no aches, nothing broken or cracked anywhere, a life promising beauty, dignity. His eyes begin to overflow.

"Damn you, Claude, this isn't the time for that." Thrasher puts a hand on the bottle and urges the man to drink. "Come on, fella. No theatrics. Wet your whistle. Enjoy."

Closing his eyes the bum drinks.

Thrasher moves away, toward the window, "Thata boy." He sucks in fresh air, gesturing to Claude to keep the bottle, have all he wants, take his time—and lighting a cigarette Thrasher looks out over the rain-glazed rooftops, there, in that direction, west . . .

Barbara and Francine were setting the Christmas table and laughing about someone named Rick the Stick who had written a love letter to someone named Charlotte. Somehow the editors of

269

the school paper got hold of the letter, thought it was a parody, printed it, and Rick the Stick's ears, which stuck out *any*way, were crimson all week. In the dining room, reporting this story among the sounds of silver and dinnerware being handled, Francine laughed until she cried.

"Is my mascara running, Mother?"

"No, Darling."

Thrasher tended the fire, red oak and hickory, and the room was expanding—he could feel the white walls moving back giving him space, the Lake Superior shoreline hanging over the sofa winding for miles toward summer, *into* summer, a deep brilliant blue, and Thrasher could smell it and smell the pine timber and the rich loam he left his tracks in, and if anyone came along right then and said, Thrasher, it's only that little tree hung with tinsel and balls you smell, he'd pick the fellow up and shake him to show he had a few screws loose—of course he could smell that timber!

And in that full mood he got out the champagne. Snow was falling past the window in fat flakes. They met at the table, laughing, beaming. The table shone with candles, china, snow-light, the glazed turkey steaming, giblet gravy, a floating galaxy of hearts and gizzards, the rich reds and yellows of fresh cranberries and buttered yams bursting their jackets, startling green asparagus spears! He raised his glass. He felt large. Any second now he believed his cheeks would crack from the clownish smile they bore. In part of his brain he stepped quickly aside, had to, he was dancing, in an orchard somewhere, whooping it up, he needed room—he held Barbara in one arm, Francine in the other, smelling apple blossoms in their hair!—and he moved closer to them to accommodate this vision. He hugged them now, spilling champagne, groaning the great good feeling that was filling his face, his chest. He wanted to pick them up, carry them off. He raised his glass again, but nothing would come out, no words. All he wanted was a simple phrase or two—here's to us, to more, much more. Anything. Lord. Somebody, help me out. He looked at them. They were waiting. Don't be afraid. Then his mouth opened and he couldn't stop, he said he wanted to come back, for good, the three of them, be together again, we can do it, don't cry, look I'm carving the turkey, it's easy, out comes the stuffing, on go the yams, the berries, these little hearts and gizzards, everything, look! And working fast he piled each plate high with the rich colors of their feast, the reds and yellows and greens, piled them higher with seconds, thirds, the creamy white meat, the nutty dark, pouring more gravy, more stars, they needed all the help they could get, he was saying, they had a long, long way to go, when Barbara put her hand on his arm.

Claude sits in his chair, head fallen back, snoring. The bottle's protected in his arms. Thrasher looks at the man. The party's over. It's time for the man to go.

"Get out," Thrasher says.

But the man continues to snore. Thrasher feels weak and light and unable to move. He wants to hear Francine and Barbara in the next room, hear them talking, he wants to go to them, take their hands.

"Look," he says, "we're alive!"

But all he hears is a man snoring.

Thrasher looks at the man, at a man who understands the beauty of sleep. Finally Thrasher goes over to him. He frees the bottle from his arms. Then he picks him up and carries him to the bed. The man continues to snore, undisturbed. Lucky man. Thrasher takes the wine and leaves.

Outside the sky is a wide bruise, but the rain has stopped. Thrasher walks, pausing now and then to drink from the bottle, stepping aside as the garbage trucks begin to come out and swallow lettuce leaves and baby shoes and the brown arrangements of bone. His legs feel stiff, as if they are all bone. He turns at the Rue de Turenne, again at the Rue des Francs-Bourgeois. He comes to the Place des Vosges, the oldest square in Paris. "Ah," he says, "the seventeenth century. Order, elegance . . ." The gate is locked. Through the bars he sees Louis XIII astride a white stone horse. Now the moon appears, turning the monument, turning everything brighter. Thrasher moves along the fence, gripping the bars as he goes. His knuckles look blue, don't they. Never mind, he wants to be in there. He wants to walk across the grass, which is against the rules. The park guards during the day keep you off it, wag a finger, speak firmly, it's not correct—dapper little soldiers, estimable women, round and round and round they stroll, keeping an eye on the likes of Thrasher—as they should!—look at him now, prowling the square, stinking, he's a bad character: *peau de vache!*—skin of a cow!

He drinks from the bottle, wipes his chin on his sleeve. His sleeve? This is not his sleeve. Nor his coat. It's the bum's coat. No wonder he's stinking.

He looks through the bars. Tell me, Louis, doesn't your ass get sore just sitting there? No? And the birdshit on your nose? No problem either? Of course not. It's a nice life you've got, symmetrical, the houses around all alike, you at the center, children at your feet, their pretty mothers, the old folks respectable, dozing, wrapped up like babies, balance, yes.

His eyes close. He sees her standing in a field of virgin prairie, gathering the wind in her hair . . . and he getting up from his bed in the dorm and walking to her window, standing there under the harvest moon, waiting beside the brilliant ivy. He has not spoken to her yet. For weeks he has watched her take her seat, watched her write her words in a blue notebook, watched her leave. Now the beaming professor has ushered them all out to the field at the edge of town, and he is watching her there too, following her, until she turns in that turning wind and says, "Listen." He looks up. Somewhere geese are flying. Under the wide, plum-colored swirls of sky he knows it. He can hear them at the edges of his heartbeat. He can smell them—marsh-ripe, fish-breathed, feather-wet—and suddenly he knows he must go there, where the blues and specklebellies are, where the Giant Canadas are.

The street is silvery, moon-sweet, and calling *wah, wahaa,* calling *ha-lonk, ha-lonk,* he starts out, slowly . . . and slowly sinks to his knees. He'd like to climb this fence and sit on the horse with Louis but, sad to say, he is bone-tired. Tail-dragging whipped. Skunked. But surely he thinks about things, his mind isn't gone, is it? About getting older? Getting a few things straight? Hold still, Thrasher, I'm going to kiss you now.

nominated by Stanley Lindberg

THE MERRY CHASE

fiction by GORDON LISH

from THE ANTIOCH REVIEW

DON'T TELL ME. Do me a favor and let me guess. Be honest with me, tell the truth, don't make me laugh. Tell me, don't make me have to tell you, do I have to tell you that when you're hot, you're hot, that when you're dead, you're dead? Because you know what I know? I know you like I know myself, I know you like the back of my hand, I know you like a book, I know you inside out. You know what? I know you like you'll never know.

You think I don't know whereof I speak?

I know, I know. I know the day will come, the day will dawn.

Didn't I tell you you never know? Because I guarantee it, no one will dance a jig, no one will do a dance, no one will cater to you so fast, or wait on you hand and foot. You think they could care less?

But I could never get enough of it, I could never get enough. Look at me, I could take a bite out of it, I could eat it up alive, but you want to make a monkey out of me, don't you? You want me to talk myself blue in the face for you, beat my head against a brick wall for you, come running when you have the least little complaint. What am I, your slave? You couldn't be happy except over my dead body? You think I don't know whereof I speak? I promise you, one day you will sing a different tune.

But in the interim, first things first. Because it won't kill you to do without, tomorrow is another day, let me look at it, let me see it, there is no time like the present, let me kiss it and make it better.

Let me tell you something, everyone in the whole wide world should only have it half as good as you.

273

You know what this is? You want to know what this is? Because this is some deal, this is some set-up, this is some joke. You could vomit from what a joke this is.

I want you to hear something, I want you to hear the unvarnished truth.

You know what you are?

That's what you are!

You sit, I'll go—I already had enough to choke a horse.

Go ahead and talk my arm off. Talk me deaf, dumb, and blind. Nobody is asking, nobody is talking, nobody wants to know. In all decency, in all honesty, in all candor, in all modesty, you have some gall, some nerve, and I mean that in all sincerity. The crust of you, my God!

I am telling you, I am pleading with you, I am down to you on bended knee—just don't get cute with me, just don't make any excuses to me—because in broad daylight, in the dead of night, at the crack of dawn.

You think the whole world is going to do a dance around you? No one is going to do a dance around you. No one even knows you are alive, they don't know you from Adam.

But if it is not one thing, then it is another.

Just who do you think you are, coming in here and lording it all over all of us? Do you think you are a law unto yourself? I am going to give you some advice. Don't flatter yourself—you are not the queen of the May, not by a long shot. Act your age—share and share alike.

Ages ago, years ago, so long ago I couldn't begin to remember, past history, ancient history—you don't want to know, another age, another life, another theory altogether.

Don't ask. Don't even begin to ask. Don't make me any promises. Don't tell me one thing and do another. Don't look at me cross-eyed. Don't look at me like that. Don't hand me that crap. Look around you, for pity's sake. Don't you know that one hand washes the other? Talk sense. Take stock.

Give me some credit for intelligence. Show me I'm not wasting my breath. Don't make me sick. You are making me sick. Why are you doing this to me? Do you get pleasure from doing this to me? Don't think I don't know what you are trying to do to me.

Don't make me do your thinking for you.

Shame on you, be ashamed of yourself, have you absolutely no shame?

Why must I always have to tell you?

Why must I always drop everything and come running?

Does nothing ever occur to you?

Can't you see with your own two eyes?

You are your own worst enemy.

What's the sense of talking to you? I might as well talk to myself. Say something. Try to look like you've got a brain in your head.

You think this is a picnic? This is no picnic. Don't stand on ceremony with me. The whole world is not going to step to your tune. I warn you—wake up before it's too late.

You know what? A little birdie just told me. You know what? You have got a lot to learn—that's what.

I can't hear myself talk. I can't hear myself think. I cannot remember from one minute to the next.

Why do I always have to tell you again and again?

Give me a minute to think. Just let me catch my breath.

Don't you ever stop to ask?

I'm going to tell you something. I'm going to give you the benefit of my advice. Do you want some good advice?

You think the sun rises and sets on you, don't you? You should get down on your hands and knees and thank God. You should count your blessings. Why don't you look around yourself and really see for once in your life? You just don't know when you're well off. You have no idea how the rest of the world lives. You are as innocent as the day you were born. You should thank your lucky stars. You should try to make amends. You should do your best to put it all out of your mind. Worry never got anybody anywhere.

But by the same token.

Whatever you do, promise me this—just promise me that you will do your best to keep an open mind.

What do I say to you, where do I start with you, how do I make myself heard? I don't know where to begin with you, I don't know where to start with you, I don't know how to impress on you the importance of every single solitary word. Thank God I am alive to tell you, thank God I am here to tell you, thank God you've got someone to tell you, I only wish I could begin to tell you, if there were only some way someone could tell you, if only there were someone here to tell you, but you don't want to listen, you don't want to learn, you don't want to know, you don't want to help yourself, you just want to have it all your own sweet way. Who can talk to you? Can anyone talk to you? You don't want anyone to talk to you. So far as you are concerned, the whole world could drop dead.

You think death is a picnic? Death is no picnic. Face facts, don't kid yourself, people are trying to talk some sense into you, it's not all just fun and fancy free, it's not all just high, wide, and handsome, it's not just a bed of roses and peaches and cream.

You take the cake, you take my breath away—you are really one for the books.

Be smart and play it down. Be smart and stay in the wings. Be smart and let somebody else carry the ball for a change.

You know what I've got to do? I've got to talk to you like a baby. I've got to talk to you like a Dutch uncle. I've got to handle you with kid gloves.

Let me tell you something no one else would have the heart to tell you. Look far and wide—because they are few and far between!

Go ahead, go to the ends of the earth, go to the highest mountain, go to any lengths, because they won't lift a finger for you—or didn't you know that some things are not for man to know, that some things are better left unsaid, that some things you shouldn't wish on a dog, not on a bet, not on your life, not in a month of Sundays?

What do you want? You want the whole world to revolve around you, you want the whole world at your beck and call? That's what you want, isn't it? Be honest with me.

Answer me this one question—how can you look at me like this?

Don't you dare act as if you didn't hear me.

You want to know what's wrong with you? This is what is wrong with you. You are going to the dogs, you are lying down with dogs, you are waking sleeping dogs—don't you know enough to leave before the last dog is dead?

When are you going to learn to leave well enough alone?

You know what you are? Let me tell you what you are. You are betwixt and between.

I'm on to you, I've got your number, I can see right through you—I warn you, don't you dare try to put anything over on me or get on my good side or lead me a merry chase.

So who's going to do your dirty work for you now? *You?* Do me a favor and don't make me laugh!

Oh, sure, you think you can rise above it, you think you can live all your life with your head in the clouds, in a cave, without rhyme or reason, without a hitch, without batting an eyelash, without blemish, without a leg to stand on, without fail, without cause, without a little bit of butter on your bread, but let me tell you something—you're all wet!

You know what? You're trying to get away with false pretenses, that's what! You think you're modesty itself, that's what! You think you look good in clothes, that's what! But you know what is wrong with you? Because I am here to tell you what is wrong with you. There is no happy medium with you, there is no live and let live with you, because talking to you is like talking to a brick wall until a person can break a blood vessel and turn blue in the face.

Pardon my French, but you know what I say?

I say put up or shut up!

Pay attention to me!

You think I am talking just to hear myself talk?

nominated by The Antioch Review

IN THE COUNTRY OF LAST THINGS

fiction by PAUL AUSTER

from THE PARIS REVIEW

THESE ARE the last things, she wrote. One by one they disappear and never come back. I can tell you of the ones I have seen, of the ones that are no more, but I doubt there will be time. It is all happening too fast now, and I cannot keep up.

I don't expect you to understand. You have seen none of this, and even if you tried, you could not imagine it. These are the last things. A house is there one day, and the next day it is gone. A street you walked down yesterday is no longer there today. Even the weather is in constant flux. A day of sun followed by a day of rain, a day of snow followed by a day of fog, warm then cool, wind then stillness, a stretch of bitter cold, and then today, in the middle of winter, an afternoon of fragrant light, warm to the point of merely sweaters. When you live in the city, you learn to take nothing for granted. Close your eyes for a moment, turn around to look at something else, and the thing that was before you is suddenly gone. Nothing lasts, you see, not even the thoughts inside you. And you mustn't waste your time looking for them. Once a thing is gone that is the end of it.

This is how I live, her letter continued. I don't eat much. Just enough to keep me going from step to step, and no more. At times my weakness is so great, I feel the next step will never come. But I manage. In spite of the lapses, I keep myself going. You should see how well I manage.

The streets of the city are everywhere, and no two streets are the same. I put one foot in front of the other, and then the other foot in front of the first, and then hope I can do it again. Nothing more than that. You must understand how it is with me now. I move. I breathe what air is given me. I eat as little as I can. No matter what anyone says, the only thing that counts is staying on your feet.

You remember what you said to me before I left. William has disappeared, you said, and no matter how hard I looked, I would never find him. Those were your words. And then I told you that I didn't care what you said, that I was going to find my brother. And then I got on that terrible boat and left you. How long ago was that? I can't remember anymore. Years and years, I think. But that is only a guess. I make no bones about it. I've lost track, and nothing will ever set it right for me.

This much is certain. If not for my hunger, I wouldn't be able to go on. You must get used to doing with as little as you can. By wanting less, you are content with less, and the less you need, the better off you are. That is what the city does to you. It turns your thoughts inside-out. It makes you want to live, and at the same time it tries to take your life away from you. There is no escape from this. Either you do or you don't. And if you do, you can't be sure of doing it the next time. And if you don't, you never will again.

I am not sure why I am writing to you now. To be honest, I have barely thought of you since I got here. But suddenly, after all this time, I feel there is something to say, and if I don't quickly write it down, my head will burst. It doesn't matter if you read it. It doesn't even matter if I send it—assuming that could be done. Perhaps it comes down to this. I am writing to you because you know nothing. Because you are far away from me and know nothing.

279

There are people so thin, she wrote, they are sometimes blown away. The winds in the city are ferocious, always gusting off the river and singing in your ears, always buffeting you back and forth, always swirling papers and garbage in your path. It's not uncommon to see the thinnest people moving about in twos and threes, sometimes whole families, bound together by ropes and chains, to ballast one another against the blasts. Others give up trying to go out altogether, hugging to the doorways and alcoves, until even the fairest sky seems a threat. Better to wait quietly in their corner, they think, than to be dashed against the stones. It is also possible to become so good at not eating that eventually you can eat nothing at all.

It is even worse for the ones who fight their hunger. Thinking about food too much can only lead to trouble. These are the ones who are obsessed, who refuse to give in to the facts. They prowl the streets at all hours, scavenging for morsels, taking enormous risks for even the smallest crumb. No matter how much they are able to find, it will never be enough. They eat without ever filling themselves, tearing into their food with animal haste, their bony fingers picking, their quivering jaws never shut. Most of it dribbles down their chins, and what they manage to swallow, they usually throw up again in a few minutes. It is a slow death, as if food were a fire, a madness, burning them up from within. They think they are eating to stay alive, but in the end they are the ones who are eaten.

As it turns out, food is a complicated business, and unless you learn to accept what is given to you, you will never be at peace with yourself. Shortages are frequent, and a food that has given you pleasure one day will more than likely be gone the next. The municipal markets are probably the safest, most reliable places to shop, but the prices are high and the selections paltry. One day there will be nothing but radishes, another day nothing but stale chocolate cake. To change your diet so often and so drastically can be very hard on the stomach. But the municipal markets have the advantage of being guarded by the police, and at least you know that what you buy there will wind up in your own stomach and not someone else's. Food theft is so common in the streets that it is not even considered a crime anymore. On top of that, the municipal markets are the only legally sanctioned form of food distribution.

There are many private food sellers around the city, but their goods can be confiscated at any time. Even those who can afford to pay the police bribes necessary to stay in business still face the constant threat of attack from thieves. Thieves also plague the customers of the private markets, and it has been statistically proven that one out of every two purchases leads to a robbery. It hardly seems worth it, I think, to risk so much for the fleeting joy of an orange or the taste of boiled ham. But the people are insatiable: hunger is a curse that comes every day, and the stomach is a bottomless pit, a hole as big as the world. The private markets, therefore, do a good business, in spite of the obstacles, picking up from one place and going to another, constantly on the move, appearing for an hour or two somewhere and then vanishing out of sight. One word of warning, however. If you must have the foods from the private markets, then be sure to avoid the renegade grocers, for fraud is rampant, and there are many people who will sell anything just to turn a profit: eggs and oranges filled with sawdust, bottles of piss pretending to be beer. No, there is nothing people will not do, and the sooner you learn that, the better off you will be.

When you walk through the streets, she went on, you must remember to take only one step at a time. Otherwise, falling is inevitable. Your eyes must be constantly open, looking up, looking down, looking ahead, looking behind, on watch for other bodies, on your guard against the unforeseeable. To collide with someone can be fatal. Two people collide and then start pounding each other with their fists. Or else, they fall to the ground and do not try to get up. Sooner or later, a moment comes when you do not try to get up anymore. Bodies ache, you see, there's no cure for that. And more terribly here than elsewhere.

The rubble is a special problem. You must learn how to manage the unseen furrows, the sudden clusters of rocks, the shallow ruts, so that you do not stumble or hurt yourself. And then there are the tolls, these worst of all, and you must use cunning to avoid them. Wherever buildings have fallen or garbage has gathered, large mounds stand in the middle of the street, blocking all passage.

Men build these barricades whenever the materials are at hand, and then they mount them, with clubs, or rifles, or bricks, and wait on their perches for people to pass by. They are in control of the street. If you want to get through, you must give the guards whatever they demand. Sometimes it is money; sometimes it is food; sometimes it is sex. Beatings are commonplace, and every now and then you hear of a murder.

New tolls go up, the old tolls disappear. You can never know which streets to take and which to avoid. Bit by bit, the city robs you of certainty. There can never be any fixed path, and you can survive only if nothing is necessary to you. Without warning, you must be able to change, to drop what you are doing, to reverse. In the end, there is nothing that is not the case. As a consequence, you must learn how to read the signs. When the eyes falter, the nose will sometimes serve. My sense of smell has become unnaturally keen. In spite of the side effects—the sudden nausea, the dizziness, the fear that comes with the rank air invading my body—it protects me when turning corners, and these can be the most dangerous moments of all. For the tolls have a particular stench that you learn to recognize, even from a great distance. Compounded of stones, of cement, and of wood, the mounds also hold garbage and chips of plaster, and the sun works on this garbage, producing a reek more intense than elsewhere, and the rain works on the plaster, logging it and melting it, so that it too exudes its own smell, and when the one works on the other, interacting in the alternate fits of dry and damp, the odor of the toll begins to blossom. The essential thing is not to become inured. For habits are deadly. Even if it is for the hundredth time, you must encounter each thing as if you have never known it before. No matter how many times, it must always be the first time. This is next to impossible, I realize, but it is an absolute rule.

You would think that sooner or later it would all come to an end. Things fall apart and vanish, and nothing new is made. People die, and babies refuse to be born. In the past year I can't remember seeing a single newborn child. And yet, there are always new people to replace the ones who have vanished. They pour in from the country and the outlying towns, dragging carts piled high with their belongings, sputtering in with broken-down cars, all of them hungry, all of them homeless. Until they have learned the ways of the city, these newcomers are easy victims. Many of them are duped out of their money before the end of the first day. Some people pay for apartments that don't exist, others are lured into giving commissions for jobs that never materialize, still others lay out their savings to buy food that turns out to be painted cardboard. These are only the most ordinary kinds of tricks. I know a man who makes his living by standing in front of the old city hall and asking for money every time one of the newcomers glances at the tower clock. If there is a dispute, his assistant, who poses as a greenhorn, pretends to go through the ritual of looking at the clock and paying him, so that the stranger will think this is the common practice. The startling thing is not that confidence men exist, but that it is so easy for them to get people to part with their money.

For those who have a place to live, there is always the danger they will lose it. Most buildings are not owned by anyone, and therefore you have no rights as a tenant; no lease, no legal leg to stand on if something goes against you. It's not uncommon for people to be forcibly evicted from their apartments and thrown out onto the street. A group barges in on you with rifles and clubs and tells you to get out, and unless you think you can overcome them, what choice do you have? This practice is known as housebreaking, and there are few people in the city who have not lost their homes in this way at one time or another. But even if you are fortunate enough to escape this particular form of eviction, you never know when you will fall prey to one of the phantom landlords. These are extortionists who terrorize nearly every neighborhood in the city, forcing people to pay protection money just to be able to stay in their apartments. They proclaim themselves owners of a building, bilk the occupants, and are almost never opposed.

For those who do not have a home, however, the situation is beyond reprieve. There is no such thing as a vacancy. But still, the rental agencies carry on a sort of business. Every day they place notices in the newspaper, advertising fraudulent apartments, in order to attract people to their offices and collect a fee from them. No one is fooled by this practice, yet there are many people willing to sink their last penny into these empty promises. They arrive outside the offices early in the morning and patiently wait in line, sometimes for hours, just to be able to sit with an agent for ten minutes and look at photographs of buildings on tree-lined streets, of comfortable rooms, of apartments furnished with carpets and soft leather chairs—peaceful scenes to evoke the smell of coffee wafting in from the kitchen, the steam of a hot bath, the bright colors of potted plants snug on the sill. It doesn't seem to matter to anyone that these pictures were taken more than ten years ago.

So many of us have become like children again. It's not that we make an effort, you understand, or that anyone is really conscious of it. But when hope disappears, when you find that you have given up hoping even for the possibility of hope, you tend to fill the empty spaces with dreams, little child-like thoughts and stories to keep you going. Even the most hardened people have trouble stopping themselves. Without fuss or prelude they break off from what they are doing, sit down, and talk about the desires that have been welling up inside them. Food, of course, is one of the favorite subjects. Often you will overhear a group of people describing a meal in meticulous detail, beginning with the soups and appetizers and slowly working their way to dessert, dwelling on each savor and spice, on all the various aromas and flavors, concentrating now on the method of preparation, now on the effect of the food itself, from the first twinge of taste on the tongue to the gradually expanding sense of peace as the food travels down the throat and arrives in the belly. These conversations sometimes go on for hours, and they have a highly rigorous protocol. You must never laugh, for example, and you must never allow your hunger to get the better of you. No outbursts, no unpremeditated sighs. That would lead to tears, and nothing spoils a food conversation more quickly than tears. For best results, you must allow your mind to leap into the words coming from the mouths of the others. If the words can consume you, you will be able to forget your present hunger and enter what people call the "arena of the sustaining nimbus." There are even those who say there is nutritional value in these food talks—given the proper concentration and an equal desire to believe in the words among those taking part.

All this belongs to the language of ghosts. There are many other possible kinds of talks in this language. Most of them begin when one person says to another: I wish. What they wish for might be anything at all, as long as it is something that cannot happen. I wish the sun would never set. I wish money would grow in my pockets. I wish the city would be like it was in the old days. You get the idea. Absurd and infantile things, with no meaning and no reality. In general, people hold to the belief that however bad things were yesterday, they were better than things are today. What they were like two days ago was even better than yesterday. The farther you go back, the more beautiful and desirable the world becomes. You drag yourself from sleep each morning to face something that is always worse than what you faced the day before, but by talking of the world that existed before you went to sleep, you can delude yourself into thinking that the present day is simply an apparition, no more or less real than the memories of all the other days you carry around inside you.

I understand why people play this game, but I myself have no taste for it. I refuse to speak the language of ghosts, and whenever I hear others speaking it, I walk away or put my hands over my ears. Yes, things have changed for me. You remember what a playful little girl I was. You could never get enough of my stories, of the worlds I used to make up for us to play inside of. The Castle of No Return, the Land of Sadness, the Forest of Forgotten Words. Do you remember them? How I loved to tell you lies, to trick you into believing my stories, and to watch your face turn serious as I led you from one outlandish scene to the next. Then I would tell you it was all made up, and you would start to cry. I think I loved those tears of yours as much as your smile. Yes, I was probably a bit wicked, even in those days, wearing the little frocks my mother used to dress me in, with my skinned and scabby knees, and my little baby's cunt with no hair. But you loved me, didn't you? You loved me until you were insane with it.

Now I am all common sense and hard calculation. I don't want to be like the others. I see what their imaginings do to them, and I will not let that happen to me. The ghost people always die in their sleep. For a month or two they walk around with a strange smile on their face, and a weird glow of otherness hovers around them, as if they've already begun to disappear. The signs are unmistakable, even the forewarning hints: the slight flush to the cheeks, the eyes suddenly a little bigger than usual, the stuporous shuffle, the foul smell from the lower body. It is probably a happy death, however. I am willing to grant them that. At times I have almost envied them. But finally, I cannot let myself go. I will not allow it. I am going to hold on for as long as I can, even if it kills me.

Other deaths are more dramatic. There are the Runners, for example, a sect of people who run through the streets as fast as they can, flailing their arms wildly about them, punching the air, screaming at the top of their lungs. Most of the time they travel in groups: six, ten, even twenty of them charging down the street together, never stopping for anything in their path, running and running until they drop from exhaustion. The point is to die as quickly as possible, to drive yourself so hard that your heart cannot stand it. The Runners say that no one would have the courage to do this on his own. By running together, each member of the group is swept along by the others, encouraged by the screams, whipped to a frenzy of self-punishing endurance. That is the irony. In order to kill yourself by running, you first have to train yourself to be a good runner. Otherwise, you would not have the strength to push yourself far enough. The Runners, however, go through arduous preparations to meet their fate, and if they happen to fall on their way to that fate, they know how to pick themselves up immediately and continue. I suppose it's a kind of religion. There are several offices throughout the city—one for each of the nine census zones—and in order to join, you must go through a series of difficult initiations: holding your breath under water, fasting, putting your hand in the flame of a candle, not speaking to anyone for seven days. Once you have been accepted, you must submit to the code of the group. This involves six to twelve months of communal living, a strict regimen of exercise and training, and a gradually reduced intake of food. By the time a member is ready to make his death run, he has simultaneously reached a point of ultimate strength and ultimate weakness. He can theoretically run forever, and at the same time his body has used up all its resources. This combination produces the desired result. You set out with your companions on the morning of the appointed day and run until you have escaped your body, running and screaming until you have flown out of yourself. Eventually, your soul wriggles free, your body drops to the ground, and you are dead. The Runners advertise that their method is over ninety percent failure-proof— which means that almost no one ever has to make a second death-run.

More common are the solitary deaths. But these, too, have been transformed into a kind of public ritual. People climb to the highest places for no other reason than to jump. The Last Leap, it is called, and I admit there is something stirring about watching one, something that seems to open a whole new world of freedom inside you: to see the body poised at the roof's edge, and then, always, the slight moment of hesitation, as if from a desire to relish those seconds, and the way your own life seems to gather in your throat, and then, unexpectedly (for you can never be sure when it will happen), the body hurls itself through the air and comes flying down to the street. You would be amazed at the enthusiasm of the crowds: to hear their frantic cheering, to see their excitement. It is as if the violence and beauty of the spectacle had wrenched them from themselves, had made them forget the paltriness of their own lives. The Last Leap is something everyone can understand, and it corresponds to everyone's inner longings: to die in a flash, to obliterate yourself in one brief and glorious moment. I sometimes think that death is the one thing we have any feeling for. It is our art form, the only way we can express ourselves.

Still, there are those of us who manage to live. For death, too, has become a source of life. With so many people thinking of how to put an end to things, meditating on the various ways to leave this world, you can imagine the opportunities for turning a profit. A clever person can live quite well off the deaths of others. For not everyone has the courage of the Runners or the Leapers, and many need to be helped along with their decision. The ability to pay for these services is naturally a precondition, and for that reason few but the wealthiest people can afford them. But business is nevertheless quite brisk, especially at the Euthanasia Clinics. These come in several different varieties, depending on how much you are willing to spend. The simplest and cheapest form takes no more than an hour or two, and it is advertised as the Return Voyage. You sign in at the Clinic, pay for your ticket at the desk, and then are taken to a small private room with a freshly made bed. An attendant tucks you in and gives you an injection, and then you drift off to sleep and never wake up. Next on the price ladder is the Journey of Marvels, which lasts anywhere from one to three days. This consists of a series of injections, spaced out at regular intervals, which gives the customer a euphoric sense of abandon and happiness, before a last, fatal injection is administered. Then there is the Pleasure Cruise, which can go on for as long as two weeks. The customers are treated to an opulent life, catered to in a manner that rivals the splendor of the old luxury hotels. There are elaborate meals, wines, entertainment, even a brothel, which serves the needs of both men and women. This runs into quite a bit of money, but for some people the chance to live the good life, even for a short while, is an irresistible temptation.

The Euthanasia Clinics are not the only way to buy your own death, however. There are the Assassination Clubs as well, and these have been growing in popularity. A person who wants to die, but who is too afraid to go through with it himself, joins the Assassination Club in his census zone for a relatively modest fee. An assassin is then assigned to him. The customer is told nothing about the arrangements, and everything about his death remains a mystery to him: the date, the place, the method to be used, the identity of his assassin. In some sense, life goes on as it always does. Death remains on the horizon, an absolute certainty, and yet inscrutable as to its specific form. Instead of old age, disease, or accident, a member of an Assassination Club can look forward to a quick and violent death in the not-too-distant future: a bullet in the brain, a knife in the back, a pair of hands around his throat in the middle of the night. The effect of all this, it seems to me, is to make one more vigilant. Death is no longer an abstraction, but a real possibility that haunts each moment of life. Rather than submit passively to the inevitable, those marked for assassination tend to become more alert, more vigorous in their movements, more filled with a sense of life—as though transformed by some new understanding of things. Many of them actually recant and opt for life again. But that is a complicated business. For once you join an Assassination Club, you are not allowed to quit. On the other hand, if you manage to kill your assassin, you can be released from your obligation—and, if you choose, be hired as an assassin yourself. That is the danger of the assassin's job and the reason why it is so well paid. It is rare for an assassin to be killed, for he is necessarily more experienced than his intended victim, but it does sometimes happen. Among the poor, especially poor young men, there are many who save up for months and even years just to be able to join an Assassination Club. The idea is to get hired as an Assassin—and therefore to lift themselves up to a better life. Few ever make it. If I told you the stories of some of these boys, you would not be able to sleep for a week.

All this leads to a great many practical problems. The question of bodies, for example. People don't die here as they did in the old days, quietly expiring in their beds or in the clean sanctuary of a hospital ward—they die wherever they happen to be, and for the most part that means the street. I am not just talking about the Runners, the Leapers, and members of the Assassination Clubs (for they amount to a mere fraction), but to vast segments of the population. Fully half the people are homeless, and they have absolutely nowhere to go. Dead bodies are therefore everywhere you turn—on the sidewalk, in doorways, in the street itself. Don't ask me to give you the details. It's enough for me to say it—even more than enough. No matter what you might think, the real problem is never a lack of pity. Nothing breaks here more readily than the heart.

Most of the bodies are naked. Scavengers roam the streets at all times, and it is never very long before a dead person is stripped of his belongings. First to go are the shoes, for these are in great demand, and very hard to find. The pockets are next to attract attention, but usually it is just everything after that, the clothes and whatever they contain. Last come the men with chisels and pliers, who wrench the gold and silver teeth from the mouth. Because there is no escaping this fact, many families take care of the stripping themselves, not wanting to leave it to strangers. In some cases, it comes from a desire to preserve the dignity of the loved one; in others it is simply a question of selfishness. But that is perhaps too subtle a point. If the gold from your husband's tooth can feed you for a month, who is to say you are wrong to pull it out? This kind of behavior goes against the grain, I know, but if you mean to survive here, then you must be able to give in on matters of principle.

Every morning, the city sends out trucks to collect the corpses. This is the chief function of the government, and more money is spent on it than anything else. All around the edges of the city are the crematoria—called transformation centers—and day and night you can see the smoke rising up into the sky. But with the streets in such bad disrepair now, and with so many of them reduced to rubble, the job becomes increasingly difficult. The men are forced to stop the trucks and go out foraging on foot, and this slows down the work considerably. On top of this, there are the frequent mechanical breakdowns of the trucks and the occasional outbursts from onlookers. Throwing stones at death-truck workers is a common occupation among the homeless. Although the workers are armed and have been known to turn their machine-guns on crowds, some of the stone-throwers are very deft at hiding themselves, and their hit-and-run tactics can sometimes bring the collection work to a complete halt. There is no coherent motive behind these attacks. They stem from anger, resentment, and boredom, and because the collection workers are the only city officials who ever make an appearance in the neighborhood, they are convenient targets. One could say that the stones represent the people's disgust with a government that does nothing for them until they are dead. But that would be going too far. The stones are an expression of unhappiness, and that is all. For there are no politics in the city as such. The people are too hungry, too distracted, too much at odds with each other for that.

The crossing took ten days, and I was the only passenger. But you know that already. You met the captain and the crew, you saw the cabin, and there's no need to go over that again. I spent my time looking at the water and the sky and hardly opened a book for the whole ten days. We came into the city at night, and it was only then that I began to panic a little. The shore was entirely black, no lights anywhere, and it felt as though we were entering an invisible world, a place where only blind people lived. But I had the address of William's office, and that reassured me somewhat. All I had to do was go there, I thought, and then things would take care of themselves. At the very least, I felt confident that I would be able to pick up William's trail. But I had not realized that the street would be gone. It wasn't that the office was empty or that the building had been abandoned. There was no building, no street, no anything at all: nothing but stones and rubbish for acres around.

This was the third census zone, I later learned, and nearly a year before some kind of epidemic had broken out there. The city government had come in, walled off the sea, and burned everything down to the ground. Or so the story went. I have since learned not to take the things I am told too seriously. It's not that people make a point of lying to you, it's just that where the past is concerned, the truth tends to get obscured rather quickly. Legends crop up within a matter of hours, tall tales circulate, and the facts are soon buried under a mountain of outlandish theories. In the city, the best approach is to believe only what your own eyes tell you. But not even that is infallible. For few things are ever what they seem to be, especially here, with so much to absorb at every step, with so many things that defy understanding. Whatever you see has the potential to wound you, to make you less than you are, as if merely by seeing a thing some part of yourself were taken away from you. Often, you feel it will be dangerous to look, and there is a tendency to avert your eyes, or even to shut them. Because of that, it is easy to get confused, to be unsure that you are really seeing the thing you think you are looking at. It could be that you are imagining it, or mixing it up with something else, or remembering something you have seen before—or perhaps even imagined before. You see how complicated it is. It is not enough simply to look and say to yourself, "I am looking at that thing." For it is one thing to do this when the object before your eyes is a pencil, say, or a crust of bread. But what happens when you find yourself looking at a dead child, at a little girl lying in the street without any clothes on, her head crushed and covered with blood? What do you say to yourself then? It is not a simple matter, you see, to state flatly and without equivocation: "I am looking at a dead child." Your mind seems to balk at forming the words, you somehow cannot bring yourself to do it. For the thing before your eyes is not something you can very easily separate from yourself.

291

That is what I mean by being wounded: you cannot merely see, for each thing somehow belongs to you, is part of the story unfolding inside you. It would be good, I suppose, to make yourself so hard that nothing could affect you anymore. But then you would be alone, so totally cut off from everyone else that life would become impossible. There are those who manage to do this here, who find the strength to turn themselves into monsters, but you would be surprised to know how few they are. Or, to put it another way: we have all become monsters, but there is almost no one without some remnant inside him of life as it once was.

That is perhaps the greatest problem of all. Life as we know it has ended, and yet no one is able to grasp what has taken its place. Those of us who were brought up somewhere else, or who are old enough to remember a world different from this one, find it an enormous struggle just to keep up from one day to the next. I am not talking only of hardships. Faced with the most ordinary occurrence, you no longer know how to act, and because you cannot act, you find yourself unable to think. The brain is in a muddle. All around you one change follows another, each day produces a new upheaval, the old assumptions are so much air and emptiness. That is the dilemma. On the one hand, you want to survive, to adapt, to make the best of things as they are. But, on the other hand, to accomplish this seems to entail killing off all those things that once made you think of yourself as human. Do you see what I am trying to say? In order to live, you must make yourself die. That is why so many people have given up. For no matter how hard they struggle, they know they are bound to lose. And at that point, it is surely a pointless thing to struggle at all.

It tends to blur in my mind now: what happened and did not, the streets for the first time, the days, the nights, the sky above me, the stones stretching beyond. I seem to remember looking up a lot, as if searching the sky for some lack, some surplus, something that made it different from other skies, as if the sky could explain the things I was seeing around me. I could be mistaken, however. Possibly I am transferring the observations of a later period onto those first days. But I doubt that it matters very much, least of all now.

After much careful study, I can safely report that the sky here is the same sky as the one above you. We have the same clouds and the same brightnesses, the same storms and the same calms, the same winds that carry everything along with them. If the effects are somewhat different here, that is strictly because of what happens below. The nights, for example, are never quite what they are at home. There is the same darkness and the same immensity, but with no feeling of stillness, only a constant undertow, a murmur that pulls you downward and thrusts you forward, without respite. And then, during the days, there is a brightness that is sometimes intolerable—a brilliance that stuns you and seems to blanch everything, all the jagged surfaces gleaming, the air itself almost a shimmer. The light forms in such a way that the colors become more and more distorted as you draw close to them. Even the shadows are agitated, with a random, hectic pulsing along the edges. You must be careful in this light not to open your eyes too wide, to squint at just the precise degree that will allow you to keep your balance. Otherwise, you will stumble as you walk, and I need not enumerate the dangers of falling. If not for the darkness, and the strange nights that descend on us, I sometimes feel the sky would burn itself out. The days end when they must, at just the moment when the sun seems to have exhausted the things it shines on. Nothing could adhere to the brightness anymore. The whole implausible world would melt away, and that would be that.

Slowly and steadily, the city seems to be consuming itself, even as it remains. There is no way to explain it. I can only record, I cannot pretend to understand. Every day in the streets you hear explosions, as if somewhere far from you a building were falling down or the sidewalk caving in. But you never see it happen. No matter how often you hear these sounds, their source remains invisible. You would think that now and then an explosion would take place in your presence. But the facts fly in the face of probability. You mustn't think that I am making it up—these noises do not begin in my head. The others hear them too, even if they don't pay much attention. Sometimes they will stop to comment on them, but they never seem worried. It's a bit better now, they might say. Or, it seems a little belligerent this afternoon. I used to ask many questions about these explosions, but I never got an answer. Nothing more than a dumb stare or a shrug of the

293

shoulders. Eventually, I learned that some things are just not asked, that even here there are subjects no one is willing to discuss.

For those at the bottom, there are the streets and the parks and the old subway stations. The streets are the worst, for there you are exposed to every hazard and inconvenience. The parks are a somewhat more settled affair, without the problem of traffic and constant passersby, but unless you are one of the fortunate ones to have a tent or a hut, you are never free of the weather. Only in the subway stations can you be sure to escape inclemencies, but there you are also forced to contend with a host of other irritations: the dampness, the crowds, and the perpetual noise of people shouting, as though mesmerized by the echoes of their own voices.

During those first weeks, it was the rain I came to fear more than anything else. Even the cold is a trifle by comparison. For that, it is simply a question of a warm coat—which I had—and moving briskly to keep the blood stimulated. I also learned the benefits to be found from newspapers, surely the best and cheapest material for insulating your clothing. On cold days, you must get up very early in the morning to be sure of finding a good place in the lines that gather in front of the newsstands. You must gauge the wait judiciously, for there is nothing worse than standing out in the cold morning air too long. If you think you will be there for more than twenty or twenty-five minutes, then the common wisdom is to move on and forget it.

Once you've bought the paper, assuming you've managed to get one, the best thing is to take a sheet, tear it into strips, and then twist them into little bundles. These knots are good for stuffing into the toes of your shoes, for blocking up windy interstices around your ankles, and for threading through holes in your clothing. For the limbs and torso, whole sheets wrapped around a number of loosely floating knots is often the best procedure. For the neck area, it is good to take a dozen or so knots and braid them together into a collar. The whole thing gives you a puffy, padded look, which has the cosmetic advantage of disguising thinness. For those who are concerned about keeping up appearances, the "paper meal," as it is called, serves as a kind of face-saving technique. People

294

literally starving to death, with caved-in stomachs and limbs like sticks, walk around trying to look as though they weigh two or three hundred pounds. No one is ever fooled by the disguise—you can spot one of these people from half a mile off—but perhaps that is not the real point. What they seem to be saying is that they know what has happened to them, and they are ashamed of it. More than anything else, their bulked-up bodies are a badge of consciousness, a sign of bitter self-awareness. They make themselves into grotesque parodies of the prosperous and well-fed, and in this frustrated, half-crazed stab at respectability, they prove that they are just the opposite of what they pretend to be—and that they know it.

The rain, however, is unconquerable. For once you get wet, you go on paying for it hours and even days afterward. There is no greater mistake than getting caught in a downpour. Not only do you run the risk of a cold, but you must suffer through innumerable discomforts: your clothes saturated with dampness, your bones as though frozen, and the ever-present danger of destroying your shoes. If staying on your feet is the single most important task, then imagine the consequences of having less than adequate shoes. And nothing affects shoes more disastrously than a good soaking. This can lead to all kinds of problems: blisters, bunions, corns, ingrown toenails, sores, malformations—and when walking becomes painful, you are as good as lost. One step and then another step and then another: that is the golden rule. If you cannot bring yourself to do even that, then you might as well just lie down right then and there and tell yourself to stop breathing.

But how to avoid the rain if it can strike at any moment? There are times, many times, when you find yourself outdoors, going from one place to another, on your way somewhere with no choice about it, period, and suddenly the sky grows dark, the clouds collide, and there you are, drenched to the skin. And even if you manage to find shelter the moment the rain begins to fall and to spare yourself this once, you still must be extremely careful after the rain stops. For then you must watch for the puddles that form in the hollows of the pavement, the lakes that sometimes emerge from the rifts, and even the mud that oozes up from below, ankle-deep and treacherous. With the streets in such poor repair, with so much that is cracked, pitted, pocked, and riven apart, there is no escaping these crises. Sooner or later, you are bound to come to a place where you have no alternative, where you are hemmed in on all sides. And not only are there the surfaces to watch for, the world that touches your feet, there are also the drippings from above, the water that slides down from the eaves, and then, even worse, the strong winds that often follow the rain, the fierce eddies of air, skimming the tops of lakes and puddles and whipping the water back into the atmosphere, driving it along like little pins, darts that prick your face and swirl around you, making it impossible to see anything at all. When the winds blow after a rain, people collide with one another more frequently, more fights break out in the streets, the very air seems charged with menace.

It would be one thing if the weather could be predicted with any degree of accuracy. Then one could make plans, know when to avoid the streets, prepare for changes in advance. But everything happens too fast here, the shifts are too abrupt, what is true one minute is no longer true the next. I have wasted much time looking for signs in the air, trying to study the atmosphere for hints of what is to follow and when: the color and heft of the clouds, the speed and direction of the wind, the smells at any given hour, the texture of the sky at night, the sprawl of the sunsets, the intensity of the dew at dawn. But nothing has ever helped me. To correlate this with that, to make a connection between an afternoon cloud and an evening wind—such things lead only to madness. You spin around in the vortex of your calculations and then, just at the moment you are convinced it will rain, the sun goes on shining for an entire day.

What you must do, then, is be prepared for anything. But opinions vary drastically on the best way to go about this. There is a small minority, for example, that believes that bad weather comes from bad thoughts. This is a rather mystical approach to the question, for it implies that thoughts can be translated directly into events in the physical world. According to them, when you think a dark or pessimistic thought, it produces a cloud in the sky. If enough people are thinking gloomy thoughts at once, then rain will begin to fall. That is the reason for all the startling shifts in the weather, they claim, and the reason why no one has been able to give a scientific explanation of our bizarre climate. Their solution is to maintain a steadfast cheerfulness, no matter how dismal the conditions around them. No frowns, no deep sighs, no tears. These people are known as the Smilers, and no sect in the city is more innocent or childlike. If a majority of the population could be converted to their beliefs, they are convinced the weather would at last begin to stabilize and that life would then improve. They are therefore always proselytizing, continually looking for new adherents, but the mildness of manner they have imposed upon themselves makes them feeble persuaders. They rarely succeed in winning anyone over, and consequently their ideas have never been put to the test—for without a great number of believers, there will not be enough good thoughts to make a difference. But this lack of proof only makes them more stubborn in their faith. I can see you shaking your head, and yes, I agree with you that these people are ridiculous and misguided. But, in the day-to-day context of the city, there is a certain force to their argument—and it is probably no more absurd than any other. As people, the Smilers tend to be refreshing company, for their gentleness and optimism are a welcome antidote to the angry bitterness you find everywhere else.

By contrast, there is another group called the Crawlers. These people believe that conditions will go on worsening until we demonstrate—in an utterly persuasive manner—how ashamed we are of how we lived in the past. Their solution is to prostrate themselves on the ground and refuse to stand up again until some sign is given to them that their penance has been deemed sufficient. What this sign is supposed to be is the subject of long theoretical debates. Some say a month of rain, others say a month of fair weather, and still others say they will not know until it is revealed to them in their hearts. There are two principal factions in this sect—the Dogs and the Snakes. The first contend that crawling on hands and knees shows adequate contrition, whereas the second hold that nothing short of moving on one's belly is good enough. Bloody fights break out often between the two groups— each vying for control of the other—but neither faction has gained much of a following, and by now I believe the sect is on the verge of dying out.

In the end, most people have no fixed opinion about these questions. If I counted up the various groups that have a coherent theory about the weather (the Drummers, the End-of-the-Worlders, the Free Associationists), I doubt they would come to

297

more than a drop in the bucket. What it boils down to mostly, I think, is pure luck. The sky is ruled by chance, by forces so complex and obscure that no one can fully explain it. If you happen to get wet in the rain, you are unlucky, and that's all there is to it. If you happen to stay dry, then so much the better. But it has nothing to do with your attitude or your beliefs. The rain makes no distinctions. At one time or another, it falls on everyone, and when it falls, everyone is equal to everyone else—no one better, no one worse, everyone equal and the same.

Bear with me. I know that I sometimes stray from the point, but unless I write down things as they occur to me, I feel I will lose them for good. My mind is not quite what it used to be. It is slower now, sluggish and less nimble, and to follow even the simplest thought very far exhausts me. This is how it begins, then, in spite of my efforts. The words come only when I think I won't be able to find them anymore, at the moment I despair of ever bringing them out again. Each day brings the same struggle, the same blankness, the same desire to forget and then not to forget. When it begins, it is never anywhere but here, never anywhere but at this limit that the pencil begins to write. The story starts and stops, goes forward and then loses itself, and between each word, what silences, what words escape and vanish, never to be seen again.

For a long time I tried not to remember anything. By confining my thoughts to the present, I was better able to manage, better able to avoid the sulks. Memory is the great trap, you see, and I did my best to hold myself back, to make sure my thoughts did not sneak off to the old days. But lately I have been slipping, a little more each day it seems, and now there are times when I will not let go: of my parents, of William, of you. I was such a wild young thing, wasn't I? I grew up too fast for my own good, and no one could tell me anything I didn't already know. Now I can think only of how I hurt my parents, and how my mother cried when I told her I was leaving. It wasn't enough that they had already lost William, now they were going to lose me as well. Please—if you see my parents, tell them I'm sorry. I need to know that someone will do that for me, and there's no one to count on but you.

Yes, there are many things I'm ashamed of. At times my life

seems nothing but a series of regrets, of wrong turnings, of irreversible mistakes. That is the problem when you begin to look back. You see yourself as you were, and you are appalled. But it's too late for apologies now, I realize that. It's too late for anything but getting on with it. These are the words, then. Sooner or later, I will try to say everything, and it makes no difference what comes when, whether the first thing is the second thing or the second thing the last. It all swirls around in my head at once, and merely to hold on to a thing long enough to say it is a victory. If this confuses you, I'm sorry. But I don't have much choice. I have to take it strictly as I can get it.

Nominated by
The Paris Review *and*
Russell Banks

THE VICTIMS

fiction by RICHARD BURGIN

from MISSISSIPPI REVIEW

IT WAS TWENTY-TWO YEARS AGO that my eighth grade baseball coach decided I should be his starting shortstop instead of Andrew Auer. As he announced the starting line-up a half hour before game time, I looked at Andy four seats away from me on the bench and saw an expression I've only seen since in children who have suffered a disappointment so great it doesn't seem comprehensible. I think it was that expression more than anything else that encouraged me to become his friend. Maybe I felt he was someone who would never hurt me. Besides, at that time I could appreciate his sensitivity while luxuriating in a secret sense of superiority. In school we were about even, but besides beating him out for shortstop, I lived in a large house with professionally successful parents, while Andy was the only child of a young divorcee who lived in one of the less fashionable parts of Newton.

For the next four years our friendship flourished. We seemed to discover the same things at the same time. By our junior year in high school I would listen to Thelonious Monk or to Mahler symphonies with him, and we would share our first attempts at writing poetry or fiction. Outside of my family, Andy was the most important person in my life. He was almost unfailingly compassionate. Even when I lost my virginity before he did, he forgave me. He became especially important to me then, because I could never confide anything like that to my sister or parents.

But a year later when he lost his, I was considerably less charitable. Andy didn't simply lose his virginity with another teenager, after all, he had an affair with a thirty-one-year-old

German woman named Lizette who seemed shockingly attractive to me. How had this happened? It was such an outrageous coup I couldn't comprehend it. She was a former model from Munich and a divorcee, while Andy was a Jewish virgin and second-string shortstop. They kept their trysts secret from everyone except me, meeting once or twice a week in her apartment for an entire summer. I was so shaken I even told my mother about it, who assured me that I, too, would have many triumphs in my life and that I should "let him have his."

Finally Lizette went back to Germany, but no sooner had she gone than I discovered that Andy scored eighty points higher than I did on his college boards, and that despite my parents paying for two years of private school for me, he got accepted by a more prestigious college. Still, Andy was far from insufferable about it. He was in his anarchistic phase then, very much under the influence of Henry Miller, and assured me all he wanted to do was to become a great writer. I somehow wasn't surprised to see him knocking on my front door four months after Antioch started, having hitchhiked all the way from Ohio and vowing never to return. I was surprised, however, that his mother didn't force him to go back. I never knew precisely what her reaction was, only that that year he stayed at home with her.

The next year Andy decided he had to live in New York. Newton, in fact, all of Massachusetts, was "too small and provincial" for a writer with his "concern for the world." As a concession to his mother he agreed to enroll in Columbia. This time he stayed about a year and a half before quitting in a rage. I never learned exactly what went wrong. He was doing well academically (his mother said he was offered a university scholarship) but he began fighting with his professors or intermittently losing his concentration in class. At night he'd suffer from insomnia. His mother called me and pleaded with me to talk him into going back to school. "Marty, you're his best friend, he'll listen to you. His uncle is going to wash his hands of the whole thing and then he'll never be able to get a degree."

I called Andy and gave him all the standard arguments (which I only half believed) for finishing school, but he wasn't convinced. He stayed in New York reading and writing and "exploring life," supported by his mother and her brother.

"If he doesn't straighten out, he'll never get a job. His mother

301

can't support him his whole life," my mother said. But getting a job, despite occasional threats from his mother and uncle, was literally the last thing on Andy's mind. Not only did he still worship Henry Miller, he'd discovered Gertrude Stein's entire "lost generation." It was both the most natural and imperative thing in the world, as he saw it, to escape "the absurd contradictions and crass materialism of America," and to move to Paris. Now his uncle did stop contributing money but in a strange turnaround Bertha defended her son's ambitions, fought with her brother, and told him not to bother calling her again. Then she left her secretarial job at a Boston hospital and began selling life insurance. She didn't enjoy her new work with its increased responsibilities, for Bertha was not a person who reacted well to pressure, but she felt she had to do it for Andy. Eventually she grew quite adept. For the next three years she was able to support him in his studio apartment in Paris. "I believe in him, Marty," she would say to me whenever I questioned her. "You know how brilliant he is. Isn't he brilliant? Isn't he as talented as anyone his age?"

"He's very bright."

"All right then. He's going to make it. He'll support himself from writing. Look at Norman Mailer, look at Gore Vidal. It can happen. He'll do it. He just needs some peace of mind to develop. He says Europe's the place, he must know. Look at Hemingway and Fitzgerald. It will happen."

At that time I had finally left Newton, and was going to graduate school at New York University. School wasn't easy for me but I was a steady, if unspectacular student. When my parents sometimes complained about how expensive my tuition was I'd feel the same envy for Andy's life that I used to feel when he was sleeping with Lizette. But it wasn't envy alone I felt. I also admired him and felt he deserved his life in a way I never could. Secretly, I'd conceded a number of things to him. He had a greater intellectual curiosity than I did. I struggled to pass my foreign language requirement at N.Y.U., but he could speak fluent French and German and was teaching himself Italian. For every book I'd read, he'd read two; not only literary books but philosophy, psychology, even books about painting or sculpture. Why *did* he need school? He also had an intensity, a generosity of spirit that I didn't. By comparison I felt petty and spiteful, even ordinary. It's true that by conventional standards I might have been considered better looking but Andy

302

had raven black hair, in fact the blackest hair and greenest eyes I'd ever seen. Even his personality made a bigger impact on people. He had a better sense of humor and was more trusting. People gravitated towards him and seemed ambivalent about me. No wonder he was able to get his way with his mother, even at the expense of her breaking off relations with her brother.

Of course there were my undeniable advantages over Andy—my family's financial success and status, the sad fact that he hadn't had any contact with his father since he was eight. But more often than not the absence of a father seemed to me one more romantic detail about Andy. It gave his life, like Gatsby's, a certain self-created quality.

While I always thought Andy remarkable I only rarely thought I was. Maybe that's why I left graduate school after I got my Master's to teach in a prep school in western Massachusetts. I was twenty-three then and felt uncomfortable taking any more money from my parents. Meanwhile, Andy and I continued to exchange letters from Northfield Mass. to Paris. In his letters he always seemed on the verge of a major breakthrough in his work. He said he was friendly with Michel Foucault, that he was contemplating going to the Sorbonne, that he was writing a novel, a screenplay, and a book on aesthetics, that he'd slept with Ingmar Bergman's daughter and a certain prominent American critic whose name I can't mention. I began to suspect he might be exaggerating but I couldn't be sure. With Andy anything seemed possible, there was never a way to prove him wrong.

That summer I visited him in Paris for two weeks. I must have been very excited since it was the first time I'd been to Europe, but what I chiefly remember is the awe, the infinite hopefulness in his face as he told me about his new life. I think we were walking in the Tuilleries, though we could just as easily have been in his studio. It is his face, the excitement in his green eyes that I am sure of, as he told me he'd increased his "overall grasp of literature exponentially. The people that I've met here are incredible, the entire ambiance—it's become my spiritual home. I only wish you could stay longer."

After a passionate description of his French female conquests he told me that his mother was now seriously involved with a very wealthy Boston businessman. Bertha was only eighteen when Andy was born, twenty-six when she was divorced. Since then

303

she'd only dated a handful of colorless men. Although she was extremely youthful and attractive I'd somehow never imagined her with anyone but Andy. I pressed him for more details but he held up his hands to stop me. "I can only talk about it so much," he said forming a short space between his thumb and index finger. "It could mean so much to her but I just don't want to say more until something definite happens."

Andy's revelation dwarfed whatever else I did in Paris, and I returned to Boston wondering how much of what he'd told me was true. Within a week, Bertha took me into her confidence and told me about "the special man in her life," Benjamin Walters, who had invested prophetically in communication systems, and was indeed a wealthy man. Not only was he rich, but he was investing in Broadway shows and other theatrical endeavors which put him in touch with people that Bertha, who'd never been out of Newton, had previously only read about. Suddenly she was eating dinner with these stars and accompanying Benjamin for quick trips to Las Vegas or Hollywood. It was clearly the adventure of her life.

Eventually I had dinner with them in the more expensive apartment she'd moved into on Beacon Hill. Benjamin Walters was overweight, shy, preoccupied with his work, but he did exude a certain gruff charm. At times he looked and acted a bit like a New England Broderick Crawford. The morning after her dinner she called me to ask me my impressions, not so much of Benjamin but of how serious I thought he was about her. It was a question she would ask me in many different ways over the next three years. Of course, I never gave her an absolute answer. I was always embarrassed, although also a little flattered when she asked my opinion. Generally I tried to encourage her because when she felt encouraged she'd be happy and she was wonderful to talk to when her basic optimism resurfaced.

Andy, meanwhile, had made some important career decisions. He'd abandoned his attempts to write novels or screenplays and concentrated instead on what he was best at, literary and social criticism. He began publishing book reviews in literary quarterlies, then longer and more theoretical essays. Within three years he was occasionally reviewing for *The New Republic* or *The Nation*.

I felt competitive and a trifle envious, though, of course, I was happy for him too. Besides, I had distractions of my own, principally a series of short, intense love affairs. As for my career, I had managed to publish a few stories in little magazines. (I thought of them, at the time, as proof of the important creative distinction between myself and Andy. So what if they appeared in magazines with circulations under a thousand. They proved I was "an artist," didn't they?). I'd also left the private school in the country and become an English instructor in a junior college in Boston. What I was concentrating on chiefly was getting tenure. I saw that as the necessary first step to anything else I wanted from life, so I methodically plugged away at it. That's how it was in those days, I was plugging away after tenure, Bertha was plugging away after Benjamin Walters, while Andy was pursuing the legacy of Edmund Wilson and making impressive progress.

Finally, after three years Bertha got discouraged, then angry that Benjamin wouldn't marry her.

"He says he's got a hang up about marriage, but I think he's just a cheapskate. He doesn't want to part with any of his big bucks. I don't care for myself, it's Andy I'm worried about."

"Andy seems to be doing fine, he's flourishing."

"Marty, I still have to support him, I may always have to help him."

"At the rate he's going he'll probably be making his own 'big bucks' from writing," I said, surprised that I was assuming the argument she usually used to defend Andy's life.

"Maybe you should give Benjamin, you know, an ultimatum of some kind," I said softly. Bertha ran her fingers through her own raven black hair, only slightly flecked with a few silver streaks. Her eyes were also sharp and green, she looked like a feminine version of Andy.

"I probably should, but the truth is, Marty, I'm afraid he'd say no. . . . Anyway, he's promised to always take care of me."

A few months later Andy moved back to New York to capitalize on his initial successes. I think we were both so busy with our careers that in some ways we had less contact than when he was in Europe. Also, I had become seriously involved with Lianne, an assistant art professor at my college, and within a few months we were virtually living together. During his last visit to Boston I only found time to have one lunch with Andy. Every time I spoke I ended up mentioning Lianne, as if my mouth took a compulsive

305

delight in pronouncing her name. When I asked Andy if he was seeing anyone he alluded to his usual list of glamorous one-night stands and then changed the subject.

I felt guilty for not spending more time with him during his visit and a month later, after a new review of his on Samuel Beckett had been published, I wrote him a long congratulatory letter.

Andy wrote me back eight pages. Typically, his references ranged from Proust to Heidegger to Miles Davis to the Abstract Expressionists. But it was the confessional part near the end that I still remember:

> You praise me for having so much to say about Beck-
> ett, but there is so much more I want to say, so much
> more inside me that I need to utter and I feel thwarted
> and ashamed that I still can't fashion it into decent prose.
> If only I could write poetry! Besides the desire to write
> something I am not disgusted with I want only three
> things in life. Happiness for my mother who has sacri-
> ficed everything for me, happiness for my friends—most
> of all for you since you are my most treasured friend—
> and a little taste of the love you have found for Lianne. I
> realize now that I have not yet been able to fall in love.

I decided to never let too much time pass without seeing Andy. That summer he was in Boston a lot and I would see him two or three times a week. He and I and Lianne would sometimes go to the movies together or walk around Harvard Square, but I was careful to not let him spend too much time with her. It was not that I didn't trust them—it was just easier for me to deal with them separately, perhaps because each required such an intense and different kind of attention. I also realized that I didn't understand Andy's sexuality—it was so ferocious yet detached, like a caged lion that was only temporarily calm. He was constantly evoking this or that starlet (usually European ones) as the apotheosis of beauty or sex appeal but the only woman I'd ever seen him express any strong emotion for was his mother. It was Bertha who could provoke his temper as no one else could, Bertha who could still induce his screaming fits the same as when he was an eighth grader, and it was Bertha whom he would still unabashedly smother with kisses, even in my presence.

306

One weekend in July, Lianne went home to visit her parents and I went to Bertha's apartment to meet Andy. We were planning to go to a literary party of some kind. When I arrived Andy was still dressing, and I saw Benjamin Walters sitting on Bertha's sofa. Corpulent, slow moving, he was wrapped in his dark blue suit like a mummy. We exchanged five minutes of awkward small talk while Bertha, dressed in a tight-fitting pink gown that showed off her slim figure, fluttered around him like a cocktail waitress. That evening she was obviously going to cook him another dinner.

"You know, I can't stand him," Andy said to me in his car as we searched for the party in Cambridge. "If it weren't for my mother I probably would have punched him out a couple of times by now."

"But he seems to make your mother happy. I've never seen her so animated."

"Of course, and that's everything to me," he said, as his voice softened. "But it's ironic that the love of my mother's life should be such a bloated, petty, ignorant, self-involved, penurious nouveau riche . . ." he searched for more adjectives and then started to laugh. "I wish for two minutes I could be Marcel Proust just to once and for all do verbal justice to Benjamin. The point is, I could forgive him for being so culturally bankrupt, but he has the chutzpah to lecture me and my mother about how I should get a job and work for him in his business. The man is actually trying to parent me. Meanwhile if he would only marry my mother she could finally stop working for once in her life, but he's too goddamn cheap to marry her and he's been sleeping with her for four years now."

"Still, you know, he might marry her and you should try to be nice to him. It can only benefit you."

"Believe me he *will* marry her. And within one year after their marriage I'll launch the most important literary magazine in America since *The Dial*. Who knows, since he has millions, I may even start a small publishing company that will only publish books of real quality."

As if sensing the pang of envy I was feeling, he quickly added, "Of course, Marty, you'll leave that little college where they're mistreating you and be my partner."

At the party there were a number of attractive women. I told Andy that I was being faithful to Lianne and that he should "go after" whoever he wanted. But Andy found something wrong with

307

every one of them. One of them was a little too plump, another looked too Jewish, a third, who was obviously pretty, he claimed had "no hips or breasts, she might turn out to be a boy."

We ended up drinking a lot at the party and then walking along the Charles River afterwards to sober up. "If Benjamin ever double-crossed my mother I think I'd be justified in killing him, don't you?" he said as we walked past a series of couples making out on the benches or on the grass by the river.

"What are you saying, are you serious?"

"You don't agree, you think that's sick?"

"I think you're too close to your mother. Can't you find a girlfriend, instead of all those one-night things?"

"You're right. It's because I know she needs me, she's given everything to me."

"But she has someone, she has Benjamin and you're still alone . . ."

"You're right, Marty. As soon as I get back to New York I'm going to work on it. I'll have a girlfriend within two weeks."

A few hours later, at 2 or 3 in the morning, I was asleep in my apartment when the phone rang. Andy's voice was saying words to me I could scarcely assimilate.

"Something unbelievable has happened. Benjamin had a heart attack. I'm calling you from the hospital. My mother's in shock."

I went to Benjamin's funeral with Bertha and Andy. Bertha cried throughout the services and then intermittently during the reception at Benjamin's brother's home. Andy was by her side every moment, his face rigid with a kind of heightened alertness.

A few days later it was determined that Benjamin hadn't left a will. As the next of kin, Benjamin's brother put in a claim for the whole estate and offered Bertha ten thousand dollars. He had grossly underestimated her. Of course, at this time palimony suits were still unheard of, and in all those years Bertha had never technically lived with Benjamin. But Bertha's claim was that Benjamin had verbally promised her his estate in lieu of marrying her, and that she had faithfully rendered to him the services of a wife.

A month later, Benjamin's brother claimed to have located a homemade will leaving him everything. The controversy wound up in court and dragged on for years with handwriting experts contradicting each other, with appeals and counter appeals. I was one of the witnesses who testified for Bertha. It was peculiar, I thought she was probably telling the truth most of the time, but the mere participation in an attempt to get someone money made me feel a little like I was committing a crime.

Since Benjamin's death Andy had moved back with his mother. Like Bertha, he became obsessed with the details of the trial. He stopped writing, and even read very little. He was too nervous to attend the various hearings. Of course it was impossible to get much pleasure from his company in those days, but in some ways our friendship was stronger than ever. Not only did he and Bertha need me as a confidant about the twists and turns of their case, but I needed them as well. I was having my own crisis. Lianne and I had broken up (I'd found out that she'd slept with someone in her department) and the pain of adjusting to living alone was worse than I'd anticipated. Also I found out I was coming up for tenure a year earlier than I'd expected and was very anxious about it. My own rate of publishing had fallen well behind my expectations. In short, listening to Bertha's and Andy's monologues about their case (as well as their occasional epiphanies about all the things they could do when they finally got their money) seemed a small price to pay for some genuine empathy for my loss of Lianne, and my troubles with tenure.

Another year passed before Bertha was finally awarded her settlement. It was far less than Andy and she had dreamed of, but it was more than a half million dollars. I had meanwhile managed to postpone the decision on my tenure for another year. What better time was there to finally discuss with Andy our long planned magazine which we both needed to revitalize our careers?

A month after the Auers won their case, when they'd returned from a short vacation in Europe, I invited Andy to dinner at a small French restaurant in Harvard Square. Perhaps because we hadn't talked about the magazine in a long time, or because I wanted it so much, I led up to it gradually. I waited until we had our main course and were on our second bottle of wine before I mentioned how much I needed to publish to get tenure. Andy stared past me and gave me a rather perfunctorily sympathetic nod. I switched to another approach and began railing against those young critics in Andy's field who were publishing everywhere and who we both knew to be mediocrities. Again he didn't take the hint.

309

"So when are we going to start working on our magazine?" I suddenly blurted out.

Andy focused his eyes on me darkly.

"About the magazine you have to understand something, Marty. It's not my money, it's my mother's. She deserves so many things and now she has a chance to get some of them. She's going to decide how every penny is spent."

"Of course, I understand. But you could ask her. I mean, it's only five or ten thousand we're talking about, initially."

"Maybe if we'd gotten the whole estate, but now? No, I won't even ask her."

"I don't understand. What have we been talking about the past four or five years?"

"I don't care about the past. My mother and I are starting a new life."

"But . . ."

"No more buts," he screamed, slamming his fist on the table. The veins stood out in his thin forehead the way they did when he'd have a temper tantrum playing baseball as a kid, or else fighting with Bertha.

"Is that why you testified at the trial? Is that why you've been my 'friend' all these years, because you want your cut? You want to rob me too, like Benjamin and his brother, and the courts, and my father. I'm nauseated! I never want to see you again . . ."

He got up from the table and left the restaurant. A few minutes later I went home, shaken. In that sleepless first night I was sure he would call and apologize. I'd seen him have these temporary rages before and then become profoundly apologetic an hour or two later. But the call didn't come. Then I thought he'd write me or that Bertha would contact me, but neither happened and soon a week had passed.

I began to wonder if I were all the things he accused me of. Who had betrayed whom? Who was the victim, Andy or myself? Yes, I had wanted to do a magazine, but I'd never made a secret of it, and it was Andy who'd suggested it first. Would I have testified for Bertha if there were no magazine involved? Of course. Would I also have listened so religiously to all his anxieties if there was no hope of my benefiting from it? I was still sure I would have. After all, we'd been friends since childhood.

310

Another week went by. I almost called him many times but my own pride and sense of justice stopped me. I finally told my parents what happened and my father shook his head and walked out of the room. My mother had a few things to say, however.

"They're the schemers, they're the opportunists. They're what they accuse you of being. I say good riddance. Andy's gotten a free ride through life. He's just jealous of you because you work like a normal person and don't live off your parents. If you ask me, they're both meshuga, and you're lucky to be rid of them."

But I didn't feel so lucky and I finally wrote Andy a long conciliatory letter. He didn't answer me and when I phoned him a week later I learned that they'd already moved.

Four years went by, maybe five. I had new love affairs, new disappointments. I didn't get tenure, but I managed to get a series of one year teaching jobs near Boston. I published a few more stories. Through the grapevine I heard that Andy and his mother had moved to Lexington, then to New Hampshire, then to Cape Cod. I was hurt by Andy, but I felt so clearly wronged that it grew easier to forget him. Eventually I only thought about him once a week or so, as if he were a relative who had died years ago. I never saw his name in print again, (although I instinctively avoided those magazines most likely to publish him) which made forgetting him still easier.

. . . Shortly after Christmas each year, the Modern Language Association holds its national convention. Although a number of academics present various papers, the main purpose of the convention is for college English chairmen to interview various candidates for their departments. Last year's convention was in New York, and I considered myself fortunate to have secured two interviews, although one was for a junior college, and the other (which was a "tenure track" job) was for a college in an obscure town in Arkansas.

After my last interview I walked out of the Hilton and began replaying the sequence of questions and answers that had just occurred five minutes ago. It was bitter cold outside. The sky looked drained as if it were too depleted of energy to send out any color that day. For no particular reason I headed east. When the wind blew it seemed to go through my neck. Around Second

311

Avenue and Fifty-fifth Street I stopped at a red light. Someone had called out my name loudly and shrilly two or three times. I turned and saw Bertha.

She was still strikingly pretty in her white fur coat, with her carefully coiffured black hair, and her green eyes under a stylish pair of sunglasses. Physically she had aged, if at all, in very subtle ways.

"Don't turn away, Marty. Come on, give me a hug. Let's forget the past, we can forgive each other, can't we?"

We embraced and at Bertha's suggestion walked into a nearby coffee shop. Once at our table we continued our small talk for another minute or two. I noticed that she looked a little sad when I told her I'd just come from a job interview.

"So, how's Andy?" I finally said.

"You'll see him tonight. I'm cooking him dinner in his loft in Soho."

"Are you . . . where are you living now?" I tried to ask diplomatically. Bertha told me matter of factly about her apartment in Sutton Place but a moment later she clutched my arm just above my wrist and said, "Promise me you'll come tonight, it will mean so much to him."

"Of course, I'll try."

"No, you have to promise. Marty, you've got to forgive him." She took off her sunglasses and wiped away a few tears. "These last five years have been a nightmare."

"I'd just heard that you moved a lot."

"You've heard of the 'wandering Jews,' right? We're setting a record."

She listed the places they'd lived in that I already knew about, and two other places that I didn't.

"What's the trouble, why do you keep moving?"

"He makes me move. One place is too isolated, the other is too noisy. He has problems now. Marty, he's not the way you remember."

"He's not working?"

"He says he's writing but I can't be sure. We wasted four years on a lousy psychiatrist—he should rot in hell. He put Andy on all the wrong medication. But now he's found a new doctor who he thinks is God. Andy can still turn it around. You know how talented he is."

"He never got a job," I said, immediately regretting my words.

"He can do it with his writing. Look at Truman Capote, look at John Updike. They never taught, they didn't need degrees. If he were healthy and writing he'd be making a million dollars . . . Marty, just promise me you'll come tonight. Here, I'll write you the address."

I went back to my hotel dazed by my meeting with Bertha and the prospect of seeing Andy in just a few hours. On my bed I closed my eyes and saw a series of pictures of my past with Andy, one at a time like paintings in a gallery; Andy in his Paris studio, Andy walking out of the movies with Lianne and me, Andy like a sentinel at Benjamin's funeral, Andy on the bench at the baseball game twenty years ago.

I forced myself to get up—I had to buy them a bottle of wine, after all, and I'd fallen asleep in my suit. Bertha was probably exaggerating about Andy's condition. Like my own mother, she was hopelessly melodramatic. . . . Andy lived on Spring Street in one of the chicest parts of Soho. He shook my hand with a quizzical but benign smile on his face.

"I'm sorry about what happened between us."

"Forget it," I said quickly.

"I guess we're both nervous," he said as he led me into the living room. Waving at me from a distance, Bertha immediately walked into a bedroom and left us alone. Andy was wearing jeans and a sports shirt and I made a joke about showing up in a suit. He laughed and handed me a glass of champagne. I noticed that his hair had receded even more than mine, and that he now had as many crow's feet around his eyes as Bertha.

"Let me show you the loft," he said, walking ahead of me. The walls were covered with paintings, prints, and photographs. Some of them, like a print by Pollock or Chagall, were of real value. He gave me a brief history of each picture but I forgot most of what he said. Where there weren't paintings, there were high white shelves completely filled with books.

"How many books do you have?" I said.

"Guess?"

"I don't know. It looks like a library."

"Ten thousand, all alphabetically arranged," he said beaming with pride. He continued his walking tour, stopping periodically to give me the history of a lamp or quilt. "I always wanted to live here, some incredible people live around me, you know," and he rattled off a list of art world luminaries. "They're here now and in the summer they go to the Hamptons. By the way, this summer my mother's going to buy a place there. She's already trying to sell the Sutton Place apartment."

We continued walking slowly in circles around the loft. I realized he was no longer nervous, but the angry wit, the edge to his personality was missing.

We finally stopped walking and sat down on a couch by a window.

"I'm sorry I didn't answer your letter," he said softly. "I don't know how much my mother told you but I've been having some troubles . . . the past few years."

"She mentioned you were seeing a doctor."

"Marty, I'm on a lot of medication. Thirteen different pills a day."

"What's the matter?"

He smiled ironically and shrugged his shoulders.

"Maybe you shouldn't spend so much time with your mother?"

"Oh, no, I'd be dead without her. I owe her everything. The only thing is she's never been able to enjoy her money. I mean, how can she be happy as long as I'm sick? My sickness is keeping her from everything she wants," he said sadly, with a strange little smile on his lips.

"So you've been living with her? . . ."

"This is the first time we've been apart in five years. It's an experiment. My doctor ordered it."

Bertha came out of the bedroom then in a bright blue skirt with a matching sweater and began making her final preparations for dinner. Andy signalled to me and we changed the subject. But it had been so long since the three of us had talked, and even longer since we'd talked about anything but "the trial", that it was awkward. When Bertha sent Andy to the store to "get some last minute things for dinner," I knew she was going to take advantage of her time alone with me to talk about Andy.

As soon as he shut the elevator door Bertha led me by the arm to the sofa by the window.

"So what do you think about Andy?"

"I don't know what to say, Bertha."

"How bad does he seem to you?"

"He seems pretty down on himself."

"Marty, his ego's on the floor. He's a thirty-five-year-old man who's never accomplished anything in his life. Think how he feels."

"So the main thing is that he's stopped writing, that's the main symptom?"

"Marty. He hasn't been with a woman in years. He sleeps twelve hours a day and he lists."

"Lists?"

"He has hundreds of rituals that he goes through every day. His doctor calls it 'listing'."

"You mean writing things down compulsively?"

"Sometimes it's that, other times it's just in his mind. His doctor calls it a 'rage for order'."

"So what do his doctors say has caused all this?"

"They contradict each other. One says it's congenital, another says something else. Between all the doctors and the moving I'm starting to go through my capital. I'm still trying to sell our house in New Hampshire. The real estate market's collapsed. I'm losing so much money with all this buying and selling I'd be ashamed to tell you."

"So stop moving."

"I shouldn't listen to him, I know. I tell him the problem's inside him, it's not where he's living."

"You gave up your job too?"

"I couldn't work. He'd call me four or five times a day at my office, every time he had a problem. It was impossible . . . Marty, you've got to be his friend again. Stay the night. He needs to know that you're his friend again."

"Of course . . ."

. . . Bertha was an exquisite cook. Her chicken crepes were so delicious that we all became engrossed in our dinner, without worrying about safe topics of conversation. By the time we got to her chocolate mousse and the champagne, we began reminiscing about our high school years and even our grammar school baseball team. Andy grew especially animated and told a couple of jokes. For a few minutes he was just like his old self. But when Bertha warned him not to drink too much because of his medication he glared at her for a moment and turned somber.

A few minutes later he got up from the table and sat down in a chair in the middle of the loft and turned on the television. I

315

continued talking with Bertha, quietly but ineffectually. Every half minute she'd turn her head and look at Andy. A little later we heard him snoring.

"This happens every night. He sits in the chair, turns on the TV and in half an hour he falls asleep."

I noticed that it was only eight-thirty.

"Well, I may as well go to sleep too," she said, yawning. "In a couple of hours he'll wake up and go to his room. I'll fix up the couch for you by the window."

"You're sure you don't want the couch? It's much bigger."

"No, no," she said, handing me my sheets and pillow. "I always sleep on that little bed in the living room when I visit him."

A half hour later Bertha and Andy were snoring in unison. I lay on the couch unable to read or sleep, feeling trapped and abandoned. I couldn't remember the last time I'd tried to go to sleep so early. When I turned off the bed lamp I started to think about Lianne. When that got too painful I began reviewing my job interviews and I thought of all the vain and foolish things I'd done to try to get tenure in a school I already had contempt for.

I got up and fixed myself a drink. Mother and son were still snoring loudly. In the vastness of the loft it echoed like a bizarre kind of church music. My mother was right, they are meshuga, I thought. But when I lay down again I began to feel sorry for them. They're the victims, I said to myself, answering my question of five years ago.

. . . I finally fell asleep, but a few hours later I woke up from a nightmare that involved both my parents and Lianne. My heart was pounding and I could hear someone pacing in the loft. When I shifted the venetian blinds there was just enough light for me to see Andy walking. I saw him making some vague and frenzied gestures in the air, like a conductor frantically cuing his wayward orchestra. I realized he was doing one of his rituals, and I watched him continue his pattern of gestures in a slow, methodical circle around his loft. When his walk brought him a few feet in front of the couch I felt an impulse to get up and stop him. I almost said, "Stop pacing, or listing or worrying. Whatever it is, just stop. Lie down in bed, next to me if you have to, but just stop."

nominated by Mississippi Review
and Elizabeth Inness-Brown

X

fiction by LEE K. ABBOTT

from THE GEORGIA REVIEW

LONG AGO NOW—but still as vital a chapter of my moral history as my first kiss (with Jane Templeton at the FFA marriage booth in the National Guard Armory) or my first love affair (with Leonna Allen, now an LPN in Lubbock, Texas)—I saw my daddy, Hobey Don Baker, Sr., do something that, until recently, was no more important to me than money is to Martians. In an event now well known to the six thousand of us who live here in Deming, New Mexico, my father struck a man and then walked from the sixteenth green of our Mimbres Valley Country Club to the men's locker room, where he destroyed two dozen sets of golf clubs, an act he carried out with the patience you need nowadays to paint by numbers or deal with lawyers from our government.

I was seventeen then, a recent graduate of our high school (where I now teach mathematics and coach JV football), and on the afternoon in question, I had been sitting at the edge of the Club pool, baking myself in the summer sunshine we are famous for. I was thinking—as I suspect all youths do—about the wonder I would become. I had a girlfriend, Pammy Jo (my wife now), a '57 Ford Fairlane 500 (yellow over black), and the knowledge that what lay before me seemed less future than fate—which is what happens when you are raised apart from the big world of horror and cross-heartedness; yet, at the moment I'd glimpsed the prize I would be—and the way it is in the storybooks I read—disaster struck: rushing up behind me, my mother ordered me to grab my shirt and thongs, and hurry out to the sixteenth green, our road hole, to see what the hell my daddy was fussing about.

"He's just chased Dottie Hightower off the course," she said. "Listen, you can hear him."

You couldn't hear him, really, just see him: a figure, six hundred yards distant, dressed in pink slacks, a black polka-dot sport shirt, and a floppy Panama hat to cover his bald spot—an outfit you'd expect to find on Las Vegas gangsters named Cheech.

"I don't hear anything," I said.

"He's out there being crazy again," she declared. "He's cussing out everybody."

We stepped closer to the chain-link fence surrounding the pool and, my mother leaning forward like a sentinel, we listened.

"You hear it?" she said. "That was language in reference to smut."

I'd heard nothing but Dub Spedding's belly-flop and an unappetizing description of what Grace Hartger said she'd eaten for dinner last night. Daddy was stomping now, turning left and right, and waving his arms. In pain perhaps, he snatched his hat off and slammed it to the turf to charge at it the way he attacked the lawnmower when it would not start.

"Look at that," Mother said.

Daddy was standing in front of Butch Newell, who still sells us our Chevrolets, and Ivy Martin, our golf pro, and pointing at Mr. Jimmy Sellers, who was sitting in his golf cart and having a beer.

"He's just missed a putt, that's all," I said. "Maybe it cost him fifty dollars."

But then—by the way she drew her beach towel around her and how her face went dark—I knew that what was going on out there had nothing to do with money.

"Maybe he's sick," I said.

His talk was vile, she said, about creatures and how we are them. "Hear that?" she howled. "That was the word *wantonness*."

I could hear birds, nearby traffic—and then, suddenly, like gunfire in a church, I heard my father. He was speaking about the world all right—how it had become an awful place, part zoo, part asylum. We were spine only, he was saying. With filth attached. We were muck, is what we were. Tissues and melts and sweats. His voice was sharp the way it became when the Luna County Democratic Party, which he was the chairman of, did something that made the Republicans look selfless.

"You get him right now," Mother said, shoving me onward.

At the pool nobody had moved: the Melcher sisters, old and also rich, were frozen; even the kids in the baby pool—the ones still in diapers, the toddlers—had stopped splashing and now stood as if they'd instantly grown very, very old.

"What do you want me to do?" I asked. This was a man who, in teaching me to box, had mashed my nose and introduced me to the noisy afterworld of unconsciousness; and he was out there, pitching his clubs into the sky and ranting.

"Scooter," my mother said, leading me by the elbow to the gate, "don't be so damned lamebrained."

I do not know now, twenty-five years later, what had ravaged my father's self-control, what had seized him as surely as devils are said to have clutched those ancient, fugitive Puritans we descend from. I can tell you Daddy was well known for his temper; and, by way of illustration, I can point to the time he broke up Mother's dinner party for Woody and Helen Knapp by storming into our dining room, his cheeks red and blue with anger, in one fist the end of a trail of toilet paper that stretched—we all soon learned—through the living room, over the petrified-wood coffee table my Aunt Dolly had picked up at an Arizona Runnin' Indian, down the hall, beside the phone stand which had belonged to Granny Floyd, and into the guest lavatory.

"Elaine," he hollered, "you come with me right now." Mother had stopped chewing her green beans. "Woody," he said, "you and Helen too. I want you to see this."

Daddy stood next to me, waving that flowery tissue like a football pennant. "And you, too, young man."

What was wrong was that Mother (or Mrs. Levisay who housecleaned Tuesday and Saturday) had put the roll on the holder backwards so it dispensed from the front, not from behind as it goddamn ought. We were a sight: the nearly five hundred pounds that were the Knapps squeezed into our bathroom with Mother and me, Daddy ordering us up close so we could see—and goddamn well remember for the rest of our miserable, imperfect lives—that there was one way, and one way only, sensible as God intended, for bathroom tissue, or anything else, to be installed.

"You wouldn't drive a car backwards, would you?" He was

319

talking to Mr. Knapp (his napkin still tucked under his chin!) who looked as hopeless and lost as any stranger can be in a bathroom. "And Helen there, she wouldn't eat soup with a fork, would she?"

I could smell us: Mother's Je Reviens, what the Pine-Sol had left, the sweat Mr. Knapp is given to when he isn't sitting still.

"Things have a purpose," my daddy was saying—shouting, actually—and pointing at the john itself. "Man, creature, invention—the whole kit'n'caboodle."

Toilet paper was flying now, shooting overhead like streamers at a Kentucky Wildcat basketball game. Mrs. Knapp, her shoulders and head draped by enough tissue to make a turban, was looking for a way out, slapping the walls, pawing blindly, and yelping in a squeak Mother said had been picked up at the Beaumont School for Girls in El Paso: "Woody, help me. Help me now."

"Remember," my father was saying, "purpose." He had arranged himself on the closed toilet seat. "This may seem small to you but, good Lord, you let the little things get away, next thing you know the big things have fallen apart. Toilet tissue one day, maybe government the next."

Another time, while I was doing the dishes—just had the glassware left, in fact—he wandered past me, whistling the tune he always used when the world worked right ("I'm an Old Cowhand"), and flung open the refrigerator. It was nearly seven, I guess, and he was about to have his after-dinner rum concoction. I was thinking about little—the TV I'd watch or that History Club essay I had to write for Mrs. Tipton. And then I heard him. "Eeeeffff."

The freezer door went bang and instantly he was at my elbow, breathing in a panic, hunched over and peering into my dishwater as if what lay at the bottom were sin itself.

"What the hell are you doing?" he hollered.

I went loose in the knees and he swept me out of the way.

"How many times I got to tell you?" he shouted. "Glasses first—water's hottest and cleanest—*then* the flatware, plates, serving dishes. Save your goddamn saucepans for last!"

I was watching the world turn black and trying to remember how to defend myself.

"Here, I'll show you." And he did: not only did he rewash all the dishes but he also—now muttering about the loss of common sense—opened every cabinet, drawer, and cupboard we have so he could spend the next five hours washing, in water so hot we were in danger of steam-burn, every item in the house associated with preparing, serving, and consuming food. Chafing dish, tureen, pressure cooker, double boiler, candy dish, meat thermometer, basting brush, strainer, lobster hammer—everything disappeared into his soapy water.

"Scrub," he said. "Hard." He was going at one dish as if it were covered with ink.

"Rinse," he said. "Hot, dammit."

A minute later he sent me to the utility room for the flimsy TV trays we own, and then he stopped. Every flat surface in the kitchen—the countertop, the tops of the freezer and the stove, the kitchen table itself, the trays—was piled high with our plates and such.

"See," he howled at last, "you see how it's done?" There he stood, arms glistening, shirt soaked, trousers damp to the knee. His eyeballs were the brightest, maddest points of reference in the entire universe; and, yes, I did see.

He even blew up one time in Korea, going off the way shotguns do, loud and spreading. Mother told me that one day, unhappy with his duties as the I Corps supply officer, he appeared at the residence of his CO, plucked his major's insignia from his shoulders, and threw them at the feet of the amazed colonel. "Pick those up, Mister," he said.

The man looked startled, so my father said that, owing to shoddiness in the world at large and the preeminence in that cold, alien place of such vices as sloth, avarice, gluttony, backstabbing, and other high crimes he'd remember later, he was quitting—which he could do, he reminded that man, on account of his non-Regular Army status as a Reserve Officer and his relation to my Uncle Lyman, then a six-term congressman from the third district of New Mexico.

"Colonel," my daddy is reported to have declared, "this is squalor, disease, violence, and hunger, and I will have no part of it."

So he had blown up in the past and would blow up many, many times after the day I am concerned with here. He would go crazy when my cousin Shirley drowned at Elephant Butte and when the Beatles appeared on the Ed Sullivan Show. Later, he exploded when Billy Sumner won the Club championship with a chip shot that bounced off the old white head of A. T. Seely. He blew up

321

when Governor George Corley Wallace used the word *nigger* on national TV, and he beat our first RCA color set with my Little League Louisville Slugger when Lyndon Johnson, jug-eared and homely as dirt, showed America his surgery scars. As he aged, my father bellowed like a tyrant when Dr. Needham told him his gall bladder had to come out, and he raged like a cyclops at the lineman from El Paso Electric who tried to string a low-voltage line across a corner of our ranch. When he was fifty, Daddy was hollering about calumny and false piety; at sixty, about the vulgar dimwits loose in the land; at seventy, about the excesses of those from the hindmost reaches of our species. Even a week before he died—which was three years ago, at seventy-four—he lay in his hospital bed, virtually screaming at his night nurse about the dreamland citizens lived in. "This is a world of ignorance and waste," he hollered. "No bridge at all over the sea which is our foreordained doom!" Yes, he had blown up before and would blow up again, so on the day I trudged across our flatland fairways, I assumed he was loco this time because, say, he'd caught Butch Newell cheating. Or that Ivy Martin had spoken unkindly about Hebrews. Or that Jimmy Sellers, whom he seemed most mad at, had gypped him on the Ramada Inn they owned as partners.

I have told Pammy Jo many times that mine was the most curious eight-minute walk I will ever take. I have read that in so-called extreme moments—those Mother associates with the words *peril* and *dire*—we humans are capable of otherwise impossible physical activity. In emergencies, we can hoist automobiles, vault like Olympians, run at leopard-like speeds. So it was with my father. As I drew nearer, my flip-flops making that silly slapping noise, I saw Daddy spin, bounce as if on springs, whirl, hop, and kick the air. He threw his ball onto the service road. He wind-milled his arms, stomped, spit on the putter he'd jammed like a stake into the heart of the green. He even dashed in a zigzag that from above might have looked like the scribbling of Arabs. I was reminded of the cartoon creatures I see on Saturday morning TV, those who race over the edge of a cliff to hang unnaturally in the air for several seconds, their expressions passing from joy to worry to true horror. And then I realized—almost, I am convinced, at the same moment he did—that Daddy was going to roar headlong at Mr. Sellers, stop in a way that would jar the innards, and cold-cock that man.

"No," I croaked, and when Daddy left off his tirade about

murkiness in the moral parts and the rupture that was our modern era, I felt something tiny and dry break free in my chest. To my knowledge, he'd never struck a man in anger before, but as he went at it now, like an honorable man with a single unbecoming task to do in life, I could see that violence—if that's all this was—was as natural to him as fear is common to us all.

"James Edward Sellers," he was shouting, "I am going to tear out your black heart."

I reached the green just as Mr. Sellers, fingering his split lip, was picking himself up. "Let's go," Daddy said, using a smile and a voice I never care again to see and hear. He seemed composed, as if he'd survived the worst in himself and was now looking forward to an eternity of deserved pleasures. "Grab my bag, Scooter," he said. Nearby, Mr. Newell and Ivy Martin had the faces you find on those who witness such calamity as auto wrecks: gray and why-filled.

"Where you going?" I asked.

He pointed: the clubhouse. "Now," he said. "This minute."

I hustled about, picking up his clubs, finding his two-iron beyond the sand trap behind the willow tree. This was over, I figured. He had been the nincompoop my mother sometimes said he was, and now he could be again that fairly handsome elder who reads books like *Historia Romania* and the biographies of dead clerics. He would, I believed, march into the clubhouse, collect himself over a mixed drink, and then reappear—as he had done several times before—at the door to the men's locker room. Into the caddy-master's hand, Daddy would place a written apology so abject with repentance and so slyly organized that when it was read over the PA, perhaps by Jimmy Sellers himself, those lounging around the pool and walking the links, as well as those in the showers or in the snack bar or in the upstairs dining room, would hush their chitchat, listen as librarians can, and afterward break into that applause which greets genuinely good news.

I was thinking this as seriously and hopefully as I now ponder issues like war and private tragedy; and yet, dragging his bag, I saw, by his squared shoulders and his purposeful stride—even by the way our sterile desert seemed white and hard as one nether world I've heard described—that he was not through.

At the men's locker room, I found the door locked. Twenty people had wedged themselves into the narrow, dim hallway; with amusement, I thought that, as he had done with Woody and Helen Knapp, Daddy had herded them here, mad and delighted, to show them the proper way to fold a bath towel or how a gentleman shines his wingtip shoes or what tie to wear with red.

"That was the trash can," Mr. Hightower said behind me.

We had heard the banging and clatter metal makes when it is drop-kicked.

Elvis Peacock was shaking his head. "Could have been the towel rack. Or that automatic hand-dryer."

You heard the crash and whang of doors slamming and a two-minute screech that Mr. Phinzy Spalding identified as the wooden rack of linen hooks that ran from the showers to the ball-washers.

Patient as preachers, they listened, and I listened to them. A jerky scraping was Dr. Weem's easy chair being dragged. Pounded. And, at last, splintered.

"What was that?" someone asked. We'd heard a deafening rattle, like gravel on a tin roof.

"Pocket change," Herb Swetman told us. "He's broken into the cigarette machine."

A glass shattered, Judge Sanders' starting pistol went off, and it was time for me to knock on the door.

"I got your clubs," I said. He was moving, spikes clicking and scratching like claws, and I had the thought that this wasn't my father at all but the boogeyman all children hear about. It was nothing to believe that what now stopped behind the door, still as the stuff inside a grave, was the scaly, hot-eyed, murder-filled monster who, over the years, was supposed to leap out of closets or flop down from trees to slay youngsters for the crimes they sometimes dream of. "What do you want me to do with them?"

I was speaking directly into the MEMBERS ONLY sign, feeling as awkward and self-conscious as I would one day feel asking Pammy Jo to marry me. Crowded behind were Frank Redman and T. Moncure Yourtees, our assistant city manager. Behind them stood the Clute brothers, Mickey and Sam, both looking as interested in this as their Pope is in carnality. Last in line, silhouetted in the doorway, stood Mr. Jimmy Sellers himself. A muscle had popped in my neck, and for a time it was impossible to breathe.

"You all right?" I asked. "Mother is real upset."

Here, then, hushed as Dr. Hammond Ellis says will be the daybreak of doom, my daddy, his face pressed against the door-

324

jamb, told me he had something special in mind. I recognized his voice as the one he'd used ten years before, when, drunk and sore-hearted with nostalgia, he had sat on the end of my bed to tell me how his brother, my Uncle Gideon (whom I am supposed to be the spitting image of), had died in the World War II Bataan Death March; it was a story of deprivation, of fortitude in the face of overwhelming sadness, and of what we human brothers—in our yellow incarnation this time—are capable of in a world slipped free of grace.

"What do you want me to do?" I asked.

"You listen carefully," he whispered.

"Yes, sir." He was my daddy and I was being polite.

He said: "I want you to break those clubs, you hear?"

The news traveled down the line behind me and returned before my mind turned completely practical: "How will you know?"

Mr. Phinzy Spalding had lit a cigar, the smoke just reaching me.

"Scooter," Daddy was saying, "I am your parent and you will do what I say." He could have been speaking to me as he had to that colonel in Korea years before.

"Yes, sir," I said.

My mother had given him these clubs—Wilson irons and Hagen woods—less than four months before, and if you know anything about golf, you know that a linkster's clubs are to him what a wand is to a magician. They had leather grips and extra-stiff shafts, and they felt, even in my clumsy grip, like a product of science and philosophy: balanced, elegant, simple as love itself. They were shiny and cost over six hundred dollars, and I told him I would begin with his wedge.

"Good idea," he said.

Snapping those clubs was neither physically nor spiritually difficult. I was strong and I was dumb. To those folks in the hallway, my actions probably seemed as ordinary as walking a straight line. Indeed, once I started, Mr. Hightower began handing me the clubs. "I'll be your assistant, Scooter," he said. He was smiling like the helpful banker he is, and I thanked him. "My pleasure," he said, "happy to do it."

There was nothing in me—doubt, aggravation, none of it. Neither fear nor joy. Neither pleasure nor satisfaction. This was work, and I was doing it. "I have your five-iron now," I called.

At my feet lay what I'd already accomplished: a gleaming pile of twisted, broken, once-expensive metal. And then I heard it: the noise I am partly here to tell about. I understand now—because I have dwelled on it and because it once happened to me—that, despite what was happening, he was still angry. Angry in a way that fell beyond ordinary expression. An anger that comes not from the heart or the brain, or another organ of sense, but from the soul itself. An anger that, looking down, angels must feel. For what he was doing, while I wrenched in half his woods and putter, was speaking, in a whisper I shall forever associate with the black half of rapture, some sort of gibberish, a jabber I can only transcribe as funny-pages gobbledygook, those dashes and stars you see in newspapers when the victim of rage empties his mind. It is X, which in the tenth-grade algebra I teach stands for the unknown— as in $x - 2 = y$. It is everything and nothing; and that day, accompanied by twenty wiser men, I heard Daddy speak it, just as yesterday I heard Dr. Hammond Ellis, our Episcopalian rector, preach about man's need for fellowship and eternal good. To be true, when I had at last fractured his putter, I believed that Daddy was mumbling as Adam and Eve were said to, in the language of Eden that Dr. Ellis insists was ours before death. Because I am old-fashioned and still a believer, I contend that my father, enraged like any animal that sleeps and eats, was speaking a babble so private, yet so universal, that it goes from your lips to the ear of God Himself; it is more breathtaking, I hold, than the wheel, fire, travel in space—all those achievements that make us, we hope, less monkey than man.

On Daddy yammered, a phenomenon those in the hall with me found as remarkable as chickens which count by twos. Mr. Hightower said my daddy was speaking Dutch. "I heard that in World War II," he said, "or maybe it's Flemish."

Frank Redman suggested it was Urdu, something he'd heard on TV the other night. "Scooter, how's your daddy know Urdu?"

Elvis Peacock, the only one besides my father to have gone to the university, said it was, well, Sanskrit, which was speech folks in piled-up headdress mutter before they zoom off to the afterlife. "Listen," he said, "I'm betting ten dollars on Sanskrit."

And so, again, we listened and were not disappointed. My father, an American of 185 pounds with bristly, graying hair and a reputation for mule-headedness, was in there—in that shambles of a locker room—yapping, if you believe the witnesses, in Basque,

326

in Mennonite, in Zulu, or in the wet yackety-yak that Hungary's millions blather when they spy the vast What-Not opening to greet them.

"Let's go in," Dr. Weems suggested at last. From their expressions, these men seemed ready to vote on it.

"Daddy," I said, "can I come in now?"

It was only midafternoon, but I felt we had waited forever.

"It's open," he said.

I sensed he was sitting, perhaps in the remains of Dr. Weem's easy chair; strangely, I expected him to be no more disturbed or disheveled than our most famous judges.

"Don't make any loud noises," Frank Redman said. "I know that man, he's liable to shoot somebody."

Slowly, I pushed open the door, stepped over the rubble of his clubs, and made room for those following me. You could see that a hurricane—a storm by the name of Hobey Don Baker, Sr.—had been through there. A bank of lockers had been tipped over, many sprung open to reveal what we in the upper class dry off with or look at when doing so. There were shampoo bottles scattered, as well as Bermuda shorts, tennis shoes, golf spikes, bottles of Johnny Walker Red and Jack Daniels, Bicycle playing cards, chips that belonged to Mr. Mickey Clute's poker game, and a nasty paperback Frank Redman wouldn't later own up to. In one corner was a soiled bundle of lady's frilly underclothes that looked worthy of ample Mrs. Hightower herself. And then Ivy Martin noticed Memo Gonzalez, the janitor, who was leaning against the wall to our right, almost facing Daddy.

"You been in here the whole time?" Ivy Martin asked.

As a group, we watched Memo nod: sure, he'd been in here. He was from Mexico—an especially bleak and depressed village, we thought—and the rumor was that he had been a thousand things in his youth: dope smuggler, highway bandito, police sergeant in Las Palomas, failed bullfighter—before Ivy brought him up here, on a green card, to sweep up and keep our clubs clean.

"We been having conversation," Memo said. "Where you been?"

Right then, you knew all the rumors were true, even those still to be invented, for you could see by the way he smoked his Lucky Strike and picked his teeth with a golf tee that he'd seen it and heard it, and that it—war, pestilence, famine, plague—had meant less to him than books mean to fish.

327

"Memo," my daddy said, "come over here, please."

I took note of one million things—the yellow light, the smell of the group I stood in, and the rusty taste coming from my stomach. I felt as apart from my father as I do now that he is dead. I wondered where my mother was and what was happening in the outer world. I thought of Pammy Jo and hoped she still loved me. I saw that Mr. Newell hadn't shaved and that Rice Hershey was the sourpuss bookkeeper Daddy said he was. A thought came, went, came back—and again I heard, in my memory, the X-language Daddy had used.

It was prayer, I thought. Or it was lunacy.

"Let's go," I said. "Mother says we're eating out tonight."

Standing, one arm around Memo's shoulders, Daddy looked, except for the hair slapped across his forehead like wet leaves, as alert and eager as he did at the breakfast table. I wanted to grab hold, say I loved him.

"Gentlemen," he was saying, "to cover expenses, I hold here a check for ten thousand dollars."

There were ooooohhh's and aaahhh's and the expressions they come from.

"If you need more, there is more."

And then he was marching past us, me running to catch up.

Now this is the modern, sad part of the story, and it is a bit about my oldest boy Buddy—who, like me in the former story, is seventeen—and how I came again to hear that double talk I thought remarkable so long ago. There is no Memo in this part, nor folks like Messrs. Redman, Hightower, and Newell, for they, like Daddy and Mother themselves, are either dead or old and mostly indoors. Mainly, though, this section is without the so-called innocent bystander because our world is utterly without bystanders, innocent or otherwise. We are all central, I believe, to events which are leading us, good and bad, to the dry paradise that is the end of things.

Buddy is like most youth these days—by turns lazy and feckless, stupid and smart-alecky, fussy and apathetic. Tall, too skinny through the chest, he speaks when spoken to and has a girlfriend named Alice Mary Tidwell who will one day be a fat but always cheerful woman. He reads periodicals like *Sports Illustrated* and what is required in school as advanced literature (which is *Silas*

Marner, verse by Shakespeare, and made-up mishmash by New York writers who haven't lived anywhere). I love him not simply because he is my flesh but because I see that in all things—his own adulthood, for example—he will be decent-hearted and serious-minded, a man who will want, as you do, to be merely and always good. More than once we have talked about this—mostly when he was a toddler. I used to sit at the end of his bed, as had my father with me, to offer my views on issues like relations among neighbors, what heft our obligations have, and how too often the heart never fits its wanting. One time, but without the dramatics my daddy enjoyed, I took him around the house, showing him what ought to be, not what was; later, when he was ten and mowing our yard, I went out, watched for a time, then stood in his path to stop him.

"What's the matter now?" he asked.

It was summer, dry but hot as fire gets, and I was partly joyful to see him sweat doing something he'd been told.

"First," I said, "you have to wear shoes. You hit a rock and no telling what'll happen."

He looked at the sandals we'd bought him in Juarez.

"And no more shorts," I added. "Long pants for the same reason."

He has his mother's blue eyes, which were fixed on me as hers often are when I rise up to put things straight in this universe.

"I'm wearing goggles," he said.

I was pleased, I told him, but then described, as Daddy had for me, how grass is cut in the ideal world.

"Starting from the outside," I began, "you go around in a square, okay? Throws the cuttings to the center and makes raking up easier."

Here it was, then, that we had a moment together, a moment which had nothing to do with yardwork; rather, it was a passage of time that, to the sentimentalist I am, seemed filled with wonder and knowledge—the first things we must pass on.

"Can I have five dollars?" he asked.

He was going to the movies, he said, with Jimmy Bullard and Clovis Barclay. I was watching his face—what it said about his inner life—and when he took the money from me, I accepted the urge, felt in the gut, to throw my arms around him and lay on the breath-defeating hug I am notorious for.

329

"Come on, Dad," he said, "don't squeeze so hard."

Mostly, however, and embarrassingly, we are not close. Like my father, I tend to lecture; like me, when I was his age, he is obliged to listen. I have talked about responsibility, the acceptance of which is a measure of our maturity and not nearly the weighty moral overcoat another might say it is, and Buddy has said, "Yes, sir." I have talked about honor, which is often seen as too ambiguous to be useful, and he has answered, "Yes, sir." I have talked about politics, which except for voting he is to avoid; and debt, which he may accept in moderation; and cleanliness, which remains a practical concern; and trust, which he must reward in others. Other times, I have warned him against tobacco, drinking with strangers, carelessness with firearms, public displays of temper, eating undercooked or fatty foods, wasting time, rudeness, sleeping in drafts, and lying when such is not called for. I have said in effect (and in a way Pammy Jo finds most amusing) that there is hardness and cruelty, confusion and turmoil; and there is knowing what's best. To all he has answered, "Yes, sir."

I have, of course, told him about his grandfather's outburst at the Country Club; to be true, I told him during that father-son talk which becomes necessary when the son acquires body hair and the shoulders broaden toward manhood. I forget the point I intended, but somewhere during a too-clinical discussion of arousal and penis length and courtship, I said, "Did you ever hear the locker-room story?" We were in our living room, him holding the well-illustrated pamphlet *Growing Up: A Young Man's Mystery* that Dr. Weems had given me. Outside, the August light was gladsome, and in here, amid palaver that made romance sound like sport among Martians, I unloaded, taking nearly two hours telling about one. Giving him names, places, and states of mind, I spent an odd instant watching his brain, as betrayed by his eyeballs, figure out what coitus had to do with madness. I watched him imagine my daddy as more than the grumpy old man he had known; and sexual congress—which, I confess, was the phrase I used—as something more than flesh attached to funny words. I told him about Memo's tattoos, which were as detailed and epic as *Spiderman* comics, and about Ivy Martin's hole-in-one afterward, and about my mother pitching turkey bones at the clock that night; and then, twilight near and our neighbors home from their trades, I watched Buddy's forehead wrinkle and his hand fidget while he thrashed about in

330

the events I had recalled, helpless as a drowning mule in his effort to establish a connection between the past and this present business of creation.

Which, in the roundabout way I think appropriate, brings us to recent hours, whose events feature a father, a son, a prophylactic, and mumbo jumbo from the start of time.

It is early April now, rainy enough to be annoying, and Pammy Jo and our youngest, Taylor, are in the eighth day of their two-week visit to her sister in El Paso. It is an absence which means that Buddy and I eat hot dogs and Kraft macaroni too often, or we visit the Triangle Drive-In for Del Cruz's chicken-fried steak in white gravy. It is an absence I feel physically, as if what I am missing from my bed and my conversation is more body part than companion. There is a larger effect, too, specifically with reference to time—which seems to stretch forward endlessly to a future ever out of reach. Time becomes inconceivable: it is reincarnation or other hocus-pocus our wishing invents. What I am saying here is that when my wife is around, I know where I am in America; and I can say to anybody that I am forty-two years old, a Scorpio (if you care), a cum laude graduate of University of New Mexico (B.S. in mathematics), a shareholder in several companies (IBM, for one), a father, a sportsman who does not care for hunting or fishing, a practicing Episcopalian, and heir to nearly two million dollars worth of baked desert rangeland (and the cattle that graze there). But when she is gone—when she visits her father in Roswell or when she attends her social workers' convention in Santa Fe—my horizon shrinks and loneliness has such weight that I am pitched forward and ever in danger of wobbling to a stop.

The other day I felt this as a restlessness to see my neighbors, a desire to be moving, so I told Buddy I was going out.

"When you gonna be back?" he asked.

It was noon and there was no reason to be anywhere—here, this continent, this world.

"I don't know, maybe I'll go to the club."

He was watching Larry Bird and the Celtics make mincemeat out of the Bullets from Washington. Plus, he had a package of Hydrox cookies and most of the milk in the house. "Have a good time," he said, and I was gone.

Yet for the next few hours, it was less I than someone else who

331

drove around Deming. First, this man who was not me found himself stopped outside a shabby duplex on Olive Street where he had been violently drunk for the first time. He had been with Donnie Bobo and Dickie Greene then and, in the company of Oso Negro and Buckhorn beer, he'd seen the night itself fly apart and burn. An hour later, he found himself on one of the line roads that head east through the scrub and brush toward Las Cruces. He had been here twice before with Bernice Ruth Ellis, and the sex they had had been fitful, not at all the hurly-burly described in *Penthouse* magazine—in part because he was married and because she was the confused daughter of our most celebrated Christian, Dr. Hammond Ellis. This infidelity occurred long ago, in the second year of my marriage, and is an episode I do not forgive myself for. It is one secret I've kept, and there are times, especially when I see Bernice and her husband Charlie Potts at the Fourth-of-July dance or at the Piggly Wiggly, when I think it did not happen at all; or that, if it did, it happened in a place—a crossroads of time and circumstance—where there was no evil or eye looking down.

Around four, I found myself at the club, one of many husbands and fathers who seemed too bored or too free. My friend Leroy Sellers (yes, Mr. Jimmy's son) was sitting on a camp stool in the pro shop, making sense out of our war with Nicaragua. Bobby Hover was there, looking like the rich real-estate broker he is; so were Joe Ben Newell, Spud Webb, Archie Meents, and Ed Fletcher—all fellows I'd grown up with or met through my exploits on the football field. In time, aided by the Scotch whiskey Spud brought from his locker, we fixed civilization up fine. After eliminating poverty, we took the starch out of the diets of fat men, dealt with dreams that terrify tyrants, turned winners into losers, fired two county commissioners, and agreed that in human beings we liked muscle, the eagle's eyesight, voices you can hear across the room, and what they teach in Sweden about freedom. Joe Ben told us about his brother who was building jet fighters for LTV in Dallas, Ed Fletcher suggested a cure for flatulence, and Spud himself took the high ground in defense of intergalactic communication with, say Venusians—a point he made by drawing our attention to the ten billion stars and planets which were said to be out there.

He was standing, I remember, and his workingman's face had taken on a blissful shine, red and wet the way yours would be were

332

you to win ten million dollars in a lottery. "There's life up there, I tell you," he said, daring each of us to contradict him. "You got to be less narrow-minded, boys."

For a moment, it was possible to believe him—to understand that out there, where light is said to bend toward time, lived creatures, like ourselves, who had our happy habits of wonder and hope.

At six-thirty, while Ed Fletcher addressed the topic of loyalty in Washington, D. C., I called Buddy to say I'd be a time yet. "No problem," he said, "I'm going over to Doug Sherwin's." I know now that he had already done it: that he had gone into our bedroom and had opened my bureau drawer, finding the plain drugstore condoms Pammy Jo and I used for birth control. I know, too, that his mind was filled with a dozen contrary notions—guilt and anxiousness and excitement; and I suspect that at the moment we in the pro shop were putting Mr. Richard Nixon on his feet again, Buddy was bringing himself to that point his *Young Man's Mystery* book calls "orgasm," which is defined as a matter of friction and fluids.

I got home late, finding eight lights burning and the TV turned to a Sunday-night movie about, near as I could tell, greed and those the victims of it. Buddy wasn't home, which was just as well because I was drunk. I have mostly forgone heavy drinking, a crutch (Pammy Jo's word) I leaned on too heavily after my father died. Nowadays, I have wine to be polite or take my alcohol mixed, for there was a time—nearly eighteen months, in fact—when I was addled enough to be drunk virtually every night; my family has said that it was truly afraid of me during this period, seeing me as a desperate sort who wouldn't watch his tongue and who heaped on others the misery he'd heaped on himself. So, unsteadily and ashamed, I made coffee and ate peanut butter, a remedy I'd heard on Phil Donahue once. I tried reading the Raymond Chandler I like, but the words, not to mention the events and the people shaped by them, kept sliding off the page. I looked at *Life* magazine but could not figure out what beasts like giraffes and African elephants were doing next to the colorful vacation homes of the rich. I thought, at last, of calling Pammy Jo, but didn't. She would hear the thing I was covering up and she would be sad. So, believing I would go to bed, I scribbled this note: "Buddy, I'm going to school tomorrow to do lesson plans; you, as promised, begin painting the garage."

My daddy claimed, especially in his rage-filled years in later life, that he'd developed the extra sense of suspicion, a faculty he likened to an awareness old-time oil men have: roughnecks, it is said, know when a well is about to come in by a "harmonic tremor," a subtle shaking of our earth heralded by a noise that causes dogs to prick up their ears. I have inherited this sense, along with bony elbows and a mouth that can be set hard as a doorknob. In our bedroom, which is as big as a $100-a-night hotel room, I knew immediately that something was wrong. My bedsheets looked too tight and the clutter on my night stand—a *National Geographic*, the Kleenex box, the clock-radio, and a water glass—seemed unfamiliar, somehow different. That organ of suspicion—which is composed, I know now, of habit and how you are taught—was well at work in me. I compare it to my dog, a pound-bred beast named Raleigh, and how sometimes he becomes three-parts attention, one-part muddle. I made my way around my room on tiptoe, feeling myself the intruder here. I have fist-fought twice in my lifetime—the last in the ninth grade with Billy Joe DeMarco when I broke my wrist—but, counting the change on my dresser and opening my jewelry box, I was ready. I heard what nighttime has to offer in these parts: Poot Tipton in his back yard next door hollering at his brother; a car going too fast on Iron Street; our air conditioner taking its own pulse. I was thinking, Who was here? and pictures came to mind of robberies and the serious prowling we suffer around here. And then, arms held as I had been taught—tight to the body, the fists on either side of the head—I went into the bathroom.

For several moments I didn't see the used condom on the water tank of the toilet. Rather, I was studying the man in the mirror who is me. It would be a cliché to say that in my face—particularly the way the cheekbones lie and how the nose goes flat at the bridge—was my father's; but there he was, at forty-five or fifty, gazing at me from a mirror my wife had paid too much for at the White House department store. It is also possible to believe that in his face lay the images, as well, of *his* father, who had gone broke at least twice, and his grandfather, who at seventy-six had been the oldest of the soldiers and civilians Black Jack Pershing had led into

Mexico in 1916 to chase the brigand Pancho Villa. Given more time, I would have seen the face before *him* and the face before that one—the faces, finally, of Ebeneezer and Jonathan, who had sailed to America in the 1700's from hamlets in France that don't exist anymore. In a way quite natural under the circumstances, I let my heart and breath go free, flipped on the lights, and looked at that room the way Chuck Gribble, our sheriff, looks at places that are the scenes of small crimes. I report to you now that I discovered the condom at that moment and took note of it, as in past years I have taken note of bad news that happens in big towns far, far away.

"Yes," I said.

It was a word which then meant no more to me than what is muttered in Paraguay. Yet I muttered it again and again—as if an official with important-looking documents had knocked on my door to say, "Are you Hobey Don Baker, Jr.?"

That night I behaved like an ignorant father. I phoned the Sherwin house, but Betty, Doug's mother, said Buddy wasn't there.

"You okay, Scooter?" she asked. "You sound funny."

For the most part, my voice was coming from my chest and, yes, it wasn't her friend talking; it was Buddy's old man. "You see him," I told her, "it's time to come home, all right?"

Sure, she said, and reminded me of the barbeque on Wednesday. "You haven't been drinking, have you, Scooter?"

I watched my hand shake and attended to the rasp my breathing made. "I'm fine, Betty, thanks."

I called Clovis Barclay and put up with Earl, his father, scolding me about how late it was. Afterwards, I stood on the street, watching our neighbors' lights go off after the late news. It would be a cool night, the clouds racing up from Chihuahua, and I hoped Buddy hadn't gone out without a jacket. I was not angry, just dislocated—as unhinged as I was when I tried to quit smoking. I heard the same noise over and over: a fierce ear-whine. I regarded heaven, which was up and far away, and hell, which was underfoot and near; and then I went indoors to make myself a camp in Buddy's room.

It is a truism that teenagers have the collector's spirit. In my time, I'd hoarded baseball cards and kept statistics on the Aggie basketball I listened to on the radio. I had trophies (swimming), drawings, and photographs of jet planes that Grumman had sent me. I had saved coins awhile—nothing special—plus books on oceans. Buddy was no different. He possessed a Zenith record player and at least one hundred albums from Fed-Mart: Motley Crue, Devo, and foreign-looking groups whose lyrics were about love, or what passed for it. On the walls—ceiling, too—were charts ("Generalized," of time and rock units) of Canada and the USA. The rocks we stood on, I learned, came from the Silurian Period. From his desk I discovered that apparently he'd never thrown away a single school assignment; you could see him, represented in thousands of pages, go from one unable to spell "garage" to one familiar with what Euclid had achieved. I am not proud of this snooping, but I had to know, and isn't knowing—even if it is painful and frightful and small—better than not knowing? And then, after I'd counted his shirts and pants, he was standing at his door.

"Hey," he said, "I read the note."

I took a second, trying to strip the age out of my voice. "Who was she?" I asked. "Was it Alice Mary?"

He stepped backwards, shaking his head as if he'd run into a cobweb. He was wearing a shirt like the checkered flag at the Indy 500 and pants that were too expensive and too tight.

"You had a girl in here tonight," I said. "I want to know who."

It was a shameful question, but I had to ask it again before I realized—my organ of suspicion, I guess—that there had been no girl, or woman; that, instead, he had indulged in what my 1949 edition of *Webster's New Collegiate Dictionary* calls, stupidly, "self-pollution," which is masturbation and is as normal to us as flying is to birds.

"In my bathroom," I said. "On top of the commode."

He went to look and while he was gone I, in my mind, began putting his books in order. Large to small. Good to bad.

"It was Pat Greathouse," he said when he returned. "You don't know her. Her old man works for the state police, a sergeant." Buddy looked defeated, as nerve-wracked as the time his Little League team was beaten and the world to him had gone topsy-turvy into chaos.

"Stop," I said. "I don't believe you."

It was true, he insisted. She sat behind him last year, in fifth-period chemistry. She had brown hair and was tall. "They live on Fir Street. It's a white place, I don't know the number."

The rocks we have in the world are formed in the Cambrian, Ordovician, and Devonian Periods. They go back six hundred million years or more, to times that were dark, silent, and wet.

"Go to bed," I said, "we'll talk about this in the morning."

His face was flushed and open, and I could see how it, too, was mine, and how I looked a generation ago.

"You're right," he said.

A fiber had snapped in my stomach—a muscle or link between nerve and bone.

"It wasn't Pat Greathouse," he was saying, "it wasn't anybody."

And then, as it had been in that men's locker room, I heard it again, our X-language, a tumbling rush of speech that if put down here would be all z's and y's and c's, the crash of tongue-thick syllables and disordered parts that everywhere is laughed at as madness. It wasn't anger I was experiencing—that word can't apply here—but sadness. Sadness that had to do with time and love. I was in the hall, several paces from Buddy's door, next to the watercolors of trees and distance we have bought as art, and the world—as it had for my father—fell away from me. Piece by piece. Element by element. A wind had come up, freezing and from twelve directions, and there was nothing hereabouts but me and my fear. I wore the cotton shirt of a civilized man and the long pants of a grown-up, but I could not think, as I am doing now, of how I came to be in this century.

"What's wrong?" Buddy asked. "Dad?"

My arm, as if on strings, went up. Down. Up again.

"Dad," he said, "you're scaring me."

I think now I was speaking, as Daddy had, of deceit and miserable hope and craftiness and forfeiture and my own ignorance and of, especially, a future too weird and horrible to ponder. I was speaking, using but controlled by X, of the mud and ooze we will one day be. If I had to translate, I would assert that, victim of a grammar composed of violence and waywardness, I said this: *We are flesh and it is fallen*. And this: *The way is the way, and there is an end*. And this: *We are matter, it must be saved*. And this: *There are dark waters all around*. And this: *Please stop, please stop*.

In those minutes in my hallway, in a home I still owe eighty thousand dollars for, while my oldest son trembled as if I had struck him, X wasn't unknown any longer. It had hair and teeth and ancient, common desires. I knew X. It was me, it was him, it was you.

Twenty-five years ago, Memo Gonzalez, to whom my daddy had given his check for ten thousand dollars, stood unmoving next to Dr. Weems's splintered chair while Daddy and I left. Jimmy Sellers, who told this to me, says there was nothing at all in Memo's face. It was stone, with the impression that the nose, mouth, and eyes had been added later. He was strong, built like a toolbox, and nobody—not even Mickey Clute, who'd wrestled heavyweight in school—thought to go over there and ask for the money. Several minutes passed—the way they do in the dentist's office—before Memo walked (*lumbered*, Jimmy says) toward Ivy Martin. He set himself in front of Mr. Martin and twenty pairs of eyes stared at the tattoos on his arms—inky, clotted designs which were of ideas he held sacred and the women he'd known. Death. Conception. Maria. "I got to be moving along, Ivy Martin," he said at last. "I quit." Whereupon he went out and, as in some fairy tales, was never seen again.

I like that moment. I like, too, the moment I had with my father in his Biscayne in the members' parking lot. I did not feel like a teenager then; rather, I felt myself to be the trustee of a dozen secrets, none of which had a name yet but all of which would be with me until there was no more me to know them. "You drive," he said. But before he gave me the keys, he touched me, squeezed me at the shoulder. In that touch, man to boy, was the knowledge that we were the same, two creatures made blind by the same light and deafened by the same noise; that his dismay was the thing I'd grow into as I had already grown into his hand-me-down trousers; that we were harmless in water, or air; that we were put here, two-legged and flawed, to keep order.

It is a moment, so help me, that I intend to re-create for Buddy when he gets home from the picture show. It will be brief, like the original, but I hope it will remain for him forever as it has remained for me.

nominated by Stanley Lindberg

AT THE DEATH OF
KENNETH REXROTH

by ELIOT WEINBERGER

from NEW DIRECTIONS

IT's A TYPICAL STORY: I was assigned, at my suggestion, to write an obituary on Kenneth Rexroth for *The Nation*, a magazine he had served for fifteen years as San Francisco correspondent. Written in the week after his death, the article was promptly rejected for "overpraising a minor writer"—and a "sexist pig" to boot. (In its place the magazine ran a lengthy piece on some sad flake from the Andy Warhol crowd.) The obituary was then sent, at the recommendation of Carol Tinker, Rexroth's widow, to the *American Poetry Review*. Two months later they replied that they would be happy to run the piece next year, and would I please send a photograph of myself to accompany it? Considering their leisure, and my mug, inappropriate to the occasion, I withdrew the article. *Sulfur* magazine, just going to press, offered to add an extra page in the front of their next issue—and there, in the obscure and sometimes honorable domain of the little magazine, is where a condensed version of my small notice of Rexroth's death finally saw print.

It's a typical story: One cannot even publish an obituary for an American poet, for the best of them die even more forlorn than they lived. In the last twenty-five years, despite the so-called "poetry boom" and the thousands of poetry books published yearly, most of the important American poets have died with most of their work unpublished or out of print. Louis Zukofsky, H.D.,

Langston Hughes, Paul Blackburn, Charles Olson, Marianne Moore, Mina Loy, Frank O'Hara, Charles Reznikoff, Jack Spicer, Lorine Niedecker, to name a few. The small group who died in print were either approved by the English Department in their lifetimes (Frost, Eliot, Cummings) or they had the fortune to be published (and kept in print) by New Directions (Williams, Patchen, Pound, Merton, and now Rexroth).

With certain exceptions, the death of an American poet inverts the reputation. Those who were heavily laureled in their lifetimes seem to vanish from their graves. Think of Tate, Ransom, MacLeish, Van Doren, Schwartz, Bogan, Jarrell, Aiken, Winters, Hillyer, and so many more. (And soon to be joined, I suspect, by Lowell, Berryman, Bishop.) For those who were dismissed or neglected in life, death becomes the primary condition for immortality. The English Department is usually too late for the funeral, but they are enthusiastic exhumers. Their critical apparatus grinds into motion and, often many years later, buoyed by exegesis, the original rises to the surface once more. Canonization is complete, and we all too easily assume that those islands were always on the map. (We've already forgotten that Williams won his only Pulitzer Prize posthumously, that the last volume of the *Cantos* was deemed unworthy of review anywhere, that H.D. at her death was remembered only for a handful of her earliest poems and that it took over 20 years for an edition of her *Collected Poems* to appear, that Marianne Moore's *Collected* was, until recently, out of print for seventeen years.)

Now, with a special issue of *Sagetrieb* ("A Journal Devoted to the Poets in the Pound-Williams-H.D. Tradition" published by the University of Maine at Orono) the ivy gates are opening to admit Mr. Rexroth. People will make a living explaining him, and the mountains of his life and work will swarm with curiosity-seekers, pedants, muckrakers and axe-grinders, all as tiny as the figures in a Chinese landscape painting. It's easy to imagine what Rexroth would have said about them—but what will they make of Rexroth? How will they take the most readable American poet of the century and render him difficult—that is, requiring explication, better known as "teachable"?

I sit with a pile of clippings: *Poetry* magazine, reviewing Rexroth's first book, comparing the poems to the license plates made by convicts, and suggesting that the poet consider another profession. Alfred Kazin calling him an "old-fashioned American sorehead." *The New Yorker,* with its usual bemused condescension, nicknaming him "Daddy-O." John Leonard in the *New York Times:* "He lives in Santa Barbara, Calif., where he professes Buddhism and meditates. Meditates? The heart sinks. If Mr. Rexroth is meditating, then he is not being the curmudgeon of old, of fond memory . . . [the] father figure to the various dandies with black fingernails."

And the obituaries: in New York, "Father Figure to Beat Poets"; in L.A., "Artist and Philosopher." A few days later, the longer assessments: Colman McCarthy, in the *Washington Post,* surprised that the newspaper obituaries "ran no longer than a few inches," but assuming that the "magazines that Rexroth wrote for—*The Nation, Commonweal, Saturday Review, Poetry*—[will] provide the full appreciations that he deserves." (None did.) Herbert Mitgang, in the *New York Times,* declaring with parenthetical snideness that he "will probably be remembered as a public personality and as an inspiration (in some circles) more than as a major poet, critic or painter."

Born in another country, Rexroth would have served as the intellectual conscience of the nation: a Paz, Neruda, MacDiarmid, Hikmet. But here, as he wrote, "There is no place for a poet in American society. No place at all for any kind of poet at all." So in his life, and at his death, he was largely seen as a crank, a colorful American eccentric who once spiced occasional magazine copy and three well-known romans-à-clef.

It is depressing that a few moments from that vast and protean life were bottled and preserved for use *ad infinitum* whenever the name of Rexroth was mentioned. How sad that he died, in the mind of America, an aged Beatnik. For what is more remote than the Beat Generation? To read *The Dharma Bums* today (where Rexroth appears as a "bow-tied wild-haired old anarchist fud," and which has dated far more than, say, Henry Miller) is to see that the Beats mainly offered an attractive selection of alternative consumer choices—red wine, Chinese food eaten with chopsticks, heterosexual sex without marriage, hitchhiking, a taste for nonrepresentational painting and jazz, occasional tolerance for gay sex, casual dress, some dabbling in meditation and Oriental philosophy and the occult, facial hair, marijuana—all of which quickly became the

341

common stuff of middle-class American weekends while, ironically, the Beats continued to retain their "wild Boho" image.

Rexroth briefly embraced the Beats (despite his famous disclaimer, "An entymologist is not a bug") as he had so many movements: the Wobblies, the John Reed Clubs, anarchism, the Communist Party (which refused him membership), civil rights, the hippies, feminism—most of which posed a far more serious threat to institutional America than the Beats. But as a political thinker and activist, he essentially belonged to "the generation of revolutionary hopelessness." More than any other poet, Rexroth's work records that history of disillusionment: the massacre of the Kronstadt sailors, Sacco and Vanzetti, the Spanish Civil War, the Hitler-Stalin pact, Hiroshima, the Moscow Trials. He wrote, in 1957:

> We thought we were the men
> Of the years of the great change,
> That we were the forerunners
> Of the normal life of mankind.
> We thought that soon all things would
> Be changed, not just economic
> And social relationship, but
> Painting, poetry, music, dance,
> Architecture, even the food
> We ate and the clothes we wore
> Would be ennobled. It will take
> Longer than we expected.

Still he clung to the vision of brotherhood exemplified by the various American Utopian communities whose history he wrote. His 1960 essay, "The Students Take Over," was dismissed by an academic critic as "mad" for "announcing a nationwide revolution among students on behalf of national and international integrity." Yet by 1969 *The Nation* would write, "What is most viable in the so-called New Left is in large part the creation of Rexroth and Paul Goodman whether the movement knows it or not." As always in Rexroth's life, the initial reaction stuck while the fact that he was proved right was forgotten: "When a prophet refuses to go crazy, he becomes quite a problem, crucifixion being as complicated as it is in humanitarian America."

His enemies were the institutions (the U.S. and Soviet states, the corporations, the universities, the church) and their products: sexual repression, academic art, racism and sexism, the charmlessness of the bourgeoisie, the myth of progress, the razing of the natural world. He was an early champion of civil rights, and his essays on black life in America are among the few from the period that have not dated. He was the first poet whose enthusiasm for tribal culture was not picked up from Frazer, Frobenius or the Musée de l'Homme, but rather from long periods of living with American Indians. And he was—almost uniquely among the WASP moderns—not only *not* anti-Semitic, but an expert on Hassidism and the Kabbalah.

Most of all, he was America's great Christian poet—a Christianity, that is, which has rarely appeared in this hemisphere: the communion of a universal brotherhood. And he was America's— how else to say it?—great American poet. For Rexroth, alone among the poets of this country, encompasses most of what there is to love in this country: ghetto street-smartness, the wilderness, populist anti-capitalism, jazz and rock & roll, the Utopian communities, the small bands at the advance guard of the various arts, the American language, and all the unmelted lumps in the melting pot.

As a poet, he had begun with "The Homestead Called Damascus," a philosophical dialogue and the only poem worth reading by an American teenager, and then veered off the track into a decade of "Cubist" experiment. Had he remained there—like say, Walter Conrad Arensberg—he would be remembered as a minor Modernist, less interesting than Mina Loy and far inferior to his French models, Reverdy and Apollinaire. But by the publication of his first book, *In What Hour*, in 1941, Rexroth had abandoned the Cubist fragments of language—while retaining the Cubist vision of the simultaneity of all times and the contiguity of all places—to write in a sparsely adorned American speech. ("I have spent my life striving to write the way I talk.") It was a poetry of direct communication, accessible to any reader, part of Rexroth's communitarian political vision, and personal adherence to the mystical traditions of Christianity (the religion of communion) rather than those of the East (the religions of liberation).

The poetry: political, religious, philosophical, erotic, elegiac; celebrations of nature and condemnations of capitalism. His long poems of interior and exterior pilgrimage are the most readable in English in this century. Though he wrote short lyrics of an erotic intensity that has not been heard in English for 300 years—worthy of the Palatine Anthology or Vidyakara's *Treasury*—he essentially belonged to the tradition of chanted poetry, not to lyric song. For some critics the poems were musically flat, yet William Carlos Williams claimed that "his ear is finer than that of anyone I have ever encountered." The way to hear Rexroth is the way he read: to jazz (or, in the later years, koto) accompaniment. The deadpan voice playing with and against the swirling music: mimetic of the poetry itself, one man walking as the world flows about him.

Curiously, his effect on poetry in his lifetime was not as a poet, but as a freelance pedagogue and tireless promoter, as energetic and inescapable as Pound: organizer of discussion groups and reading series and radio programs; responsible for bringing Levertov, Snyder, Rothenberg, Tarn, Antin, Ferlinghetti and others to New Directions; advocate journalist, editor and anthologist. Though Gary Snyder can be read almost as a translation of Rexroth; though it is difficult to imagine Allen Ginsberg's "Howl" without the example of "Thou Shalt Not Kill"; though everyone has read the Chinese and Japanese translations; it seems that few, even among poets, have read "The Phoenix and the Tortoise," "The Dragon and the Unicorn," "The Heart's Garden, The Garden's Heart," "On Flower Wreath Hill," or more than a scattering of the short poems.

The result is that Rexroth at his death was among the best known and least read of American poets. It is a sad distinction that he shares, not coincidentally, with the poet he most resembles, Hugh MacDiarmid. (I speak of MacDiarmid's reputation outside of Scotland.) Except for MacDiarmid's orthodox Marxism and Rexroth's heterodox Christianity, which are mutually exclusive, both were practitioners of short lyrics and long discursive and discoursive poems, both were boundless erudites, and both are formed out of the conjunction of twentieth-century science, Eastern philosophy, radical politics, heterosexual eroticism, and close observation of the natural world. (The resemblance, strangely, went beyond intellectual affinity: Rexroth claimed that he was often mistaken for MacDiarmid in the streets of Edinburgh.)

I suspect that the neglect of Rexroth and MacDiarmid is due to the fact that both are, at heart, outside of (despite their varying sympathies for) the "Pound-Williams-H. D. tradition." Their spiritual grandfathers were Wordsworth and Whitman: the life of the mind on the open road. [It is, by the way, how one writes the Chinese *tao:* the character for "head" over the character for "road."] MacDiarmid may have been sunk by his galactic vocabulary, but Rexroth? One guess is that Rexroth was ignored because, by writing poetry that anyone who reads can read, he subverted the system, the postwar university-literary complex. Poets, especially the advance guard, driven to the fringes of society, have developed an unspoken cultishness: a secret fidelity to the "unacknowledged legislator" myth and a tendency toward private languages that are mutually respected rather than shared. The university professors, for their part, enjoy the power of ferreting out the sources and inside information, being the holders of the keys and the decoder rings—playing George Smiley to the poet's Karla. Rexroth blew the circuits by presenting complex thought in a simple language. The English Dept. has no use for "simple" poets, and the Creative Writing School no use for complex thought. He remained an unpinned butterfly.

Nevertheless, there is no question that American literary history will have to be rewritten to accommodate Rexroth, that postwar American poetry is the "Rexroth Era" as much (and as little) as the earlier decades are the "Pound Era." And it will have to take into account one of the more startling transformations in American letters: that Rexroth, the great celebrant of heterosexual love (and for some, a "sexist pig") devoted the last years of his life to becoming a woman poet.

He translated two anthologies of Chinese and Japanese women poets; edited and translated the contemporary Japanese woman poet Kazuko Shiraishi and—his finest translation—the Sung Dynasty poet Li Ch'ing-chao; and he invented a young Japanese poet named Marichiko, a woman in Kyoto, and wrote her poems in Japanese and English.

The Marichiko poems are particularly extraordinary. The text is chronological: in a series of short poems, the narrator longs for, sometimes meets, dreams of and loses her lover, and then grows old. Although Marichiko is identified as a "contemporary woman," only two artifacts of the modern world (insecticide and pachinko games) appear in the poems; most of the imagery is pastoral and the undressed clothes are traditional. The narrator is defined only

345

in relation to her lover, and of her lover we learn absolutely nothing, including gender. All that exists is passion:

> Your tongue thrums and moves
> Into me, and I become
> Hollow and blaze with
> Whirling light, like the inside
> Of a vast expanding pearl.

It is America's first Tantric poetry: through passion, the dissolution of the world (within the poem, the identities of the narrator and her lover, and all external circumstances; outside the poem, the identity of Marichiko herself) and the final dissolution of passion itself:

> Some day in six inches of
> Ashes will be all
> That's left of our passionate minds,
> Of all the world created
> By our love, its origins
> And passing away.

The Marichiko poems, together with the Li Ch'ing-chao translations, are masterworks of remembered passion. Their only equal in American poetry is the late work of H.D., "Hermetic Definition" and "Winter Love"—both writers in their old age, a woman and a man as woman. Man as woman: a renunciation of identity, a transcendence of self. As Pound recanted the *Cantos* and fell into silence; as Zukofsky ended "A" by giving up the authorship of the poem; Rexroth became the *other*.

Pound left us, in Canto 120, with a vision of paradise and the despair of one who cannot enter paradise. Zukofsky left us with a black hole, 80 *Flowers*, an impossible density that few will ever attempt to penetrate. And now Rexroth, speaking through the mask of Li Ch'ing-chao, has left us with passion and melancholy, the ecstasies of one woman (man) in a world seemingly forever on the verge of ruin:

> Red lotus incense fades on
> The jeweled carpet. Autumn

346

Comes again. Gently I open
My silk dress and float alone
On the orchid boat. Who can
Take a letter beyond the clouds?
Only the wild geese come back
And write their ideograms
On the sky under the full
Moon that floods the West Chamber.
Flowers, after their kind, flutter
And scatter. Water after
Its nature, when spilt, at last
Gathers again in one place.
Creatures of the same species
Long for each other. But we
Are far apart and I have
Grown learned in sorrow.
Nothing can make it dissolve
And go away. One moment,
It is on my eyebrows.
The next, it weighs on my heart.

nominated by John Allman

TURTLE, SWAN

by MARK DOTY

from CRAZYHORSE

Because the road to our house
is a backroad, meadowlands punctuated
by gravel quarry and lumberyard,
there are unexpected travelers
some nights on our way home from work.
Once, on the lawn of the Tool

and Die Company, a swan;
the word doesn't convey the shock
of the thing, white architecture
rippling like a pond's rain-pocked skin,
beak lifting to hiss at my approach.
Magisterial, set down in elegant authority.

he let us know exactly how close we might come.
After a week of long rains
that filled the marsh until it poured
across the road to make in low woods
a new heaven for toads,
a snapping turtle lumbered down the center

of the asphalt like an ambulatory helmet.
His long tail dragged, blunt head jutting out
of the lapidary prehistoric sleep of shell.
We'd have lifted him from the road
but thought he might bend his long neck back
to snap. I tried herding him; he rushed,

though we didn't think those blocky legs
could hurry—then ambled back
to the center of the road, a target
for kids who'd delight in the crush
of something slow with the look
of primeval invulnerability. He turned

the blunt spearpoint of his jaws,
puffing his undermouth like a bullfrog,
and snapped at your shoe,
vising a beakful of—thank God—
leather. You had to shake him loose. We left him
to his own devices, talked on the way home

of what must lead him to a new marsh
or old home ground. The next day you saw,
one town over, remains of shell
in front of the little liquor store. I argued
it was too far from where we'd seen him,
too small to be his . . . though who could tell

what the day's heat might have taken
from his body. For days he became a stain,
a blotch that could have been merely
oil. I did not want to believe that
was what we saw alive in the firm center
of his authority and right

to walk the center of the road,
head up like a missionary moving certainly
into the country of his hopes.
In the movies of this small town
I stopped for popcorn while you went ahead
to claim seats. When I entered the cool dark

349

I saw straight couples everywhere,
no single silhouette who might be you.
I walked those two aisles too small
to lose anyone and thought of a book
I read in seventh grade, *Stranger than Science*,
in which a man simply walked away,

at a picnic, and was,
in the act of striding forward
to examine a flower, gone.
By the time the previews ended
I was nearly in tears—then realized
the head of one half the couple in the first row

was only your leather jacket propped in the seat
that would be mine. I don't think I remember
anything of the first half of the movie.
I don't know what happened to the swan. I read every week
of some man's lover showing
the first symptoms, the night sweat

or casual flu, and then the wasting begins
and the disappearance a day at a time.
I don't know what happened to the swan;
I don't know if the stain on the street
was our turtle or some other. I don't know
where these things we meet and know briefly

as well as we can or they will let us
go. I only know that I do not want you
—you with your white and muscular wings
that rise and ripple beneath or above me,
your magnificent neck, eyes the deep mottled autumnal colors
of polished tortoise—I do not want you ever to die.

nominated by Crazyhorse *and Maura Stanton*

THE FOUNDRY GARDEN

by STANLEY PLUMLY

from THE OHIO REVIEW

Myths of the landscape—
the sun going down in the mouths of the furnaces,
the fires banked and cooling, ticking into dark, here and there
    the sudden flaring into roses,
then the light across the long factory of the field, the split and
    rusted castings,
across the low slant tin-roofs of the buildings, across fallow
    and tar and burnt potato ground. . . .
Everything a little still on fire, in sunlight, then smoke, then
    cinder,
then the milling back to earth, rich earth, the silica of ash.
The times I can taste the iron in the air, the gray wash like
    exhaust,
    smell the burn-off,
my eyes begin to tear, and I'm leaning against a wall short of
    breath,
my heart as large as my father's, alone in such poverty my body
    scars
    the light.
Arable fields, waste and stony places, waysides—
the day he got the job at the Wellbaum and Company Foundry
    he wept,
and later, in the truck, pulled the plug on a bottle.
In the metallurgy of ore and coal and limestone, in the conversion
    of the green world to gray,

in the face of the blue-white fire, I remember the fencerow,
    the white campion,
calyx and coronal scales, and the hawthornes, cut to the size of
    hedge,
the haws so deep in the blood of the season they bled.
The year we were poor enough to dig potatoes we had to drive
    there,
then wait for the men to leave who let the fires go out.
There'd be one good hour of daylight, the rough straight rows
    running into shade.
We'd work the ground until the sun was a single line.
I can see my father now cut in half by the horizon, coming toward
    me, both arms weighted down.
I can see him bending over, gone.
Later, in the summer, I'd have painted the dead rust undulant
    sides
    of all the buildings aluminum,
which in the morning threw a glare, like a glaze of water, on the
    garden.

nominated by Joan Murray

IT

by HOWARD MOSS

from THE ANTIOCH REVIEW

It was a question of whether it couldn't
See you or you see it, that surface
That was more than a surface, crooning its jokes,
Like "Hello, stranger!" and "Sir, you're up!"

And sometimes, "Darling, where have you been?"
Cosying back to you in your bathrobe,
Slightly sick and wanting you home
To give it hot tea and toast in bed,

Wanting you there, and I mean always,
Waiting for hours until you'd appear
To give it life, some reason for
Existing at all, it would often say,

Watching you shave into a snowy
Newness of flesh, watching you comb
Hair there was less and less of, swearing
"I'll never breathe a word of this to anyone,"

Confessing its hopes only to you:
"Clean me, please. Or dirty me further.
Or break me in two. Or make me whole.
I'll never leave you. Never, never."

nominated by David St. John

353

COOKING

by JAMES HATHAWAY

from BLOOMSBURY REVIEW

Half across the house, I smell the pot I left
simmering. My wife, who is in the kitchen,
does not notice the smell, but I do, my senses
cleared by distance, the subtle complexities
of chicken, lamb and herb sorting themselves out,
rolling out their details like an old and sacramental list.

Through the grape leaf skin of the dolma,
the story of onion is spilling forth, the raw
vegetable brutalized by knife and heat, giving up
its essence, changing. Perhaps it remembers
the soft, black-muck onion fields, I don't know,
the sun slanting in long warm shadows in the evening,

the dive and rush of swallows twittering overhead,
but here it says its last, undeniable words,
sings them with the parsley, the grape and the rice,
combining to tell all the earth knows. Cooking,
it seems to me now, is unbearably sad: it's the best
moment coming, the squash blossom opening and closing,

huge and golden, the history of loss.

nominated by The Bloomsbury Review
and Naomi Shihab Nye

THE POET AT SEVENTEEN

by LARRY LEVIS

from QUARTERLY WEST

My youth? I hear it mostly in the long, volleying
Echoes of billiards in the pool halls where
I spent it all, extravagantly, believing
My delicate touch on a cue would last for years.

Outside the vineyards vanished under rain,
And the trees held still or seemed to hold their breath
When the men I worked with, pruning orchards, sang
Their lost songs: *Amapola; La Paloma;*

Jalisco, No Te Rajes—the corny tunes
Their sons would just as soon forget, at recess,
Where they lounged apart in small groups of their own.
Still, even when they laughed, they laughed in Spanish.

I hated high school then, & on weekends drove
A tractor through the widowed fields. It was so boring
I memorized poems above the engine's monotone.
Sometimes whole days slipped past without my noticing.

And birds of all kinds flew in front of me then.
I learned to tell them apart by their empty squabblings,
The slightest change in plumage, or the inflection
Of a call. And why not admit it? I was happy

Then. I believed in no one. I had the kind
Of solitude the world usually allows
Only to kings & criminals who are extinct,
Who disdain this world, & who rot, corrupt & shallow

As fields I disced: I turned up the same gray
Earth for years. Still, the land made a glum raisin
Each autumn, & made that little hell of days—
The vines must have seemed like cages to the Mexicans

Who were paid seven cents a tray for the grapes
They picked. Inside the vines it was hot, & spiders
Strummed their emptiness: Black Widow, Daddy Longlegs.
The vine canes whipped our faces. None of us cared.

And the girls I tried to talk to after class
Sailed by, then each night lay enthroned in my bed,
With nothing on but the jewels of their embarrassment.
Eyes, lips, dreams. No one. The sky & the road.

A life like that? It seemed to go on forever—
Reading poems in school, then driving a stuttering tractor
Warm afternoons, then billiards on blue October
Nights. The thick stars. But mostly now I remember

The trees, wearing their mysterious yellow sullenness
Like party dresses. And parties I didn't attend.
And then the first ice hung like spider lattices
Or the embroideries of Great Aunt No One.

And then the first dark entering the trees—
And inside, the adults with their cocktails before dinner,
The way they always seemed afraid of something,
And sat so rigidly, although the land was theirs.

nominated by Quarterly West

MOLLY'S DOG

fiction by ALICE ADAMS

from ONTARIO REVIEW

ACCUSTOMED TO EXTREMES of mood, which she experienced less as 'swings' than as plunges, or more rarely as soarings, Molly Harper, a newly retired screenwriter, was nevertheless quite overwhelmed by the blackness—the horror, really, with which, one dark pre-dawn hour, she viewed a minor trip, a jaunt from San Francisco to Carmel, to which she had very much looked forward. It was to be a weekend, simply, at an inn where in fact she had often stayed before, with various lovers (Molly's emotional past had been strenuous). This time she was to travel with Sandy Norris, an old non-lover friend, who owned a bookstore. (Sandy usually had at least a part-time lover of his own, one in a series of nice young men.)

Before her film job, and her move to Los Angeles, Molly had been a poet, a good one—even, one year, a Yale Younger Poet. But she was living, then, from hand to mouth, from one idiot job to another. (Sandy was a friend from that era; they began as neighbors in a shabby North Beach apartment building, long since demolished.) As she had approached middle-age, though, being broke all the time seemed undignified, if not downright scary. It wore her down, and she grabbed at the film work and moved down to L.A. Some years of that life were wearing in another way, she found, and she moved from Malibu back up to San Francisco, with a little saved money, and her three beautiful, cross old cats. And hopes for a new and calmer life. She meant to start seriously writing again.

In her pre-trip waking nightmare, though, which was convincing in the way that such an hour's imaginings always are (one sees the

357

truth, and sees that any sunnier ideas are chimerical, delusions) at three, or four a.m., Molly pictured the two of them, as they would be in tawdry, ridiculous Carmel: herself, a scrawny sun-dried older woman, and Sandy, her wheezing, chain-smoking fat queer friend. There would be some silly awkwardness about sleeping arrangements, and instead of making love they would drink too much.

And, fatally, she thought of another weekend, in that same inn, years back: she remembered entering one of the cabins with a lover, and as soon as he, the lover, had closed the door they had turned to each other and kissed, and laughed and hurried off to bed. Contrast enough to make her nearly weep—and she knew, too, at four in the morning, that her cherished view of a meadow, and the river, the sea, would now be blocked by condominiums, or something.

This trip, she realized too late, at dawn, was to represent a serious error in judgment, one more in a lifetime of dark mistakes. It would weigh down and quite possibly sink her friendship with Sandy, and she put a high value on friendship. Their one previous lapse, hers and Sandy's, which occurred when she stopped smoking and he did not (according to Sandy she had been most unpleasant about it, and perhaps she had been) had made Molly extremely unhappy.

But, good friends as she and Sandy were, why on earth a weekend together? The very frivolousness with which this plan had been hit upon seemed ominous; simply, Sandy had said that funnily enough he had never been to Carmel, and Molly had said that she knew a nifty place to stay. And so, why not? they said. A long time ago, when they both were poor, either of them would have given anything for such a weekend (though not with each other) and perhaps that was how things should be, Molly judged, at almost five. And she thought of all the poor lovers, who could never go anywhere at all, who quarrel from sheer claustrophobia.

Not surprisingly, the next morning Molly felt considerably better, although imperfectly rested. But with almost her accustomed daytime energy she set about getting ready for the trip, doing several things simultaneously, as was her tendency: packing clothes and breakfast food (the cabins were equipped with little kitchens, she remembered), straightening up her flat and arranging the cats' quarters on her porch.

By two in the afternoon, the hour established for their departure, Molly was ready to go, if a little sleepy; fatigue had begun to cut into her energy. Well, she was not twenty any more, or thirty or forty, even, she told herself, tolerantly.

Sandy telephoned at two-fifteen. In his raspy voice he apologized; his assistant had been late getting in, he still had a couple of things to do. He would pick her up at three, three-thirty at the latest.

Irritating: Molly had sometimes thought that Sandy's habitual lateness was his way of establishing control; at other times she thought that he was simply tardy, as she herself was punctual (but why?). However, wanting a good start to their weekend, she told him that was really okay; it did not matter what time they got to Carmel, did it?

She had begun a rereading of *Howards End*, which she planned to take along, and now she found that the book was even better than she remembered it as being, from the wonderful assurance of the first sentence, "We may as well begin with Helen's letter to her sister—" Sitting in her sunny window, with her sleeping cats, Molly managed to be wholly absorbed in her reading—not in waiting for Sandy, nor in thinking, especially, of Carmel.

Just past four he arrived at her door: Sandy, in his pressed blue blazer, thin hair combed flat, his reddish face bright. Letting him in, brushing cheeks in the kiss of friends, Molly thought how nice he looked, after all: his kind blue eyes, sad witty mouth.

He apologized for lateness. "I absolutely had to take a shower," he said, with his just-crooked smile.

"Well, it's really all right. I'd begun *Howards End* again. I'd forgotten how wonderful it is."

"Oh well. *Forster*."

Thus began one of the rambling conversations, more bookish gossip than 'literary,' which formed, perhaps, the core of their friendship, its reliable staple. In a scattered way they ran about, conversationally, among favorite old novels, discussing characters not quite as intimates but certainly as contemporaries, as alive. *Was* Margaret Schlegal somewhat prudish? Sandy felt that she was; Molly took a more sympathetic view of her shyness. Such talk, highly pleasurable and reassuring to them both, carried Molly and Sandy, in his small green car, past the dull first half of their trip: down the Bayshore Highway, past San Jose and Gilroy, and took them to where (Molly well remembered) it all became beautiful. Broad stretches of bright green early summer fields; distant hills, grayish blue; and then islands of sweeping dark liveoaks.

At the outskirts of Carmel itself a little of her pre-dawn apprehension came back to Molly, as they drove past those imitation Cotswold cottages, fake-Spanish haciendas, or bright little gingerbread houses. And the main drag. Ocean Avenue, with its shops—all that tweed and pewter, 'imported' jams and tea. More tourists than ever before, of course, in their bright synthetic tourist clothes, their bulging shopping bags—Japanese, French, German, English tourists, taking home their awful wares.

"You turn left next, on Dolores," Molly instructed, and then heard herself begin nervously to babble. "Of course if the place has really been wrecked we don't have to stay for two nights, do we. We could go on down to Big Sur, or just go home, for heaven's sake."

"In any case, sweetie, if they've wrecked it, it won't be your fault." Sandy laughed, and wheezed, and coughed. He had been smoking all the way down, which Molly had succeeded in not mentioning.

Before them, then, was their destination: the Inn, with its clump of white cottages. And the meadow. So far, nothing that Molly could see had changed. No condominiums. Everything as remembered.

They were given the cabin farthest from the central office, the one nearest the meadow, and the river and the sea. A small bedroom, smaller kitchen, and in the living room a studio couch. Big windows, and that view.

"Obviously, the bedroom is yours," Sandy magnanimously declared, plunking down his bag on the studio couch.

"*Well*," was all for the moment that Molly could say, as she put her small bag down in the bedroom, and went into the kitchen with the sack of breakfast things. From the little window she looked out to the meadow, saw that it was pink now with wildflowers, in the early June dusk. Three large brown cows were grazing out there, near where the river must be. Farther out she could see the wide, gray-white strip of beach, and the dark blue, turbulent sea. On the other side of the meadow were soft green hills, on which—yes, one might have known—new houses had arisen. But somehow inoffensively; they blended. And beyond the beach was the sharp, rocky silhouette of Point Lobos, crashing waves, leaping foam. All blindingly undiminished: a miraculous gift.

Sandy came into the kitchen, bearing bottles. Beaming Sandy, saying, "Mol, this is the most divine place. We must celebrate your choice. Immediately."

They settled in the living room with their drinks, with that view before them; the almost imperceptibly graying sky, the meadow, band of sand, the sea. And, as she found that she often did, with Sandy, Molly began to say what had just come into her mind. "You wouldn't believe how stupid I was, as a very young woman," she prefaced, laughing a little. "Once I came down here with a lawyer, from San Francisco, terribly rich. Quite famous, actually." (The same man with whom she had so quickly rushed off to bed, on their arrival—as she did not tell Sandy.) "Married, of course. The first part of my foolishness. And I was really broke at the time—*broke*, I was poor as hell, being a typist to support my poetry habit. You remember. But I absolutely insisted on bringing all the food for that stolen, illicit weekend, can you imagine? What on earth was I trying to prove? Casseroles of crabmeat, endive for salads. Honestly, how crazy I was!"

Sandy laughed agreeably, and remarked a little plaintively that for him she had only brought breakfast food. But he was not especially interested in that old, nutty view of her, Molly saw—and resolved that that would be her last 'past' story. Customarily they did not discuss their love affairs.

She asked, "Shall we walk out on the beach tomorrow?"

"But of course."

Later they drove to a good French restaurant, where they drank a little too much wine, but they did not get drunk. And their two reflections, seen in a big mirror across the tiny room, looked perfectly all right: Molly, gray-haired, dark-eyed and thin, in her nice flowered silk dress; and Sandy, tidy and alert, a small plump man, in a neat navy blazer.

After dinner they drove along the beach, the cold white sand ghostly in the moonlight. Past enormous millionaire houses, and blackened windbent cypresses. Past the broad sloping river beach, and then back to their cabin, with its huge view of stars.

In her narrow bed, in the very small but private bedroom, Molly thought again, for a little while, of that very silly early self of hers: how eagerly self-defeating she had been—how foolish, in love. But she felt a certain tolerance now for that young person, herself, and she even smiled as she thought of all that intensity, that driven waste of emotion. In many ways middle age is preferable, she thought.

In the morning, they met the dog.

After breakfast they had decided to walk on the river beach, partly since Molly remembered that beach as being far less populated than the main beach was. Local families brought their children there. Or their dogs, or both.

Despite its visibility from their cabin, the river beach was actually a fair distance off, and so instead of walking there they drove, for maybe three or four miles. They parked and got out, and were pleased to see that no one else was there. Just a couple of dogs, who seemed not to be there together: a plumy, oversized friendly Irish setter, who ran right over to Molly and Sandy; and a smaller, long-legged, thin-tailed dark gray dog, with very tall ears—a shy young dog, who kept her distance, running a wide circle around them, after the setter had ambled off somewhere else. As they neared the water, the gray dog sidled over to sniff at them, her ears flattened, seeming to indicate a lowering of suspicion. She allowed herself to be patted, briefly; she seemed to smile.

Molly and Sandy walked near the edge of the water; the dog ran ahead of them.

The day was glorious, windy, bright blue, and perfectly clear; they could see the small pines and cypresses that struggled to grow from the steep sharp rocks of Point Lobos, could see fishing boats far out on the deep azure ocean. From time to time the dog would run back in their direction, and then she would rush toward a receding wave, chasing it backwards in a seeming happy frenzy. Assuming her (then) to live nearby, Molly almost enviously wondered at her sheer delight in what must be familiar. The dog barked at each wave, and ran after every one as though it were something new and marvelous.

362

Sandy picked up a stick and threw it forward. The dog ran after the stick, picked it up and shook it several times, and then, in a tentative way, she carried it back toward Sandy and Molly—not dropping it, though. Sandy had to take it from her mouth. He threw it again, and the dog ran off in that direction.

The wind from the sea was strong, and fairly chilling. Molly wished she had a warmer sweater, and she chided herself: she could have remembered that Carmel was cold, along with her less practical memories. She noted that Sandy's ears were red, and saw him rub his hands together. But she thought, I hope he won't want to leave soon, it's so beautiful. And such a nice dog. (Just that, at that moment: a very nice dog.)

The dog, seeming for the moment to have abandoned the stick game, rushed at a just-alighted flock of seagulls, who then rose from the wet waves'-edged sand with what must have been (to a dog) a most gratifying flapping of wings, with cluckings of alarm.

Molly and Sandy were now close to the mouth of the river, the gorge cut into the beach, as water emptied into the sea. Impossible to cross—although Molly could remember when one could, when she and whatever companion had jumped easily over some water, and had then walked much farther down the beach. Now she and Sandy simply stopped there, and regarded the newish houses that were built up on the nearby hills. And they said to each other:

"What a view those people must have!"

"Actually the houses aren't too bad."

"There must be some sort of design control."

"I'm sure."

"Shall we buy a couple? A few million should take care of it."

"Oh sure, let's."

They laughed.

They turned around to find the dog waiting for them, in a dog's classic pose of readiness: her forelegs outstretched in the sand, rump and tail up in the air. Her eyes brown and intelligent, appraising, perhaps affectionate.

"Sandy, throw her another stick."

"You do it this time."

"Well, I don't throw awfully well."

"Honestly, Mol, she won't mind."

Molly poked through a brown tangle of seaweed and small broken sticks, somewhat back from the waves. The only stick that would do was too long, but she picked it up and threw it anyway. It was true that she did not throw very well, and the wind made a poor throw worse: the stick landed only a few feet away. But the dog ran after it, and then ran about with the stick in her mouth, shaking it, holding it high up as she ran, like a trophy.

Sandy and Molly walked more slowly now, against the wind. To their right was the meadow, across which they could just make out the cottages where they were staying. Ahead was a cluster of large, many-windowed ocean-front houses—in one of which, presumably, their dog lived.

Once their walk was over, they had planned to go into Carmel and buy some wine and picnic things, and to drive out into the valley for lunch. They began to talk about this now, and then Sandy said that first he would like to go by the Mission. "I've never seen it," he explained.

"Oh well, sure."

From time to time on that return walk one or the other of them would pick up a stick and throw it for the dog, who sometimes lost a stick and then looked back to them for another. Who stayed fairly near them but maintained, still, a certain shy independence.

She was wearing a collar (Molly and Sandy were later to reassure each other as to this) but at that time, on the beach, neither of them saw any reason to examine it. Besides, the dog never came quite that close. It would have somehow seemed presumptuous to grab her and read her collar's inscription.

In a grateful way Molly was thinking, again, how reliable the beauty of that place had turned out to be: their meadow view, and now the river beach.

They neared the parking lot, and Sandy's small green car.

An older woman, heavy and rather bent, was just coming into the lot, walking her toy poodle, on a leash. *Their* dog ran over for a restrained sniff, and then ambled back to where Molly and Sandy were getting into the car.

"Pretty dog!" the woman called out to them. "I never saw one with such long ears!"

"Yes—she's not ours."

"She isn't lost, is she?"

"Oh no, she has a collar."

Sandy started up the car; he backed up and out of the parking lot, slowly. Glancing back, Molly saw that the dog seemed to be leaving too, heading home, probably.

But a few blocks later—by then Sandy was driving somewhat faster—for some reason Molly looked back again, and there was the dog. Still. Racing. Following them.

She looked over to Sandy and saw that he too had seen the dog, in the rear-view mirror.

Feeling her glance, apparently, he frowned. "She'll go on home in a minute," he said.

Molly closed her eyes, aware of violent feelings within herself, somewhere: anguish? dread? She could no more name them than she could locate the emotion.

She looked back again, and there was the dog, although she saw now much farther—hopelessly far behind them. A small gray dot. Racing. Still.

Sandy turned right in the direction of the Mission, as they had planned. They drove past placid houses with their beds of too-bright, unnatural flowers, too yellow or too pink. Clean glass windows, neat shingles. Trim lawns. Many houses, all much alike, and roads, and turns in roads.

As they reached the Mission, its parking area was crowded with tour busses, campers, vans and ordinary cars.

There was no dog behind them.

"You go on in," Molly said. "I've seen it pretty often. I'll wait out here in the sun."

She seated herself on a stone bench near the edge of the parking area—in the sun, beside a bright clump of bougainvillea, and she told herself that by now surely the dog had turned around and gone on home, or back to the beach. And that even if she and Sandy had turned and gone back to her, or stopped and waited for her, eventually they would have had to leave her, somewhere.

Sandy came out, unenthusiastic about the church, and they drove into town to buy sandwiches and wine.

In the grocery store, where everything took a very long time, it occurred to Molly that probably they should have checked back along the river beach road, just to make sure that the dog was no longer there. But by then it was too late.

They drove out into the valley; they found a nice sunny place for a picnic, next to the river, the river that ran on to their beach, and the sea. After a glass of wine Molly was able to ask, "You don't really think she was lost, do you?"

But why would Sandy know, any more than she herself did? At that moment Molly hated her habit of dependence on men for knowledge—any knowledge, any man. But at least, for the moment, he was kind. "Oh, I really don't think so," he said. "She's probably home by now." And he mentioned the collar.

Late that afternoon, in the deepening, cooling June dusk, the river beach was diminishingly visible from their cabin, where Molly and Sandy sat with their pre-dinner drinks. At first, from time to time, it was possible to see people walking out there: small stick figures, against a mild pink sunset sky. Once, Molly was sure that one of the walkers had a dog along. But it was impossible, at that distance, and in the receding light, to identify an animal's markings, or the shape of its ears.

They had dinner in the inn's long dining room, from which it was by then too dark to see the beach. They drank too much, and they had a silly outworn argument about Sandy's smoking, during which he accused her of being bossy; she said that he was inconsiderate.

Waking at some time in the night, from a shallow, winy sleep, Molly thought of the dog out there on the beach, how cold it must be, by now—the hard chilled sand and stinging waves. From her bed she could hear the sea's relentless crash.

The pain that she experienced then was as familiar as it was acute.

They had said that they would leave fairly early on Sunday morning and go home by way of Santa Cruz: a look at the town, maybe lunch, and a brief tour of the university there. And so, after breakfast, Molly and Sandy began to pull their belongings together.

Tentatively (but was there a shade of mischief, of teasing in his voice? could he sense what she was feeling?) Sandy asked, "I guess we won't go by the river beach?"

"No."

They drove out from the inn, up and onto the highway; they left Carmel. But as soon as they were passing Monterey, Pacific Grove, it began to seem intolerable to Molly that they had not

366

gone back to the beach. Although she realized that either seeing or *not* seeing the dog would have been terrible.

If she now demanded that Sandy turn around and go back, would he do it? Probably not, she concluded; his face had a set, stubborn look. But Molly wondered about that, off and on, all the way to Santa Cruz.

For lunch they had sandwiches in a rather scruffy, open-air place; they drove up to and in and around the handsome, almost deserted university; and then, anxious not to return to the freeway, they took off on a road whose sign listed, among other destinations, San Francisco.

Wild Country: thickly wooded, steeply mountainous. Occasionally through an opening in the trees they could glimpse some sheer cliff, gray sharp rocks; once a distant small green secret meadow. A proper habitat for mountain lions, Molly thought, or deer, at least, and huge black birds. "It reminds me of something," she told Sandy, disconsolately. "Maybe even someplace I've only read about."

"Or a movie," he agreed. "God knows it's melodramatic."

Then Molly remembered: it was indeed a movie that this savage scenery made her think of, and a movie that she herself had done the screenplay for. About a quarrelling alcoholic couple, Americans, who were lost in wild Mexican mountains. As she had originally written it, they remained lost, presumably to die there. Only, the producer saw fit to change all that, and he had them romantically rescued by some good-natured Mexican bandits.

They had reached a crossroads, where there were no signs at all. The narrow, white roads all led off into the woods. To Molly, the one on the right looked most logical, as a choice, and she said so, but Sandy took the middle one. "You really like to be in charge, don't you," he rather unpleasantly remarked, lighting a cigarette.

There had been a lot of news in the local papers about a murderer who attacked and then horribly killed hikers and campers, in those very Santa Cruz mountains, Molly suddenly thought. She rolled up her window and locked the door, and she thought again of the ending of her movie. She tended to believe that one's fate, or doom, had a certain logic to it; even, that it was possibly written out somewhere, even if by one's self. Most lives, including their endings, made a certain sort of sense, she thought.

The gray dog then came back powerfully, vividly to her mind:

the small heart pounding in that thin, narrow rib cage, as she ran, ran after their car. Unbearable: Molly's own heart hurt, as she closed her eyes and tightened her hands into fists.

"Well, Christ," exploded Sandy, at that moment. "We've come to a dead end. Look!"

They had; the road ended abruptly, it simply stopped, in a heavy grove of cypresses and redwoods. There was barely space to turn around.

Not saying, Why didn't you take the other road, Molly instead cried out, uncontrollably, "But why didn't we go back for the dog?"

"Jesus, Molly." Red-faced with the effort he was making, Sandy glared. "That's what we most need right now. Some stray bitch in the car with us."

"What do you mean, stray bitch? She chose us—she wanted to come with us."

"How stupid you are! I had no idea."

"You're so selfish!" she shouted.

Totally silent, then, in the finally righted but possibly still lost car, they stared at each other: a moment of pure dislike.

And then, "Three mangy cats, and now you want a dog," Sandy muttered. He started off, too fast, in the direction of the cross-roads. At which they made another turn.

Silently they travelled through more woods, past more steep gorges and ravines, on the road that Molly had thought they should have taken in the first place.

She had been right; they soon came to a group of signs which said that they were heading toward Saratoga. They were neither to die in the woods nor to be rescued by bandits. Nor murdered. And, some miles past Saratoga, Molly apologized. "Actually I have a sort of headache," she lied.

"I'm sorry, too, Mol. And you know I like your cats." Which was quite possibly also a lie.

They got home safely, of course.

But somehow, after that trip, their friendship, Molly and Sandy's, either 'lapsed' again, or perhaps it was permanently diminished; Molly was not sure. One or the other of them would forget to call, until days or weeks had gone by, and then their conversation would be guilty, apologetic.

And at first, back in town, despite the familiar and comforting presences of her cats, Molly continued to think with a painful obsessiveness of that beach dog, especially in early hours of sleeplessness. She imagined going back to Carmel alone to look for her; of advertising in the Carmel paper, describing a young female with gray markings. Tall ears.

However she did none of those things. She simply went on with her calm new life, as before, with her cats. She wrote some poems.

But, although she had ceased to be plagued by her vision of the dog (running, endlessly running, growing smaller in the distance) she did not forget her.

And she thought of Carmel, now, in a vaguely painful way, as a place where she had lost, or left something of infinite value. A place to which she would not go back.

nominated by Ontario Review *and Robert Phillips*

SOMETHING GOOD FOR GINNIE

fiction by MARY HOOD

from THE GEORGIA REVIEW

THE SUMMER Ginger Daniels was twelve years old she no longer needed her mother's feet on the gas or brake pedal to help her drive. She could do it all, big enough and willing. Her mother never knew how to stop her except by going along. Ginnie pushed it to the limit and past, on the straight stretches through the pinelands between black-water ditches, cutting a swath through the swarming lovebugs, her mother riding beside her, not thinking, just answering, "Sure, Baby," if Ginnie asked was she happy "*now*, this exact very minute I mean *now?*"

Neither of them knew if Harve Powell ever got elected, but they laughed about his sturdy ads rusting away several to a mile: YOU CAN TRUST HARVE POWELL IN CONGRESS. "I don't know about Congress, but he sure was thorough with his *signs*," her mother said. Several times they started to count them, but lost track—something else always caught their attention. What difference did it make anyway? They didn't come from around there.

"That was before my time," Ginnie said.

"Don't wish your life away," her mother warned.

On their getaway sprees they sang to the radio and laughed and yelled at cattle in the fields—miles before their courage drooped and they had to turn back. Sometimes they picked berries or wildflowers. Ginnie teased the pitcher plants and sundews with the tip of a reed. She knew just how little or how much it took to cause the involuntary carnivorous snap of the fly traps. She ran through the congregation of sulfur butterflies and they settled on her like petals shattered by wind.

Her mother always told her she was going to be beautiful, a heartbreaker. "If you could *see* yourself," she'd say.

Long before she qualified for her learner's permit, Ginnie was driving solo.

"Why do you *let* her?" someone asked Mrs. Daniels, before her fall.

"She's going to anyway," Ginnie's mother said. "I want her to know how."

When Ginnie was thirteen, her mother fell out of a live oak on a camping trip, way out on a limb after a bird's nest for Ginnie. She broke her back on a POSTED sign, but they couldn't operate immediately; she had to be detoxed first. This was down in Jacksonville, and when the hospital released her, she went to a halfway house. She didn't come back to Georgia right away. Ginnie's father, Doc Daniels, told people it was snakebite. He knew better, and so did the ones around Dover Bluff who always kept up with things like that.

Word got back across the state line that Doc's wife had been feeding her habit straight from his shelves. As long as something's possible, rumor doesn't stop to ask, *Is it true?* His pharmacy— never number one in town before that—endured harder times afterward. He couldn't afford to reopen the snack bar, closed since integration, or to stock more than a few of any of the items that lay dusting and yellowing toward their expiration dates on the sparse shelves. Most of his regular customers kept charge accounts, usually delinquent, with hard cash trickling in a few dollars at a time from oldtimers who didn't feel like driving out to the new mall or from tourists who sometimes stopped to ask directions back to the Interstate.

He had a Coke machine out on the sidewalk which brought in a little income, not much, not reliably. More often, vandals picked the coin box and made off with the profits—and small change made a big difference some weeks. That made Doc shrewd, restless. He got a gun and kept it in his cash drawer. There was room.

He had returned to Dover Bluff several years earlier—had packed up his life entire and moved back home to become his father's partner—even though his father and the store were both failing, and they had never been able to work together before. There was still friction, but not like the kind after his mother died that had driven Doc all the way to North Georgia to establish himself there. Doc had come back thinking that he could turn around the losses, and things had looked pretty good—until the new Interstate opened and business moved east. His father died the second year of their partnership, but Doc left the sign up: *Daniels & Son, Drugs*. Ginnie was Doc's only child.

Now, with both his parents gone, Doc got restless again. Dover Bluff was a dead end for him, and his wife had never given up hoping they'd move back to the mountains. Doc decided she was right; he was finally free to please himself, and a fresh start for him meant a fresh start for all of them. They stuck it out in South Georgia for another year, making their plans, then moved back to Deerfield, north of Atlanta, where Ginnie had been born.

Doc leased a brand-new building at the plaza south of town and built them a house out in the country—no neighbors—on land they had bought years before, thinking of retirement someday. They returned to Deerfield the year Ginnie was supposed to start her junior year. The high school was six miles away. Everything was six miles away, "or more," Ginnie's mother fretted.

"A girl needs friends," Mrs. Daniels said, standing at the window, watching the woods. She no longer used her walker, just a cane.

Ginnie said she didn't care, so long as they didn't make her ride the bus. She wouldn't go to school if she had to ride the bus.

Her mother said, "Be happy, Baby, be happy," and Doc said he'd see.

Her first car was a fifteen-year-old Falcon. "I won't," she said. "I'd rather be dead in a ditch."

"You're the type," he agreed.

Ginnie's mother had a more practical approach. "What'll it take?"

Ginnie knew, exactly. "Red," she said. "I want it painted red. New seatcovers. And shag. And a tape deck."

"Jesus Holy Christ," Doc said. "You want me to rob a bank?"

Ginnie didn't back down: "You want me to, *I* will."

"She doesn't mean that," Ginnie's mother told Doc.

Ginnie said, tightening her barette, "I didn't want to go to school anyway. Boring."

"They're going to like you, Sugar," her mother said. "You make friends easy, and you already know these kids, went to grade school with them. Remember sixth-grade Talent Night at PTA? They liked you best."

"Well, that's what counts," Doc said.

Mrs. Daniels picked up the keys to the Falcon and offered them to Doc. "It won't always be like this," she said. "This is just the beginning. Look ahead, that's where to look."

When Doc didn't take the keys, and Ginnie stood with her arms crossed, head tilted, not looking, her mother said, "Your daddy finished fifth in his class. He's going to make it right for us, he just hasn't found his niche yet."

"Well, here we all are," Ginnie said, "Hillbilly Heaven."

"When you get back into things—" her mother began.

"Just shut up, both of you," Doc said. "Will you?" He grabbed the keys and went out, cutting along fast down the hill and through the woods.

"He's probably going to throw them into Noonday Creek," Ginnie said, just as he turned back. They could see the white of his tunic flashing far off, a flag of surrender.

"You mustn't hurt people's feelings," her mother told Ginnie. "You won't be able to keep friends if you play like that."

Ginnie watched her father walking slowly back. He didn't come in. He got in the Falcon and drove, hard, toward town. She turned from the window and said, "He's going to do it! Every last bit!"

Her mother hugged her, held and held her. "We love you, Baby."

Ginnie was sixteen when Gid Massey fell in love with her. Gid was a man already. Around school they called him "Drool Lips," but he didn't drool. It was just their way of singling him out. He was a strong, tough, slow man who guarded the parking lot, served in the lunchroom, and swept the halls. He was out in the parking lot the first morning of Ginnie's junior year. She wheeled in, late, and backed between two school buses, into the one remaining space, skilled and cool, indifferent to him standing there, watching. After that, he waited to see her arrive, even though she was usually late,

373

past the first bell. He never waved or spoke. When her arms were full of books, she kicked the car door shut. When she had gone, he'd go over and wipe off the scuff on the paint her shoe had left. Her name was on the door, in pink: *Ginnie*. The *i*'s were dotted with hearts.

Gid stopped by the office one day to see if anyone had claimed a ballpoint pen he'd turned in; he always turned in whatever he found, even money. They teased him. Was he going to write a book?

"Letter," he told them, earnest. He talked slowly, thickly. It sounded as if he said *Let ha*.

Behind his back, they smiled. "He's all right," they said, meaning "not dangerous," meaning "good-natured," meaning "too bad the speech therapist hadn't helped him and a hearing aid couldn't."

Gid watched Ginnie a long time before he wrote that first letter. For practice he ruled the page off, the whole brown grocery sack page, using a two-by-four scrap for a straightedge. He practiced on the scratch sheet till he got it right. He kept the note in his pocket, folded no bigger than a coin. Every day at lunch when he saw Ginnie coming by for her milk, he reached deep and touched that folded paper, but he didn't give it to her. He'd hand her a carton of milk instead, just as always, saying, "Here for you," with an intense look that made Ginnie and her friends exchange sly grins. Once Ginnie said, "You'd think it was heart's blood," and everyone laughed. Gid laughed too, the watchful, mirroring, uncertain, count-me-in laugh of the deaf.

After lunch Ginnie always worked for an hour in the school library, shelving books. He knew that. He had seen her. He had found her with his fugitive glance as he pushed his wide broom by the open door, a glimpse only with each pass he made up and down the oiled planks of the dim hall. He looked from dark into light to find her—the afternoon sun silvering the hair on her arms as she stood watering the philodendron, straightening the magazines on the table, giving the globe a spin as she dusted the quiet world. Ginnie worked in the library every day that semester, penance for misbehavior in study hall. They kept their eye on her, kept her busy. They caught her once in the stacks, kissing Jack Taylor's pale wrist—he'd just had the cast removed. After that, they kept her in plain sight, up front.

Gid Massey swept past now, and she turned, about to notice

him in his plaid jacket, pants tucked inside his laced-up boots like a Marine, his head with its lamb's curls ducked over his work, over his secrets.

"Hunnay," Ginnie drawled, loud enough for the other worker to hear and laugh. Ginnie patted her heart, mimicking agitation. She fanned herself with a limp *Geographic*. Anything for a laugh.

She wasn't the one who found the note. The other girl did, and brought it to Ginnie the moment Mrs. Grant's back was turned. It was folded and smudged and tied with blue sewing thread—and it was for "GINNIE," the N's backward. Ginnie wouldn't read it right then. Let them wonder. She knew how to play things for all they were worth.

All it said, and it made her smile in contempt when she at last unfolded and read it, was PLEASE. The S was backward too. The next day, she stood at the door of the library as he swept. He tossed a little note ahead of his broom; she might pick it up or not. If not, he'd sweep it away. She let him wonder. She let it go almost past, then she plucked it up and pocketed it, her eyes drugged and shining with her secrets. It never mattered much what the fun was, to Ginnie, so long as she had a part in it. This note was longer:

LIKE YOU GINNIE YOU GOOD THANK YOU
YOU FREND GIDEON

Ginnie wasn't afraid of him. She'd never been afraid of anything but missing out. She banked each little thread-wrapped message from Gid in her majorette boots, along with her birth-control pills and her stash of marijuana. She couldn't wear the boots any more—they were from long ago. She kept them stuffed with newspapers, the perfect hiding place. Before her parents gave up on stopping her, she used to hide her cigarettes in the boots, too. She smoked in public now, anywhere or any time she wanted. Even at school. That's how she got thrown out of study hall. Three days suspension for not using the smoking area, and a semester in the library—in the peace and quiet and order of Mrs. Grant's cedar-oiled rooms, among timeless and treasured-up thoughts— because of how she had sassed Mrs. Pilcher, the study-hall keeper, who wouldn't have her back. The library was a compromise. It had taken a little for Ginnie to get used to Mrs. Grant and the silence. She had to learn how to look busy, to keep the librarian off her back.

"I thought things were going better with me and you," Mrs. Grant said, the day she found the fifth note. Gid had left it in plain sight on the poetry shelf.

"Between you and *I*," Ginnie said. "Isn't that correct?"

"No, it isn't, but how would you know?" Mrs. Grant said, walking her to the principal's office. Ginnie had the note, but Mrs. Grant wanted it back.

"It's a federal offense to tamper with the mails," Ginnie said.

"No way, Sister," Mrs. Grant said. "No stamp, no postmark. You lose that round too."

Ginnie opened the note and wound the thread tightly around her finger, round and round.

"Untie it," Mrs. Grant said. "It'll cut off the circulation and your finger will turn black and fall off and you won't be able to wear a wedding ring."

Ginnie laughed. "What do you care?"

"Hush now," said Mrs. Grant, as they entered the office.

Ginnie said, "You're not my mama."

The principal brought it all to a head by saying, "Last chance," and reaching for the note.

In the hall, Gid Massey swept by, not looking in, but knowing. He couldn't hear much of what was going on, but he knew Ginnie was in trouble, and he hated them for making her unhappy. He leaned against the wall, trying to hear what the secretary was telling Doc on the phone. He caught Ginnie's voice, too, but no words. The principal said, "If you *don't*—"

There was a struggle and a chair overturned. Gid heard the principal cry, "Stop her!" and "Don't let her swallow!" and then things speeded up. The school nurse came running and, as the door swung shut behind her, he saw Ginnie's foot rising through the air to kick. The nurse came back out into the hall, calling, "Mr. Massey! Come help us."

He went in and helped hold Ginnie.

"She's having a fit," the nurse said.

When Doc got there, he took one look at her and said, "She's just kidding. Let her go."

Gid had been holding her up in the air, her feet just off the floor, strong but not hurting her. He wouldn't hurt her. If they had laid a

376

hand on her, he'd have struck them down. Mrs. Grant glanced at Gid's eyes, then looked again, wiser. Gid set Ginnie gently down. Her legs didn't buckle and she didn't run.

She turned to Gid and said, "I ate it. The whole thing."

Then they knew who had been writing to her, and they also knew that she hadn't been trying to protect him at all, simply defying them.

"If *we* had said *eat it*, she'd have found a way to publish it on the front page of the *Enterprise*," Mrs. Grant said.

Ginnie said, "This isn't Russia. I don't have to stay here."

The three o'clock bell rang. "I'm walking," she told them. "I'm sixteen."

"Are you dropping out?" Doc asked, grabbing her arm.

"Some of it's up to us, not Ginnie," the principal reminded her.

"We must get to the bottom of this," Mrs. Grant said.

Gid stood there, watching them talk fast.

"That man is dangerous," Mrs. Grant said, pointing. Gid stepped back, but he didn't relax till Doc released Ginnie; his fingers left marks on her arm.

"We'll just talk it through," the principal said, bringing in another chair. To Gid he said, "You may go." Behind Gid's back, he mouthed to Mrs. Grant, "Fired."

Ginnie saw. She took the principal's desk chair, tipped it back as she unraveled the thread from her finger. The bloodless white skin pinked and plumped with each heartbeat.

"Why do you like trouble?" Mrs. Grant wondered.

Gid didn't shut the door as he went out. In the halls, there was the afternoon chaos of lockers slamming and bus lines and laughter and scraps of song, the roar of normalcy.

"First of all . . .," the principal said, closing the door on all that.

It was a lengthy conference.

Ginnie rode out a three-day suspension and then was back in class. She didn't see Gid for a long time afterward, but he was watching her. After he lost his job at school, he found work at a sawmill. He stayed gone from Deerfield during the weeks, but he was back in town on Saturdays. That's whose boots left the tracks in the driveway by their mailbox, that's who left kindling on their porch. It was Gid who waited in the woods behind the Baptist Church and watched Ginnie smoking a last cigarette before services, her

Sunday shoes flashing like glass, her legs still summer-tan under her choir robe, her hair caught tidy in enameled combs. He saved her cigarette butts, her lips printed on the filter in Frosted Plum.

When she started going with Dean Teague, Gid watched more closely. Some weeks she left church with other boys from school; it wasn't always Dean. They went to dinner at Pizza Hut and sometimes Gid followed them, on his bicycle. He never came close.

Ginnie was popular.

Her mother said, "Baby, now don't give these little old boys heart failure. Don't play them off one against the other."

Meaning what? Fickle? Ginnie just laughed: "Mama, you know anybody but a baby can eat two french fries at once."

At Christmas Ginnie got a card from Gid, a big satiny one proclaiming HAPPY CHRISTMAS BIRTHDAY TO A WONDER-FUL DAUGHTER. He had bought it—the most expensive card in the store—from Ginnie's father himself. Gid counted the sawmill dollars into Doc's clean palm, laid the exact change for tax on top, and didn't understand why Doc asked him, twice, "You know what this says?" and read it to him, like Gid couldn't read.

Gid didn't get mad. He thought Doc meant, "Are your intentions serious?"

He liked the card. He knew it was Jesus' birthday, so that was the birthday part of it. And he liked the red satin, like a valentine, and the gold shining on it—that was the Christmas part of it. And he knew Ginnie was a wonderful daughter, and Doc must be so proud to be her father. "Good," he told Doc. "Happy."

Doc rang up the sale. He was uneasy with Gid so near the cash drawer stuffed with holiday money. Doc got the pistol and laid it on the counter in plain sight. "Anything else?" he asked, business-like. "Card like that takes extra stamps."

Gid shook his head, no, no. "Take," he said, taking. He smiled.

Ginnie saw his boot tracks and knew, even before she opened the mailbox and found the card. She was furious as she read what he had written inside:

ALAWAYS LOVE YOU HAPPY DAY YOU LOVE GID.

It wasn't funny any more. When it was happening at school, there had been an audience. Now it was boring. It was nothing.

378

What was she getting out of it? And yet sometimes she thought of how he had lifted her in his arms in the principal's office. That had been interesting. And how he had taken her side, had stood for her and by her. Strong as that, he could be trained, broken. He could serve. "There's something good worth getting at in any soul," her mother always said. Ginnie wanted to get at it if she could; maybe he would be harder to solve than most, but that made it more of a challenge. Once she had seen a man on TV take down a whole round factory chimney by chipping the mortar from the bricks, one course at a time, row on row. When the chimney fell, it swooned in slow motion, ending in rubble. The man was famous for it. He had stood there, just beyond reach of the topmost fallen bricks and rising dust, smiling.

So she went from wishing Gid would get lost forever to watching for him on the road or in town. She went from wanting everyone to see them together—so that they could laugh behind his trusting back—to not wanting to see him at all again, and then, finally, to wanting to see him alone. He wasn't hard to find, once she made up her mind. Everyone knew Gid.

After New Year's, she drove to where they said he lived. She had never been by there before and was just going to look, not stop. But she decided to stop—why not?—and parked behind an old barn, a field over, prying off a hubcap and tossing it into the briars at the turn, in case she needed an alibi. She was always losing hubcaps.

Gid was living as a squatter in an abandoned houseboat, atilt in a cornfield gone to sedge and scrub oak. She had to be careful where she stepped; there were tires and junk everywhere. She could see where his garden had been, outlined in stones, his scarecrow slumped in a broken lawn chair. He'd staked his beans on a bedspring. Everywhere were aluminum cans he'd salvaged from the ditches for scrap. The doghouse was made of sawmill slabs, and the ax he cut kindling with was deep in a stump. His small dog didn't scare her.

The snow had about melted; only the roots of the trees wore little rinds of it. She made a snowball around a rock and threw it at his window. It missed, thudding softly against the houseboat's siding. Gid couldn't hear well, she knew, but she wouldn't shout. She was sure he was in there, so she kicked on the crumpled pontoon, kicked and kicked, till he finally felt it and opened the door. He looked down, not knowing what to do, not even saying hello.

"Come out or ask me in," she told him. He read her lips, puzzled, then jumped to the ground—there were no steps—and they stood in the sunlight while the dog barked and leaped.

"I don't know what you want with me," she said, suddenly wanting to kick Gid instead of the boat. She talked too fast for him to catch it all. She beat at him with her fists and he let her.

She had all his notes in her coat pockets. She took them out and flung them. Then she tore his big red Christmas card into pieces and scattered it on the wind. When a car drove by on the high road, she turned her back and raised her hood over her hair. She wasn't afraid, and she wasn't being discreet; she just didn't want to be stopped.

"Invite me in, dammit!" She didn't wait for him to help her; she planted her boot on the sill and drew herself up by the door frame, strong.

"Oh, God," she said, when she saw how he had painted everything red, barn red. "Massacre," she said.

He had nailed the ceiling over with raw boards. The quilts were folded across the foot of his neat bed. Things looked clean. He even had a few books, missing their covers, that looked as if he had found them in the ditches as he hunted cans. An oil lamp stood on his table, nothing special. He had framed a picture of her, from the newspaper. She shook her head.

He chunked more wood into the fire and latched the stove door, taking his time adjusting the draft. Then he looked at her with those trusting-dog eyes. "Trouble?" he guessed. *Tubba* was how it sounded.

Ginnie laughed. "No trouble at all," she told him. He was slow-blooded, like a lizard in winter. She knew it would be up to her to warm him to living speed. Funny how he acted, standing there looking proud.

"You love this dump, don't you?" she said, checking the old Coleman icebox for beer. No beer. She'd bring some next time.

As she drew him down, down with her cool hands, she warned, "No future, and my terms."

"Friend," he said. It sounded like *fend*.

"All human beings are is animals who can talk," she told him, peeling the watchcap from his big furry skull. "And you can't even talk."

She teased him till he was crazy, till he barked, till he sweated, crawling after her on all fours. She rode him bareback. "Lady Godiva," she called herself. He was "Tennessee Stud." She sang it to him, till he knew the tune. He couldn't sing, but he could keep time. She tied him to the table. She learned him by heart. They played like that for hours, till the sun headed down. She wasn't afraid of a knock on the door. She wasn't afraid of anything. If anyone had come to that grounded boat then, she'd have answered the door herself, wild as God made her.

"As God made me," she asked Gid, "how'd he do?"

"Howdy do," Gid said.

They ate canned soup afterward—she had interrupted his lunch—and she drove home by dark. She warned him again, as she left: "No future, my terms."

Gid couldn't hear her.

Ginnie wasn't crazy about Dean Teague. She could make him do some things, but sometimes he wouldn't. It took her a little time to figure out whether he meant no for now or no forever. Not about sex, but about dope. And not because his father was the police chief, but because he ran on the track team. It would have been something to get him to smoke, or some other thing, to have him beg her for a light or a line. She couldn't make him, though. She liked him better when she couldn't make him, till she figured out she never would be able to. Then he wasn't much fun any more, and she told him so.

She told Jeff Davis about him too. "He's just no fun," she said.

"Why is that?" Jeff asked. He was like a little pony you train on a course to take each jump with a mere flick of the whip. He wanted to know why so he wouldn't make the same mistake. But Ginnie wouldn't say. That was better for business.

She ran Jeff ragged. She called him "Reb," and made him feel special, and called him "Manny," and let her hands rove as they were driving up to Hammermill to the basketball tournament. She rode so close to him she could feel him heating up. It was going to be almost too easy.

Excited, Jeff drove wild. He wasn't used to dope, and he ran them into the ditch, lightheaded. He was almost crying to get out of there, before his father found out. He went all around the car checking on the paint. All he needed was a wrecker, but he beat his hands on the roof of the car, and cursed his luck, and cried.

He even made her put the Miller in the woods, out of sight in case the Law should happen by. "I'm not drunk," he said, over and over. She would have had time to finish the grass, but he knocked the roach out of her hand into the mud and stomped it out of sight. He wasn't thinking party any more.

The first one to stop by was Buck Gilbert. Ginnie told Jeff farewell, and she and Buck drove off for help.

At the first house Buck slowed. "What're you doing?" she said.

"Telephone," Buck said.

"Let the little jerk sweat," Ginnie said. "He's already wasted enough of my precious time."

Buck put the bigfooted four-wheeler in gear and gunned the truck on by. Ginnie liked the way it wallowed on the curves as though it might roll over, but Buck knew how to drive it. He laid it around in the gravel, full circle, twice—no accident the first time, more fun the second. She wanted to try it. He let her. She sat in his lap, the way she had learned to drive in her mother's own lap. She had the hang of it soon.

She wasn't drunk and she wasn't high. She was willing. "Let's go back," she said. "See if he's still sitting in the mud."

They wheeled around and headed back. The ditch was empty, though, and the mud tracks headed south. "Home to his daddy," Ginnie said. She got out and ran into the woods and found the beer she'd stashed.

Buck had the 4×4 turned around, nosing back toward the north.

"Well all right," she yelled. "Party time!"

"Satisfactory," he said, finishing off one of the ponies and tossing the bottle. It shattered into smoke on the road behind them.

Buck knew where to find others in a party mood, so they never made it to the tournament. They hung out at the video arcade for an hour or two—nobody was watching the clock. Then, in a convoy, they headed down to the thousand acres where the off-road vehicles churned up the mud on weekends.

They had picked up Johnny Bates and Chris Olds. "Love makes room," Ginnie said. She sat across their laps, her back against the door, washing down Chris's pills with Johnny's vodka. Buck was tailgating the Trans-Am ahead of them. "Kiss it! Kiss it!" Ginnie urged, bracing herself for the collision, but the 4×4 was too tall; Buck ran right over the car's trunk, and they had to stop—the whole convoy—and discuss it. The other driver was so stoned he couldn't even walk straight; when Buck pushed him down, he crawled on the road, trying to get up. "Like a spider," Ginnie said. "Step on him." She stomped, just at his fingertips. He rolled away and staggered to his feet, as she climbed into the 4×4 and revved the engine. "Where's your balls?" she called, backing the truck off the Trans-Am. Buck and Johnny and Chris jumped on board, laughing. The boy in the road didn't step out of the way. The 4×4 grazed him, and he grabbed onto the hood, trying to haul himself up. "Bullfighting!" Ginnie said, jerking the wheel sharply left, then right. He slid away into the dark. Everybody was laughing. Ginnie drove on, leading the pack now.

They prowled on down to the landing, where there was moon enough to party. Ginnie felt the light hit her arms like blows as the shadows of the pines laddered over her flesh. "I *feel* it!" she said, jumping from the truck, spinning, savoring. She fell in the sand and sat, looking around. She didn't even get up when the headlights of another truck swung across the sky and headed toward her. The other truck's radio was on the same station as theirs. Full blast.

They danced, then, Ginnie and the others. She didn't know quite who they were, but she liked them. She wanted to take off her clothes and dance on the dock in the moonlight. She wanted to swim all the way to Thompson Beach. She was the only one. It was still winter.

When the fight started, Ginnie pitched right in. She didn't like the other girl and began tearing at her face and clothes and calling her "slut" and "whore" and kicking sand and cursing. She found a pine limb and wielded it like a bat, trying for serious damage. The girl was screaming and crying loud enough to turn the lights on in the windows across the cove. They could hear sirens far off, nearing.

Buck and Chris got Ginnie into the truck and got out of there— not waiting for Johnny, who had disappeared as soon as the fight started. They pulled into a side road, lights off, till the deputies had passed.

Ginnie didn't want to go home. She thought of Gid's houseboat. It wasn't far.

"Let's stop here," she dared.

She knew Gid wasn't there except on weekends. He boarded up at Dixon now, since it was too far to commute weekdays on his bicycle. Too cold.

"It's abandoned," Ginnie said, crawling up inside. She lit the lamp and turned to give a hand to Chris.

He climbed up, looked around, and whistled. "I know this guy," Chris said. "He—"

"He's dandruff on the shoulders of life," Ginnie said.

Buck was wild enough for anything, and Ginnie was ready, but Chris edged toward the door, saying, "I need air."

"Did you say prayer?" Ginnie asked, her scorn so sudden and hot it made her want to kill him. He was the one she wanted right then, Chris. She'd make him.

She stood blocking the open door, all the night behind her, dark, nothing to break her fall. "Say the word," she teased. She didn't lay a hand on him, just waited for him to try to get past. She could change anybody's mind.

"What're you doing these days, Ginnie?" Chris asked, as if they were meeting on the street at noon. "Found one that fits yet?"

She looked at their faces as they laughed at her, Buck laughing louder.

"Y'all just get out!" she screamed, kicking at them wildly. "Out!" She was still raging and cursing as the 4×4 roared away.

After they had gone, she trashed Gid's houseboat, broke and tore and spattered and fouled it from bow to stern. Then she made a fire in the stove, stoking it till the flue glowed red, and left the place to find its own fate. It would look like an accident. She knew Chris and Buck wouldn't tell. If they did, what could they prove?

She cut across the sedgefields toward home. It was miles, and she had blisters the size of silver dollars on both heels by the time she got there, sober and vomit-hollowed, her hair tangled with burrs. She chewed some Dentyne and thought fast. There was a light on. She began crying.

Her mother met her at the door and cried too.

Ginnie told her, "I've walked miles. I made them let me out. They weren't Christians, Mama. They weren't good boys at all."

"Did they hurt you, Baby?"

384

"I'd die first," she said.

Doc didn't do anything except turn out the yard light, lock the door, and listen. He knew Ginnie well enough not to swear out warrants. He knew where the birth-control pills missing from his inventory were going. He never challenged her, just went on pretending she was who she thought they thought she was. "We all ought to be in bed," he said.

"Let her talk it out," Ginnie's mother said. "Talk it out, Honey." She drew Ginnie to her, shoulder to shoulder, so alike that time was the only thing that made the difference: Before and After, Doc thought, clicking the three-way bulb to low.

Ginnie said, "I just want to put it behind me, you know? Like, it's over." She bent to pry off her boots and look at her heels.

"Vitamin E," Mrs. Daniels said, going to the cabinet to get a capsule. She believed in *Prevention*; she kept a stack of the magazines by her bed, and could rattle off the names of vitamins and minerals and their uses the way some people name saints and their miracles. She might question Doc about some vitamin controversy, but she believed in miller's bran, aloe vera, and D-alpha tocopherol with the same blind faith she put in Ginnie: a wholesomeness never to be doubted, and possibilities worth any expense. If Doc was a realist, and hated talking things out, just getting on with it instead, his wife had a softer eye and heart. Maybe she didn't really know her daughter. She didn't worry; she trusted. Not to trust seemed dishonorable; when doubt shaded in, and chilled her, she turned her mind's channel to another station, just like she did the TV. She kept herself busy, living in a world of her own making, putting her own crazy captions to the pictures in the news, watching TV for hours with the sound off. When they were driving along and passed a road-killed animal, she said, "Probably just playing possum," even if you could *smell* it. Doc always said, "Goddam!" and laughed. "What'll it take to convince you?" he wondered.

Mrs. Daniels came back with the vitamin E. "There won't be any scars, if you'll just start this early." She knelt and helped smear the oil on Ginnie's wounded heels.

Ginnie laid her hand on her mother's head. "Mama," she said. "Did you save the receipt for these boots? They're going back."

"Tomorrow," her mother said. "First thing."

"It's already tomorrow," Doc said.

Mrs. Daniels stood and wiped her hands. "It may already be tomorrow, but it's never too late." She headed for the kitchen to cook them something special for breakfast.

"I bet you didn't sleep a wink all night," Ginnie said to Doc. She tossed her ruined boots over by the hearth and sat down in Doc's recliner, shoving it all the way back. She looked up at him. "Your bags have bags." Doc had been about to yawn, but he forced it into a smile.

"Slept great. Your mother got me up when you came home."

Doc never slept great. Sometimes he woke in the night and felt like breaking things, or shooting up the whole world, every lying thieving cheat in it. He'd been burglarized again, and often, and not always petty thefts: they knew what they wanted, what was worth anything. He had changed his whole anti-theft system after the Bland boy broke in and stole the drugs that killed him. He'd installed alarm systems connected to the police direct by radio signal, and new deadbolts and wires on the windows. From time to time he bought another gun and registered it. What more could a man do? All that trouble and expense at work, and at home, Ginnie and her mother would be unruffled, calmly paging through their catalogs for custom curtains, brass bedsteads, Fair Isle sweaters, Hummel figurines . . .

"What do you say, Daddy?" Ginnie sounded serious. Doc hadn't been listening. He tried to catch up, then decided against asking her flat out. She had something to say? He waited to hear more.

"I'm going to graduate next year," she vowed. "I'm going to settle down and study and make me some A's. What do you say?"

Her mother, in the kitchen making banana waffles from scratch, always a big deal out of something, deliverance this time, hummed "Come Thou Fount of Many Blessings," beating eggs in time.

"This is the turning point of my *life*," Ginnie told him. "You hear me?"

"I'm listening," Doc said. The anniversary clock chimed six-thirty.

"What do you say to Beta Club and some A's and all that Glee Club stuff and a diploma and graduation with my class and all that?"

Doc bent and picked a section of briar from the toe of Ginnie's boot.

"How much will it cost me?"

Ginnie didn't even open her eyes.

"Have you seen the new T-roof-Z's?"

He flung the bit of briar in the fireplace. "No way," he said. He laughed. "Not for straight *A*'s and perfect attendance." He took off his glasses and polished them, settling them back on his face again, giving the room a clear hard look. "You should have started sooner."

"I'm starting now," she said.

"No sale," he told her. "Besides, I thought you were dropping out. Going to cosmetology school or something."

"You say that like it was worm-farming, Daddy," Ginnie said. "People change."

In the first light, she looked like herself at ten, scolded too hard, afraid to raise her face to their anger and disappointment. He didn't really believe in evil, born in, unchangeable. People could change. We all start off even, her mother was always saying. Some of us learn a little slower and whose fault is that?

The recliner snapped upright and Ginnie sat staring at her hands.

"Shit!" She held her hand out for him to see. "I broke my fingernail getting off those damn boots."

Doc didn't move and Ginnie glanced up. Then he reached over to the cat's scratching post and handed it to her. "Here," he said.

She couldn't believe her eyes and ears. She looked at him as at a stranger. He *was!*

"Daddy?"

She was gifted, he knew, by all her test scores. Genius. *Under-challenged,* they had told him and his wife. "Keep her busy," they had said. "Keep her motivated." He resumed himself. "T-roof-Z?" he said, thinking it over.

To help him calculate, she asked, "Can you stroke it? Are you good for it?"

"I'll tell you the truth," he said. "I don't think *you* are."

Ginnie reclined her chair again, smiling. "I guess it's up to me."

She was asleep at breakfast time. Her mother called, then came to see. She laid an afghan over Ginnie and tiptoed back to the kitchen to serve Doc. "Sleeping like a baby, like an angel." She moved around to Doc's chair and poured his coffee. She set the pot down and hugged him, rocked him to her, and let him go.

"She's going to straighten up," she told Doc. "This time she's on her way. I pray it for her all the time: something good for Ginnie."

Doc said, "It's her deal, and she knows it."

387

"I'm happy, *happy!* Thank you, Doc. Thank you, God," she said, and then sat down and cried. She was still crying, and Ginnie was still asleep, when Doc left for work.

Ginnie didn't see Gid much any more. After his boat burned—it went down as accidental—he took a permanent place at Dixon and didn't even come back on weekends. He was saving his money, had an account in the bank—one of the mill workers helped him open it—and he was careful of his pay. He planned to marry Ginnie. She had plans of her own.

She quit dating. Quit partying. Dropped out of sight except for school and church. In the afternoons, twice a week, Jordan Kilgore came to the house to tutor her in geometry. This was Doc's idea. Jordan was fifteen, sprouting his first manly bristles and nervous around Ginnie, who was a little older and beyond wild hope. Jordan lived with his grandfather, who owned the yacht club across the lake, but he didn't go to school at Deerfield. He went to Atlanta to special classes for the gifted. He was already taking college courses twice a week. Those were the afternoons he had free to help Ginnie. He was a virgin, Ginnie could tell—as much fun as a newborn kitten. She played little games all through the lessons; he never even suspected. She'd let the top button on her blouse gape, and then button it quick, shy. She wore scent on her hands so when he went home, her flavor was on his books. She didn't have anything in mind, just to drive him crazy a little and pass off time. On lesson days she wore her daintiest clothes, no leather, no makeup, no angora, no jeans. She wore dresses or full skirts and eyelet and never said *damn*. When his cat died, she cried and came down to the lesson with her eyes red and swollen.

On her birthday in March he gave her a silver cross set with aquamarines, for studying so hard.

She kissed it and said, "I'll wear it always, when I marry, forever, I'll never take it off!" She let him clasp it, his hands clumsy and slow, tangling in the stray curls she had left out as she pinned her hair up. When it was fastened, she had him kiss it too, and she dropped it down her blouse, out of sight, but known.

"You look like a valentine," he said.

She looked down at the tucks and laces and white white shirt-front and bit her lip. "Thank you," she said.

"Ginnie," he said, hurting. They were alone.

388

She shook her head. "Let's pray," she said. But it was too much, too strong. They embraced, and she let him—soft lips! untrained shy questing shy lips—kiss her. He quivered like a horse wearing its first saddle. She was almost bored, but not quite. She drew away, and stood, tucking her blouse in and smoothing her hair. "We mustn't."

"I have wicked thoughts," she said, as he looked away. "But we have just an hour, and it's for geometry."

"You—you're making progress," he agreed. He turned to the lesson.

"I think about you all the time!" she said, just as his mind had gotten fixed on the matter at hand. Ginnie was having trouble proving triangles. "I dream about you," she said. She checked the clock. Her mother was at a luncheon.

He drew a triangle. "I dream about you too," he said.

He could smell her shampoo. He leaned into the fragrance, inhaling, all the time drawing another triangle inside the first triangle, and numbering from one to ten.

"Tell me," she whispered, stopping his pencil with her fingertip. He leaned away.

"What do you dream?" She got up and went to the window and looked out. "What did you do with those magazines?"

"They—I burned them."

"Daddy has more. New ones. He keeps them under the counter. You have to ask, people always ask."

"They're trash," he said.

"Slime," Ginnie agreed. "Filth. Don't think about them!" She watched as his color burned higher. "Do you dream about them? Things like that?"

Her mother's car was turning in the driveway. Ginnie slapped her book closed. "We ought to burn them all! It could be—" she drew a breath, "—*noble,* like Jesus running the moneylenders out of the temple." He gathered his papers and books. They hadn't done a thing for the hour except those two triangles, one inside the other.

"Don't tell!" she cautioned him, and ran outside to meet her mother. He passed them in the drive as they were picking daffodils. He was on his ten-speed, bent forward, his bookbag strapped across his back, his legs strong on the hill.

Ginnie's mother worried what he'd do when it rained. Ginnie

389

said, "With an uncle who's a bishop and a granddaddy who's got a wad on his hip the size of Stone Mountain, he could have a Porsche if he wanted it, if he knew how to ask."

Doc was paying Jordan five dollars an hour for the tutoring. Sometimes Ginnie borrowed a little of it, just a few dollars now and then. "I'll pay you back," she always promised. "Somehow."

"He's a darling boy," Ginnie's mother agreed.

All through Lent she tormented him like that, till she left the note in his book. Unsigned. Who could prove a thing if it went wrong? "Tonight, back door at Doc's, midnight, god's sake don't leave your bike in plain view." She typed it at school, in a spare moment.

He'll never show, Ginnie thought. And if he did, she'd think of something.

She left her car at the roller rink, and walked back to town. Two, three blocks, no street lights till the post office, where the sidewalk began.

Anne Summerday, charge nurse for the 11 to 7 shift at Tri-County Hospital, saw Ginnie walking along the road toward town, all in white. Anne pulled alongside the girl, thinking she might be a nurse in some kind of trouble. When she saw it was Ginnie, dressed like a bride in a dream, vacant-eyed, ghostly, she knew better. "Anything the matter?"

Ginnie said, "One of your headlights is out."

"I meant with you—need any help? Anything?"

"Nothing radical," Ginnie said. "Just airing it out, y'know?" She played with the ribbons at her waist. "Massive weather, hunh?" She blew a gum bubble, perfected it, inhaled it whole, and popped it with a blink of her eyes. Then started over.

"Take care of yourself," Anne told her.

"Not going far," Ginnie assured her.

"It's dark as an egg's inside," Ginnie complained as Jordan came in. She had opened the door at his third tap. She groped over to the partition between the storeroom and the pharmacy, pulling open the golden plastic curtains that served for a door. An eerie light, green as the aurora, streamed through the gap she made.

"I can't stay," Jordan said.

Her eyes glinted alien in the strange light that pulsed from a cosmetic display in the front of the store.

390

"Why did you come?"

"I shouldn't be here."

She shoved him away toward the door. "That one-eyed grand-daddy of yours, I bet, calling frog and you hop." She covered her eye with her hand and tilted her head at him, saying in a mocking mannish voice, "Jordan, boy, you better love Jesus, my Jesus yes!" She had smoked a roach on the way. He couldn't ever catch up with her.

"I do!"

"*I do!*" she mocked. "Is this a wedding?"

She slipped into the store and brought back a hairbrush and handed it to him. "Do me," she said.

He began stroking her hair, too lightly, tangling as he went, then smoother, firmer, from her crown to her waist.

"How I like it," she said, leaning into the stroke.

"You smell like clover," he noticed.

She spit out her bubblegum and stuck it under a shelf. "Sweet Honesty," she said. "Avon. I don't sell it any more. Daddy says it's competition for the store." She took the hairbrush from him and threw it over a pile of cartons in the corner. It scuttered out of sight.

"Everything in this store is *mine*," she told Jordan. "I can help myself. What would you like to have?"

"I have to go now," he said.

"You ought to teach your folks a lesson," she told him.

"How?" Like a man in a dream, he kept on walking toward the cavemouth, his heart pounding.

"Make them afraid. Afraid you'll die. Afraid you'll run away." She turned to face him and got close. "You scared of me?"

"No."

She laughed. "Miles to go to mean it," she said. She drew the cross he had given her up from her blouse, saying, "Feel, it's as warm as I am."

He touched it but didn't touch her.

"I could wash your feet and dry them with my hair," she suggested. "I think as highly of you as I do of Jesus." She said, "Take off your shoes."

She didn't figure he would. There was a slight film of sweat on his face.

"Do you really believe God made me out of your ribs?" She put

391

her hand out and touched his chest. "I just want to see the scar," she said.

He thought he heard something.

"What could you hear?" she said. "Your heart?" She leaned her ear and listened.

Ginnie heard something else.

"Did you lock the door?" she wondered.

"I—"

"*Did* you?"

"I—"

A flashlight beam prowled across the ceiling over their heads. They ducked to the floor. "Night watchman!" he whispered.

"No," Ginnie said. "There isn't one. It's somebody breaking in!" She almost laughed aloud. Luck! She couldn't think fast enough. She was excited and almost danced. Which way? Which way? "In here," she decided, and they crept around behind the curtains into the store and waited. Ginnie leaned around to look.

"Get behind me," Jordan said.

"You! In there! I heard you!"

"Daddy!" Ginnie breathed. "Oh shit!"

Doc kicked the door open and yelled, "Freeze!" just as Jordan stepped forward, his hands out in the dark. "It's all right, sir," he began to say.

Doc fired, both barrels.

The impact knocked Jordan backward, the ribs Ginnie had touched a moment ago gone like the plastic curtain in their faces, and then Jordan fell. There was nothing between Ginnie and Doc but that spilled blood.

Ginnie didn't scream but once, then she bent there, trying to pull her skirt out of Jordan's grip. Doc stood looking down.

"*Goddam mess,*" he said.

Jordan tried to say something, but he couldn't remember what. He rested. When the sirens neared, he asked, "Who's hurt?"

When Ginnie said, "This didn't happen," he asked, "Who is it?" already forgetting, with each emptying pulse, time running backward as it ran down.

"You're hurt," Doc told him, facing facts. The emergency unit arrived.

"I'm not afraid," Jordan said. The technician stripped back Jordan's sleeve to start plasma.

"Take it easy, son," the attendant said. "Stay with us." They lifted him up and even then Jordan was awake, gripping Ginnie's skirt. She rode beside him in the ambulance.

"Notify trauma," they radioed ahead.

Ginnie said, "I need to wash my hands," and someone gave her a towelette. There were bits of the curtain in her hair. They kept drifting randomly down.

Doc said, mile after mile after mile, "It was self-defense."

In emergency, they all waited together. Jordan's grandfather was there, his sports coat pulled on over his pajamas, no socks on his pale feet, the elastic to his eye patch lost in a rumple of white hair under the yachting cap. Doc sat in the corner on a straight chair. Ginnie stood at the window, looking down at traffic. She had washed her face and arms. All of the blood was Jordan's. She hadn't got even one pellet, she was that lucky.

Jordan's grandfather said, "Seven units of blood already."

A policeman was standing in the doorway, filling out reports. Doc answered most of the questions. Ginnie moved back and forth in front of the windows, like a fox in a cage. Finally she sat. She drew another chair over and propped her feet on it.

From the hall, footsteps brought them all to attention. A woman looked in at them, waiting. Her left hand was cupped to catch her cigarette ash, her eyes witness to some unspeakable anxiety. She looked at them all, one by one, then studied the policeman's insignia, the flag on his sleeve, his badge. She shook her head, lost in her own anguish, tears brimming. "Mine's not a police matter," she said, going on by, down the hall, out of sight.

Jordan's grandfather said, "Sonofabitch!" and pounded his fist into his thigh. He passed his hands over his face, and blinked at Doc.

"I thought he was reaching for a gun," Doc said.

At the door, the policeman cleared his throat.

They looked at him, for news. He said, "I was just clearing my throat."

"They ought to have a TV in here," Ginnie said.

"I could see them moving around—the silhouettes, you know?" Doc spoke to the Deputy. "I did what I thought right at the time."

Jordan's grandfather said, "He was born right here in this hospital."

393

Doc said, "She was too."

Jordan's grandfather said, "The night you made her, you should have shot it in the sink instead."

Ginnie laughed.

Doc didn't. He jumped up so fast his chair turned over. The two men kept hitting each other, and sobbing, till the orderlies and the officer pulled them apart. The old man sat down, still crisp with anger, and pressed his handkerchief to his lip. A nurse brought Doc a plastic glove filled with ice for his eye.

Doc blew his nose.

Ginnie shook out her dress and sat again. "This was a Laura Ashley," she explained. She looked down inside the blouse, then stood and shook her skirt. The cross didn't fall out. It was gone. "And I lost my necklace too," she said. She started looking for it on the floor.

"Sit down and shut up," Doc told her.

It was another hour before the surgeon came in. He was as bloody as Ginnie. He paused a moment, then said, "Kilgore?" and the old man stood, slowly, but tall.

"Alive," the doctor said. "I came to let you know we've had a look around. It's bad, couldn't have been much worse. Spine's not hurt, but the bleeding has to be stopped. We do that, he's got a chance. I don't kid you, abdominal's second only to head for tricky. We're layered, not toys. And he's a mess. We have to stop the leaks first. Then we might have a chance," he said. "A chance."

"I'll be here," his grandfather said, in a different voice, and not as tall.

"It'll be hours. There's a snack bar down the hall; we'll keep you posted." At the door he turned back and said, "Good luck."

"And to you the same," the old man said.

When the surgeon had gone, he told Doc, "I don't want you here, none of y'all. I don't want to see you." He looked at Ginnie, "I don't want to *smell* you."

Doc said to Ginnie, low as prayer, "Not a word."

They walked with the lawman to their car. Doc wasn't under arrest; charges pending. "But you'll both have to answer some more questions," the officer told them.

"I'm not going anywhere," Doc said.

Afterward, as they drove home, Ginnie said, "I guess this cooks it about the Datsun for graduation, doesn't it."

"Could you cry for that?" Doc wondered. "Could you?"

The bright moon stared down at itself in the river as they crossed. It was almost dawn.

"This'll put your mother back at Brawner's," Doc said. "If they sue, we're looking at Chapter 7 bankruptcy."

Ginnie clicked on the radio. Doc cut it off instantly. "For God's sake!"

Not that she was listening for news. There wouldn't be any, not for three days. Jordan lived three days. No lawsuits.

Gid didn't die until the next summer, and Ginnie didn't know anything about it at the time. Doc had double-mortgaged to send her away to finish high school at Tallulah, and then she spent the summer at a mountain camp, lifeguarding.

She heard about Gid casually, soon after returning home, and she didn't ask any questions. She went to the library and read about it on microfilm. He had been riding a lumber truck, atop the piled wood. He was leaning against the cab, not watching where he was going, just looking back at the road he had already traveled; they went under a low railroad bridge and he was killed instantly. It made her feel funny, reading about it like that. She hadn't thought of him in a long time.

Home again, she went to her room and got her majorette boots out of their box, dumping the newspaper stuffing on the bed. There wasn't much to sort through. She didn't even have to hide her pills any more.

She found the matchbox crammed in the left toe, filled to roundness with cotton. In the center of that cotton was the ring. It wasn't worth anything. All its pawnable worth had fallen from it the day it arrived in the mail. She had carried the little package upstairs to open it and had dropped it on the bathroom floor. The laid-on stone, turquoise paste, had crumbled off. The silver was so thin the brass showed through. It had a coppery smell, like blood. Its flashiness was plated on, and inside, engraved within its tarnished perfect greening circle was "REMEBER GIDEON." He'd paid for that. It still made her laugh. She said it: "Remeber." Had the engraver made the mistake, or Gid? When she stepped on the broken blue stone from the ring, it had powdered to dust. She had cleaned it off the floor with a tissue and flushed it away.

She had never worn the ring and had never seen Gid again. A

week later she had gone away to school. Now she tried it on, and it fit so tight it frightened her. She had to work it off with soapy water.

She put it back in the box and headed downstairs, with the box in her pocket. As she went by her mother's door, her mother called, over the top of her latest Harlequin, "Seat belt!"

The Datsun was backed into the garage. She opened the door and drove out, leaving rubber on the cement. That was for her mother, listening upstairs. She tapped the horn at the end of the drive. That was for the dogs. They jumped in and rode with her, nosing out the T-roof, taking the air.

It was a fine day, a late autumn day. The lake wasn't busy—a few sails on the far channel, a bassboat on the west cove, and no skiers. She let the dogs out to run; they drank from the lake and chased each other clumsily along the muddy shore, turning over rocks, sniffing at debris. Ginnie stood at the car a moment watching them. She left the door open, sliding the keys on their jailer's bracelet onto her wrist, walking easily down to the water and along the littered and slippery beach. The "Private" sign nailed to the dock stuck up just enough so she could clean the mud off her boots on its sharp edge. The wood was so sun-warm she could feel it through her soles. A kingfisher buzzed her, and flew past, settling on the reef-warning, looking this way, then that, at the green reflection of the pines in the water. Out in the channel the lake was blue as the sky. The dock dipped under Ginnie's feet, slow, drowsy, on the lapping rim of the lake.

She shaded her eyes and looked as far as she could, claiming it all. She felt as free and right as she did in her own home. The untrammeling world was widening in ripples around her, and she was the stone at the center that sets things moving. She took out the box from her pocket and shook the ring out of its cotton, like a seed. The cotton blew away, and the lake took it, dragged it down slowly. She held the ring on her palm in the sun till it burned hot, hotter than her blood. Then she tossed it as far as she could, out past the low-water reef. It skipped once—plook!—and vanished. The dogs chewed up the matchbox, playing on past her, barking off on trails into the woods. Ginnie stood there a moment in that impersonal vantage and solitude, breathing deep.

She reached high over her head and clawed the sky, then folded up, right at the edge of the dock which tipped a little with her hundred pounds. Her hands smelled brassy. She dipped them in the lake, troubling the clear water, then drew them up, splashing her cheeks with the cool. Refreshed, she looked up, as though something on the horizon had caught her attention. She stood flinging the last drops from her hands, drying them on her skirt. She walked back to the car, whistling the dogs in, and churned the car slowly uphill through that sand onto the lane between the windbreak pines, heading toward the main road in no particular hurry. It wasn't life or death.

nominated by The Georgia Review *and Ellen Wilbur*

THE NOISE THE HAIRLESS MAKE

by STEPHEN DOBYNS

from SONORA REVIEW

How difficult to be an angel.
In order to forgive, they have no memory.
In order to be good, they're always forgetting.
How else could heaven be run? Still,
it needs to be full of teachers and textbooks
imported from God's own basement, since only
in hell is memory exact. In one classroom,
a dozen angels scratch their heads as their teacher
displays the cross-section of a human skull,
saying, Here is the sadness, here
the anger, here's where laughter is kept.
And the angels think, How strange, and take notes
and would temper their forgiveness if it weren't
all forgotten by the afternoon. Sometimes
a bunch fly down to earth with their teacher
who wants them to study a living example and
this evening they find a man lying in a doorway
in an alley in Detroit. They stand around
chewing their pencils as their teacher says,
This is the stick he uses to beat his wife,
this is the bottle he drinks from when he
wants to forget, this is the Detroit Tigers

T-shirt he wears whenever he's sad, this is
the electric kazoo he plays in order to weep.
And the angels think, How peculiar, and wonder
whether to temper their forgiveness or just
let it ride which really doesn't matter since
they forget the question as soon as it's asked.
But their muttering wakes the man in the doorway
who looks to see a flock of doves departing
over the trash cans. And because he dreamed
of betrayal and pursuit, of defeat in battle,
the death of friends, he heaves a bottle at them
and it breaks under a streetlight so the light
reflects on its hundred broken pieces with such
a multi-colored twinkling that the man laughs.
From their place on a brick wall, the angels
watch and one asks, What good arc thcy? Thcn
others take up the cry, What good are they,
what good are they? But as fast as they articulate
the question it's forgotten and their teacher,
a minor demon, returns with them to heaven.
But the man, still chuckling, sits in his doorway,
and the rats in their dumpsters hear this sound
like stones rattling or metal banging together,
and they see how the man is by himself without
food or companions, without work or family
or a real bed for his body. They creep back
to their holes and practice little laughs
that sound like coughing or a dog throwing up
as once more they uselessly try to imitate
the noise the hairless make when defeated.

nominated by Stuart Dybek

WHAT ARE THE DAYS

by COLETTE INEZ

from POETRY NORTHWEST

They are pilferers
stealing our resolve,
Thomas broods aloud.

Or stones
to use for good or ill,
says James sitting
on a rock with Peter.

Soon, the dreamer
comes along saying:
all days are brothers.

Aren't days fish
swimming to shore?
asks Simon, the fisherman
mending his nets.

They are coins to hoard
or to spend, Judas frowns,
and looks at his palms.

Twaddle, says Martha
running to fix supper.
You talkers, get me a hen,
get me an egg.

I bet you think
all the days are women
pouring wine and honey.

They are what they are,
says the hammerer of nails,
securing thieves and the dreamer
to the cross, nothing more.

nominated by Peter Cooley

THE THEME OF THE THREE CASKETS

by WILLIAM MATTHEWS

from THE IOWA REVIEW

> *Men and women are two locked caskets,*
> *each of which contains the key to the other.*
> *Isak Dinesen*

One gold, one silver, one lead: who thinks
this test easy has already flunked.

Or, you have three daughters, two humming-
birds and the youngest, Cordelia, a grackle.

And here's Cinderella, the ash-princess.
Three guesses, three wishes, three strikes and

you're out. You've been practicing for this
for years, jumping rope, counting out,

learning to waltz, games and puzzles,
tests and chores. And work, in which strain

and ease fill and drain the body like air
having its way with the lungs. And now?

Your palms are mossy with sweat.
The more you think the less you understand.

It's your only life you must choose, daily.

*   *   *

Freud, father of psychoanalysis,
the study of self-deception and survival,
saw the wish-fulfillment in this theme:

that we can choose death and make what we can't
refuse a trophy to self-knowledge, grey,
malleable, dense with low tensile strength

and poisonous in every compound.
And that a vote for death elects love.
If death is the mother of love (Freud wrote

more, and more lovingly, on mothers
than on fathers), she is also the mother
of envy and gossip and spite, and she

loves her children equally. It isn't mom
who folds us finally in her arms,
and it is we who are elected.

*   *   *

Is love the reward, or the test itself?

That kind of thought speeds our swift lives
along. The August air is stale in

the slack leaves, and a new moon thin
as a fingernail paring tilts orange

and low in the rusty sky, and the city
is thick with trysts and spats

and the banked blue fires of TV sets,
and the anger and depression that bead

on the body like an acid dew when it's hot.
Tonight it seems that love is what's

missing, the better half. But think
with your body: not to be dead is to be

sexual, vivid, tender and harsh, a riot
of mixed feelings, and able to choose.

nominated by Susan Mitchell

MARIA MITCHELL IN THE GREAT BEYOND WITH MARILYN MONROE

by CAROLE OLES

from NIGHT WATCHES: INVENTIONS ON THE LIFE OF MARIA MITCHELL (Alice James Books) and PRAIRIE SCHOONER

What would my life have been with your face?
Once someone said I had good eyes. Mostly
on canvas, in photographs, I half turned away.
The camera, they say, was your most faithful lover.

> No one ever told me I was pretty when I was
> a little girl. All little girls should be told
> they're pretty, even if they aren't.

Little girls should hear the truth.
No one could make a beauty of me. I knew.
And Quaker Discipline decreed: "Be not conformed
to this world, but be ye transformed
by the renewing of your mind."
A child in my closet-size study, I hung a sign—
Maria is busy. Do not knock.

> When I was 8 my foster family made me wash
> every dish for 5 cents a month.

Dear child, how could fame repair such loss,
your mother's mind broken like her parents'
and brother's before. Though a woman, I
faltered when Mother's mind cast off from me.

    The same year, at the boardinghouse the nice
    man showed me a game, and when

I saw! They disbelieved, and you began to stammer.
What man on earth isn't selfish?
My sister died thankful never to have been naked
before her husband. I never married.
Come walk with me. Smell the ocean
and pick daphne, grapes, heart's ease.

    Do you know how I got here? Three days before
    at a party I wrote in the guest book
    under Residence, *Nowhere*.

And now you live everywhere at once
whose ambition was to be men's earthly star.
Here are stars you can trust:
Sirius, Canopus, Arcturus, Vega, Capella,
Betelgeuse, Altair, Aldebaran.
Say these, Norma Jeane.
We are women learning together.

nominated by Ted Wilentz and Joyce Carol Oates

OUTSTANDING WRITERS

(The editors also wish to mention the following important works published by small presses last year. Listing is alphabetical by author's last name.)

NONFICTION

Sourdoughs, Filibusters, and a One-Eared Mule — Will Baker (Georgia Review)

Seven Prose Pieces — Stephen Berg (TriQuarterly)

A North American Memoir: Revenge — Clark Blaise (North American Review)

Looking Behind Crane — David Bradley (Southern Review)

Edward Thomas and Modernism — David Bromwich (Raritan Review)

Elizabeth Bishop's Dream Houses — David Bromwich (Raritan Review)

The Mont Blanc Pen — Frederick Busch (Seattle Review)

The Intentional Alligator — Hayden Carruth (Georgia Review)

The Education of Daisy's Father — Alexander Cockburn (Grand Street)

Telephone — Nicholas Delbanco (Salmagundi)

The Passing of Jazz's Old Guard — Gerald Early (Kenyon Review)

Tradition and The Practice of Poetry — T.S. Eliot (Southern Review)

Academic Criticism and Contemporary Literature — Reginald Gibbons (TriQuarterly)

Fear and the Absent "Other" — Louise Glück (Southern Review)

The Essential Gesture: Writers and Responsibility — Nadine Gordimer (Granta)

Place and Displacement: Reflections on Some Recent Poetry from Northern Ireland — Seamus Heaney (Agni Review)

FICTION

Etiquette — Will Baker (Black Warrior Review)
The Fish — Russell Banks (Agni Review)
The Eleventh Floor — Charles Baxter (Writer's Forum)
Big Grey — Geoffrey Becker (West Branch)
Times Square — Joe David Bellamy (Mid-American Review)
Play Me Something — John Berger (Threepenny Review)
The Ex-Class Agent — Carol Bly (TriQuarterly)
Kitchen Man — Arthur Boatin (Western Humanities Review)
Dancing In The Movies — Robert Boswell (TriQuarterly)
A Good Deal — Rosellen Brown (Massachusetts Review)
Scoring — Carole Bubash (TriQuarterly)
Embalming Mom — Janet Burroway (Apalachee Quarterly)
Dog Song — Frederick Busch (Georgia Review)
Greetings From A Far-Flung Place — Frederick Busch (Crazy-
    horse)
Semi-Blue — Francois Camoin (Crosscurrents)
Tilson Ezekiel Alias Ti-Zek — Jan Carew (NER/BLQ)
At the Hop — Ron Carlson (Missouri Review)
The Governor's Ball — Ron Carlson (TriQuarterly)
Twelve Tales From the Life of Jirac Disslerov — George Chambers
    (Northwest Review)
Stories — Maxine Chernoff (Black Ice)
The Tennessee Waltz — Alan Cheuse (Quarterly West)
Two Chapters from *The Chocolate Soldier* — Cyrus Colter (Tri-
    Quarterly)
That F'kucken Karl Marx — Robert Coover (Fiction International)
Monologue of the Movie Mogul — Michael Covino (Paris Review)
The China Doll — Ann Deagon (Chattahoochee Review)
Under the Wheat — Rick Demarinis (*Graywolf Annual*, Graywolf
    Press)
Eternity — Thomas M. Disch (Shenandoah)
The Postcard — Stephen Dixon (2 plus 2)
Grace — J.D. Dolan (Mississippi Review)
The Zulus — Rita Dove (*Fifth Sunday. Stories*, Callaloo)
The Performance — Sergei Dovlatov (Partisan Review)
What They See — Eileen Drew (Nimrod)
Fire Ants — Gerald Duff (Ploughshares)
Eskimos — B.H. Friedman (Fiction International)
Tornadoes — Gary Gildner (Grand Street)
The Dragon's Tale — Laurence Gonzales (NER/BLQ)
Open Possibilities — Roberta Gordon (Confrontation)

The Bequest — Joyce Carol Oates (NER/BLWQ)
Getting To Know The Weather — Pamela Painter (Sewanee Review)
Confessions of a Bad Girl — Bette Pesetsky (Ontario Review)
The Value of Diamonds — Eileen Pollack (Agni Review)
Typical Day in A Desirable Woman's Life — Leon Rooke (Grand Street)
Kiss The Father — Sarah Rossiter (Massachusetts Review)
Shadow Bands — Jeanne Schinto (Ontario Review)
Passover — Sheila M. Schwartz (MSS)
Down Under — Steven Schwartz (Virginia Quarterly Review)
Milk River — Ellie Scott (Writer's Forum)
You Leave Them — Mona Simpson (Paris Review)
Rough-and-Tumble Mercies — Sharon Sheehe Stark (Agni Review)
Desert — Nancy Stouffer (Fiction Network)
Flights — Linda Svendsen (Western Humanities Review)
Cubicles — Tricia Tunstall (Fiction Network)
The Yellow Banana — Patricia Volk (*The Yellow Banana*, Word Beat Press)
The Mummies of Guanajuato — Gloria Weaver (Story Quarterly)
The Interpreter — Gordon Weaver (TriQuarterly)
A Feather in The Breath of God — Paul West (Conjunctions)
The Order of Virility — Curtis White (Epoch)
Homefronts — Gayle Whittier (Story Quarterly)
President's Commission on Holiday Verse Directive #81-A-406 — David Wilk (Open Places)
Dirt Angel — Jeanne Wilmot (North American Review)
Payment in Kind — Robley Wilson Jr. (Sewanee Review)
Coming Attractions — Tobias Wolff (Antaeus)
The People I Know — Nancy Zafris (Black Warrior Review)
Birds — Zirana Zatelli (Translation)

POETRY

Rehearsal — Jennifer Atkinson (Sonora Review)
Rest Stop — David Baker (Cimarron Review)
The Oriental Rug — Peter Balakian (Poetry)
Song For A Little Bit of Breath — Marvin Bell (Breadloaf Anthology)

411

Minus Tide — Helena Minton (Alice James Books)
Nail Bag — Robert Morgan (Poetry)
Islands — Leslie Norris (Tar River Poetry)
Gardener — Naomi Shihab Nye (Open Theater)
Poem for Basho — Ed Ochester (North American Review)
Sunrise — Mary Oliver (Partisan Review)
The Guard: 1934 — Eric Pankey (Tendril)
Morning Star — Cesare Pavese (New Rivers Press)
Why Are We Clothed? — Molly Peacock (New Letters)
The Marriage — Ken Poyner (Calliope)
According to Ovid — Bin Ramke (Poetry)
Necessity — Keith Ratzlaff (Indiana Review)
Screens — Christopher Reid (Grand Street)
Lies — David Rivard (Crazyhorse)
The Days Inside the Night — Alane Rollings (Antioch Review)
Easy The Life of the Mouth — Nancy Schoenberger (Columbia)
Rumors of Suicide — Rebecca Seiferle (Indiana Review)
Chinese Architecture — Aleda Shirley (Georgia Review)
Hanging Out the Wash — Betsy Sholl (Agni Review)
The Game of Jack Straws — Jane Shore (Yale Review)
High Holy Days — Jane Shore (Rowan Tree Press)
Monkey Bridge — Charlie Smith (Black Warrior Review)
Thinking Like a Child — Gary Soto (Threepenny Review)
Song of Renunciation — Elizabeth Spires (Scarab Press)
An Essay on Liberation — David St. John (Partisan Review)
Victim — Joan Swift (Dragon Gate Press)
Miniatures — Lee Upton (Poetry)
Banking the Fire — Pamela Uschuk (Bloomsbury Review Reader)
Devoid of Ornament or Rhetoric of Any Kind — Robert Venturi
    (Poetry East)
The Labor of Buscando La Forma — Alma Luz Villanueva (Ameri-
    can Poetry Review)
The Trust — Ellen Bryant Voigt (Pequod)
Storm Figure — Derek Walcott (Antaeus)
Fencing — Ronald Wallace (Heatherstone Press)
The Garden of Eden — Ralph Wilson (Georgia Review)
A Journal of True Confessions — Charles Wright (Paris Review)
The Street — Franz Wright (Ploughshares)
Painting the House — Dean Young (Ohio Review)

413

OUTSTANDING SMALL PRESSES

(These presses made or received nominations for this edition of *The Pushcart Prize*. See the *International Directory of Little Magazines and Small Presses*, Dustbooks, Box 1056, Paradise, CA 95969, for subscription rates, manuscript requirements and a complete international listing of small presses.)

A

AWP Newsletter, c/o Old Dominion University, Norfolk, VA 23508
Abacus, See Potes & Poets Press
Abbey, 5360 Fallriver Row Court, Columbia, MD 21044
Abraxus, 215 Gregory St., Madison, WI 53711
ACTS, 324 Bartlett St., #9, San Francisco, CA 94110
Adastra Press, 101 Strong St., Easthampton, MA 01027
Adler Publishing Co., P.O. Box 9342, Rochester, NY 14604
Aegina Press, 4937 Humphrey Rd., Huntington, W.VA 25704
Afro-American Studies Program, Univ. of Mississippi Press, Oxford, MS 38677
The Agni Review, P.O. Box 660, Amherst, MA 01004
Ahsahta Press, English Dept., Boise State Univ., Boise, ID 83725
Alcatraz, 354 Hoover Rd., Soquel, CA 95073
Alice James Books, 138 Mt. Auburn St., Cambridge, MA 02138
Allegheny Review, Box 2074, Allegheny College, Meadville, PA 19136
Ally, 234 Street #6, Santa Cruz, CA 95060

Alternate Routes, Box 367, 1600 Campus Rd., Los Angeles, CA 90041

Alyson Publications, 40 Plympton St., Boston, MA 02118

Amelia Magazine, 329 "E" St., Bakersfield, CA 93304

American Book Review, Box 188, Cooper Sta., New York, NY 10003

American Poetry Press, P.O. Box 2013, Upper Darby, PA 19082

American Poetry Review, 1616 Walnut St., Rm. 405, Philadelphia, PA 19103

American Studies Press, Inc., 13511 Palmwood La., Tampa, FL 33624

The American Voice, Heyburn Bldg., Ste. 1215, Broadway at 4th, Louisville, KY 40202

Anemone, Box 656, Newburyport, MA 01950

Angeltread, Rt. 1, Box 137, Marion, KY 42064

Another Chicago Magazine, Box 11223, Chicago, IL 60611

Ansuda Publications, P.O. Box 158, Harris, IA 51345

Antaeus, 18 West 30th St., New York, NY 10001

Antietam Review, 33 W. Washington St., Hagerstown, MD 21740

The Antigonish Review, St. Francis Xavier Univ., Antigonish, Nova Scotia, B2G, 1CO, CANADA

The Antioch Review, P.O. Box 148, Yellow Springs, OH 45387

Apalachee Quarterly, P.O. Box 20106, Tallahassee, FL 32304

Applezaba Press, P.O. Box 4134, Long Beach, CA 90804

Artful Dodge, P.O. Box 1473, Bloomington, IN 47402

Ascent, 100 English Bldg., Univ. of Illinois, Urbana, IL 61801

Asphodel, 613 Howard Ave., Pitman, NJ 08071

Atticus Review, 720 Heber Ave., Calexico, CA 92231

AVATAR, St. Mary's College of Maryland, St. Mary's City, MD 20686

The Axe Factory Review, P.O. Box 11186, Philadelphia, PA 19136

B

Bamberger Books, P.O. Box 1126, Flint, MI 48501

Bannack Publishing Co., P.O. Box 50460, Billings, MT 59105

Barnwood Press, Rt. 2, Box 11C, Daleville, IN 47334

B-City, 619 W. Surf St., Chicago, IL 60657

Beacon Review, 2921 E. Madison St., Seattle, WA 78112

Le Beacon Review, 621 Holt Ave., Dept. PP, Iowa City, IA 52240

Beekman Hill Press, 342 E. 51st St., 3A, New York, NY 10022

Before the Rapture Press, P.O. Box A3604, Chicago, IL 60690

The Bellingham Review, 412 N. State St., Bellingham, WA 98225

Bellowing Ark, P.O. Box 45637, Seattle, WA 98415

The Beloit Poetry Journal, RFD 2, Box 154, Ellsworth, ME 04605

Bennington Review, Bennington College, Bennington, VT 05201

Berkeley Poetry Review, 1601 Sunnyvale Ave., #25, Walnut Creek, CA 94596

Berkeley Poets Cooperative, P.O. Box 459, Berkeley, CA 94701

Between C & D, 255 E. 7th St., New York, NY 10009

Bieler Press, Studio One, 4th Fl., 212 2nd St., N, Minneapolis, MN 55401

Bits Press, English Dept., Case Western Reserve Univ., Cleveland, OH 44106

Bitterroot, P.O. Box 489, Spring Glen, NY 12483

BkMk Press, 107 Cockefair Hall, 5100 Rockhill Rd., Kansas City, MO 64110

Black Bear Publications, P.O. Box 373, Croydon, PA 19020

Black Buzzard Press, 4705 S. 8th Rd., Arlington, VA 22204

Black Ice Press, 6022 Sunnyview Rd., NE, Salem, OR 97305

Black Sparrow Press, P.O. Box 3993, Santa Barbara, CA 93130

Black Warrior Review, P.O. Box 2936, University, AL 35486

Blackwell's Press, 2925B Freedom Blvd., Watsonville, CA 95076

Blind Alleys, See 7th Son Press

The Bloomsbury Review, P.O. Box 8928, Denver, CO 80201

Blue Begonia Press, 225 S. 15th Ave., Yakima, WA 98902

The Blue Cloud Quarterly, Blue Cloud Abbey, Marvin, SD 57251

Blue Scarab Press, 243 S. 8th St., Pocatello, ID 83201

The Blue Sky Journal, 1710 Decker Rd., Malibu, CA 90265

Bluefish, P.O. Box 1601, Southampton, NY 11968

Blueline, Blue Mountain Lake, NY 12812

Bogg Publications, 422 N. Cleveland, Arlington, VA 22201

Book Forum, 38 E. 76 St., New York, NY 10021

The Boston Review, 33 Harrison Ave., Boston, MA 02111

Bottomfish Magazine, DeAnza College, 21250 Stevens Creek Blvd., Cupertino, CA 95014

Breitenbush Books, P.O. Box 02137, Portland, OR 97202

Brick Books, P.O. Box 219, Ilderton, Ontario, N0M 2A0, CANADA

Brooklyn Review, English Dept., Brooklyn College, Brooklyn, NY 11210

Broomstick, 3543 18th St., San Francisco, CA 94110

Burning Deck, 71 Elmgrove Ave., Providence, RI 02906

C

Cache Review, P.O. Box 3505, Tucson, AZ 85722

Caesura, English Dept., Auburn University, Auburn, AL 36849

Cafe Solo, 7975 San Marcos Ave., Atascadero, CA 93422

Calapooya Collage, The Monmouth Inst., W. Ore. St. College, Monmouth, OR 97361

Caldwell Publications, 2612 N. Powhatan St., Arlington, VA 22207

California Quarterly, 100 Sproul Hall, Univ. of Calif., Davis, CA 95616

Callaloo, English Dept., Univ. of Kentucky, Lexington, KY 40506

Calliope, Creative Writing Program, Roger Williams College, Bristol, RI, 02809

Calyx, P.O. Box B, Corvallis, OR 97339

The Camel Press, HC80, Box 160, Big Cove Tannery, PA 17212

Canadian Literature, Univ. of British Columbia, 2029 West Mall, Vancouver, BC V6T 1W5, CANADA

Candle, See Tiptoe Publishing

Canyon Publishing Co., 8561 Eatough Ave., Canoga Park, CA 91304

The Cape Rock, English Dept. Southeast Missouri State, Cape Girardeau, MO 63701

Caribbean Review, Florida Internat'l Univ., Tamiami Trail, Miami, FL 33199

Carolina Quarterly, Greenlaw Hall 066-A, Univ. of N.C., Chapel Hill, NC 27514

Carolina Wren Press, 300 Barclay Rd., Chapel Hill, NC 27514

Celtic Heritage Press, 59-10 Queens Blvd., 9B, Woodside, NY 11377

The Centennial Review, 110 Morrill Hall, Michigan State Univ., East Lansing, MI 48824

The Chariton Review, N.E. Missouri State Univ., Kirksville, MO 63501

The Chattahoochee Review, 2101 Womack Rd., Dunwoody, GA 30338

The Chauncy Press, Turtle Pond Rd., Saranac Lake, NY 12983

Chelsea, Box 5880, Grand Central Sta., New York, NY 10163

Chouteau Review, Box 10016, Kansas City, MO 64111

Cimarron Review, Oklahoma State Univ., Stillwater, OK 74074

Cincinnati Poetry Review, English Dept., 069, Univ. of Cincinnati, Cincinnati, OH 45221

City Newspaper, 250 N. Goodman St., Rochester, NY 14607

Clay & Pine, English & Foreign Language Dept., Georgia Southwestern College, Americus, GA 31709

Cleveland State University Poetry Center, English Dept., Euclid Ave. at 24th St., Cleveland, OH 44115

Clockwatch Review, 737 Penbrook Way, Hartland, WI 53029

Cloud Marauder Press, 1422 Bonita St., Berkeley, CA 94709

Coastline Publishing, P.O. Box 223062, Carmel, CA 93922

Cobblestone, 20 Grove St., Peterborough, NH 03458

Coffee House Press, P.O. Box 10870, Minneapolis, MN 55440

Cold-drill, Boise State Univ., English Dept., Boise, ID 83725

Colorado Review, 322 Eddy, English Dept., Colorado State Univ., Fort Collins, CO 80523

Comet Halley Press, 376 W. Park, #22, El Cajon, CA 92020

Compages, P.O. Box 26517, San Francisco, CA 94126

Confluence Press, Inc., Spalding Hall, LCSC Campus, Lewiston, ID 83501

Confrontation, C. W. Post, L. I. University, Greenvale, NY 11548

Conjunctions, 33 West 9th St., New York, NY 10011

Connecticut Poetry Review, P.O. Box 3783, New Haven, CT 06525

Connecticut River Review, 30 Burr Farms Rd., Westport, CT 06880

Contact II, P.O. Box 451, Bowling Green Sta., New York, NY 10004

Copper Canyon Press, P.O. Box 271, Port Townsend, WA 98368

Cotton Boll/The Atlanta Review, Sandy Springs, P.O. Box 76757, Atlanta, GA 30358

The Cotton Lane Press, 2 Cotton Lane, Augusta, GA 30902

Cottonwood, Box J, KS Union, Univ. of Kansas, Lawrence, KS 66045

Countryman Press, P.O. Box 175, Woodstock, VT 05091

Coydog Review, 203 Halton Lane, Watsonville, CA 95076

Coyote Love Press, 27 Deering St., Portland, ME 04101

Crab Creek Review, 806 N. 42, Seattle, WA 98103

Crawlspace Press, 908 W. 5th St., Belvidere, IL 61008

Crazyhorse, English Dept., Univ. of Arkansas, Little Rock, AR 72204

Creeping Bent, 433 W. Market St., Bethlehem, PA 18018

The Crescent Review, P.O. Box 15065, Winston-Salem, NC 27113

Critique, P.O. Box 11451, Santa Rosa, CA 95406

Crone's Own Press, 310 Driver St., Durham, NC 27703

Crosscurrents, 2200 Glastonbury Rd., Westlake Village, CA 91361

The Crossing Press, Trumansburg, NY 14886

Croton Review, P.O. Box 277, Croton-on-Hudson, NY 10520

Cumberland Poetry Review, P.O. Box 120128, Acklen Sta., Nashville, TN 17212

Curbstone Press, 321 Jackson St., Willimantic, CT 06226

CutBank, English Dept., Univ. of Montana, Missoula, MT 59812

D

The Dalkey Archive Press, 1817 79th Ave., Elmwood Park, IL 60635

Denver Quarterly, English Dept., Univ. of Denver, Denver, CO 80208

Descant, P.O. Box 314, Sta. P, Toronto M5S 2S8, Ontario, CANADA

Devil Mountain Books, P.O. Box 4115, Walnut Creek, CA 94596

The Difficulties, 1695 Brady Lake Rd., Kent, OH 44240

The Dog Ear Press, P.O. Box 143, South Harpswell, ME 04079

Dog River Review, P.O. Box 125, Parkdale, OR 97041

Dolphin-Moon Press, P.O. Box 22262, Baltimore, MD 21203

Dragon Gate, Inc., 508 Lincoln St., Port Townsend, WA 98368

Druid Press, 2724 Shades Crest Rd., Birmingham, AL 35216

Drumm (Chris) Books, P.O. Box 445, Polk City, IA 50226

E

Ecco Press, 18 W. 30th St., New York, NY 10001
Electrum Magazine, 2222 Silk Tree Dr., Tustin, CA 92680
Ellis Press, P.O. Box 1413, Peoria, IL 61655
L'Epervier Press, 4522 Sunnyside North, Seattle, WA 98103
Epoch, 251 Goldwin Smith Hall, Cornell Univ., Ithaca, NY 14853
Erie Street Press, 221 S. Clinton, Oak Park, IL 60302
Exile Press, P.O. Box 1768, Novato, CA 94948
Expresso Tilt, 108 Chatham Lane, Newark, DE 19713
Exquisite Corpse, 630 Lakeland Dr., Baton Rouge, LA 70802

F

FM Five, P.O. Box 882108, San Francisco, CA 94188
Fablewaves Press, P.O. Box 7874, Van Nuys, CA 94109
Falling Water Press, P.O. Box 4554, Ann Arbor, MI 48106
Farmer's Market, P.O. Box 1272, Galesburg, IL 61402
Fell Swoop, English Dept., UNO, New Orleans, LA 70122
Feminist Studies, c/o Women's Studies Program, Univ. of Maryland, College Park, MD 20742
Fergusson, Anne, 132 Martel Crescent, Vankleek Hill, Ontario K0B 1R0 CANADA
The Fessenden Review, 1259 El Camino Real, Ste. 108, Menlo Park, CA 94025
Fiction, English Dept., CCNY, New York, NY 10031
Fiction International, San Diego State Univ., San Diego, CA 92182
Fiction Network, P.O. Box 5651, San Francisco, CA 94101
Field, Rice Hall, Oberlin College, Oberlin, OH 44074
Films in Review, 245 E. 72nd St., New York, NY 10021
Fine Madness, P.O. Box 15176, Seattle, WA 98115
Five Fingers Review, 100 Valencia St., Ste. 303, San Francisco, CA 94103
The Florida Review, English Dept., Univ. of Central Florida, Orlando, FL 32816
Folio, Dept. of Literature, 227 Gray Hall, The American Univ., Washington, DC 20010

Footwork, Passaic County Community College, College Blvd., Paterson, NJ 07509

Forced Exposure, 76 Bromfield St., Watertown, MA 02172

Ford-Brown & Co., Publishers, P.O. Box 600574, Houston, TX 77260

Forum, English Dept., RB 248, Ball State Univ., Muncie, IN 47303

Four Zoas Night House, Ltd., P.O. Box 111, Ashuelot, NH 03441

Friends of the Durango Public Library, 2908 Cedar Ave., Durango, CO 81301

Frontiers, Women Studies Program, Univ. of Colorado, Boulder, CO 80309

G

Galileo Press, 15201 Wheeler Lane, Sparks, MD 21152

Gargoyle/Paycock Press, P.O. Box 3567, Washington, DC 20007

The Georgia Review, Univ. of Georgia, Athens, GA 30602

Godine, David R., Publisher, 306 Dartmouth St., Boston, MA 02116

Graham House Review, Box 5000, Colgate Univ., Hamilton, NY 13346

Grand Street, 50 Riverside Dr., New York, NY 10024

Granta, 44a Hobson St., Cambridge, CB1, 1NL, ENGLAND

Graywolf Press, 370 Selby Ave., RM. 203, St. Paul, MN 55102

Great River Review, 211 West 7th, Winona, MN 55987

Green Key Press, P.O. Box 3801, Seminole, FL 33542

Greenfield Review, RD 1, P.O. Box 80, Greenfield Center, NY 12833

Green's Magazine, P.O. Box 3236, Regina, Saskatchewan, S4P 3H1, CANADA

The Greensboro Review, English Dept., Univ. of North Carolina, Greensboro, NC 27412

Guild Press, P.O. Box 22583, Robbinsdale, MN 55422

The Gutenberg Press, P.O. Box 26345, San Francisco, CA 94126

Gypsy, 1101 Avalon Dr., #J, El Paso, TX 79925

H

Hawaii Review, English Dept., 1733 Donaghho Rd., Univ. of Hawaii, Honolulu, HI 96822

The Hayeck Press, 25 Patrol Ct., Woodside, CA 94062

Heartland, c/o Fairbanks Daily News-Miner, P.O. Box 710, Fairbanks, AK 99707

Heatherstone Press, Meadville, PA

Heirloom Books, Box 15472, Detroit, MI 48215

Helaine Victoria Press, 4080 Dynasty Lane, Martinsville, IN 46151

Helicon Nine, P.O. Box 22412, Kansas City, MO 64113

Helix Press, 4410 Hickey, Corpus Christi, TX 78413

Hemlocks and Balsams, P.O. Box 128, Lees-McRae College, Banner Elk, NC 28604

Hermes House Press, 127 W. 15th St., Apt. 3F, New York, NY 10011

Heyday Books, Box 9145, Berkeley, CA 94709

Hiram Poetry Review, P.O. Box 162, Hiram, OH 44234

Hit & Run Press, 1725 Springbrook Rd., Lafayette, CA 94549

Hob Nob, 715 Dorsea Rd., Lancaster, PA 17601

Hog Ranch Press, 1621 W. Odell, Casper, WY 82604

The Hollins Critic, P.O. Box 9538, Hollins College, VA 24020

Holy Cow! Press, P.O. Box 2692, Iowa City, IA 52244

Home Planet News, P.O. Box 415, Stuyvesant Sta., New York, NY 10009

Hour Publishing, 24 Westminster, #3, Venice, CA 90291

Hubbub, 5344 SE 38th, Portland, OR 97202

The Hudson Review, 684 Park Ave., New York, NY 10021

Humana Press, Crescent Manor, P.O. Box 2148, Clifton, NJ 07015

Hunter House, Inc., Publishers, P.O. Box 1302, Claremont, CA 91711

I

Ikon Press, P.O. Box 1355, Stuyvesant Sta., New York, NY 10009

Illinois Libertarian, 822 Tacker St., Des Plains, IL 60016

Image Magazine, P.O. Box 28048, St. Louis, MO 63119

Images, English Dept., Wright State Univ., Dayton, OH 45435
Imagine Publishers, 645 Beacon St., Ste. 7, Boston, MA 02215
Indiana Review, 316 N. Jordan Ave., Indiana Univ., Bloomington, IN 47405
Indra's Net, 78 Center St., Geneseo, NY 14454
Inkblot, 1506 Bonita, Berkeley, CA 94709
Inlet, English Dept., Virginia Wesleyan College, Norfolk, VA 23502
Insight Press, Box 25, Ocotillo, CA 92259
Invisible City, See Red Hill Press
Iris, 27 Chestnut St., Binghamton, NY 13905
Iron, 5 Marden Terrace, Cullercoats, North Shields, Tyne & Wear, NE30, 4PD, ENGLAND
Ironwood, P.O. Box 40907, Tucson, AZ 85717

J

Jam Today, P.O. Box 249, Northfield, VT 05663
James Dickey Newsletter, DeKalb Community College, 2101 Womack Rd., Dunwoody, GA 30338
Jewish Currents, 22 East 17th St., Ste. 601, New York, NY 10003
Journal of New Jersey Poets, English Dept., 285 Madison Ave., Fairleigh Dickinson Univ., Madison, NJ 07940
Joydeism Press, P.O. Box 14, Point Arena, CA 95468
Jukebox Terrorists with Typewriters, See Young Whippersnapper Press
Juniper Press, 1310 Shorewood Dr., LaCrosse, WI 54601

K

KSOR Guide to the Arts, 1250 Siskiyou Blvd., Ashland, OR 97520
Kansas Quarterly, English Dept., Denison Hall, Kansas State Univ., Manhattan, KS 66506
The Kenyon Review, Kenyon College, Gambier, OH 43022
Kickapoo Press, P.O. Box 1443, Peoria, IL 61655
The Kindred Spirit, Rt. 2, Box 111, St. John, KS 67576
Kinraddie Press, 521 Agua Fria, Sante Fe, NM 87501

L

La Jolla Poets Press, 3280 Via Alicante, La Jolla, CA 92037

Lake Street Review Press, Box 7188, Powderhorn Sta., Minneapolis, MN 55407

Latitude 30'18", 1124B Reagan Terrace, Austin, TX 78704

Laurel Review, West Virginia Wesleyan College, Buckhannon, W.VA 26201

Legerete, P.O. Drawer 1410, Daphne, AL 36526

Library Trends, See David R. Godine, Publisher

Lintel, Box 8609, Roanoke, VA 24014

LIPS, P.O. Box 1345, Montclair, NJ 07042

The Literary Review, Fairleigh Dickinson Univ., 285 Madison Ave., Madison, NJ 07940

Little Free Press, Rt. 2, Box 136A, Cushing, MN 56443

The Little Magazine, P.O. Box 78, Pleasantville, NY 10570

The Lockhart Press, Box 1207, Port Townsend, WA 98368

The Loft Press, 42 Sherman Ave., Glens Falls, NY 12801

Logbridge-Rhodes, P.O. Box 3254, Durango, CO 81301

Long Pond Review, English Dept., Suffolk Community College, Selden, NY 11784

The Long Story, 11 Kingston St., North Andover, MA 01845

Lost and Found Times, 137 Leland Ave., Columbus, OH 43214

The Louisville Review, English Dept., 315 Bingham Humanities, Univ. of Louisville, Louisville, KY 40292

The Lunchroom Press, P.O. Box 36027, Grosse Pointe Farms, MI 48236

M

MSS, SUNY, Binghamton, NY 13901

The Madison Review, English Dept., H. C. White Hall, 600 N. Park St., Madison, WI 53706

Madrona Publishers, Inc., P.O. Box 22667, Seattle, WA 98122

Magazine, School of Humanities, S.F. State Univ., San Francisco, CA 94132

The Magazine of Speculative Poetry, P.O. Box 564, Beloit, WI 53511

The Malahat Review, Univ. of Victoria, P.O. Box 1700, Victoria, B.C. V8W 2Y2 CANADA

Manhattan Poetry Review, 36 Sutton Place South, New York, NY 10022

Manhattan Review, 304 3rd Ave., 4A, New York, NY 10010

Manic d Press, 1853 Stockton, San Francisco, CA 94133

MANNA, 4318 Minter School Rd., Sanford, NC 27330

Manuscript 30, English Dept., Los Angeles Valley College, 5800 Fulton Ave., Van Nuys, CA 91401

The Massachusetts Review, Memorial Hall, Univ. of Mass., Amherst, MA 01003

MATI, See Ommation Press

Media History Digest, 11 W. 19th St., New York, NY 10011

Memphis State Review, English Dept., Memphis State Univ., Memphis, TN 38152

Menu, See The Lunchroom Press

Merton Press, Suite 604, Atlantic Bank Bldg., St. Augustine, FL 32084

M'godolim, 2921 E. Madison St., #5PP, Seattle, WA 98112

Mho & Mho Works, P.O. Box 33135, San Diego, CA 92103

Michigan Quarterly Review, Univ. of Michigan, 3032 Rackham Bldg., Ann Arbor, MI 48109

Mickle Street Review, Box 417, Bethlehem, PA 18016

Mid-American Review, English Dept., Bowling Green St. Univ., Bowling Green, OH 43403

Midland Review, English Dept., Oklahoma State Univ., Stillwater, OK 740

Midwest Arts & Literature, P.O. Box 1623, Jefferson City, MO 65102

Midwest Poetry Review, Box 776, Rock Island, IL 61201

Midwest Quarterly, Pittsburg State Univ., Pittsburg, KS 66762

Milkweed Chronicle, P.O. Box 24303, Minneapolis, MN 55424

Millers River Publishing Co., Box 159, Athol, MA 01331

Mississippi Mud, 1336 SE Marion St., Portland, OR 97202

Mississippi Review, Box 5144, Southern Sta., Hattiesburg, MS 39406

Missouri Review, English Dept., 231 Arts & Sc., Univ. of Missouri, Columbia, MO 65211

Modern Haiku, P.O. Box 1752, Madison, WI 53701

Momo's Press, 45 Sheridan St., San Francisco, CA 94103

Moveable Feast Press, P.O. Box 5057, El Dorado Hills, CA 95030

Moving Parts Press, 419A Maple St., Santa Cruz, CA 95060

Mr. Cogito Press, P.O. Box 627, Pacific Univ., Forest Grove, OR 97116

Murphy & Broad Publishing Co., 425 30th St., Ste. B, Newport Beach, CA 92663

Mylabris Press, Ltd., P.O. Box 20725, New York, NY 10025

N

NRG, 6735 SE 78th, Portland, OR 97206

The Naiad Press, Inc., P.O. Box 10543, Tallahassee, FL 32302

Naked Man, English Dept., K.U., Lawrence, KS 66045

NEBO, English Dept., Arkansas Tech. Univ., Russelville, AR 72801

The Nebraska Review, Univ. of Nebraska at Omaha, Omaha, NE 68182

New Collage Magazine, 5700 No. Miami Trail, Sarasota, FL 33580

New Directions, 80 Eighth Ave., New York, NY 10011

New England Review & Bread Loaf Quarterly, Box 170, Hanover, NH 03755

New England Sampler, RFD 1, Box M119, Brooks, ME 04921

New Letters, Univ. of Missouri-K.C., Kansas City, MO 64110

New Oregon Review, 537 NE Lincoln St., Hillsboro, OR 97123

New Orleans Review, Loyola Univ., New Orleans, LA 70118

New Poets Series, Inc., 541 Piccadilly, Baltimore, MD 21204

New Rivers Press, 1602 Selby Ave., St. Paul, MN 55104

New Society Publishers, 4722 Baltimore Ave., Philadelphia, PA 19143

The New York Quarterly, NPF, 305 Neville Hall, Univ. of Maine, Orono, ME 04469

Nimrod, 2210 S. Main, Tulsa, OK 74114

No Aplogies, Box 1852, Brown Univ., Providence, RI 02912

North American Review, Univ. of No. Iowa, Cedar Falls, IA 50614

North Carolina Haiku Society Press, P.O. Box 14247, Raleigh, NC 27620

North Dakota Quarterly, Box 8237, Univ. of North Dakota, Grand Forks, ND 58202

Northeast, See Juniper Press

Northwest Magazine, The Oregonian, 1320 SW Broadway, Portland, OR 97201

Northwest Review, 369 PLC, Univ. of Oregon, Eugene, OR 97403

O

O.ARS, P.O. Box 179, Cambridge, MA 02238

The Ohio Review, Ellis Hall, Ohio Univ., Athens, OH 45701

Oink!, 1446 W. Jarvis, Chicago, IL 60626

Old Red Kimono, P.O. Box 1864, Rome, GA 30163

Omega Press, P.O. Box 574, Lebanon Springs, NY 12114

Ommation Press, 5548 N. Sawyer, Chicago, IL 60625

The Ontario Review, 9 Honey Brook Dr., Princeton, NJ 08540

Open Places, Box 2085, Stephens College, Columbia, MO 65215

Orphic Lute, 1021 E. Little Back River Rd., Hampton, VA 23669

Osiris, Box 297, Deerfield, MA 01342

Other Voices, 820 Ridge Rd., Highland Park, IL 60035

Ouroboros, 40 Grove Ave., Ottawa, K1S 3A6, Ontario, CANADA

Outerbridge, College of Staten Island, 715 Ocean Terrace, Staten Island, NY 10301

Overman, Marjorie, Publishing, 323 E. Cavanaugh St., Wallace, NC 28466

Owl Creek Press, 1520 N. 45th St., #205, Seattle, WA 98103

Ox Head Press, 414 N. 6th St., Marshall, MN 56258

P

Pacific Arts & Letters, P.O. Box 640394, San Francisco, CA 94164

Paideuma, 305 Neville Hall, Univ. of Maine, Orono, ME 04469

Painted Bride Quarterly, 230 Vine St., Philadelphia, PA 19106

Pangaea, The Open Theatre, P.O. Box 422, Austin, TX 78767

Pangloss Papers, Box 18917, Los Angeles, CA 90018

Parabola, 150 Fifth Ave., New York, NY 10011

Paris Review, 45-39 171 Place, Flushing, NY 11358

Parnassus, P.O. Box 1384, Forest Park, GA 30051

Partisan Review, 141 Bay State Rd., Boston, MA 02215

Passages North, Bonifas Arts Center, Escanaba, MI 49829

PAX, 217 Pershing Ave., San Antonio, TX 78209

Pembroke Magazine, P.O. Box 60, PSU, Pembroke, NC 28372

The Pennsylvania Review, Univ. of Pittsburgh, English Dept./526 C.L., Pittsburgh, PA 15260

Pequod, 305 Neville Hall, Univ. of Maine, Orono, ME 04469

Perivale Press, 13830 Erwin St., Van Nuys, CA 91401

Philadelphia Poets, 330 Bainbridge St., Apt. 13, Philadelphia, PA 19147

Phrygian Press, 58-09 205th St., Bayside, NY 11364

Piedmont Literary Review, 724 Bartholomew St., New Orleans, LA 70117

Pig Iron Press, P.O. Box 237, Youngstown, OH 44501

Pinchpenny, 4851 Q St., Sacramento, CA 95819

Pine Press, Box 530, RD 1, Landisburg, PA 17040

Pivot, P.O. Box 542, Shepherdstown, W.VA 25443

Place of Herons Press, P.O. Box 1952, Austin, TX 78767

Plains Poetry Journal, Box 2337, Bismarck, ND 58502

Plainsong, Box U245, West Kentucky Univ., Bowling Green, KY 42101

Plainswoman, P.O. Box 8027, Grand Forks, ND 58202

Planet Detroit, 8214 St. Mary's, Detroit, MI 48228

Ploughshares, Box 529, Cambridge, MA 02139

Plunkett Lake Press, 551 Franklin St., Cambridge, MA 02139

Poet & Critic, 203 Ross Hall, ISU, Ames, IA 50011

Poetic Justice, 8220 Rayford Dr., Los Angeles, CA 90045

Poetics Journal, 2639 Russell St., Berkeley, CA 94705

Poetry, Box 4348, Chicago, IL 60680

Poetry Australia, Market Place, Berrima, N.S.W. 2577, AUSTRA-LIA

Poetry Canada Review, 307 Coxwell Ave., Toronto, Ont., M4L 3B5, CANADA

Poetry East, Star Rte. 1, Box 50, Earlysville, VA 22936

Poetry/LA, P.O. Box 84271, Los Angeles, CA 90073

The Poetry Miscellany, English Dept., Univ. of Tenn., Chatta-nooga, TN 37403

Poetry Northwest, Univ. of Washington, 4045 Brooklyn Ave., NE, JA-15, Seattle, WA 98105

Poetry Projects, 312 Park St., Huron, OH 44839

The Poetry Review, 15 Gramercy Park, New York, NY 10003

Porter Gulch Review, English Dept., Cabrillo College, Aptos, CA 95003

Potes & Poets Press, Inc., 181 Edgemont Ave., Elmwood, CT 06110

Prairie Schooner, 201 Andrews, Univ. of Nebraska, Lincoln, NE 68588

Primavera, 1212 E. 59th St., Chicago, IL 60637

Proof Rock, P.O. Box 607, Halifax, VA 24558

Prophetic Voices, 94 Santa Maria Dr., Novato, CA 94947

Puckerbrush Review, 76 Main St., Orono, ME 04473

Puerto del Sol, College of Arts & Sc., Box 3E, N.M. State Univ., Las Cruces, NM 88001

Q

The Quarry Press, P.O. Box 1061, Kingston, Ontario, K7L 4Y5, CANADA

Quarry West, Porter College, Univ. of California, Santa Cruz, CA 95064

Quarterly West, 312 Olpin Union, Univ. of Utah, Salt Lake City, UT 84112

Quarto, 608 Lewison Hall, Columbia Univ., New York, NY 10027

Queen's Quarterly, Queen's Univ., Kingston, Ontario, K7L 3N6, CANADA

Quill, Univ. of Tampa, Box 2749, 401 W. Kennedy Blvd., Tampa, FL 33606

R

Raccoon, 1407 Union Ave., Ste. 401, Memphis, TN 38104

The Raddle Moon, 9060 Ardmore Dr., Sidney, B.C., V8L 3S1 CANADA

RAJAH, 4024 Mod. Language Bldg., Univ. of Michigan, Ann Arbor, MI 48109

Rampike, 95 Rivercrest Rd., Toronto, Ontario, M6S 4H7, CANADA

Raritan, Rutgers Univ., 165 College Ave., New Brunswick, NJ 08903

Raw Dog Press, 2-34 Aspen Way, Doylestown, PA 18901

Real Fiction, 298 9th Ave., San Francisco, CA 94118

Realities Library, 2745 Monterey Hwy #76, San Jose, CA 95111

The Reaper, 325 Ocean View Ave., Santa Cruz, CA 95062
Rebis Press, P.O. Box 2233, Berkeley, CA 94702
Red Bass, P.O. Box 10258, Tallahassee, FL 32302
Red Dust, Inc., P.O. Box 630, New York, NY 10028
Red Herring Press, 1009 W. Church St., Champaign, IL 61821
Red Hill Press, P.O. Box 2853, San Francisco, CA 94126
Red Sky Press, P.O. Box 10313, Seattle, WA 98101
Renaissance House, 541 Oak St., P.O. Box 177, Frederick, CO 80530
Rhyme Time/Story Time, P.O. Box 2377, Coeur d'Alene, ID 83814
The Ridgeway Press, P.O. Box 120, Roseville, MI 48066
River City Review, P.O. Box 34275, Louisville, KY 40232
River Styx, 14 S. Euclid St., St. Louis, MO 63108
Riverside Quarterly, P.O. Box 833-044, Richardson, TX 75083
The Round Table, 206 Sherman St., Wayne, NE 68787
Rowan Tree Press, 124 Chestnut St., Boston, MA 02108
Rubicon, McGill Univ., 853 Sherbrooke St., W, Montreal, QUE, H3A 2T6 CANADA

S

Sachem Press, P.O. Box 9, Old Chatham, NY 12136
Sagetrieb, 305 Neville Hall, Univ. of Maine, Orono, ME 04469
Salmagundi, Skidmore College, Saratoga Springs, NY 12866
Salome, See Ommation Press
The Salvage, The Gutenberg Dump, P.O. Box 578, Haines, AK 99827
Samisdat, Box 129, Richford, VT 05476
San Francisco Review of Books, P.O. Box 33-0090, San Francisco, CA 94133
Saturday Press, P.O. Box 884, Upper Montclair, NJ 07043
Scarab Press, Salisbury State College, Salisbury, MD
SCORE, 595 Merritt, #2, Oakland, CA 94610
Sea Pen Press & Paper Mill, 2228 NE 46th St., Seattle, WA 98105
Seal Press, 312 S. Washington, Seattle, WA 98104
The Seattle Review, Padelford Hall, GN-30, Univ. of Washington, Seattle, WA 98195
Second Coming Press, P.O. Box 31249, San Francisco, CA 94131
The Seneca Review, Hobart & William Smith Colleges, Geneva, NY 14456

7th Son Press, P.O. Box 13224, Baltimore, MD 21203

Sewanee Review, Univ. of the South, Sewanee, TN 37375

Shadow Press, P.O. Box 8803, Minneapolis, MN 55408

Shady Acre Press, Rt. 5, Box 201, Roanoke, VA 24014

Shameless Hussy Press, Box 3092, Berkeley, CA 94703

Shankpainter, Fine Arts Center, Provincetown, MA

Sheba Review, See Midwest Arts & Lit.

Shenandoah, P.O. Box 722, Lexington, VA 24450

Sign of the Times, P.O. Box 6464, Portland, OR 97228

Simon & Pierre Oublishing Co., Ltd., P.O. Box 280, Adelaide St. Sta., Toronto, Ont., M5C 2J4, CANADA

Sing Heavenly Muse!, P.O. Box 13299, Minneapolis, MN 55414

SITES, 446 W. 20 St., New York, NY 10011

Slipstream, Box 2071, New Market Sta., Niagara Falls, NY 14301

Small Pond Magazine, P.O. Box 664, Stratford, CT 06497

Soho Arts Weekly, 318 E. 6th St., New York, NY 10003

Sojourner, 143 Albany St., Cambridge, MA 02139

Solution Journal, 11 Greenfield Ave., Stratford, CT 06497

Sonora Review, English Dept., Univ. of Arizona, Tucson, AZ 85721

SOS Books, 1821 Kalorama Rd., NW, Washington, DC 20009

Soundings East, Salem State College, 352 Lafayette St., Salem, MA 01970

South Carolina Review, English Dept., Clemson Univ., Clemson, SC 29631

South Dakota Review, Univ. of South Dakota, Vermillion, SD 57069

Southeastern FRONT, 565 17th St., NW, Cleveland, TN 37311

Southern Humanities Review, 9088 Haley Center, Auburn Univ., Auburn, AL 36849

Southern Poetry Review, Univ. of North Carolina, Charlotte, NC 28223

The Southern Review, 43 Allen Hall, Louisiana St. Univ., Baton Rouge, LA 70803

Southwest Review, Box 4374, So. Methodist Univ., Dallas, TX 75275

Sou'wester, So. Illinois Univ., Edwardsville, IL 62026

Space and Time, 138 W. 70th St., Apt. 4B, New York, NY 10023

Spiraling Books, 12431 Camilla St., Whittier, CA 90601

Spirit that Moves Us Press, P.O. Box 1585, Iowa City, IA 52244

Spoon River Poetry Press, See Ellis Press

St. Andrews Press, Laurinburg, NC 28352

Stand Magazine, 179 Wingrove Rd., Newcastle upon Tyne, NE4 9DA UK

State Street Press, 67 State St., Pittsford, NY 14534

Stepping Stones Press, Box 1856, Harlem, NY 10027

The Stone, Greenpeace/Monterey Bay, 1112 Ocean St., Santa Cruz, CA 95060

Stone Country, P.O. Box 132, Menemsha, MA 02552

Story County Books, Box 355, Ames, IA 50010

Story Quarterly, P.O. Box 1416, Northbrook, IL 60065

Sulfur, 852 S. Bedford St., Los Angeles, CA 90035

Sun Dog, Florida State Univ., 406 Williams, Tallahassee, FL 32306

Sun Magazine, 412 W. Rosemary St., Chapel Hill, NC 27514

Sunrust Magazine, See Dawn Valley Press

Sunstone, P.O. Box 2321, Santa Fe, NM 87501

Swale, Phoebus Publications, P.O. Box 12052, Broadway Sta., Seattle, WA 98102

Swallow's Tale Press, P.O. Box 930040, Norcross, GA 30093

T

Tamarisk, 1200 Forrell Terrace, Rahway, NJ 07065

Taplinger Publishing Co., Inc., 132 W. 22nd St., New York, NY 10011

Tar River Poetry, English Dept., East Carolina Univ., Greenville, NC 27834

Telescope, See Galileo Press

Temenos, Box 687, Sta. Q, Toronto, Ontario, M4T 2N5, CANADA

Tendril, Box 512, Green Harbor, MA 02041

The Texas Review. Sam Houston State Univ., Huntsville, TX 77341

13th Moon, Box 309, Cathedral Sta., New York, NY 10025

This, 2020 9th Ave., Oakland, CA 94606

Thistledown Press, Ltd., 668 East Place, Saskatoon, Saskatchewan, CANADA S7J 2Z5

Thorndike Press, P.O. Box 157, Thorndike, ME 04986

Thornfield Press, 21 Steele Ave., Staten Island, New York, NY 10305

The Threepenny Review, P.O. Box 9131, Berkeley, CA 94709

Tiger Stream Press, P.O. Box 96, Pismo Beach, CA 93449

Tilted Planet Press, P.O. Box 8646, Austin, TX 78713

Tiptoe Publishing, 12 KM E. of 101 at Wilderness, P.O. Box 206, Naselle, WA 98638

Tombouctou, Box 265, Bolinas, CA 94924

Tompson & Rutter, Inc., P.O. Box 297, Grantham, NH 03753

Touchstone, P.O. Box 42331, Houston, TX 77042

Translation, Translation Ctr/307A Mathematics Bldg., Columbia Univ., New York, NY 10027

Trilobite Press, 1015 West Oak, Denton, TX 76201

TriQuarterly, Northwestern Univ., 1735 Benson Ave., Evanston, IL 60201

Trivia, P.O. Box 606, N. Amherst, MA 01059

Truly Fine Press, P.O. Box 891, Bemidji, MN 56601

2 Plus 2, See Mylabris Press

U

U.S. 1, Box 441, Kingston, NJ 08528

Unicorn Press, Inc., P.O. Box 3307, Greensboro, NC 27402

University Editions, 4937 Humphrey Rd., Huntington, W.VA 25704

V

Vagabond Press, #1 Morris Way, Eburg, WA 98926

Vanity Press, 160 6th Ave., New York, NY 10013

The View After Dark, 577 S. High St., Columbus, OH 43215

Vimach Associates, 3039 Indianola Ave., Columbus, OH 43202

Virginia Quarterly Review, One West Range, Charlottesville, VA 22903

Viva Baja, P.O. Box 11630, Costa Mesa, CA 92627

The Volcano Review, 6714 Belmont, Houston, TX 77005

W

Walt Whitman Quarterly Review, Univ. of Iowa, Iowa City, IA 52242

Wampeter Press, Box 512, Green Harbor, MA 02041

Washington Review, Box 50132, Washington, DC 20004

Washington Writers Publishing House, P.O. Box 50068, Washington, DC 20004

Water Mark Press, 138 Duane St., New York, NY 10013

Waterways, 799 Greenwich St., New York, NY 10014

Waves, 79 Denham Dr., Richmond Hill, Ontario, L4C 6H9, CANADA

Wayland Press, 2640 E. 12th Ave., Box 715, Denver, Co 80206

Webster Review, Webster Univ., 470 E. Lockwood, Webster Groves, MO 63119

West Anglia Publications, P.O. Box 2683, La Jolla, CA 92038

West Branch, English Dept., Bucknell Univ., Lewisburg, PA 17837

West End Press, Box 291477, Los Angeles, CA 90029

Western Humanities Review, Univ. of Utah, Salt Lake City, UT 84112

Westgate, 8 Bernstein Blvd., Center Moriches, NY 11934

White Pine Press, 73 Putnam St., Buffalo, NY 14213

White, Stewart W., 105 Shore Acres, SW, Tacoma, WA 98498

The Willow Bee, Box 9, Saratoga, NY 82331

Willow Springs Magazine, P.O. Box 1063, (PUB), E.W.U., Cheney, WA 99004

The Windless Orchard, English Dept., Indiana Univ., Fort Wayne, IN 46805

Wisconsin Academy Review, 1922 University Ave., Madison, Wi 53705

Wisla Publishers, P.O. Box 65042, Baton Rouge, LA 70896

The Women's Review of Books, Wellesley College, Ctr. for Research on Women, Wellesley, MA 02181

The Worcester Review, 19 Walnut Hill Dr., Worcester, MA 01602

Word Beat Press, P.O. Box 10509, Tallahassee, FL 32302

The Wormwood Review, P.O. Box 8840, Stockton, CA 85284

Writers Forum, Univ. of Colorado, Colorado Springs, CO 80907

X

Xanadu, Box 773, Huntington, NY 11743

Y

The Yale Review, 1902A Yale Sta., New Haven, CT 06520
Yarrow, English Dept., Lytle Hall, Kutztown St. Univ., Kutztown, PA 19530
Yellow Silk, P.O. Box 6374, Albany, CA 94706
Yes Press, P.O. Box 91, Waynesboro, TN 38485
Young Whippersnapper Press, 171 Lincoln Ave., Amherst, MA 01002

Z

Zephyr Press, 13 Robinson St., Somerville, MA 02145
ZYZZYVA, 55 Sutter St., Ste. 400, San Francisco, CA 94104

INDEX

The following is a listing in alphabetical order by author's last name of works reprinted in the first eleven *Pushcart Prize* editions.

438

442

446

CONTRIBUTORS' NOTES

LEE K. ABBOTT has published two collections of stories and his third, *Strangers in Paradise,* is due from Putnams in 1987. He won the St. Lawrence Award for Fiction in 1981.

ALICE ADAMS is the author most recently of two books from Knopf, *Superior Women* (1984) and *Return Trips* (1986).

PAUL AUSTER's story is part of a series to be published by Sun & Moon Press. He lives in Brooklyn, New York.

DONALD BARTHELME has published many books of fiction, most recently *Overnight to Many Distant Cities*. He teaches at the University of Houston.

GINA BERRIAULT lives in Sausalito, California and is author of the novel, *The Descant,* recently reissued by North Point Press.

WENDELL BERRY is the author of several books from North Point Press. His essay in this issue is also available as a booklet from Guardian Press, Box 272, Brookfield, NY 13314.

LINDA BIERDS lives in Seattle, and has published in many journals including *The Massachusetts Review, The New Yorker* and elsewhere. She works at Seattle's Woodland Park Zoo and The University of Washington.

RICHARD BURGIN is founder and editor of *Boulevard,* a journal of contemporary writing. He lives in Philadelphia.

HENRY CARLILE has been employed as a millworker, clerk, commercial fisherman, shipfitter, military bandsman, guest poetry editor and visiting instructor. His work has appeared in *Fiddlehead, The Portland Reviw, Tar River Poetry, Chowder Review* and others. He lives in Portland, Oregon.

HAYDEN CARRUTH teaches at Bucknell. His *Selected Poems* was just published by Macmillan.

ANTONIO CISNEROS lives in Lima, Peru and teaches at the University of San Marcos there. He is the author of eight poetry collections and is editor of the political monthly, *Thirty Days*.

STEPHEN DOBYNS' sixth book of poetry, *Cemetery Nights*, is just out from Viking.

MARK DOTY teaches at Vermont College. His work has appeared in *Ploughshares, Poetry* and elsewhere.

JOHN DRURY is author of the collection, *Fire In The Wax Museum*, and lives in Cincinnati. His work has appeared in *Poetry, Shenandoah, Hudson Review* and elsewhere.

ANDRE DUBUS lives in Bradford, Massachusetts. His most recent collection of stories, *The Last Worthless Evening*, is just out from David Godine, Publisher.

RICHARD FORD lives in Coahoma, Mississippi. He is the author of the novel, *The Sportswriter*, and the forthcoming fiction collection, *Rock Springs*.

GARY GILDNER is the author of *The Crush* (Ecco, 1983) and the forthcoming novel, *The Second Bridge*, and story collection, *A Week In South Dakota* (Algonquin Books).

DANIEL HALPERN is editor of Ecco Press.

JAMES HATHAWAY lives in Chandler, Arizona and has published in *Poetry East, Greenfield Review, New Letters* and elsewhere.

AMY HEMPEL is contributing editor to *Vanity Fair*. She lives in New York and is at work on a collection of short fiction.

EDWARD HIRSCH is the author of two poetry collections from Knopf and teaches at the University of Houston.

LINDA HOGAN recently received a National Endowment for the Arts fellowship. Her *Seeing Through The Sun* (University of Massachusetts Press) won the American Book Award for 1986.

GARRETT KAORU HONGO teaches at the University of Missouri and co-edits poetry for *The Missouri Review*. He is the author of *Yellow Light* (Wesleyan).

MARY HOOD's second collection of stories, *And Venus Is Blue*, has just been published by Ticknor & Fields. Her stories and essays have appeared in *Kenyon Review, Georgia Review, Harpers, North American Review* and elsewhere.

LYNDA HULL is an associate editor of *Crazyhorse* and lives in Provincetown, Massachusetts.

COLETTE INEZ is the author of three collections of poetry and has received fellowships from The Guggenheim Foundation, The National Endowment for the Arts and The Rockefeller Foundation.

DENIS JOHNSON's new novel, *The Stars at Noon*, is just out and a collection of poems will shortly follow. He lives in Boonville, California.

DORIANNE LAUX has published in ZYZZYVA, *Tendril*, *Yellow Silk* and elsewhere. She lives in Berkeley, California. She is a student at Mills College.

LI-YOUNG LEE was born in Indonesia and lives in Chicago, where he is employed as a jewelry maker. His first book is forthcoming from BOA Editions.

LARRY LEVIS teaches at The University of Utah and has published four volumes of poetry, most recently with The University of Pittsburgh Press. He has won fellowships from The National Endowment for the Arts, The Guggenheim Foundation and others.

GORDON LISH is an editor at Alfred Knopf Inc., and the author most recently of the novel, *Peru* (Dutton, 1985).

JOHN LOGAN is the author of the collections *Only The Dreamer Can Change the Dream,* and *The Bridge of Change.* His pamphlet of poems, *The Transformation,* just appeared from Pancake Press, San Francisco.

D.R. MACDONALD has published in *TriQuarterly, Epoch* and elsewhere. He is completing a collection of short stories and he lives in Palo Alto, California.

WILLIAM MATTHEWS' most recent book is *A Happy Childhood* (Atlantic-Little Brown). He lives in New York City.

HERBERT MORRIS is the author of *Peru,* (1983) and *Dream Palace* (1986), both from Harper and Row.

HOWARD MOSS is the poetry editor of *The New Yorker* and author of the poetry collection, *Rules of Sleep* (Atheneum, 1984).

CAROLE OLES lives in Newton, Massachusetts and has published in *Poetry* and elsewhere.

LUCIA PERILLO recently graduated from Syracuse University where she won two Raymond Carver awards for her poetry and fiction. She works as a park ranger in the Northwest.

STANLEY PLUMLY has published five books of poetry, most recently *Summer Celestial.* He directs the Creative Writing program at the University of Maryland.

FRANCINE PROSE's most recent novel is *Bigfoot Dreams.* She lives in upstate New York.

MONA SIMPSON has published in *Ploughshares, The Iowa Review, North American Review* and elsewhere. Her first novel is due from Knopf.

TOM SLEIGH lives in Cambridge, Massachusetts and publishes in *Antaeus* and elsewhere.

ARTHUR SMITH teaches at The University of Tennessee at Knoxville. This poem is from his first collection of poetry, winner of the 1985 Norma Farber First book Award from the Poetry Society of America.

TED SOLOTAROFF is an editor at Harper and Row and is past editor of *New American Review.*

ANA LYDIA VEGA lives in Rio Piedras, Puerto Rico. Her *Pasion de Historia* won the Juan Rulfo International Prize in 1984.

MARILYN WANIEK is the author of two volumes of poetry and teaches at the University of Connecticut, Storrs.

ELIOT WEINBERGER has translated work by Borges, Paz and Aridjis, His *Works On Paper*, a collection of his own essays, is just out from New Directions.

TOBIAS WOLFF received the PEN/Faulkner Award for his short novel, *The Barracks Thief* (Ecco, 1985). He teaches at Syracuse University.

DON ZACHARIA is the author of *The Match Trick* (Linden Press) and is at work on a new novel. His work has appeared in *Partisan Review* and *Epoch*.